The Tracks
- a refuge -

Alex W MacLeod

Printed and bound in Canada by Friesens

Book Design & Typesetting: Kevin Estey Design

Library and Archives Canada Cataloguing in Publication

The Tracks a refuge
Alex MacLeod

ISBN 978-0-9949142-0-0

CHAPTER ONE

Mothers often get enemas just before the birth of their child; otherwise, the baby could be born in a pile of shit. Juliette Cameron found comfort in this.

Juliette didn't live at The Tracks in Sterling Reserve during the hot, muggy summer of nineteen fifty-one. The Tracks was a railroad spur line abandoned by Glover Metals Mining Company. They left five derelict rail cars on the wrong side of a broken down bridge. People began living in the abandoned cars.

The residents of the cars disposed of their body wastes more or less satisfactorily. Ronnie, the least satisfactory, moved into an empty car in mid-July. Ronnie just slid open the door of his rail car to piss. He walked ten or twenty feet from the tracks to squat and shit.

Archie MacKenzie was the most genteel. He used the toilet in his caboose originally intended to drop human waste directly onto the tracks from a moving train. Archie ran a discharge pipe to a hole he dug in the woods fifty feet from the tracks. Sewage disposal from the other cars fell somewhere between Ronnie's and Archie's sensibilities.

Lank and Irma Graham lived in the dining car with their ten-month-old daughter. Lank could fix cars, do carpentry, plumbing or cooking when sober but he was usually drunk. Lank would drink anything but most days he drank a brew made from water and baker's yeast with sugar, molasses, rice, potato, corn syrup or any combination of these fuels for alcohol fermentation. Many of the locals made moonshine from a brew like that but Lank never got to the distillation. He drank it early before it completed fermentation. Lank often got sick. The cloudy, smelly moonshine wash made him throw up, knocked him down and gave him diarrhea. Other than that Lank was charming and disarming.

Archie completed a Bachelors degree in philosophy and a Masters in English while Lank worked as a handyman around St Francis Xavier University. The two men became good friends and drinking buddies.

Archie saw the potential for The Tracks becoming a small co-op community when his first job took him to Sterling Reserve. A Masters degree got him a job as a commissioned salesman for a meat packing company. He made twice the money in half the time selling in the larger centers of Halifax and Truro but he liked traveling to the little places. He liked the idea of a town built around a run-down silver mine. Archie drove his Chevy Sedan Delivery along the eastern shore of Nova Scotia, turned inland at Brookfield and found Sterling Reserve at the end of the road. The name of the town was forward-looking. In nineteen thirty-five, Glover Metals Mining Company had reserved the silver mine for exploitation at a later date. But Sterling Reserve's future had passed. The silver mine closed during the Second World War when rising labor costs made the marginally productive mine unprofitable.

A railway spur line across the river from Sterling Reserve became known as The Tracks. Glover Metals operated a coalmine at The Tracks. They used up the small coal deposit to run the silver mine and heat the houses in Sterling Reserve. The railroad bridge across the Tillman River became too rickety for coal cars. Glover Metals didn't have the money or the energy to fix it. They closed both mines. The Canadian National Railway considered the bridge okay for empty cars. The CNR parked five cars that needed repair on the spur line, out of the way. By the time CNR got back to the railcars on the other side of the river, the bridge had deteriorated too much for any rail traffic. Archie MacKenzie saw those cars when he arrived in Sterling Reserve. He saw them as great places to live. Archie quit his job, moved into the caboose and convinced his old friend Lank to join him at The Tracks.

Lank's wife, Irma, complained about the smell around The Tracks. "That fuckin' Ronnie. You could step in his shit three times a day. He don't care."

Archie had suffered the stink quietly but said, "Yes yes, there are a good number of people living here now and you with the baby, we need some facilities. Do you want to build an outhouse?"

"Oh yes. I do. You mean a community outhouse?"

"I don't think building individual outhouses would be good because, well, would Ronnie build one?"

"Gotcha. When do we start?"

"Let's make plans today and start tomorrow."

In the morning they hacked out a hole for the outhouse. Archie's slow, deliberate pace made it difficult to tell if he was working or resting. Irma worked fiercely, swinging the pick wildly at the hard earth and thrusting the short-handled shovel into the ground like a treasure hunter who just heard her shovel hit a strongbox. Archie raised the pick slowly and let it fall into the ground of its own weight. He put the shovel blade on the ground and pushed it in with his foot while probing for obstructions, which in that ground could be rocks, lumps of coal, roots or discarded pieces of metal. Archie scooped up his shovel full of dirt and placed it away from the hole with a smooth motion ending in an outstretched right arm twisting the shovel and emptying the dirt precisely where he wanted it to be. Irma flung the dirt out of the hole.

Irma and Lank and baby Lacie struggled to get by. Lank didn't spend much money on alcohol, being willing to drink almost anything but it interfered with his ability to work. People took their cars to Lank for repairs. Lank lay on his back on the ground, bent his long body over the engine and changed tires in the snow. If he wasn't drunk he did whatever work came to him. Irma made twenty dollars every Tuesday cleaning Richard Johnson's house and jerking him off. She worked around the house all afternoon wearing only a slip and masturbated him at the end of her working day. Irma washed her whole body in Richard Johnson's kitchen sink as he drifted into his after-sex sleep. She had to wake him up to get the twenty dollars before going home to feed Lacie. Lank had supper ready when she got back to the old CNR dining car they lived in.

Richard Johnson bragged about this but even the guys at the White Rose gas station didn't want to hear it. Reggie, the proprietor, told him to shut up and go home. Richard Johnson said, "She's the best lookin' woman around here. You fellas just wish she'd give you a hand job." Reggie's little brother Mark beat him, dragged him outside and threw him up against the gas pumps. After that Richard Johnson bought his gas at the Esso in Brookfield and got Lank to do the work on his car. The men who hung around the White Rose garage agreed that it was a shame Lank would do that.

Archie and Irma dug an eight by three foot hole in a day. They cut the hole neatly into the stoney ground. By the time they finished, most of The Tracks people were helping or hanging around. They picked up the best stones they could find and carried them to the hole to square up the rim as a foundation. It was a big event and as the sun quit the sky over The Tracks, Ronnie said, "Let's make a fire and have a drink. It's on me." That meant Ronnie offered his moonshine, which had a good reputation. Irma brought out a bag of last year's shriveled potatoes. She cleaned them off a bit and threw them in the campfire. Everyone took care of their own potatoes, turning them with a stick so they wouldn't burn on one side. The fire-roasted skins cooked crispy and dark with smoke but the inside was steaming white. They ate them with lots of salt and fat left over from frying cheap cuts of pork. City McKinnon had a couple of pounds of mutton scraps. A sharp metallic knock on the side of his rail car woke him early that morning. When he slid the heavy steel door open, he found the mutton on the steps to his boxcar. It was typical of the gifts City received; some anonymous, some presented with great flourish by superior benefactors and some offered humbly by gentle souls. Sterling Reserve had few refrigerators and not many residents of Sterling Reserve liked lamb; fewer liked mutton. When one of the local sheep got butchered, City got mutton. Lank cooked the mutton in an odd looking vessel made out of an oil pan from a derelict Mercury. He added spices and some fresh herbs from one of Archie's raised gardens. When the meat was done, Lank saved the fat in a can for future cooking. He dumped a mixture of flour, sugar, oatmeal and baking soda with raspberries into the pan to make bannock.

Irma brought out wine for City because he wouldn't drink Ronnie's strong moonshine. If you asked for wine at the Brookfield liquor store, the closest one to Sterling Reserve, the guy behind the counter passed you a bottle of Chateau Gai Scotia Port. If you gave a local wine drinker a glass of viniferous wine, he'd scrunch up his face and say, "That's right sour." Chateau Gai Scotia Port may have had a brief passing acquaintance with a grape but the twenty percent alcohol and extreme sweetness came from white sugar. City loved the stuff.

Everyone ate well and got drunker than usual. After sneaking back to his caboose twice to refill his moonshine cup with Anne Bonnie rum, Archie took the quart bottle out. It lasted ten minutes. Even little Lacie had a drink.

Irma said, "She likes the strong drink. When she takes a drink of juice, she likes a spot of moonshine in it, if I got any around. That ain't often, the way Lank drinks. She'll sleep good tonight after that little drink of rum."

City said, "My Jesus girl, she's not a year old." Irma shrugged as if she was just a spectator to her baby's growing up.

 Archie said, "Irma, drink isn't good for children. Perhaps it's no good for anyone."

"Oh, why you drinkin' then?"

"I suppose we do a lot of things we shouldn't."

"Should, shouldn't, I can't tell."

Archie lowered his head. "Yes yes, that's the way." He emptied his cup.

"Oh shit, here comes Custard. Don't give him anything to drink. He can't hold liquor, that's for sure." Ronnie put his gallon jug of shine behind him so Custard wouldn't see it.

Archie said, "Give him a break. Custard is crazy as a loon; he needs a break."

"I'll give him a break. I'll break his god damn head." Irma brandished a wine bottle. "He stole a whole cake that Lank made. He coulda asked me for some but he took the whole thing. City found two thirds of it on the ground over by the bridge. Custard just threw it away."

Custard called himself James Terrecci. Most people believed he made up the name. The new RCMP officer in Brookfield said that Custard often renamed himself. They knew of Solomon MacLeod, James L Freidberg and Lance Stone as aliases from Halifax, Truro and Fredericksburg, Virginia. But where ever he went, the name Custard Head waited for him there. It followed him around, it stuck to him and he hated it.

Custard Head lived with an older couple in Sterling Reserve. That year the Robinsons did not have the meager income provided by the province for housing foster children. Mrs. Robinson genuinely loved children but they really needed the money so she took in Custard Head. The Robinsons got paid by someone, Custard Head's family or perhaps some government agency or charity.

Custard Head was also known as Headache, Tap Head and Tard but at The Tracks they called him by his first name, Custard. They believed at The Tracks that Custard was involved in two deaths. As a passenger on a motorcycle, people saw him hitting and shaking the driver just before a fatal head-on collision with a car. In another incident a ten-year-old girl died when Custard's car hit her. Custard, the only witness, claimed that she darted out in front of him. The limited evidence at the scene did not refute or substantiate his claim but everyone from the little village in Maine agreed that she was a smart, careful little girl.

Custard's own death concerned him most. An attempted suicide, using an oxyacetilene torch, left a gruesome scar from his lower jaw to the top of his head. It took away the sight in his right eye. Custard had a pronounced limp caused by landing on his feet after jumping from a second story balcony. Both wrists had wounds and a failed or pretended attempt to stick a large knife into his heart mangled his left pectoral muscle. Most often he walked in front of moving cars in his failed suicide attempts. It became a pattern. He jumped into the path of a slow moving car, received a glancing blow and often got a few dollars from the driver for his scrapes and bruises.

Custard limped up to the partiers around the fire. "I'm starving to death. I'm going to die from no food."

"Here have some bannock. That'll stick to your ribs." Irma passed him a square of Lank's latest creation. He took it, turned it around in his hand and threw it in the fire.

"I don't like that."

Irma stood up, setting her beautiful face within inches of Custard's disfigured head. "You get the fuck away from here, you goddamn fairy."

Custard began to whine, a high-pitched noise calculated to cause maximum annoyance. "I want to drink. I want some of your illegal moonshine or I'll tell the police about it."

Ronnie, two inches shorter than Custard, picked him up by the ass of his pants and by his long hair. Custard kicked and screamed. Ronnie carried him over the bridge to drop him on the Sterling Reserve side of the Tillman River. He said a few words which seemed to create fear in Custard. When Ronnie walked back toward the campfire, Custard began to wail. Ronnie went back and said another few words to Custard who went quiet and limped away. He was bent over. Custard's balls suffered from Ronnie's carrying technique.

Archie said, "A bit hard on him, weren't you?"

Irma spoke for Ronnie, "Custard is the nastiest prick around. He's doubly annoying with them slinky, womanly ways. Ronnie done him a service by dragging him outa here, else I probably woulda killed the cocksucker."

Irma scared Archie a bit. She was a wild woman. He addressed the campfire crowd, "If anyone can find some boards and other materials tomorrow we should get started. We need tarpaper, shingles and a window. Two windows would be nice; small windows that could open. I got two by fours but they're old and not so good. We need something for sills, too. I may be able to get some two by six to laminate for sills." He put on his jacket. It was getting cold.

"Look at him, will ye." Irma laughed. "He's not got a spot of dirt on. Archie, I'm insulted. You weren't wearin' a tie all afternoon."

"Please accept my apologies Madame. My tie clip fell once and I worried if it happened again, your shovel would eat it up."

"Your goddamn hands are clean. I got dirt and sand up my arse."

Irma was a mess. She started the job in a tattered old dress which became a ragged old dress by noon. Her face and hair displayed a day of dirty work. She emptied stones out of her cut-off rubber boots at least twenty times during the process of digging the hole. Archie wore a dark gray suit. Archie always wore suits. His shoes got a bit dirty but otherwise you could not tell he had been anywhere near dirt all day.

"We got 'er done though, Archie. The tortoise and the hare. In the end we did the same amount of work I guess but at the finish line, the tortoise looks a damn bit better. The hare's got all kindsa dirt in her hair."

Lank looked at his wife, dirty but beautiful in shadows and firelight.

"We should put a sink in 'er. Put it in now and worry about connecting up later."

"Oh yeah, that'd be great. Maybe make a step for little ones to reach the sink."

"Yes, yes." Archie rolled cigarettes and passed them around. "A sink is a great idea. We should dig a little trench for the sink drain to direct it away from the shit pile under the outhouse. Too much liquid in there would make it smell worse."

City asked, "Why did you dig such a big jeesly hole anyway?"

"It's going to be a three-seater my man."

"What? Are you going to have parties in there?"

Irma said, "One hole is gonna be small enough for kids and there'll be a mama and a papa hole. Look around you, man. There are a lot of different sized arses in the world."

The campfire party slowly broke up. They went back to their cars to sleep, to digest or to drink a bit more at home, alone. Archie had a substantial glass of pretty good Scotch which he drank slowly while reading an old issue of Tribune magazine. He liked Scotch but it sometimes gave him heartburn. He went to bed with two Tums in his mouth.

Archie woke at eight in the morning with a dusty mouth. His blood vessels felt dusty. Two glasses of water and two cups of tea later, he ate his morning oatmeal. When he stepped outside, a flatbed one-ton truck rattled across the bridge. The bridge had planks laid over the tracks so they could drive on it. The one-ton left a cloud of smoke behind. Archie saw lumber, a door, several windows and a section of roof just the right size for the outhouse, piled up on the flatbed. /this looks like trouble/

Lank jumped out of the truck. "Good morning Arch. Jimmy Fox had this truck hanging around for near a year, waitin' for him to swap the engine. I told him I'd do it for five dollars if he'd loan me the truck for a week a year."

"Great, but where did you get this stuff?"

"The blue house. I asked Elliott and he said to fill our boots, cause the house is gone to hell anyway."

"I don't know Lank. What will the company think of this?"

"To hell with them. They don't care and I don't care if they do care."

"We're all squatters on their land."

"Yeah, yeah I know. It's too late now. I cut that section of roof out with a chainsaw. The roof on the other side was leakin' and there were two more windows broke that Elliott wasn't going to fix. Elliott took some stuff too."

Glover Metals still owned the blue house and most of the houses in Sterling Reserve. Glover Metals Mining Company was a family-owned English corporation. The company, a going concern up to the Second World War, sold off all their other enterprises shortly after closing the silver mine at Sterling Reserve. Elliott Bruce lived in a little shack next door to the blue house. He sent letters to the company's official address in Manchester. First he offered one thousand dollars for the house, then fifteen hundred. He reoffered the fifteen hundred in a third letter with a picture of the house showing that he had boarded up some broken windows. Six months later he sent the final letter with pictures of the roof which had shingles missing and pictures of rain leaking through the roof on the inside of the house. Elliott offered them eighteen hundred. In the only reply he got from the company, the president wrote, "No. How many times do I have to tell you? No. I will not sell the house to you."

In nineteen fifty-one, eighteen hundred dollars was a lot to offer for a run-down house in a town which lost its only reason for being. A mining town without a mine at the dead end of a road and a railway track was not prime real estate. Generally, the people of Sterling Reserve did not like Glover Metals when they operated the mines and liked them even less since they left. Elliott Bruce, who worked as a foreman in the silver mine, said of the Glover family, "They're half crazy and the other half is stupid. They look like three generations of brother and sister intermarriage."

Lank said, "I cut out the good part of the roof. We just eased it down one side with ropes. Worked slick."

"Well, since you pretty much destroyed the house, we might as well get pipes and stuff from there too."

"I didn't destroy it. It was leakin'. Windows and roof leakin' and most of the plaster down and everthin' startin' to rot, okay?"

"Okay, yes yes. Okay."

"The Curries jumped on it when we left. So, maybe, we should wait till they pick at the bones first."

"Oh yes, don't get involved with them." Archie laughed. "I'm sure those poor idiots will get blamed for it all, anyway."

"Archie, come look at the door."

Lank had the front door from the blue house. Built of oak with a frosted window panel, the panel had one little peek-a-boo square of clear glass in a frame set in the larger frosted glass panel. The peek-a-boo part had a curtain."

Archie said, "Oh yes. Yes, that's worth the risk. We'll have the best shit house in Canada."

CHAPTER TWO

Ronnie recognized the knock as someone tapping on the steel door of his rail car with a half empty bottle. He slid the door open and saw twenty-three-year-old Juliette Cameron in a light dress and open jacket.

"Somebody tell ya to knock like that?"

"Knock like what?"

"With the bottle."

"No, what is it, a secret code? My hands are full of bottles. See, each of them is full with a bottle."

"What do ya want?"

"A place to sleep. They say it is going to be cold tonight."

"If you're cold, button your coat."

"Fuck off then." Juliette turned to go but spun back around like a dancer. "Would you like some cloudberries? I am tired of carrying them around." She passed the quart milk bottle full of amber berries up to him. "They are absolutely delicious this late in the year." Her smile surprised Ronnie. He thought she was mad at him.

"Never touch the stuff." Ronnie grabbed the handhold by the side of his door; pivoted down and picked the wine bottle out of Juliette's other hand.

"Come on up. You can stay here." As Juliette pulled herself up into the boxcar, Ronnie unscrewed the top with the edge of his hand in a quick rolling motion. The bottle cap spun in the air over Juliette's shoulder. Ronnie drank half of the remaining sweet port and exhaled with the ghost of a whistle. "First one today."

She took the bottle from him with some force and drained the rest of it with one open-throated swallow. "Last one today, given my dire circumstances." She put the bottle on the floor. Ronnie kicked it out the door toward the small scattering of remainders from his two months at The Tracks.

"I am Juliette Cameron."

"G' day to ya. My name's Ronnie."

"Well, thank you Ronnie for inviting me in. I was not sure about it for a while there."

"People here know I got lots of moonshine; at least I had lots of moonshine. Some of them knock on my door with a half-empty bottle of something or other when they know they're gonna run out."

"Well, good shine is the purest of drinks."

"I had twenty-five jugs, a gallon each. I got them in Antigonish. Planned to sell it in Halifax but my car broke down in Brookfield. A guy lives here at The Tracks can fix cars good and don't charge an arm and a leg. Lank, do you know Lank?"

"No, I know only Ronnie."

"What do ya mean?"

"You, Ronnie, you are the only person I have met in Sterling Reserve. I got a ride on a fish truck as far as Brookfield and walked up here."

"That's a long fuckin' walk."

"Yes, I had time to pick cloud berries after I drank my milk. I planned to take the train up the valley and maybe walk over here on the Sterling Reserve branch line. Instead, I got my coat from my bag, put my high heels in it and stashed the bag in the station at The Harbour. The road along the shore is beautiful. I love this part of the world."

"You're pretty, like a movie star."

"Thank you, sir. Oh, the dress, I left a wedding in Halifax to come up here."

"Yeah, okay, ah, do you want a cup?"

"Tea?"

"Oh no, I mean a cuppa shine."

"Yes, that would be pleasant but I thought you were guarding it."

"Not any more. I'm leavin' here soon. Lank's got my car fixed, I guess, so now I have to find some shine I can get on credit so I can sell it to pay Lank. He owes for some parts he put on it. It was noisy when I bought it but I didn't know what was wrong until half the cylinders weren't working. Lank says the head was cracked."

"Ford Flathead V-8?"

"Yeah, how'd ya know?"

"I saw it out there by that next railcar. Did he get a new head or new engine?"

"He got a good used engine. Said he did something, ah, yeah, put in a new water pump; different one, better I guess. The car's only two years old." Ronnie poured substantial amounts of moonshine into stained teacups. "What'll ya have in that?"

"Oh, nothing thanks. Yes, too bad about the Ford. This is good shine. I have a few extra dollars. How much do you charge for a quart?"

"I don't sell quarts. There's two and a half gallons left. You can have them for ten dollars."

"That is too cheap for good moonshine. You probably paid that when you bought it in bulk from the family."

Ronnie looked alarmed. "How'd ya know where I bought it? I never said where I got it."

"You told me Antigonish. I failed out at St. FX partly because of too much of the Gillis's moonshine." Juliette found a box to sit on.

"You know a lot. You been to college. You're smart, I guess."

"Not smart enough to avoid this." Juliette raised her cup of shine. She drank it straight. Ronnie mixed his down with a bit of apple juice.

"You're a hard drinker, eh?"

"No, not so much lately. I am going to have a baby I guess, and I get sick easily. Thanks for the offer but I could not carry two gallons of moonshine."

"Where ya going?"

"This is where I was going. I need a place to live. I might go to Halifax, or Montréal. Perhaps to the States or I may crawl back to Glace Bay and try to look repentant. There is no good reason to choose one place over another."

"Look, I'm movin' out, probably tomorrow or Wednesday. For fifteen bucks you can have the shine and the car."

"Five dollars for a car?"

"This here, this train car, my home sweet home for the last two months. I don't own it or nothin'. I just took it 'cause it was empty but you can't have it unless it's empty or I give it to you. What do you say, fifteen dollars?"

Juliette reached into her brown messenger satchel and pulled out fifteen dollars. "Here is the fifteen. I might forget I paid you if I get drunk. Will you remember?"

He laughed, "I won't forget. That brings my fortune up to seventeen dollars and twenty-six cents. Why did ya come to my car?"

"I thought it might be presumptuous to choose the palatial caboose next door. Who lives there, the mayor?"

Ronnie laughed and coughed. A loosely rolled cigarette hung from his mouth. He didn't remove it for talking or coughing, just for drinking. Ronnie tilted his head and closed one eye to avoid the smoke snaking up from his cigarette. "Yeah, he's mayor of The Tracks, Mayor MacKenzie. Jesus, ya'd think he was a Prime Minister, the way he goes around. What did you mean presumt...?"

"Presumptuous: it means forward, asking too much." She leaned back against the wall.

"Yeah, okay, that's what I thought." Ronnie sat in a rocking chair held together with tape.

Juliette's stilted speech irritated certain people but it never seemed to bother those like Ronnie who spoke in careless local dialects. Ronnie told her that he was a driving bootlegger. He bought quality moonshine or bought rum from Saint Pierre, a French protectorate off Newfoundland's south coast. Ronnie resold the booze in Halifax to a dozen customers who were small-scale retailers themselves.

Ronnie couldn't read or write. He lived with his mother on the old family farm at East Bay, Cape Breton, when he wasn't on the road or in jail. At thirty years old, he had spent a cumulative thirty-seven months in jail for bootlegging or beating up customers who hadn't paid. Ronnie supported himself, his mother and his older brother who "… ain't too smart and he's got nerves, so he can't work much. He'll milk the cow but won't collect the eggs 'cause he's scared of the chickens."

"I remember one time…" Ronnie chuckled and coughed so much he had to take the cigarette out of his mouth. "I remember I got caught once. I always made sure, there on the farm, I had lotsa firewood cut and dried and lotsa potatoes and cabbage stored and flour and sugar in case I'd have to go away for a time. They searched the house. They never done that before but they found five twenty-pound bags of sugar. The Bulls charged me with makin' moonshine along with sellin' it. That was a separate charge. When I got to court, I says to the judge, 'I never made no moonshine. I only bought that much sugar and flour to get my mother and brother through, if I got caught.' I says to him, 'I don't know how to make moonshine and the stuff I sell is good-quality shine made by people who knows what they're doin'.' He asked the court clerk to bring one of the gallon jugs of shine up to him. They had a dozen jugs of shine and five bags of sugar in the courtroom for evidence. The Crown prosecutor wanted to put me away for two years. He said I was a danger to children, stole from the province, all kinds of stuff. He almost had me convinced I was a rotten guy. Anyway, the judge drinks all the water in his glass up there on his judge's desk and he pours, it must've been three shots of moonshine, into the glass. He sniffs it, takes a little sip, then a bigger drink, then he polishes it off in one drink. Then he says, 'The defendant didn't make this beverage.' He called it 'this beverage'. He sentenced me to two weeks and three months suspended. The court clerk guy went back up to the judge's desk and like, put his hand out for the jug of shine but the judge just didn't pay no attention. We all had to stand up when he's leavin' and he took the jug of my moonshine with him. I figure twenty-three and a half months of freedom was pretty good pay for a jug of shine. Anyway, they gave the sugar back to me."

Ronnie talked about himself and about The Tracks and her new neighbor, Archie Mackenzie. Archie lived in the caboose surrounded by a low wooden fence. The fence had an eight-inch plank on top to make it comfortable for sitting. The caboose and fence were freshly painted red with white trim. He had extra windows installed in the caboose, all with curtains. The two larger windows had Venetian blinds. Whereas the other five cars at The Tracks were surrounded by rough shale and gravel, pit rock really, Archie's yard had raised beds made of railway ties. One held a selection of small pruned conifers and hardwoods, indigenous to the area. Another had remains of the summer's vegetable crop with parsley and basil still fresh and green. Another bed contained a small apple tree and a bush of local berries. The fourth bed contained several thorny wild plants: burdock, thistle, small thorn bushes and black raspberry canes.

Archie usually wore very good-looking suits. When he worked in his garden, digging holes or patching the roof, he took precautions in order to stay clean. His shoes were not of the same high quality as his suits but he kept them clean and polished.

Archie moved slowly, talked slowly and rested often. He smoked a pipe occasionally and drank most afternoons, getting quite drunk once or twice a week. When drunk, he moved more slowly, talked less and rested more often.

A wind-powered electrical generator stuck out of the caboose roof. Archie built it from a forty-gallon copper tank cut in half, the axle of a wrecked Prefect, an aluminum shaft and some belts and pulleys. When the wind blew, this contraption turned an old Chevy generator charging two car batteries to power lights and a radio.

Juliette and Ronnie drank a lot of moonshine. They decided to trust each other in the way you can trust a stranger. Stranger trust doesn't matter much unless you are dead wrong about it. Easy freewheeling talk flowed between them with no shared past to sputter and block the conversation. Ronnie and Juliette had a night of convivial drinking except for the ten minutes of hostility Ronnie passed through on his way to extreme drunkenness, and the few minutes of morose self-deprecation Juliette passed into before passing out.

* * *

She opened her eyes in the morning and didn't see Ronnie. As consciousness and memory returned, Ronnie did not. Juliette remained on the floor in her clothes under a mildewed blanket for an hour, hoping the nausea would settle out. When she finally got up, she couldn't get the heavy sliding door opened quickly. Juliette threw up on the threshold of her new home. She slumped down on the broken rocking chair Ronnie left behind.

"This here is your car now."

Juliette saw a tall thin man outside the partly open door. "Why, because I threw up on it?"

"No, because Ronnie left this morning. He told me and Archie, that's the guy lives in the caboose, that you could have the car and everything in it. I'm Lank. I live right there with my wife and daughter." Lank smiled. He made few hand gestures but spoke with his whole body. His knees flexed continually, seemingly sideways as well as bending forward and back like knees should. His pigeon chest thrust out then withdrew, his shoulders circled and his head bobbed. To Juliette, it looked like some sort of discomfort crawled around inside his clothes and tickled him to the edge of pain. Lank seemed glad to be there, thrilled to be alive, amazed at every word said and awed by another tick of the clock. Lank bowed his head slightly, turned to one side or the other and then brought it up to meet Juliette's gaze with his whole bearded face and pale, lucent blue eyes. This head-bobbing exercise took about two seconds. Each time that he cycled through it to the point where he looked up again, Juliette felt relief that he had gotten through another one. He was, however, very handsome.

"Thank you Lank and thanks to Ronnie wherever he may be." She got up from the rocking chair.

"Yeah, I hope he is in his car that I fixed up for him and I hope he is happily on his way. There's a shit… I mean an outhouse over there if you feel the need again."

"Yes, I have been there. I just did not make it that time. It is a great outhouse, fabulous really." Juliette recalled Ronnie describing Lank's participation in the design and building of the outhouse and how proud he was of Irma's part in it. "I have got to lie down for a bit of time. My name is Juliette Cameron."

"Yeah, you go lie down. You'll get over it. Ronnie's shine is strong but it's good. You'll be fine enough in no time."

"I will see you; so long." She started sliding the door closed but decided against that in favor of the fresh air, her vomit being more inside the car than outside. "I'll clean that up later." she added weakly. Lank's head bobbed and he smiled.

After another hour of sleep, Juliette woke up tired and hungry. Her predicament was not unfamiliar, a cold dirty place, no food, not much money and getting over being too drunk. She put herself through it often. She crawled back under the dirty blanket, masturbated and slid off to sleep again.

Juliette woke after forty-five minutes but didn't get up. She was daydream awake, drifting into pieces of sleep, easily ducking the slabs of memory and expectation that tried to corner her and force her to take a stand. Juliette enjoyed these afternoons of recovery from a night of heavy drinking. It wasn't the return to strength she looked forward to but this drifting nowhere with her limbs, her torso strewn on something, covered by something, and the little tingle between her legs that drew her hands there to enjoy. She conjured up old lovers, passersby, pictures she had seen and mixed them with the feel of her own thin body and horny smells. It overwhelmed the smell of vomit, booze and failure. Another heavy, sultry, slow orgasm flushed through her. The third one was always hard to come by, requiring strained images of sex pushed past the borders into badness and perversion. She'd have to vigorously stroke her upper vagina, rapidly massaging with the first two fingers of both hands, squeezing and abusing. The effort was unattractive. She let the world seep into her senses along with the underlying presence of The Tracks; the smell of steel, dust and creosote.

***

Juliette cleaned up the doorway with an oily rag and some toilet paper. Seeing nobody about, she slinked off to the outhouse. The sun blinded her but the brisk October air refreshed. She squinted, eyes almost completely closed, on the way back from the outhouse. But the inside of her car was dismal. The kerosene lamps that looked so warm during last night's drunkenness hung dirty on the walls beneath black streaks of soot. The brakeman's lamp on the one small table was so dirty that Juliette doubted any light would penetrate the smoky glass. The open sliding door made a wide gap but its light died where it fell. In the areas untouched by the direct light nothing could be clearly discerned. She had recovered enough to be able to think, /at least I have moonshine/

A knock on the side of her railcar announced a dark blue suit with a gray pinstripe. A man carrying a biscuit tin filled with steaming soup occupied the suit.

"You must be Archie?"

"And you're Juliette."

"Yes I am Juliette Cameron. You bring a gift."

"Yes yes, it's bean and barley soup. It's got some potatoes, some ham and onions and it could keep you going for a week."

"Well, I am a hungry girl and I thank you very much."

He said, "Yes yes, when people arrive here at The Tracks, it's not because they have a lot of money. Being broke and hungry seems to be the entrance fee. The folks here will generally help out a bit as long as no one takes advantage of our moderate generosity."

"Well you, Archie, with your suit and tie and your shoes which must have been offended, I am sure, by my doorway, can line up the rules and define the zeitgeist in short order."

Archie laughed and grinned the sheepish grin of the just caught. "Yes yes, I suppose I presented a gift of humble food with caveats." His smile opened up as his embarrassment became mirth. "If you partake of the bean soup, you'll have adopted the liturgy of The Tracks. We'll have a ceremony and you'll become exactly like the rest of us."

"From what I have seen and heard, I think that is a wide range. I might just fit in."

"It's a good spot. I've got everything I want right here."

Juliette questioned, "Boredom?"

"Pardon me."

"Having everything you want, that would seem to preclude any further excitement."

"Yes yes. I suppose I'll have to watch what I say to you. Perhaps what I should have said is that I feel… I find a pleasing sufficiency here."

"Yes. It may be necessary for me to get over my substantial hangover to sort 'everything I want' from 'pleasing sufficiency'. I look forward to that."

"Looking forward to the sorting out, or the pleasing sufficiency?"

"I will have to watch what I say to you."

"Okay, I'll leave you now. I live next door so don't be a stranger."
Archie started to leave but turned back. "Since we're being frank, I
really don't like visitors a lot but, well, I am, I suppose, neighborly."

Juliette said, "Me though, I am friendly when sober and annoyingly
gregarious when drunk. You will have to watch out for me.
But I cannot be insulted, it is not in me, so do not worry about
offending."

Archie said, "Bye."

"Toot toot, thanks for the soup."

Juliette was amazed at how Archie's half-broken front tooth added
such color and honesty to his already unabashed smile; a delightful,
good-looking fellow.

Juliette's new home had originally been a parcel car but got
converted to an insulated cold car. A crude window covered the
hole where the refrigeration unit had been.

Ronnie had eagerly told Juliette the history of the car. It became
a cold car in order to transport the remains of sailors who died
on a storm-wrecked fishing boat trying to make it to port at the
difficult harbour of Lockeport. The coffins were bound for Halifax,
Lunenburg, New Bedford and Gloucester. Juliette wondered if she
recognized or imagined the smell of dead humans and disinfectant.
She wondered if this steel box she adopted as home would do her
harm, wear her down.

She found a spoon among the things that Ronnie left behind.
Juliette ate the soup directly from the biscuit tin. The fading label
said, 'NABISCO PREMIUM SALTINES thin crisp crackers'. /
another tin with the thin crisp crackers would be nice/ But the plain,

unimaginative soup settled out any traces of nausea.

Sunshine, coming through the sliding door opening, made a parallelogram on the far wall. Dust danced slowly in the little breeze. Juliette put on her worn blue shoes and stepped down to the gravel track bed. Slouched against the corrugated steel of her new home, she closed her eyes. Through many trials Juliette established that it took six minutes for the booze-shot eyes to allow for sunlight. Less than six minutes and she suffered hours of aching behind her eyes; more than six minutes and people inquired about her health, which was just a pain in the ass. Juliette enjoyed the heat and the light pressing her skin, burning the toxins from her body and spirit. Opening her eyes confirmed the feeling that someone watched her.

"Yes maid, you'd best get the sun while it's still around. My name is Irma."

"Hello Irma. I am Juliette Cameron and that must be Lacie staring at the new girl from the safety of your arms."

"Jesus yes. She generally don't notice much as far away as you are, unless it's movin' but she locked on to you some quick."

Juliette walked over to them. Irma stood on a well-made doorstep in front of a dining car.

"I have windows."

Irma said, "Yeah that crazy Ronnie never opened up the part of the car with the windows. I guess that was the living quarters for the parcel man or Postman, whatever he was."

"Oh that makes me feel great. Living in a windowless box… I did not look forward to that." The baby, just one-year-old, gave a little cackle as Juliette spoke. A tiny hand stuck out from the blanket.

"Holy holy, likes you don't she now? Gonna shake the pretty lady's hand are you, Lacie?"

"How do you do, Lacie? I am pleased to meet you." Juliette took her hand, kissed it and made an elaborate bow. Mother and daughter chuckled. Juliette had no idea what to do next. She never really liked or understood children even when she was one herself.

"You're scared of babies."

"What?"

"You're going to have one, ain't ya?"

"Yes. I am not exactly afraid of them. I just do not know how to deal with children."

"Well girl, it's not common knowledge. It's a blessing that you know you don't know. I believe it's incommunicable knowledge that nobody can tell ye about, except the baby. So to that end, here, you hold her because I gotta go to the toilet and she ain't dressed for it. She'll lose that blanket pretty quick when she gets crawlin' around."

Irma passed Lacie to Juliette and strolled to the outhouse with her arms loosely swinging. The light cotton skirt that she wore, the easy motion of her hips and the bounce in her step took Juliette's eye. /*effortlessly sexy*/

"You know that your mother has just the loveliest arse. Will you have an arse like that?"

Lacie cooed and bobbled and smiled.

"You are an easy study, kid. You look pleased. Is everyone here good-looking and smart?"

Lacie was indeed not dressed. Under the blanket she wore only a thin plaid diaper, roughly cut from an old dress but Lacie didn't like the blanket. "You want to get a tan, is that it little Lacie? Actually you are not little at all."

Juliette let her squirm out of the blanket and then placed it underneath her in case the homemade diaper was asked to perform beyond its capacity. She carried Lacie up and down The Tracks speaking to her, "Oh this one is beyond unusual. This is fucking nuts. What is it, a coal car with a pickup truck welded on top? It does the job though, or looks like it does the job. What a contraption. I think I may like it here. Do you like it here, Lacie, the not-so-little?" Juliette concluded over the next few months that Lacie's mother rarely arrived; she just appeared. When Juliette turned to walk back to her car, Irma stood a few steps away.

"I had a friend at home who was a stiff skater. At Isle aux Morts, there's lots of places to skate but not many skates. Nancy had a real nice pair of white ones that she didn't like to share. She loaned them to me though. That was great because my brothers' old skates were way too big and falling right apart, indeed they were. Everybody told Nancy that you had to be relaxed in order to skate but fallin' scared her. She stayed right stiff. She never fell, just by her effort, by sheer force of will. Nancy was able to skate the way you're not supposed to be able to skate. Are ye like that?"

Juliette paused before answering. "Did Nancy enjoy skating?"

"She loved it. She said she loved it."

"I don't like babies. They make me nervous. Was Nancy generally stiff or just when she skated?"

"No, I guess no but she was afraid of danger. She could meet people and be happy and fine even at exams and stuff at the school but if we were driving crazy or out on the boats acting the fool, she got stiff. Oh yeah she hated being out on the rocks. But like, with babies, she wasn't stiff at all."

"No, I am not generally stiff. Maybe I have some things that make me rigid but I can only think of one offhand, babies. No I really

31

cannot think of anything else, just babies and little kids in general. But that is okay. Walking around with Lacie is not daunting. In fact I feel quite comfortable with her. It surprises me that you think I feel stiff."

"It's the way you're talking' maid. It's like you're deliverin' a lecture in a tavern."

"Yes I see. I do that deliberately. Is baby talk good for kids? Do they ask for it? I have no understanding of it, really."

"Guaranteed, automatic you'll talk baby babble when you gets your own."

"Fuck off, Irma. How would you know what I will do? I bet you a chocolate cake I will not speak to my child in baby talk."

Irma raised her eyebrows. "With boiled icing?"

"Most certainly, my dear."

"You're on girl. I can taste it now. You don't have a man, do ya?

"Not at the moment but it only takes a moment."

"I can see that. Lank said you were beautiful and he's right."

Juliette was embarrassed. "I do not mean that. When I get drunk my standards get lower. Well, actually when drunk, my standards disappear. I got drunk and some fellow I cannot remember knocked me up."

"Are ya gonna keep it?"

"I am not sure. I guess I will just fall into it. Lately my decisions seem to make themselves without much participation on my part."

Irma finally took Lacie back and said, "That makes good sense, maid. Ya know it means you're going to keep your baby?"

"It seemed to be so unlike me to have a child, to be a mother. No, motherhood did not fit with me so I guess I thought I could not get pregnant."

"Lacie sure likes you. What do you want a girl or boy?"

Juliette said, "Oh rats. I hope it is not a boy. I do not like children much but I dislike boys."

Irma laughed a deep conspiratorial laugh. "You're an evil one, you are."

"And you have got that greasy grin yourself."

"Ah so ya knows some Newfy talk. Ye also knows Monte House, don't ya?"

"Monte was my deckhand."

Irma said, "Yes I thought it might be you he talked about was his skipper. I knew the name was Cameron and I thought maybe it was Juliette he talked about. By the Jesus, he always raved about you. The best captain and the most beautiful woman in the world if you'd listen to Monte."

Juliette smiled. "Monte from Isle aux Morts. Some of the guys called him Monte Mort."

"Yeah, they teased him a lot out around home, too. Yes maid, he got teased for having had a woman for a skipper."

"I was not a woman, more a girl. I started as skipper at seventeen. Monte was on my old boat with me and moved onto my new one when I bought her. He is a very pleasant man. He did not work especially hard but he did not need to. Monte has a great feel for a boat. Most of us plod around on a boat but Monte moves with grace."

Irma rewrapped Lacie in the blanket. As she listened to Juliette her eyes glistened with the beginnings of tears. She bowed her head to avoid detection but then looked straight into Juliette's eyes, sniffling. "I ner' ever heard no one call Monte House a man. He's just one of the boys around the Bay. I ain't never heard no one praise him before. He's been a little guy like, and they teased him relentless and he didn't take it good so they always kept at him."

"Yes I have seen that. He is not stupid; he is a dreamer. He sees beauty in seagulls. He sees beauty. I like him a lot."

"If ever I see him again, I'll be tellin' him in front of the others that his skipper from Glace Bay spoke very highly of him."

"From what you said, Monte is not ashamed to speak well of me. I know at least one of my old crew who will not admit to working with a female skipper even though he caught more fish with me than with anybody else."

Irma bounced Lacie, who began to fuss. "Monte told me that. Said he made real good money fishing on your boat. I'll be going now, Lacie wants feedin' and I don't take my tits out in public, leastways not to feed a baby." Juliette laughed and Irma smirked that greasy grin. She took Juliette's hand, "I hope you stays on here a good long while."

"It feels good to talk to you and it was a pleasure to hold your baby."

Irma took her child back to the old dining car. Juliette went to the outhouse. She tried the middle seat but the hole was a bit large for comfort so she sat on the right, the smallest hole, designed for children. The bowel movement came quickly. She felt all of last night's over-drinking being expelled. Juliette became something like lonely. She'd like to be still talking with Irma, maybe even with Lacie. She'd like to be over-drinking again.

CHAPTER THREE

A warm excitement filled Archie with possibilities. His new neighbor had him jumping. That he felt something like being in love excited him a bit but not much. 'In love' comes and goes. Juliette restored a balance at The Tracks. Ronnie was an interesting character but not the right sort. Archie didn't closely define what Ronnie lacked as a resident of The Tracks. He hesitated to drop in on his own conundrum, the irreconcilable democracy versus elitism.

Archie attended St. FX, the same Nova Scotia university where Juliette spent two years. He studied the co-op and internationalist movements of Jimmy Tompkins and Moses Coady. These Catholic priests taught that communities, business, housing and government should be people's initiatives. An educated populace could run it all; no need for top-heavy capitalism or the Marxist dictatorship of the proletariat. However, an intellectual elitism hovered over the Antigonish Movement. Father Jimmy Tompkins didn't usually say hello when he met someone new. He would more likely ask, "Do you read?" Not everyone in Nova Scotia did read in the nineteen-forties and Father Jimmy wasn't much interested in talking to anyone who did not read and only those who read Latin or ancient Greek could really catch his attention.

Archie believed that these wonderful dreamers tried to gloss over differences among people. In Archie's view, a lot of people couldn't really be educated because they weren't intelligent enough, diligent enough or they didn't care. Archie rejected the idea that everyone who had the curiosity to give a fuck, should give a fuck. Knowledge could make you evil rather than leading you to the good, as Socrates believed. Archie loved democratic ideals but loving it doesn't make it work; doesn't make it workable.

As the first resident of The Tracks, he invited his good friend Lank to join him and live in another car. By the time Lank arrived in Sterling Reserve he had a girlfriend and they planned to marry. It took Archie some time to realize that Irma was brilliant. After seeing her and Juliette talking, he wondered what they thought of each other. He hoped this would work. He hoped Juliette would stay. Archie wanted The Tracks to become a haven for non-academics who could think, discuss and learn. Ronnie was non-academic but no intellectual. Juliette Cameron looked like full-card bingo.

Archie made attempts to bend the population mix in the little community toward his conception of an interesting gathering of thinking people. He promoted The Tracks to those he thought might fit and tried to subtly discourage people who would bring it down to a mere stationary hobo camp. Lank, however, told any strangers he met that an empty car waited for them at The Tracks. Archie could not bring himself to ask his old friend not to do this. Lank would stop, if he asked him to but Archie had trouble admitting to himself that he disapproved of the random democratizing effect of inviting anybody to live in the next available rail car. He certainly could not admit that to Lank.

Archie also liked drinking buddies. Juliette would make a great drinking buddy. His excitement caused sensations of a smile inside his mouth, a tickling in his chest and pleasant electric jitters in his legs and groin. Door locked, lights off and curtains closed, he lit a candle and went to the brakeman's box to get a cloth bag with a small jar in it. The jar contained a yellow powder. Archie would see the pinkish tinge in the yellow after he smoked a bit of it. He might, inadvertently, leave an opium pipe hanging around after getting stoned, so he smoked it in his regular pipe. Archie smoked the pipe tobacco to get it hot, added a quarter teaspoon of opium on top and took a deep, long drag. Two puffs, a decent radio station and he enjoyed the rest of the night.

He picked up CJCB from Cape Breton and got a mix of jazz and popular music. Sarah Vaughan followed Les Paul and Mary

Ford. Archie sat perfectly still in his chair as the musical phrases twirled around his head. All the faults of his converted car radio disappeared. The musicians entered the room. Every note fell perfectly. He switched the radio off when the news came on. Looking for another station seemed like insurmountable effort.

Archie never knew how stoned he would get, partly because of the inconsistent quality of the opium and because he never carefully measured the amount he used. He drifted off into an opium sleep that quickly turned to erotic half-waking dreams. The new woman, in the car next to his, whirled through the sumptuous dreams. An hour later, he puffed up again. One drag of opium and tobacco removed time. Archie knew it was morning when he heard a knock on his door but he had no sense of any duration between his last puff and the morning knocking. He looked out a window to see Irma and she saw him.

"Come out for breakfast, my dear. Juliette's got a huge scoff on."

Archie got cleaned up and dressed. The slight worry about detection of his infrequent opium use evaporated as he brushed his teeth. Cleaning the teeth brings innocence and goodness. He walked toward Juliette's car. Irma met him. "Bring a chair with ya, Archie. We're a bit short of chairs. Good day there Archie; are ya hearin' and not heedin' or… Have ya made it to the morning yet, Archie?"

Archie often felt discomfort around Irma. She was so blatantly sexy and she seemed to have made it her quest to take his clothes away. She wanted him exposed. Irma assumed that if you kept something from her that automatically made it her business.

Archie managed his anger, "Irma, are you trying to make me regret waking up?"

"Well, my son, we need another chair. I'll go get it." She headed for his car but he didn't remember putting the pipe and lamp away.

"Stay they hell out of my car unless you're invited."

"Sure, proper thing."

His heart fell to his shoes. Irma quickly walked back to Juliette's car. Archie didn't like direct confrontation. He preferred the appearance of running smoothly but Irma was so sexually electric and so willing to exercise all of her power all of the time. Her being Lank's wife complicated matters. Irma had made clear signs that she wanted to have sex with Archie. Although tempted, he resisted fucking his best friend's wife and became very glad of that. Archie didn't trust her and he believed she would use it against him somehow if he succumbed to her advances. Irma's attractiveness made him feel somehow diminished that he hadn't taken the bait. He liked her and enjoyed time spent with Irma but she often pushed when he wanted to be left alone. He would not apologize for yelling at her, thinking it restored a certain balance; telling her where the limits were.

Archie stepped up into the parcel car and Juliette said welcome and good morning. She told him to have a seat. The chair she offered must have been Irma's, who made a movement a bit like stomping her foot. She stood with her arms folded trying to dissipate some internal heat. Archie accepted the chair as graciously as he could, thinking that Juliette knew of the tiff and chose his side. He still felt stoned, tentative and unsure of his footing but it lifted him up to think that Juliette took his side. The smells of breakfast hit him. He recognized cinnamon and bacon and coffee, so rich he thought the opium made it smell like that.

Lank held Lacie, who sucked on some sort of spiced apple slices. "Arch, buddy, you've gotta try the coffee. I spent fifteen minutes crushing coffee beans. It's out of this world."

Archie did not want to seem naïve but then decided that disarmingly frank would work well. "I don't think I've ever seen a coffee bean."

Juliette passed a small can to him. "These are very heavily roasted. My father gets them from a customer of his in France. Father Jimmy doesn't drink coffee so he sends them to me when he can find me. I carried some in my satchel for a couple of weeks now. This is the first time I stopped long enough to use them. Try one. They are bitter but a great flavor." Archie chewed one. It reminded him of the burnt flavor of his pipe tobacco after the opium had flared out. Archie was getting his bearings in this little breakfast society. The unpredictable effects of the opium would sometimes cause him to be dazzled by simple things, unable to act. In some other minute, the opium made him feel like he could do anything. A large ball of colored yarn occupied his head but it started to congeal into something like a brain.

"Oh Irma, I'm sorry. I must've taken your chair." He got up. Irma unfolded her arms, sat down and said, "I'll take her, Lank."

Archie realized that in one day, Juliette made the car clean and cozy. The other section, with the windows, was opened up and cleaned up. Juliette had the coal stove going. She used wood scraps and small limbs picked up in the woods. She had cleaned the lamps and Ronnie's kerosene heater. The walls, floor and the sparse furniture didn't sparkle but a quite presentable railcar home surrounded Archie and friends. Conviviality tamped down his anger and his mistrust of Irma.

"Juliette, the car looks great. Did you do all this yourself?"

"Yes, being itinerant for more than a year taught me how to quickly fix up a run-down place to something close to livability."

"Well a rail car is an odd container for a person to live in. You made it look very homey in a short time."

Irma said, "Yes you have, girl. This was a shit hole when Ronnie lived here. It always smelled of kerosene and piss. Our place is far from perfect but Ronnie was just looking for temporary shelter, I guess."

Lank said, "We all look for temporary shelter; we all want to come in from the cold, find a place to rest."

Archie was stoned again, dumped right back into it by Lank's words. Coming down often happened like this. It drained away slowly but then an opium wave rolled back. He liked that but wanted to gather his thoughts together.

Juliette brought out plates of various colors and sizes, all stacked high with breakfast. "Archie, I had no chance to ask what you wanted, so by default, you get the whole works. Here, the shelf along here is a great place to keep your plate. I tried it, and it is a bit high for me but it should be perfect elbow leaning for you."

It was. The shelf along the length of the wall must have acted as a counter for the parcel man. The plate of food contained fried potatoes with onions and spices that he could not identify, little strips of smoked mackerel, and scrambled egg, also strangely spiced. A green mush sat on the rim of his plate as well as pieces of fried apple and banana with maple syrup on top. City McKinnon said, "My Jesus Lord, where'd you get the pesto, girl? I ain't seen pesto since I come back from overseas in forty-five."

"I hitchhiked to Halifax yesterday and got some stuff."

City said, "Where'd you get this in Halifax?" At that same time, Lank said, "You hitchhiked to Halifax besides cleaning up this pigsty? Oh sorry. I didn't mean to call your place a pigsty. I mean it's not a pigsty." Juliette stopped him from talking with a light kiss on his lips.

"It was a pig house, Lank, and as I told Archie, I am too much of a tramp to ever be insulted."

Irma snapped "What kind of tramp, maid? The kind that goes around kissin' my husband?"

"Since he is your husband, love, I will not fuck him but he is a very kissable guy and I would like to be able to do that in this sort of spontaneous fashion as long as it does not get your knickers in a knot."

Irma laughed, throwing her head back. She was most sexy when she did this. "I was just kiddin' girl. You go ahead and fuck with him. I'd be proud to have you underneath my old man." Irma threw her head back and laughed again. Archie had tasted the green mush at the same time he saw Juliette's gentle kiss. The opium flood came back. He was glad because it would be at least a week before he got high on opium again. These little remnants were precious. Archie watched Lank squirm like a little kid after the kiss. He never understood how that man could be simultaneously nervous and delighted most of the time. The warmth he felt for Lank filled the room and he thought /this is a wonderful day/ these are wonderful people/

He said, "Yes yes, I also want to know where the, what is it, pesto, came from. My God, what a taste."

Juliette said, "Put it on your eggs. It is a little strong by itself. Fuck, I forgot to make toast."

"Sit your arse down. We don't need no toast. But you'll have to sit on the floor as Mayor MacKenzie was too stingy to bring a chair to breakfast."

"I would have brought a chair but I was afraid Irma would sit in it and well, then I'd have to destroy it." Irma skillfully flicked a piece of potato at Archie's face with a slingshot fork. Archie half expected the fork so he was ready and caught the potato in his left hand, picked it out of his hand with his fork and ate it. "These potatoes are delicious. What's on them?"

Everyone laughed. Irma said, "It's my spit, love." and she enjoyed another big throaty laugh.

Juliette held Lacie on her hip like a real mother. "Okay stop that, children. You must behave. The pesto came from a little Greek store on Spring Garden Road and I put wilted rosemary on the potato. I stole some from your planter. Don't you use it?"

"No, I don't ever cook anything special."

Lank said, "You know I ain't seen Archie move that fast since we played baseball. He can run like a bugger you know."

City said, "No need to rush. More hurry, less speed."

"You never cook anything special?"

"No, I can't cook. Boiling an egg is a challenge for me. You've already had my best dish; a can of bean and barley soup is the best I can do."

"That was good. However, with a little less salt and some garlic and basil it would be great. If you do not have a natural knack for cooking, follow a recipe, the amounts, the cooking times. It is only chemistry."

Archie said, "I could never match Lank's cooking no matter how hard I tried and now there's you. It's a total mystery to me how you can make anything taste this good."

Irma said, "You two should have a cookoff."

Lank answered, "Competition is for fools. You only get to enjoy half of it."

Archie remembered that being around Lank felt a bit like being stoned.

City said, "When a boxer gets a big whack in the jaw, it must hurt some bad."

Juliette served coffee and tea while bouncing Lacie on her hip. "She is heavy."

"I'll take her, girl."

"No, love, I have to practice." She dipped her finger in a little pitcher of cream, letting Lacie lick it off.

Archie sipped coffee, "I don't want to sound like a hick but I guess I am, and since Lank never cooked me a breakfast as good, this is the best breakfast I ever had, by far."

Juliette said thank you with her head bowed. She accepted the compliment with what Archie saw as sweet humility, happy to have given something, glad to be appreciated.

Lank said, "Me too. I'd remember if I had a breakfast this good. Thanks Juliette."

Juliette seemed to try to make herself even smaller.

Irma said, "It was shit. I threw mine at Archie." She laughed that deep laugh, fierce freedom and abandon.

The breakfast party broke up but Lacie and Archie stayed. He didn't really know what to say. She impressed him so much. Juliette was beautiful and erotically interesting and seemed like a genuine good soul. If she proved to be amenable to having sex, would he do it? A pregnant woman so dangerously easy to love, he'd have a family in no time. It's great to feel free and jump into things but jumping in so often takes your freedom away. Archie smoked opium but he kept it down to once or twice a month and never did it twice in one week. He considered getting high a freeing experience but trepidation about the possibility of becoming locked into a habit kept Archie a conservative opium user.

Lacie took all of Juliette's time and attention while Archie cleaned greasy dishes in a large bowl of cold water. "She tried to hook me into babysitting when she first came here and Lacie was only two months or something. If you went over there now, you might find Lank at home but Irma will be long gone. You won't see her till tonight. Perhaps I'm gossiping, running down the neighbors but I feel it's just fair warning. When the child gets hungry, there won't be much you can do."

"Does she have anything but her mother's milk? I don't know a fucking thing about these little creatures."

Archie shook his head. "I think she has some solid food but I don't know what. I know she drinks moonshine with flat 7-Up or something."

"You mean Lacie?"

"I'm afraid so."

Juliette said, "Godamn. I have some cream. I can warm it up but how will I get it in her. She needs to suck on something, right? Fuck it. I am taking her home. Trickery pisses me off."

Juliette came back with Lacie still on her hip. She also had a baby bottle. "Amazing, they just dumped her on me. I do not know my head for my hole when it comes to kids."

"It isn't they who dumped her. It's Irma. She likely told Lank you volunteered and everything was under control. He hates to accuse her of lying. I think he has to do it so much that he doesn't want to push his luck."

"It all sounds a little bit ugly."

"Yes yes, she threatens sometimes to up and leave and Lank can let the baby suck on his tits. That's pretty much a quote."

Juliette said, "I really like her but she is strong medicine. She sounds treacherous."

"Treacherous is a good word. I feel like such a busybody saying these things."

"Archie, I can see that you follow the same rule that I go by. If someone is likely to take advantage of somebody else that somebody else should be warned, unless the somebody else deserves it."

"Yes yes, all ethical rules need caveats. There's always an 'unless.'"

Juliette put warm water in the cream. Lacie was happy with that. "Sorry not-so-little Lacie. We do not serve alcohol to minors here. You are lovely. I hope mine comes out good. If mine is a boy, do not let him screw you until you are at least three."

Archie chuckled and said, "My my, it sounds like you plan to stay here for a while."

"I am unpredictable Archie; however, when I cleaned up the car, it felt good. I wondered if that business about the bodies being transported in this car would bother me but I took a good look at it and, unless there are actual ghosts, I will be fine on that account. I never thought about living in a train car, a railway car, whatever one should call it. However, when I first heard about this place a couple of weeks ago, I thought about, well, the concept. I had lived on boats that were not going anywhere and there is a je ne sais quoi about using some means of transport as a more or less stationary abode. What is that? What do you think about it?"

"Yes yes, I never really understood the reason or reasons. When I first saw the place, The Tracks, it was immediately attractive. Run-down houses or other run-down buildings wouldn't seem so attractive. Wait now, maybe some building that had another intended purpose, like a garage or a church maybe but that might be complicated. Hmm."

Juliette said, "I think of James Joyce in the Martello Tower. Perhaps it is an avoidance of expectation or, I guess, the avoidance of having the way you live already planned out. A regular house was designed as a place to live by you or by somebody else. Yes, the house is planned as a place to live, a rational plan. It is usually a conventionally-rational plan. The house expects a certain kind of behavior. If you have a room which has certain characteristics; you have to ask yourself what that room intends you to do in there. Let us say it is a dining room. You will probably use it for that but if you did not have a dining room, you might like to eat with a plate on your lap."

"What do you…"

"Oh, wait. I have to say this. A friend showed me around her place once. It was an old farmhouse, not very big. It had this little room with a little window; the borning room. They had a room for having your children." Juliette chuckled. Archie saw the brave, wide-open ability to experience delight. Juliette's eyes, her entire mien lit up in talking about her encounter with the odd little room at her friend's house. But Archie realized that Lacie caused the delight by chewing on Juliette's chin. "What an expectation to stuff into a new wife's life. The borning room; always waiting for you to use it."

"When is your baby due?"

"Sometime in the spring, I suppose. I will need a doctor. Any recommendations?"

"Yes. We have one doctor here and I recommend him. George Lawley, good man."

"Good. I should see your Dr. Lawley."

Archie, still a little high, heard the absurd silence of the real conversation they should be having. He wasn't a bold man. But it made him feel dishonest when sexual attraction wasn't acknowledged. He could see the value of dancing around the topic but it made him feel fraudulent. He never figured out a proper way to do it and he expected this wouldn't be right either.

"Juliette, are we going to have a love affair or is that something that doesn't interest you?"

"No we are not. Again, I find myself unpredictable but my thoughts are that I have never been good at maintaining friendships with people I had sex with. You are attractive to me but keeping that at bay has its own pleasures. How do you feel about that?"

"Good, yes good. It's kind of a relief. It would seem terribly complicated to have even an offhand sort of coupling. Maybe that's partly because it would be so easy." Archie added quickly, "I'm not insinuating you are easy."

"I suppose I am, at least when I am drunk. It would seem propitious to be able to visit each other for tea and screwing but it would not work out for either of us."

 Archie said, "Okay, we've got that straightened out. What were we talking about?"

"I forgot. I am thinking about what your cock might look like."

Archie laughed. How intimidating that would sound coming from Irma but it was sweet from Juliette. He also thought this could be new to him, a friend he could talk to. There are things you don't talk about with other men and things you don't talk to women about when you're romantically involved. "My cock, Juliette, is the best thing you will never see. What's going on for you today?"

She said, "There must be fish in this river."

"There's gaspereau, trout, a salmon run and eels."

"Do you know any good holes?"

Archie smiled and said, "I can show you where to get fish. We can walk up about a half mile through the woods on this side of the river. There's a good spot there." They agreed to go fishing the next morning.

***

It was a dismal, rainy day just on the edge of snowing. Juliette wore rubber boots she borrowed from Irma when she took Lacie back at midnight. She borrowed a jacket from Archie. Archie wore rubber boots and an oilskin coat with a suit underneath. Under the suit jacket he wore a sweater as a concession to comfort. Archie moved with deliberation. He liked to think ahead and he gave himself the time to do so. His path was easy. They avoided the worst of the thickets and rough terrain.

Juliette said, "You got here just as quickly as someone in a rush."

"I think so. I was quick and jerky and highly energetic as a child. I had to contain my rambunctiousness. The nuns kept after me to slow down. By the time I reached grade nine, they were telling me to hurry up but I got stuck at this pace. It's not a real choice anymore. It's just the way I've become." Archie liked to stand on a riverbank fishing. They both caught a few rainbow trout and after some fly-fishing pointers from Archie, Juliette landed a good-sized salmon. They spoke very little. Archie liked that.

"Shall we go back? With the size of that salmon, you'll have to give some away."

"Oh, I should I suppose but after I cook it, I can keep it for a long time in this weather. I could eat fish exclusively. Are you a fan?"

"I like salmon and trout, almost any fish really. These trout though, a couple of them have eggs and I don't like that. The fish seems softer. I guess some people eat the eggs."

She had her gear packed up, ready to return to The Tracks. "I will take the eggs and some of the guts too. I make a very salty, stinky sauce that I use in all kinds of cooking. It gives what I refer to as a strong bottom flavor to meat dishes."

"Now that sounds thoroughly unpleasant."

When they got to The Tracks, she knocked and poked her head into the dining car. "I will bring some baked salmon for your supper, if you like that sort of thing."

"Yes maid. You can borrow my boots anytime."

Archie waited for Juliette. "How are you going to bake it? You don't have an oven."

"Oh yes, that is a detail I overlooked. It is not raining too hard. I have some dry wood under my car. I can make planked salmon outside."

"No, use my oven."

"Perhaps we should be careful to maintain a distance. We are only a few feet of track away from each other. We do not want to be living in each other's shoes." Juliette cleaned all of the fish and kept the spawn and some of the offal for fish sauce and gave all of the trout back to Archie. He went to his car feeling spurned. She hadn't accepted his offer to use his oven, didn't volunteer to bring him cooked salmon nor did she say thanks for the fishing trip. They were his fishing spots. He never even told Lank about them. Archie hated cooking fish.

CHAPTER FOUR

Dear Archie

It started to feel like a date, a lovely date that could easily have continued on to a pleasant dinner, some drinks, more drinks and casual screwing. I can easily walk away from love affairs, especially the brief ones. I do not want to walk away from here. This place, The Tracks, feels like it arrived in my life just in time.

I am pregnant because I did not take care to avoid pregnancy. I cannot fuck this up. I own a fishing boat that provides a meager income, good enough for a stationary hobo. The Tracks grants a new start for me and, dare I say, for my baby.

Given the right circumstances, circumstances like a few drinks, I could have sex with anybody here, except for City and the kid of course. I am that kind of a girl. Anyway, I wish this was a love letter. I would make it irresistibly persuasive.

Thank you for the great day on the beautiful Tillman. Fly fishing could be as habit-forming as sex and liquor.

Your friend
Juliette

Juliette sent three letters of rejection to would-be lovers; she did it face to face at least five times and twice by telephone. Her attractiveness and apparent availability made it necessary. Juliette got quite good at these rejections, phrasing it all so that nobody would be bruised but she avoided lies. Archie had agreed they should not be lovers but Juliette suspected he'd respond to any inviting move.

"Did you get my note?"

"Yes yes. We can maintain a friendship without getting involved. I'm sure we can."

"Would you like to go fishing on the ocean?"

Archie smiled, "Yes sure, if it's a nice day and not too rough, I'm game."

"That is not the kind of fishing I had in mind. Most of my crew likes to take time off around Christmas and prices are good then. It would be a ten or twelve day trip all told."

"Oh hell no, I couldn't do that. I'd shit my pants. The ocean is not my element."

"Well, you would not want to be on my boat. She is quite lively. How do you think Lank would be at that sort of thing?"

"No drinking while at sea, I presume?"

"That is correct."

"He wouldn't like that. He might… let's just say he wouldn't like that. Irma's done some fishing, I'm pretty sure."

"Yes I know, mostly in bays, not offshore. But she is Irma."

Archie slowly bobbed his head. "Oh yes, she's Irma."

"I think perhaps I will ask her. She could make six hundred dollars. They could use that."

Archie gave a little whistle, "That's good money and, yes they could use a boost."

Archie had enough work and enough money for his tastes. He occasionally filled in as driver or helper on the Coca-Cola truck and did a bit of finish carpentry. But most of the work came from his close friend, Cliff, a successful lawyer. The suits Archie wore also came from Cliff who bought two or three new suits a year and wore them for only a few years, then gave them to his friend. Archie did research for Cliff's law firm, medical research on insurance claims, business research for corporate commercial matters and sometimes actual sleuthing to find out who told the truth about whom. He liked the variety. It just popped up and he did it until it was finished. Spurts of employment suited Archie. He expected that any real job would eventually creep toward drudgery. Whether he did research or carpentry, Archie wore a suit and he never rushed.

Juliette said, "I planned a grilled cheese sandwich for lunch. Could I interest you in one of those? Blue cheese with chives and basil, okay?"

"I usually have two pieces of white bread with Velveeta in the middle but I guess I could lower my standards."

***

Irma jumped at the chance to go fishing. Juliette's regular crew took Slipper to Sheet Harbour in mid-December and went home for Christmas. On December twenty-second, Juliette, Irma and the regular first mate landed a big catch in Boston. They refreshed and re-provisioned in time to sail on Christmas morning. Slipper unloaded a good catch in Halifax the day before New Year's Eve. Prices were holiday-season high and Juliette hadn't lost her touch as Slipper skipper. She found the fish, avoided the worst weather, got good prices and did it all quickly with a skeleton crew. Irma and the first mate started having sex on the first day out but, when Slipper got to Georges Bank, they were too tired for anything but work and the few hours of sleep they got each day.

Irma was a fierce worker. Juliette worried because she would go at it with no mind for anyone's safety, particularly her own. But they made it to shore without injuries. When Juliette passed eleven hundred and eighteen dollars to Irma after computing the shares, Irma said, "Don't tell Lank how much I made."

"What a crew makes is their own business. I do not tell anyone but I always considered it sleazy for the men to not tell their wives what they made. I tend to avoid having sleazy people on my boat."

Archie, Lank and Lacie picked them up in Halifax. The first mate stayed with the boat, waiting for the regular skipper and crew. He knew he earned more in the last two weeks than he would earn in the next three months. While Irma fussed with Lacie, Juliette told Archie and Lank how much they caught, what they sold it for and how the boat share, skipper share and crew share got divided. "So after fuel, provisions and all my boat expenses, I made twenty-eight hundred dollars, thanks in no small part to the fact that Irma works like a mad woman." The math was easy. Lank knew how much Irma made.

The first time Irma got her alone, she demanded, "Why'd you do that? It's my money. I worked for it."

"I did not tell your husband you fucked with Larry."

"I don't give a Jesus if you do."

"It is your money; you worked hard for it. I indirectly revealed the amount you earned. I disliked doing that but it... it did not seem right, Irma. I knew you would tell Lank you made three hundred or something. Maybe I owe you an apology but you wanted to force me into conniving against Lank. I know he tells you what he earns and he shares with you and Lacie. Anyway, you were good crew except that you are a wild woman."

"I don't blame you for tellin' him. What the fuck? Who cares? Thanks for the work. I know you did me a big favor. You coulda got a professional. Slipper is a great boat for you but she's a ship that suits me, too. You get there quick, put up with the liveliness till you got 'er loaded and get to market quick. I like that too."

"I'll keep you in mind for another trip if it comes up but we will have to go over some safety rules and how not to gaff the fish, things like that."

"Good enough. I'll do whatever you ask aboard the Slipper, skipper. Oh yeah, I'm goin' down to Richard Johnson's and telling' him that I won't be cleaning for him no more but if he pays me twenty bucks, he can lick my arse." Irma tossed her head back and that wild, throaty laugh went up to the sky. It showed her crowded front teeth. She was so feline, playful and beautiful but well equipped for attack. Irma had Juliette's admiration but not her trust.

***

That Christmas, while Irma and Juliette were fishing, Sterling Reserve became angry and unhappy. On the Friday afternoon before school holidays began, Custard drove his Ford at high speed into the driveway of the Robinsons' house where he lived. He burst into the kitchen and told Clara Robinson that the little Whitney girl's legs got crushed at the train yard.

Six-year-old Alice Whitney was the sweetest part of Clara Robinson's life. Alice lived next door. She was a lovely child who genuinely liked Clara but Alice did not like Custard. When she heard the news, Clara Robinson gathered herself together. She did not cry. She bravely walked next door ready to give her all, just to help a little bit. Clara, a conservative and pious Anglican and a mild-mannered woman, told Dr. Lawley, "I saw little Alice in the kitchen wearing the skirt she wore to school. Her beautiful little legs were still attached to the rest of her and she walked up to me and said, 'Hi.' I said, 'You're all right.' and she said to me, 'What do you mean?' I was so happy but I marched straight back to my house and confronted that crazy bastard and he told me he just said it. It wasn't a mistake or rumors he heard; he just said it. Well doctor, I threw his clothes out in the yard. He's gone from my house for good. God forgive me, I hope he freezes in the snow. He's an evil thing."

Custard remained in Sterling Reserve, at first living in his Ford, then in the coal hopper car at The Tracks. That car provided grim shelter during the summer of 1950 for a young woman named Mary and her nine-year-old child. Mary climbed up the ladder, lifted a heavy section of hopper-car cover in order to climb down another ladder to a cold steel floor that was slanted on both sides. Archie and Lank hoisted the cab of an old truck to the top of the hopper car, removed one of the covers and welded the truck on top. It gave Mary and her little girl light, windows that could be opened, and a door. They also built a crude floor sixteen feet along the length of the hopper car and put a wood stove in it. Still, Lank and Archie were relieved when Mary went home to her parents before winter set in.

Custard used the wood stove in the hopper car for heat but he didn't cook. He ate cookies and other sweets purchased at Percy Donovan's store and ate things from cans: beans, canned stew, corned beef. He ate all those things cold.

On January fourth, two weeks after the Alice Whitney incident, Custard arrived at the hospital's emergency parking space. His horn blared, and the body of a Sterling Reserve boy lay in the back seat of his car. The boy rode his bicycle on the road to Brookfield. The roads were dry but hard frozen snow, piled up along the sides by the snowplow, made bike riding difficult. Custard claimed that the boy swerved in front of him. There were no other witnesses. At the hospital, Custard's exaggerated femininity, arm waving, wailing and blaming the boy for having done this to him, made observers quite certain that Custard enjoyed the notoriety.

A few days after Christmas, the two RCMP officers stationed at Brookfield pursued Custard's car as he drove from Sterling Reserve toward Brookfield. Since the death of the boy, he drove with exaggerated caution at very low speeds. Custard made hand signals to indicate a left or right turn, not only for turns but for curves in the road. The police officers saw him extend his arm out the window signaling his approach to a gradual thirty-degree curve that stretched over a quarter of a mile. They didn't find it funny. The young policemen had given themselves an assignment.

A man from Sterling Reserve drove by as the police finished up their work on Custard's car. They broke the lights, windows, carburetor and distributor on the Ford. They followed the witness, pulled him over and politely asked him not to report it or talk about it. He assured them he'd keep their secret. The man didn't exactly keep his promise to be quiet but someone else claimed to see Custard smashing up his own car and police radio records showed no police cars in the area that afternoon. Custard's accusations did not get investigated and the few rumors about police involvement were quelled.

***

The general area got a lot of rain that winter but in Sterling Reserve it all came down as snow. Juliette sank into contentment when the snow swirled outside the parcel car windows. She had enough money to be comfortable and generous with her hospitality. Pregnancy treated her well. She felt more at ease and less inclined to search out something new, some next thing. Juliette missed drinking but not as much as she expected. Three drinks made her nauseous. Never having understood the point of drinking one or two drinks, she just didn't bother. The thought of a drunken baby in her womb was creepy.

Late in the fall she, Archie, Irma and Lank built a small veranda on the back of her car. Juliette often sat there in a nightdress and bundled up in blankets to drink her morning coffee. Sometimes a light breeze or the morning sun melted enough snow to cause it to slip off the pine trees. A cascading shower of snow flashed a diffuse white light and fell so slowly through the light and shadows among the evergreens that it looked like it fell upward. She laughed that these sights caused joy in her.

 Most days had snow. It came in storms with blizzard conditions and it came out of a few clouds on a sunny day. If Juliette hadn't made tracks in the snow going to the outhouse by noon, someone checked on her, usually Archie. She kept a chamber pot with a cover that could take her through a whole day but she got to the outhouse by ten o'clock to avoid morning visitors. Juliette made a lot of convivial meals for the little community on The Tracks. She invited Lank, Irma or Archie or any combination for breakfast, lunch, tea or dinner. She and Lank often cooked together in the dining car, which had a great kitchen. They invited City to some larger gatherings and Juliette often brought food to him. City wasn't a sparkling conversationalist and he was a lonely man, making him a good source of guilt but not a good source of entertainment.

However, a dinner at Juliette's with Lank, Irma, Archie, his lawyer friend Cliff and George Lawley was a thrilling occasion. Any topic might come up for discussion. They spoke about religion, agriculture, war and philosophy. They asked why men's balls can be appealing despite their ugliness, does family loyalty, extended, become racism, is reason the worst guide and did medicine become body snatching because doctors assumed ownership of their patients. Archie felt an edgy enthusiasm for the after-dinner discussions at Juliette's.

On such a night, after an exploration of Plato's distortion of Socrates' teachings, Irma and Lank began to dance. They had no music but they danced something between jitterbug and tango. Juliette began to sing and bang on a pot held between her legs. She sang Louis Jordan songs and melancholy versions of Stephen Foster. Irma and Lank danced. Lank's jittery, directionless movement disappeared. He became graceful. The dance accentuated Irma's sexuality. She acted flirtatious and sexually aggressive at these gatherings but when she danced, the eroticism lacked self-consciousness. A Presbyterian couldn't object.

Archie sang a Cape Breton ballad about a river. Juliette was the only sober person there; Lacie retired early in Juliette's bed with a small amount of milk and moonshine in her belly. Archie finished his song. Juliette sat on the arm of his chair, leaned her considerable stomach and herself on him, and put her arm around his neck. "Now, I know that I will always love you, Mr. MacKenzie." He looked for evidence that she was kidding but saw none. She held him against her with one arm and put her hand on his heart under his jacket, inside his shirt. It caught the attention of the others.

"Thank you, Juliette. That song is the best of me."

"The best of us all."

***

Everyone left at the same time. They didn't realize how much snow came down. The wind blew hard, right along the tracks, in the direction of Sterling Reserve. Juliette got dressed and took a relaxing five minutes in the outhouse. The blizzard filled in her tracks during those five minutes. She could not see the faint glow of her oil lamps inside the parcel car and Archie's brighter electric lights did not penetrate. Juliette guessed he was still up but the whiteout obscured his lights. Cliff stayed at Archie's but George Lawley set out to walk home. She worried about George loosing his way. He was drunker than usual when he left the caboose.

Juliette used the compass on her fishing boat only to confirm what she already knew about direction. She concluded her dead reckoning in her head before she calculated and put it on a chart. Juliette's sense of direction and distance was extraordinary even among fishing captains. She didn't consciously pay attention to the cues. The information came in and got worked out in her brain with very little effort. If she took the time to isolate what led one way rather than another, it amazed her how many subtle items of information she calculated and balanced to set a course.

On a calm, foggy night at dead low tide with no visibility, she took her boat and crew into an unfamiliar bay north of Portland, Maine. She set a course and then checked the boat compass. It disagreed. Juliette went to a handheld compass. It agreed with the boat compass. If she was right, the compass would take her into some shoals; if the compasses were right, her own course would lead onto a rocky shore. The clanging bouys didn't clang and the groaners didn't groan on the flat calm waters. The chart showed a marker, a groaner, one mile ahead on her course. If she was wrong, the rocky shore lay not much more than a hundred feet beyond that. A very bad weather forecast made anchoring an unattractive option. The compasses persisted in their readings but they became a bit fluttery and Juliette trusted her own reckoning more. Fog can distort sound direction and little evidence came from the still water. They saw nothing through the dense fog but smell is often enhanced in damp, windless weather. She smelled the burning of birch firewood and maple at different points, which told her they ran close to the little village because the smoke from each house had not come enough distance to co-mingle. That information tended to confirm her course.

As they came close to the mark, Juliette wound the high-revving diesel up to full power. The fully-loaded Slipper dug a hole in the water and made a huge wake. She wanted to rock the buoy in Slipper's wake so that it would make noise. She would then cut the engine in order to hear the groaner. If her course was wrong, there would be no groaner buoy. The not entirely reliable depth sounder began to confirm her course. They saw it and heard its first sad groans at the same time. It passed four feet from their port gunwhale. Slipper's bow wave had set it groaning. A crew member said, "Pretty good chart."

It was a standing joke among Juliette's crew. Hitting close to a buoy in bad visibility usually occasioned a compliment to the skipper but they complimented the chart's accuracy for showing the buoys right on Juliette's course. Slipper continued to the wharf in the village as the compass began to agree with Juliette. They made it to the only bar in town before last call. The bartender told Juliette that compasses often go wacky in their little bay.

She started out tracking George Lawley by following the slight change in color of the snow where it filled in his footprints. She traced the change in texture where his boots beat down the snow.

The wind replaced it with lighter stuff. She followed him, with relief, across the bridge. He obviously experienced some difficulties locating it but made it across. In a few minutes she found him halfway down the riverbank on the Sterling Reserve side.

"Hi George. Too white to see much?"

"That you, Juliette?"

"Yes, I am here. I will walk you home."

"It's too slippery. I can't get up from here."

"Go a few feet to your right and you should come across a rope from that old eel weir. You can pull yourself up on that."

George got up to the top of the riverbank, weasing and coughing. "Jesus Juliette…I thought I was done. Shit… I figured I'd die…in the snow."

"You had quite a climb. Walk behind me when you catch your breath."

Juliette broke a path, zigzagging to avoid the deepest snow. George had no reference point except for the swaying green overcoat in front of him. His own doorstep was the first thing he recognized.

"Home, George."

He whispered, "Not so loud. Ann will be awake worrying about me being in the presence of two beautiful women. She doesn't need to hear that one of them walked me home."

Juliette gave him a silent wave but he grabbed her coat, "Thanks. I enjoyed a great night at your place and you probably saved my drunken life."

"How many lives do you figure you saved as a doctor, George?"

"Six for sure. I'm not so sure about the not-so-sures but I killed a kid with the wrong medication. I had no way of knowing beforehand."

"It must feel good to have saved six lives."

"Yeah, I think about it when I'm doubting my worth. It helps."

"Good night, my friend."

Juliette enjoyed the walk home thinking about capability, duty and voluntary assistance. She thought about how her capabilities dwindled away with drunkenness until the capacity for consciousness left her. Why this didn't bother her much was a mystery.

By eight o'clock in the morning the snow had refashioned the landscape. Drifts mounded up six feet high in places, sculptured by the night's wind. The snow stopped, the wind died and it got cold. A beautiful winter day began. Juliette used milk in her coffee because she ran out of cream. The milk was on the edge of souring. She reached out a window and stuck it in a snowdrift to stay cold. / *pancakes/great for pancakes/cooking absolves the sins of sour/*

She climbed onto Archie's roof with a covered dish of pancakes and bacon. Juliette enjoyed the irony of a stationary parade of rail cars led by a caboose. She tapped on the window of the cupola and gave Archie ten or fifteen seconds to compose himself before peeking in. He stood with the small shovel from the coal skuttle mounded up with the cheap brown coal he sometimes scrounged from the old mine. Juliette could tell by the smoke that only wood burned in his stove so far and she guessed that Archie had been up for about fifteen minutes. He looked engagingly sloppy in pajama bottoms and a loose old sweater, bent over but looking up at the cupola with curiosity, close to alarm. He saw her brushing snow off the window. Archie put the lignite and the shovel back in the coalscuttle, slowly climbed up to the cupola and slid the window open.

"There seems to be a pregnant lady on my roof."

"Yes, good morning. The drifts are too high to charge through. I took the high road. Your breakfast, sir."

"Holy jumpins, you're kidding. Aren't you an absolute angel?"

"Oo, I was an angel last night. I followed George because of the storm. I thought he might get lost. I found him halfway down the riverbank and he could not get back up. Do not mention it to anyone, please. He may be embarrassed but I just had to tell you. I am excited like a kid that I may have saved the life of a friend."

"You are an angel. Have you made breakfast for everybody?"

"Oh oh, I forgot about Cliff. He is here, is he?"

"Yes, Cliff 's still asleep. We can share."

"No, I will have some for him in twenty minutes, perhaps half an hour. I am going to deliver to the Grahams and City. Oh please do not put the brown shit in the stove yet. It will choke me to death on my way back."

"Okay okay."

"Toot, toot."

She delivered the other breakfasts. City's was a challenge. She had to walk through the deep snow past Custard's coal car with the pickup welded on top. Juliette wanted to avoid Custard. She felt good, and pretending to be nice to Custard would ruin that. She had quite a struggle along the ground to get to City's dismal boxcar with its one window. She banged on his door for three minutes before he responded sleepy-eyed, disheveled and wearing dirty longjohns.

"Oh my God, wasn't it a terbl' night. I near stayed awake all night. I thought the boxcar was gonna tip right up over. Oh my God, what a night. Lordy, look at that. My my, all the snow. How in the world will we ever get out?"

Juliette lied, "I would like to stay and talk but I have something cooking on the stove. I brought breakfast."

"Oh my golly, isn't that nice? Oh, too bad you can't stay and have some with me. I could make some tea if I can get that blessed stove going. It's only got one…"

"I have to go City. I will see you." She turned to trudge through her footprints past Custard's car.

"Okay girl, thanks for, er, ah what is it? Oh my, pancakes. I love pancakes, yes I do."

Before climbing back on the dining car roof, she turned and waved, "Enjoy the pancakes." /*shit*/*I could spend an hour with him* /*sometime* /*no*/ *boredom hurts* / City was a lonely, boring man getting fat on bread and pork trimmings given to him by the grocer in Sterling Reserve. She felt the usual tinge of guilt running away from City but his speech drilled into her like a badly played fiddle, like a new mystery noise from the engine of a fishing boat. City's voice wouldn't let you settle. Guilt for Juliette was like jealousy for Juliette. Both passed very quickly leaving no permanent impression. By the time she reached her car to cook Cliff 's pancakes and bacon, she forgot City and thought about Cliff and Archie's grinning faces saying something like she was as cute as a button and as sweet as hot rum and honey. After the breakfast deliveries, Juliette settled down in the parcel car with her coffee. No cream left, no milk left, so she used canned evaporated milk in her coffee. She didn't like the taste but it reminded Juliette of life aboard a longliner, while she sat in the warm comfort of her parcel car; no danger, no responsibility.

***

Irma was a great help during Juliette's pregnancy mostly because of her repeated message, "Don't worry girl, that's just normal." But Juliette did worry about having a child to care for. She worried about her reliability, her drinking habit and mostly about worrying. Juliette feared she would worry about every little thing, make the child fearful and make herself bitter and defeated like so many mothers. But Irma made a great tutor in the not giving a fuck department.

It surprised her daily how good she felt nearing the end of her pregnancy. She even liked to put her hands on the sides of 'me and my kid', that bulb of a belly in front of her. She felt cheery, perhaps optimistic. Anxiety became a surface thing rather than a deep feeling.

George Lawley was resigned and phlegmatic but a very good doctor. He listened to whatever Juliette had to say. His understanding went past symptoms already paired with diagnoses. The science of medicine gave George a toolbox; the art of medicine was his job.

Juliette always paid George. Many in the area could not afford to. When he started off in the Glover Metals Mining days, the mineworkers had a checkoff. The doctor's salary got deducted from their pay. The monthly checkoff amount came to George and the company-owned hospital. It was a good company in those days; a great company compared to the other mining outfits in Nova Scotia.

"No Juliette, you keep that."

"George, if you do not take what I owe you, I will give it to the CCF party election fund. That is the deal." George took the money. He didn't object to the left-leaning policies of the CCF; he just thought they were all idiots. George knew Juliette would follow through on the threat. She would do it in his name and give him the receipt.

Juliette followed a simple political view. When a women's party existed, she would vote for it. Nova Scotia had three men's parties and four more or less viable men's parties ran federally but no women's parties. They all talked man talk. Everywhere in Canada the number of women candidates came to less than five percent. She said to Archie, "Voting never worked for me anyway. Had I voted in every election since I reached twenty-one, I would not have made any difference. Not once did someone get elected by only one vote."

"Juliette, that's an old story but what if everyone thought like that. There could be no democracy."

"If everyone else thought like that, I would vote. I would have all the power. Voting is not a real exercise in politics. Bribery, coercion, assassination and sabotage are unfortunately much more effective political tools for the common woman or the common man."

"Maybe those of us who vote are less common."

"Oh Archie, you know I cannot be insulted."

"Yes, that was stupid. I'm sorry. Your point is all too powerful. It may be true but I hate it. If not democracy then what? If the people can't have power in an orderly fashion, what's the use?"

"Indeed, what is the use?"

****

During a Friday night dinner at Lank and Irma's car, Juliette had two glasses of wine and felt okay, so she had a third and a fourth. No one really noticed but it made her a little tipsy and she enjoyed the evening in the old way. She must have looked more receptive because Cliff told her that he would be available to her as a long-term lover. He told her that he would not expect to be her exclusive lover but anyway she wanted it, would be fine with him. "I am not a super passionate man. I'm not crazed for sex but it is clear to me that I'm in love with you. I'll be around if you're ever ready for me."

Rather than answer him, she had a glass of rum.

****

In March, winter dissolved into all kinds of weather, except sunshine. During a three-week period of dismal skies, things took a downturn at The Tracks. City was ill, more listless than usual and unable to eat much, a big change for him. Juliette wanted to help but she got stuck in the mud of early spring. She drank occasionally and worried about getting the baby drunk. Juliette didn't get rip-roaring drunk like her pre-pregnant days but she felt vulnerable to her habit.

Lank and Irma lived on her earnings from the Christmas fishing trip. Lank couldn't work on cars down at The Tracks because of the snowy winter. He worked a few days at the White Rose station but Lank and Irma ran out of money after getting accustomed to the relative wealth they had enjoyed. Irma asked Juliette to get her a fishing job but it was tough for a woman to get a job on a boat. Irma avoided regular jobs. She wanted to work hard for a quick buck. Lank slowly got back to working on cars but the Grahams remained pretty broke. Irma berated Lank for not supporting his family. Archie grew to dislike her as well as distrust her.

He had his own problems with the opposite sex. A seventeen-year-old high school student from Sterling Reserve became Archie's latest girlfriend. Her parents hated the idea of their daughter going out with an 'old man from The Tracks'.

Ellen got off the school bus from Brookfield at three-thirty and headed to Archie's car. At about six o'clock, she went home for supper and to argue with her parents and then back to Archie's. Sometimes Ellen stayed over all night. Archie was embarrassed at having such a young girlfriend but he liked her a lot and nobody at The Tracks objected to such a thing.

Her father, a salesman, got a job in Dartmouth selling Rexair vacuum cleaners with a Fuller Brush route on the side. The family planned to move. "Ellen, I'm too young to get married." was Archie's answer to her wish to move in with him. Ellen had no alternative but to go with her family and finish her grade twelve in Dartmouth. Their parting made Archie sad. It made Ellen bitter.

"I guess father was right all along. You were just taking advantage of me." Archie thought that maybe they were right. He missed her a great deal and almost succumbed. Juliette talked him out of asking her to come back to finish school.

"So what would you do, kick her out at the end of June? She might be pregnant by then anyway; where would that leave you?"

"We had our ways of avoiding babies. We never had intercourse without a French safe, unless it was two days before or two days after her period."

"Very careful but accidents do occur. Anyway Archie, if you ask her back, you might just as well get married because you will be. She should have a chance at life before she gets tied down to an old fucker like you."

"I know you're right, Juliette but..."

"But you are cunt struck, right."

"My God, sometimes you're crude."

Juliette backed off a bit. "Archie, I am not saying that you are not perhaps in love but you have been in love before. You will get over it. Give Ellen a chance to get over it. At the risk of appearing even more crude, she is very attractive now but inclined toward chubby. Her parents are both overweight; her mother is downright fat. Say all you will about the enduring power of love but I know you. You will want something else when you are in your forties, as horny as ever, and she is fat."

He glared at her but the rum made him mellow. His energy for the argument waned. "Shit. I know goddamn well it can't work. I miss her a lot. She's just a kid but I miss her."

"I know, I know. You can feel just as strongly for someone young. It adds zest really."

Archie said, "Zest it had. My mind is made up. It's over. Thanks for the, I was going to say, sober second thoughts but we're not real sober, either one of us."

"I drink too fucking much but I will have one more before I go and put my belly to bed."

"You think Ellen's chubby?"

Juliette smiled, "Quite voluptuously so, right now but watch out."

"I suppose."

✱✱✱

The walk to the outhouse amused Juliette. She imagined what she looked like, a small pregnant woman staggering a bit. The rum didn't really cause the staggering; it just exaggerated the side-to-side wobble she had adopted in the last two weeks. Juliette usually waited until she got home alone before talking to her belly but she couldn't help saying, "You are bigger and heavier than I am, kid. I hope you do not get fat. No need to worry, I suppose. I would never let a fat guy screw me, no matter how drunk I got."

In her car for the night she had a glass of moonshine and water and slept much more soundly than usual. It took two cups of coffee to get her going in the morning. She gave her last gallon of moonshine to Lank. It posed too great a temptation and Lank could save some money or save himself from his own half-fermented home brew. It worked well for Lank but too often Juliette popped over in the evening for a nip of shine.

The weather got better with some blue-sky days. City settled into being a sick man. Cliff and Archie double dated with two stylish ladies from Halifax and it was salve for Archie's wounded heart. The Grahams continued to argue about money but Lank was able to get back to work, fixing cars. A change in the weather, a brightening up of things, restored Juliette's blood and brain. She had developed a great affection for little Lacie and gladly relieved Irma of her motherly duties. Lacie became a person, still very little and stupid and helpless but a unique thing, unlike a baby. Babies looked formless to Juliette. Their faces were potatoes and their legs badly-made sausages. Lacie developed an appearance and personality that distinguished her from other one-year olds. When she had Lacie in her home, Juliette felt the presence of three: her, Lacie and the child in her belly.

***

Custard bragged that he found a home at The Tracks and that they loved him there. He was quite wrong about that. City hated him. Irma felt angry that he lived at The Tracks and Archie considered Custard treacherous and disgusting. Lank just avoided him. Juliette spent time talking to Custard but not out of friendship. She didn't find him shocking but simply one of those many unpleasant, undesirable things we come across, not ordinary but not all that unusual. She spoke to Archie, "I assume that he murdered people and he may open up to me about it. I want to know what kind of evidence would be needed to convict the silly prick before he kills some other kid. Is that the kind of pro bono project Cliff might be interested in?"

Criminal law didn't interest Cliff but Juliette did. He came down to visit Archie. The three of them drank and talked about Custard and the law. He confirmed that it was difficult to get information that would convict him; even a direct admission of guilt to Juliette would be of little use in court. However, she could, perhaps, gather some information the police could use in an investigation.

The three of them, Cliff, Archie and Juliette, got along very well but she could sometimes feel a little out of place because they got drunk and she didn't. Cliff asked, "Do you really get sick if you have more than two drinks?"

"Earlier on, I just got sick. Now about half the time, if I drink any amount, I will not feel good the next day. It is okay really. If I did not get sick, the baby might be drunk half the time. That cannot be good for a human during the early, indoor stage of life."

Cliff said, "It must be a tiny thing. You don't look eight or nine months pregnant; you don't look pregnant at all hardly."

Archie said, "I've never understood that phrase 'not at all hardly' but then, you're a lawyer and it's your job to not be understood."

"I'll need more whisky to put up with you, MacKenzie."

Cliff walked Juliette the few feet to the door of the parcel car. He told Archie later that he experienced the usual trepidation about whether to kiss her good night but Juliette shattered the ice by saying that Dr. Lawley told her the distance between her vagina and uterus was unusually short and having sex might be dangerous for the baby. "But maybe we could do that after I get unpregnant." Cliff kissed her good night.

***

A few days later Juliette's sliding door flew open and a wild-eyed Irma came in with Lacie in her arms. Lacie was simpering. "Take her. I'm going to kill that bastard." Irma ran out leaving Juliette holding Lacie. Juliette assumed 'that bastard' was Lank and 'kill' was an overstatement until she heard glass breaking farther down the tracks. She dumped Lacie in the crib Archie made for the upcoming baby and ran as fast as her swollen belly allowed. She reached Custard's hopper car as Irma climbed up the ladder. A window on the truck cab was broken. Juliette grabbed both of Irma's ankles. "Stop. Do not go in there!"

"Let go, you fuckin' bitch. I'm gonna kill Custard."

Juliette let go of her ankles, struck her firmly behind both knees and caught Irma as she fell backwards. Juliette held her tightly and spoke softly into her ear. "He is probably waiting with a knife. He also has a four-foot steel bar in there and he says it is for protection. If he does not kill you, you will kill him and go to jail for murder or manslaughter. Either way Custard wins and Lacie loses her mom." In three minutes, Irma and Juliette were back with Lacie in the parcel car.

"Thanks, girl. Thank you, thank you Juls. Oh Jesus, I don't know who else could have stopped me. I would've killed that fucker or he would've killed me. Wouldn't that make the miserable creature happy? I was coming back from the outhouse, just to pee. I wasn't gone more than a minute. There was his nibs hightailing it out of my car and Lacie inside ballin' for all her might. You know she don't cry. I don't know what the miserable fucker done to her. Jesus, Mary and Joseph, I don't want to think about it. Soon as I get a clear chance that jeesly pack of shit is gonna be dead. Soon's I get a clear chance."

CHAPTER FIVE

The outhouse remained a cooperative effort. Juliette provided toilet paper, Lank and Irma kept it clean and tidy, City made a dirty mess and Archie kept it smelling okay. On most days, he sprinkled some lime in the holes and about once a week added old hay to compost beneath the holes. The outhouse smelled like a reasonably clean barn.

Juliette arrived at the outhouse while Archie scattered lime.

"Just a minute Juliette, I'm flushing."

"Well, I just got a dozen rolls of paper. I forgot to bring them over."

"Good. We were down to one roll and the Cape Breton Post. Okay, the procedure is complete. Fill your boots."

"But that is why I am here, to avoid filling my boots."

Archie laughed. "May your piss be delivered with the same easy-flowing alacrity as your wit. Does 'alacrity' fit there?"

"Fits there. Got to go."

Archie liked these silly exchanges with his good friend. Through late March and early April, Juliette and Archie took advantage of frosty nights and sunny days, perfect for gathering sap for maple syrup. They built a brick and steel firebox with a two-stage evaporator on top. The evaporator was a diesel fuel tank cut in two. In her advanced pregnancy, Juliette remained a hard worker and they usually came home with a half-gallon of maple syrup after a five-hour day in the sugar bush a mile from The Tracks. A day spent in amongst the big old rock maples with Juliette was a great day for Archie.

The last time they boiled sap, she said to him, "It is not the work; it is where the work takes you. People say they like fishing but I think it is the ocean, the light. With sportfishing, it is the river we love. You can go out hunting deer in the worst kind of weather and love it because you would not normally go in the woods for a pleasure stroll on a rainy day but the woods in the rain gets in your soul. Here, the two of us work together. Instead of sitting around drinking in railcars, we celebrate in the sugar maple cathedral with a cherished companion.

***

Juliette came over to Archie's where he fiddled with his gate hinges.

"Yes, 'alacrity' worked there. It is a lot like cheerful. A willingness to get at it, and I suppose, an easy flow in doing something. Thanks for the compliment."

"You're welcome. Do you look these things up or is it all in your head?"

"Ah yees, I knows me words rate good, bye. I allees gits me le'ers roit." Juliette laughed. "It is a Cape Breton disease. We love to do accents but we are all hopeless at it. Unless we have a strong local accent, a Cape Bretoner cannot do a Cape Breton accent but we will try upper-class British, Chinese, whatever; we will try it. But a Cape Bretoner cannot do accents. Newfoundlanders, now they can do anything. Some of them can put on the accents from twenty different Bay settlements, Paris French, Acadians and Quebeckers speaking English. They can do Mark Twain, Texas, Boston or Jamaica."

"I never heard Irma do accents."

"No? Oh she is a killer. She is great. Irma does a fabulous Orsen Welles."

"Hmm. Miss Cameron, would you like to come in for a cup of tea?"

"Yes, lovely, thanks."

One cup of tea led to three glasses of rum. Archie was only a little concerned. Juliette no longer got sick from alcohol and the image of a baby getting drunk in the womb; he could never take it seriously. It was just too comical.

"I guess I had heard of the Glace Bay Camerons, Cameron Fisheries."

"My baby and I are the last of the line."

"Stop me if I'm prying but your father was a legendary drinker too, is that right?"

"Yes, Father Jimmy is a legend. Like most legends, not all of it is true."

"A legend is always true even though it may be entirely fictional."

Juliette laughed the little laugh, her mannered laugh. She used it to acknowledge something witty.

"Why do you call your dad Father Jimmy? That was Dr. Tompkins' nickname."

"I call my dad Father Jimmy to piss off my grandmother. I refer to her as old Isobel, which also pisses her off. She would prefer the title of Grandmother."

"I don't guess many grandmothers enjoy being called old."

"Right. Anyway, Father Jimmy likes to work and play and he does not really separate the two very much, which is nice. He is not deep and not very strong. My father accepts old Isobel as the authority in the family. She gets things on people so she can later blackmail or manipulate them into doing what she wants and I think she has gotten Father Jimmy's balls. She hides them in a drawer somewhere. He puts up weak arguments against her proposals or whatever she whines about. They have an unspoken agreement that she will be obeyed but nobody admits that. Isobel has a talent for knowing what people will not admit. I believe that I scare her because I will admit to anything."

"You're so proud of having no pride."

The real laugh came out, the spontaneous, unfastened laugh. Archie realized she was getting drunk. "You are right Archie, I am proud of having no pride even though it is not true. What are you proud of Archie? Certainly not your past. That is a sealed tomb, it seems."

"I don't talk about it, no."

"That must mean that it is too dull or too exciting."

"Ah, I don't talk about it."

"Okay, okay. We will not talk about your past. I will not ask now or ever. Remind me of this promise. I am getting a bit tipsy. What is this lovely stuff you slipped into my rum diet?"

"It's Cognac. I got it from one of Cliff's clients who is particularly grateful for some research I did."

"Great. I should have asked which brand it is. Wonderful stuff."

"Prunier. Are you a connoisseur of Cognac?"

"I have certainly had my share. If it is French and it has alcohol in it, Glace Bay fishermen drink it. We would stop in at St. Pierre or buy it in Newfoundland. The Newfs have always smuggled to and from St. Pierre. I have not had Prunier. Perhaps it costs too much for a fisherman."

Archie said, "Cliff tells me this stuff is ridiculously expensive. I love it so much I would pay a dollar more a bottle than I do for Anne Bonnie rum. I think I'll keep on drinking until I pass out. It's funny. We're having a good time, enjoying each other's company, I would say, and at times like this, we want to dull the brain with drunkenness."

"Too true but I should not drink much more. The little one is probably drunk already." She looked down at her glass, almost empty. "But I will have another, if you are, and you do not mind."

"Oh yes. Pour away. I need to piss, Miss."

When Archie got back from his little washroom, he saw that both glasses had larger drinks than he poured. He also noted that the rum bottle was moved and that some dark rum drained down the inside of the bottle. The aura around Juliette told him she was recovering from a substantial gulp of straight spirits. Living at The Tracks and having the largest continuous supply of alcohol made him keenly aware of these sorts of clues. Half of the Cognac was gone and the remaining half didn't have much chance of survival left out in the open. Archie took a little run at casual tidying up. He took off his suit jacket and tie, hung them in the closet and put some dishes away. He also picked up the Cognac and rum and put them in a cupboard. He took out a half gallon of Gillis family moonshine. He figured Juliette would drink to oblivion and he preferred she did it with good moonshine rather than cheap fortified wine or some half-fermented concoction she might have at home. Despite Archie's attempted discretion, Juliette looked down at her feet when he exchanged the good liquor for moonshine. He could see her caught in the anxiety and urgency that last call brings to a drunkard.

More conversation and more of the moonshine elixir eased a drunk's shame at passing her decisions over to alcohol. Archie didn't remember getting in his bed but he woke up at three in the morning.

Juliette came up into consciousness on the caboose floor, drunk and in need of a shit. She went out to the mild spring night barefoot, thinking about the pressure of walking barefoot in late fall with a hoarfrost on the ground; walking on the frosted tips of the grasses, crushing them down to their damp base and the cool earth. But this was spring, everything soft, with no edges. Bits of light, coming from here and there, had no edges. It felt like walking on a cool cushion of water and air. But that early morning in spring was sweet, with the slowly penetrating mist and her wet feet. She could imagine them steaming like the back of a hard-working horse on a winter day.

Juliette started out in the wrong direction towards her rail car rather than the outhouse. The mistake brought her a quiet amusement. She drank for these moments or at least these moments provided her best reason for drinking. The feeling she had there outside Archie's gate was the reward for drinking. Maybe not ample reward but Juliette once again felt grateful for this swelling of the soul to fill the body. Her nipples got hard. An electric sizzle coursed through her thighs and groin up to her chest and shoulders. She thought of sex, not particular sex, not a fantasy or memory but some touch of the moment.

Juliette didn't simply turn around to go in the other direction toward the outhouse; she turned three hundred and sixty degrees once, twice, three times, maybe more. Her loosely apprehended goal was to finish the turns facing the outhouse in an exotic, legs apart, ass stuck out, palms forward pose. /the tango/some eastern dance/ After a few turns, she staggered and felt the need to defecate grabbing and stabbing at her stomach and wringing out her breath. She needed lots of air but it seemed to get stuck on the way to her lungs. /too drunk for spinning/ She crawled and stumbled to the outhouse. The pain became more dizzying than the booze. Euphoria cycled to misery. The outhouse smells welcomed her, composting piss and shit softened by the lime and old hay Archie added.

As her pregnancy ran its course, she started sitting on the medium-sized hole rather than the kids hole, which suited her skinny ass. Her bottom hadn't gotten any bigger through the pregnancy but she had that belly and just followed it to the medium-sized hole.

***

Juliette: I remember terrible pain and gasping at the beginning of the bowel movement. I do not know but something dropped first. I passed out and when I came around I tried to call for help but I did not make any noise. I heard the other little voice so I went down on the floor to look in. I could not make anything out, could not discern what happened. It felt like a horror movie. I could not hold on to a thought. I tried to pick you up but my arms were too straight, too rigid or something. I did not know if I was dreaming or what. The circumstances overwhelmed me, completely. I clearly remember that, when Archie came into my mind, I knew what a drowning person must feel when they put their feet down and touch bottom. I got out of there but fell down right away. Around my ankles, my underpants tripped me up. I began to pull them up but they were wet, slimy wet. I took them off and ran to Archie's. Running required more energy than my body had left. I leaned on his gate. I could only manage to scream 'my baby, my baby'.

Archie: I knew Juliette's voice and I knew she was desperate but the more panicky the situation, the more I feel like I should be relaxed, so I can handle it sensibly, or perhaps it's just cowardice and I'm hoping someone else will get there first.

***

Juliette's screams awakened Archie at three AM. He heard only screaming, no words. He woke clearheaded but he needed to pee and he did so and then put on his underwear, pants, shirt, a jacket, socks and shoes.

Archie finally got outside to find Juliette crying and stumbling down the tracks. Stopping her, he saw blood and mucus, which he took to be a miscarriage.

"My baby is in the shitter."

Archie held her. "It's all right, you're okay. It's all right."

"No no, my baby is in the outhouse. Go get it."

"What, you mean it's alive?"

"Yes. I think so. Go."

Archie ran. It hurt his knees and he tried to remember the last time he ran.

**

Archie: I heard the little cry or laugh or maybe a gurgle. My heart jumped, you know that quick little pump when something special happens and I remember it as excitement I felt, not apprehension or anxiety. I looked down the middle hole and there you were on your back in the pale pitbank light. You were moving your arms around. I reached in and picked you up, so tiny. Not really slippery like I expected. You looked at me; we looked at each other. I lifted you out of the hole. There was some shit, your mother's I guess, on your left arm. You were surely smiling; I think laughing. In fact, I think you were saying 'gotcha, you're mine'.

**

Archie carried the baby to Juliette. Irma arrived. Archie asked, "Is the Austin running?"

"Yeah. I think there's a nurse at the hospital." Irma rushed off to the dining car.

"That is my baby." Juliette's voice was hoarse, meek and tentative.

"Oh yes, here Juliette. Wait, I'll wipe the dirt off. Look, look a girl."

"I have a daughter. How do I hold her?"

"Like this, I guess."

Irma returned with a baby blanket. "That's good, Juls, cradle it gentle like that."

"What do I do with this?"

"Here maid, just put the baby in the blanket; put that in, too. The doctor will snip it off."

Archie said, "Can we get Lank?"

"Yeah. I want to clean Juls up too. Nurse Ingram might be on night duty at the hospital. She's some fuss budget bitch."

Archie and Irma showed no alarm. Irma remembered that Lank fell asleep in the Austin. She shook him awake.

"Lank, get up. You gotta drive to the hospital. Don't step in that." He had been sick right outside the driver's door. A half empty jug of Lank juice sat on the passenger seat.

"What, what? Lacie all right?"

"Yeah. Juls had her baby."

"Oh yeah, oh my. I have to connect the battery. She'll run." He had the car going in less than a minute. Lank shook off the cold, the cramps in his limbs from hours spent crunched up in the tiny Austin, and the sludge of drunken sleep.

Archie helped Juliette over to the sputtering Austin. Irma got some clothes from Juliette's place and then returned to her dining car.

***

Archie: Your mother got in the back of the baby Austin on the passenger side. I should have sat in the front or gone around to the other door but Juliette was holding you cradled in her right arm so I made her slide over in the back of that little Austin so I'd be close to you. I really didn't think I'd ever want to take my eyes off of you. (chuckle) I felt a little embarrassed, really.

***

Irma returned to the car with a kettle of tepid water. She drove the car because she was sober. "I was gonna get you 'n the little one cleaned up some but you're in here now. I'll wash you up when we get there."

Lank, in the front seat, had clothes piled on his lap. He looked back at Juliette and the baby, smiled at them and then gave Irma some instructions. "She can jump out of third gear so you have to hold 'er in." He glared at the half jug of Lank juice by his feet while he spoke. The Austin began to lose power in spurts and then roar ahead again. "Put it in second and keep the revs up. Use the choke; put it half closed." Irma did all these things. She expected such procedures in Lank's old wrecks. The little pinkish gray car lunged ahead and then its progress almost completely died like a small boat hitting a big wave. The forward surges came accompanied with harsh noises and black smoke spitting out of the tiny tailpipe. The engine died a quarter of a mile below the hospital.

"Turn 'er over for a few seconds, dear. No, okay that's enough. I siphoned that gas from an old truck in the Harbour and got water in the tank for my troubles. I'll have to bleed the gas line. It'll take three or four minutes."

Archie said, "No this is good. We can walk up. I can carry you both if you can't walk."

"No, I can walk."

Irma turned around to see Juliette trying to wipe tears away. She straightened her hair. The baby nuzzled and quickly burrowed into her mother. "It wants your breast."

"What?"

"The baby's hungry; wants some milk. Open up. Pull up your sweater."

"Oh Jesus; well, I..."

Irma got out of the car, opened the back door and pulled up Juliette's sweater. She pushed her forward a bit to undo her bra. Irma gently took the baby's head and put it on her mother's left breast. The little girl settled into her first feeding. Juliette stopped crying and looked at the small creature. Oblivious to Irma removing her bloodstained skirt and cleaning her up, she just looked at the baby in stunned wonderment. Irma got the kettle of water from the trunk and washed Juliette below the waist with a towel. She fiddled with her hair, cleaned her face and put on some lipstick and rouge for her cheeks from a little make-up stash she kept in the glove compartment of the Austin. Irma got the skirt she took from the parcel car. It was part of a bunch of clothes Ronnie sold to Juliette. He got them from a girl in Halifax in exchange for a gallon of moonshine. They were obviously stolen from a very good ladieswear store. The subdued grey linen-wool skirt fell a bit below the knees. The skirt and the burgundy silk blouse Irma put on Juliette screamed 'understated good taste'. Irma took a jacket from the pile of clothes, not a perfect match in color but of the same quality as the skirt. "Sorry Juls, hon. I forgot to get shoes for ya."

Juliette said. "Thank you."

*　*　*

Archie: Several times she said, 'thank you' as she fed you and Irma cleaned and dressed her. I wasn't sure if she said it to Irma or to you.

*　*　*

The old gas needed to be drained. Lank would just let it run into the ditch. Irma removed the cap and threw the bottle of Lank juice in the ditch. "Sorry, honey but you've got work to do tonight."

"Yeah, okay yeah. You're right." But the jug landed on its side, did not break and not much of the murky fluid spilled. Lank noticed.

"Irma, could you clean the baby's arm, the left one. It's a bit dirty."

"Yes, sure Archie. Give me that little arm. Oh it is dirty. My yes, what a cutie you is."

"She's a girl." Archie picked up the baby so that Juliette could get out of the car where she had been washed and dressed.

"Oh, what a beautiful girl." Irma stopped her busyness and fussing with Juliette's hair and aligning her expensive jacket. She gazed at the baby. Irma showed no sign of her usual saucy and sexy urgency.

Irma's face softened. Lank cooed, smiled and clicked his tongue at the little girl.

"Here Juls, rinse your mouth out with this; get the booze smell on the run. Oh careful, don't spill it on you my dear. "You just had a baby and already you look like…. you look better than a movie star, even without no shoes." Once again Juliette said softly, "Thank you."

"I gotta get home. Lacie's alone."

***

Juliette: I heard Irma say she had to get back because Lacie was alone and I realized you cannot leave a child alone. That and 'the baby wants your breast' jarred me. I never got a real grasp of those things before. Except for Irma, I had no friends with babies. I did know that I would need to feed and care for you. Well you know, knowledge that does not touch you is just information. Archie held my arm. We walked up the hill. He had you in his other arm. I got out of fishing because of the responsibility of keeping my crew safe and productive. That was fuck-all compared to this. I just kept walking with Archie. The fatigue from the birth and the drunkenness passed but I worried that without Archie I might have been frozen, catatonic.

Victoria: What's that mean?

Juliette: The word? Catatonic?

Victoria: Yeah.

Juliette: Unable to move. There is a classification of mental illness called catatonic schizophrenia. I imagine it is simply not being able to find that key to get started; the mind's decisions get in the way of the body.

Irma and Lank watched them walk toward the hospital. "She got no underwear, no shoes, lots of booze still left in both of them and they look regal, don't they?"

Lank grinned. "The royal family of The Tracks. What's that make us, dear?"

The Sterling Reserve hospital was a leftover from the silver days, well built, well-equipped, abandoned by Glover Metals Mining, and later revived by the people who needed it. The hospital had only six beds, two in private rooms and a four-bed ward. An airy lounge could be converted to an emergency ward for up to twenty-one patients on foldaway cots.

Old Arlen Glover had seen industrial disasters in England during his youth and he cared about such things. No disaster occurred at Sterling Reserve but the hospital served the people and the company well. After the mine closures, Glover Mining leased the building to the Province of Nova Scotia. It was run by two registered nurses, a flow of student nurses, occasional fill-ins from the Sisters of St. Martha in Antigonish, Dr. Lawley and a lot of help from here and there. The patient load from Sterling Reserve, Brookfield and some of the communities nearby provided hospital funding for salaries but equipment maintenance was always a struggle. Volunteer work, fundraising and endowments were vital. Many patients could not pay hospital fees but George Lawley never turned anyone away.

***

At four AM on April twenty-first, nineteen fifty-two, student Nurse Marsh was on duty. She wore a uniform. A white bib apron wrapped almost all the way around her like a skirt. Under the apron she wore a light blue dress of very serviceable cotton. On her head, two bobby pins held a starched little white cap in place.

Nurse Marsh was a young woman, too womanly for her age. Her black hair accented pale, splotchy skin. Descriptions of Nurse Marsh were often followed by, "But she's got a heart of gold and she's a good worker."

"Oh, a new baby. You're, ah, Mrs. Cameron?"

"Miss Juliette Cameron and this is my daughter, Victoria Elizabeth."

"Oh, what a beautiful name. She sounds like a princess."

"Two queens actually. She is named after two queens and I suppose Queen Victoria's great, great, granddaughter Princess Elizabeth who has ascended to the throne but is not yet crowned so you are right. My baby is only a princess yet."

Nurse Marsh took a clipboard off its hook at the nurses' station. She checked things off on an admissions sheet, creating the first record of Victoria Elizabeth. Nurse Marsh loved children and old people but those in between childhood and old age were, perhaps, too much of a challenge for her. The admissions sheet comforted the nurse. It shielded her from the glare shining off the Princess and her mother who was surely a goddess. She glanced up from the clipboard at Juliette Cameron and winced with bashful unworthiness. Nurse Marsh showed no bitterness toward Juliette Cameron for possessing all of the qualities she didn't have: beauty, style, ease and grace. She recognized these things and they were marvelous to her any time she saw them in other people. Juliette Cameron's gracious charm thrilled Nurse Marsh.

"And your address, ah, if you don't mind?"

Juliette held the baby. "Simply Sterling Reserve, Nova Scotia."

"Ster…ling Re…serve No..va Scotia. Ah, thank you Miss Cameron. I'll call Dr. Lawley and yes, please yes, come in here to the examination room, please."

***

Archie, Juliette and Victoria Elizabeth were left in the large, bright examination room. "Archie, help me please. I want to get up on the stretcher but my body resists the effort. Should I feed her?"

"Yes yes, wouldn't hurt. Lie on your back and put her on your belly." But Juliette and Victoria Elizabeth curled up together on the stretcher, finding positions that required no energy expenditure.

"She gives me the creeps. The nurse I mean. The way she looks at me, I think she wants to eat the afterbirth."

"Maybe not when you tell her where it is."

"Fuck off, Archie."

"What are you going to do? Nobody knows, not even Lank or Irma. Nobody knows that she was born in the outhouse. Not a good thing for people to know about her. No need to tell."

"No need to hide. Maybe, I do not know. You decide. How wonderful. I have a little wonder girl. Magic. From my point of view, that is."

"Mine too. It's crazy. I feel a weird level of affection for her, attachment."

"Ooh Victoria, we like that kind of talk."

***

But Victoria did not respond. There was no smile, no cooing nor any baby arm waving. Her encounter with the outside world had been a busy time for Victoria Elizabeth. She had so much to learn and so little to learn it with. She needed to relax and solidify those connections.

Archie said, "Okay. She was born at your place. It came on suddenly. Ah … you delivered and walked to my place with the baby. No I walked to your place to get the baby from the crib. I'll fix up with Lank and Irma whatever they saw or supposed. Better for the child."

"Hmm."

***

Dr. Lawley came in the examination room. Through the years, George Lawley allowed his style of dressing to follow his body and his demeanor. By nineteen fifty-two, he looked round-shouldered, overweight, rumpled and crumpled. His gait showed a trace of shuffling. The effect was an appearance of tired defeat. As a young man he was athletic and a smart dresser. George acknowledged to Juliette and Archie that a lot of things slipped away in his pursuit of comfort. Nurse Marsh was awestruck by the appearance of the three people from The Tracks but George laughed.

"What's up, George?"

"Well, Archie, I'm laughing at myself. Early-morning visitors, right after a birth, are usually a bit disheveled but I should have expected that you two would look elegant. If there was a way to make money in a hospital these days, I would go back home to get my Kodak and take a snapshot of you and Juliette and the baby. I could use it as a commercial advertisement for the hospital. Good morning to you, Archie. Is she asleep?"

"Yes, good morning, George. Yes, she and she are asleep."

"Everything went well?"

"Very well, it seems."

"Good. The baby looks good."

"Oh yes, she has already eaten and managed to charm everyone."

"Are you going to stay for the exam?"

"Oh no, George. I've already told you I'm not the father, not a lover or anything. We are just good friends."

"I know, I know. It's the 'just good friends' part that throws me off. I've used that line."

"Right. Well anyway, you examine and I'll make tea. Would you like tea?"

"Wonderful idea, and ask Nurse Marsh to come in, please. I don't really need her in here but she'll fuss and want to make the tea. I don't tell her where I keep my good tea. She'd give it away to everyone."

"I'll ask her to come in."

By the time Archie had tea ready, Dr. Lawley finished his examination and pronounced mother and child healthy and compliant. Nurse Marsh bathed both of them.

"Juliette told us she didn't know anything about babies. That she doesn't know what to do. I suggested all she had to do was stay sober for twenty years. She's going to give it a try. We do home visits with new mothers. Nurse Marsh will do that for Juliette starting this morning after she gets off shift. That will be eight o'clock unless something dire comes up.

"How did Juliette react to that?"

"Good. She seemed happy about that."

***

Victoria: How did you react to that?

Juliette: I remember. I am just trying to verbalize it. I do not know. Well, I do know. I was happy to have you. You were my baby and you filled me up the first time I held you. In the outhouse, you were just a medical problem. When I held you, a very big feeling bubbled up in me, quite complex but not hard to figure out. But the responsibility. I expected to be inadequate. It all scared me. So to answer your question, I wanted Lorraine Marsh on our side. My first assessment of her was grossly unfair and way off the mark. She acted kindly and I needed her. I knew nothing. Irma was great, truly outstanding on that morning but she was, and probably still is, a wild woman, about as maternal as the common cuckoo.

Anyway, I had gone through a long period of time where I accepted my own weaknesses. That morning everything looked new for me.

Victoria: Gotta stop. The tape's running out.

CHAPTER SIX

Lorraine Marsh visited the Cameron household more often than her duties to the hospital home-extension program called for. Victoria Elizabeth was a pleasant baby with lots of smiles and gesticulations that ellicited goos and gaws from her adult audiences. Nurse Marsh and Juliette did not become friends. Juliette didn't entirely trust the 'heart of gold and a hard worker' ethic. Nurse Marsh was too nursey but both women cared for Victoria Elizabeth like loyal allies.

Loyalty is cowardice. Juliette formed this opinion in her teens and maintained it throughout her life. She considered patriotism, team loyalty, family ties and churches extentions of the grappling fear we need to survive childhood or old age. A couple married forty or more years, whose dedication to each other inspired admiration from most people, made Juliette feel embarrassed for them.

She watched herself feel the warmth of Nurse Marsh's loyalty and then carefully counted up the fees payable for that feeling.

"Lorraine calls me Miss Cameron and it is full of accusation, 'you fornicator, you slut.'"

"Lord Jesus girl, don't let them sort bother you. They're all over the fuckin' place. The judgementors, I calls them. They can't burn us at the stake no more. I wouldn't worry about her."

"Irma, my dear, you would not worry if you had a live grenade up your ass."

"I'm no worrier, that's for sure. Best way, if ya asks me."

"Lorraine looks at Victoria like she is the Christ child but I do not think she believes I am the Virgin Mother."

"I bet the Virgin Mary, Mother of God had the same problem as you. She was drunk when she got knocked up and she just couldn't remember."

Juliette didn't appreciate special efforts and acts of kindness in the way that Lorraine Marsh expected. These kindnesses became attachments, leeches. If the offerings were accepted, they had to be put in a jar to keep them from reattaching and sucking blood. Juliette usually spotted a lie when someone said 'don't mention it' or 'it was nothing, really'; it was always something.

A shared good time is an event, a burst of glory. But one must guard against attempts to make it into a constituent of the dull gray cement used to keep alliances and relationships together. A helping hand calls for a 'thank you' and no residual indebtedness. Otherwise it is trade. It becomes contract with attendant accounting. Contract is fine but cost, delivery time, offer and acceptance should be clearly acknowledged. Nurse Marsh had made the comment to Juliette that it was a shame Victoria's father didn't contribute, at least to send a bit of money.

"Well, Lorraine, that is not your business and it would be impossible. How could Victoria's father send me a bit of money? I do not know who he is and he does not know he fertilized an egg that became Victoria. Because he fucked me he owes me a living is a prostitutional proposition. It becomes insidiously toxic otherwise."

Lorraine did not respond. This sort of attitude she associated with the sort of person who would not express it with big words. Juliette put a clean diaper on the baby and she pricked Victoria with a safety pin. "Aacck!"

"Oh sorry, Victoria."

"Miss Cameron, that's the first time I've heard you apologize to anyone for anything." Nurse Marsh stared and did not flinch. This was not her usual dutiful look. A defiant Lorraine Marsh did not avert her eyes. Lorraine's hard, honest stare surprised and pleased Juliette. However, what Irma called 'that greasy grin' appeared on Juliette's lips.

"You are quite right, Lorraine. It was entirely inappropriate for me to say that. I take that back, Victoria, my lovely. Please, return my apology to me." Victoria said, "Eeshhd" and the eeshhd bubbled out all over her chin.

"Thank you, lovely. I expected you to share my opinion of my apology."

Nurse Marsh passed a warmed bottle of milk to Juliette. "Perhaps she'd like some of this."

"Thank you, Lorraine. It looks like you are about to leave."

"Yes, I'll be back Thursday morning at nine."

"I hope I am awake. I know she will be." The nurse's demeanor had returned to obsequious. Juliette stepped toward her. "Lorraine, I apparently fucked up by making a joke of your comment about my reticence in apologies. We are so different that we must be tolerant of our differences. Perhaps I talk too much but this is really all I have to say." She put her hand on Lorraine Marsh's cheek and kissed her on the lips. "Until Thursday, then."

"Goodbye. Bye bye, Victoria."

"Eeiisss."

∗∗∗

Custard avoided the serious-looking nurse. He had spent no time in mental hospitals, avoiding those houses of suffering by wandering. He expected that a diagnosis would mean long-term care. He'd get locked up for the rest of his life. When Nurse Marsh was around

The Tracks, Custard kept out of sight. Juliette became preoccupied with Custard because he was preoccupied with her and her baby. She had few remaining dishes. Custard took them over the months and he began to take the baby's things. Juliette fashioned a screen door to fit over the sliding door opening. It locked on the inside to keep Custard out.

On the first night of July, the mosquitoes arrived. The locals told her the daytime black flies diminished and the nocturnal mosquitoes took over in July. The mosquitoes showed up on time. They sounded desperate and military outside the screen. Juliette was happy with her design and handiwork until she headed for the outhouse and realized the screen locked behind her with Victoria inside the parcel car. Juliette had never been good at holding her water. When she formed the intention to pee, it was difficult to roll it back but she decided to deal with the baby on the other side of the locked screen rather than going to the outhouse. Whistling or singing sometimes worked to keep her mind off the urination urge but her mind filled up with getting the screen off. Piss dribbled down Juliette's leg and into her shoe. The choice to get mad or find it funny presented itself. She chose funny. She wore a long skirt and no underwear. Juliette didn't bother squatting, just lifted her skirt, legs apart and let it go. It made her smile that our own piss can smell all right but other peoples' urine stinks.

The screen was built to withstand pushing from the outside. It needed to be pried and Archie would have the tools for that. He wasn't home and he padlocked his little shed behind the caboose because of Custard's pilfering. But Juliette was good with locks. The diaper safety pin she had in the waistband of her skirt got her past the padlock. Archie's prybar got her through the wooden latch that held the screen door closed. Victoria slept quietly, not a movement, not a sound. The baby always seemed to be bathed in light. Juliette wondered how much of that came from a mother's biological focus and how much was behavioral, the mother paying more attention, unconsciously placing the child in a more lighted area, things like that. She put the screen back in place but the lock no longer worked. After Victoria's early hours of the morning feeding, Juliette headed for the outhouse again. A few seconds of enjoying the balmy summer air disappeared with the buzzing and biting of mosquitoes. The reports about the Tillman River area said that mosquitoes lasted for only three to four weeks but on these early July nights they were most vicious. Juliette decided to put the chamber pot under her bed. Those things worked better in winter when cool, dry air keeps the smell down but Juliette would prefer to walk to the outhouse naked in a blizzard than to brave those hungry little beasts.

After her own breakfast and before Victoria's breakfast, she cleaned up a bit. Custard tried the screen door and found it unlocked. He walked in, hands waving and, "Oh my God she's beautiful." Custard squealed and asked, "Do you have a cigarette for me?" Then, "Oh, they want to kill me." And, "Oh my god, girl."

"Get away from the baby."

"But Julie, I love her."

"Get out, Custard."

"Oh please. I'm alone. I want my own baby. You have Victoria and you're just mean to me." He reached for Victoria.

"Get away from her. Get out! Fuck off now!"

Custard grabbed Victoria's foot and pulled her out of the crib bumping her head on the railing. Juliette put all of her light weight and all of her considerable strength into her small fist. She drove it into Custard's lower back. The lack of resistance from the man's back surprised her. His legs collapsed, Custard fell to the floor and Victoria fell, head first, back into her crib with no protest to the rough handling. Custard tried his usual high-pitched siren wail but it came out in short breathy yelps. He banged his head. Custard tried to get up on all fours but it looked like his legs didn't work. Juliette figured she probably broke his back. Custard banged his head on the floor a few times and gasped out his last cry for sympathy, "Blood. I cut my head, maybe my ear."

"I am going to kill you now. What is your real name? I would like to say goodbye."

"Allister."

She kissed him on his scarred cheek. "Goodbye Allister." His good eye looked up at her but she could not discern the meaning of the look. The hard cast-iron handle of the frying pan shocked Juliette's wrist as it smashed Custard's skull. She swung in a wide arc that landed squarely on the side of his head. The odd sound, she assumed, was skull bone breaking. Juliette heard one exhalation from Custard and then the silence of a lifeless aggregation of meat and bones.

She picked up Victoria. The child's head was just above her mother's shoulder. Juliette walked out of the parcel car. Victoria looked backward at the world receding and she may have noticed Archie walking slowly and deliberately toward Juliette's car. Archie was responding to the commotion he'd heard. He cleared his thoat. Juliette didn't turn around but said, "Nothing you want to know about." and continued walking to Lank and Irma's car. When she entered the dining car, the baby happily babbled and Juliette happily talked back. "We will need to get a net to keep those pesky flies off your pretty skin."

"Lank, I need your help. I just assisted Custard in his last suicide attempt. Could you help me dump the body in West Pit? Irma does not need to know about it."

"What, he's dead? You killed him?"

Irma spoke from the next compartment, "What don't I need to know about?"

"Custard killed himself at my place and I helped him along."

"Yeah, I don't need to know about it."

"I want Lank's help in dumping the body."

"West Pit. I'd say that would be good."

"Yes, that is what I planned."

Irma said, "Since I know about it, I may as well become an accessory in case you piss me off someday and I squeal on you."

Juliette said, "Good point. We will take the girls with us to the burial."

Lank suggested that they get the old duffel bag Custard used and put some of his stuff in it.

"Yeah, Archie told me that Custard talked about going to Saskatchewan. Saskatchewan or the bottom of West Pit, who'd know the difference?"

Irma hugged Juliette. "Thanks for doin' it, girl. I feel a lot better. I thought I wanted to do it myself but I know I ain't going to feel like I missed anything. Thanks, Juls. It was just a matter of time before I got to it and I probably would've fucked it up."

Juliette closed up the parcel car until nightfall. At dusk Archie knocked on the dining car door. Irma answered the door. Archie said, "I'm going to get City. We'll sit over by the monument and drink wine. Do you have some cigarettes so he can smoke, too?"

"Yes, sure, just a minute." Irma whispered to Juliette as she went for smokes, "Does Archie know about this?"

"Not specifically, no. Do not say anything about it."

"Here we are, Sir. Five tailor-mades. Big night for City."

"Oh, we're just going to watch the cars go by."

"Okay, yeah, good."

"Thanks for the cigarettes."

"You bet."

Lank asked, "What's that all about?"

"Archie knows something's up so he's going to keep City busy and make sure nobody comes across the bridge."

"Leave it to Archie."

"Yeah, I admit, he's good in a pickle. He thinks it all through."

The three of them got Custard in the small back seat of the Baby Austin. That was enough accessory work for Irma. She and Lacie did not go to the funeral. It was Victoria's second drive in the Austin. She bounced on her mother's lap in the front seat while the potato sack that covered Custard's head slapped with the breeze in the back seat. Lank and Juliette dragged the body out of the car and dropped it down the shaft. Custard's duffel bag, with all the things in it that he might've taken on his trip to the prairies, went in on top. They heard the dull thud as the bag hit the body.

"She ain't so deep anymore. It's gotten filled up with trash. Should we say a few words?"

"Sure. We sincerely regret any discomfort and inconvenience we may be causing the rats of West Pit."

Lank laughed and coughed and Victoria burbled. They got in the Austin and drove to The Tracks in silence. When they got out of the car, Lank said, "I should take some trash out to West Pit tomorrow. Some stuff on top wouldn't hurt."

Juliette touched his arm. "Yes, very good." She fished in her pocket and got a dollar. "Here Lank, would you mind getting him a couple of packs of smokes? Sweet Caporal was his brand."

"Sure thing, Juls."

She got out of the Austin with the taste of tears in her throat.

CHAPTER SEVEN

Juliette: No, you were on my mind, not Custard. He was dead. I killed him. The next day was another day. It did not strike me as a big thing then and it does not seem like a big thing now.

Victoria: You're not proud of it, are you?

Juliette: No. I am not a proud woman.

Juliette knew Custard didn't try to kill himself. He inserted himself in the lives of others more than they wanted. Did she murder him for that? Did she defend her child? Did she rid the earth of a mean prick who had already killed two or three times? Bugs, spiders, bees and wasps got picked up and brought outside rather than killed in Juliette's parcel car. But houseflies, mosquitoes, mice, shiny red centipedes and Custard, she killed in the parcel car. Killing was not a good thing but she killed a lot of fish in her life for nothing but money. The usual excuses for killing humans did not impress her. War and execution of criminals she found objectionable but universal rules for humans broke apart when you applied pressure. /principles are only inclinations with a history/

At The Tracks the season of clear air and well-defined shadows began. The Custard questions passed through Juliette but they had no substantial weight. She didn't worry about paying for her crime. Archie mentioned Saskatchewan to City and he took it from there. When Custard hadn't appeared around The Tracks for a week, City went into his hopper car and authoritatively confirmed to anyone who would listen that Custard packed up and went out West. City gradually retrieved the items Custard stole from here and there, righteously returning them to their owners. He got a couple of weeks filled with thank yous and idle chat in gratitude for his rescue of spoons, ashtrays and wrenches.

Victoria's presence and the sun on her skin were gifts to Juliette. She sat down on the squared-up chunks of pine logs that replaced the railway tie steps. She had thrown ashes and clay on the ties under her car to get rid of the creosote smell. It worked. Archie did the same. Irma gradually covered up the creosote ties under the dining car but it took a long time. Irma didn't seem to go at anything around The Tracks with any vigor.

Victoria seemed less irritable on this sunny day. She started teething. Her mother didn't really know what teething meant but expected that if she asked Irma, she'd get a response like, "What the fuck, girl; what do you know? Where you been all your life?" It would be said in humor and Juliette would have responded with a clever insight or a self-deprecating joke but sometimes cleverness and self-deprecation just take too much energy. She asked Nurse Marsh about teething. Lorraine was willing and honored to answer all baby questions. Early in the morning Juliette's first post-birth period began, bringing the thorough relief that sometimes came with menses. The dark tension and prickly sensitivity she felt before her period drained away with the blood of an unfertilized potential sibling for Victoria. She thought of Custard and she thought of cigarettes. Thoughts of euthanasia, murder, morality, sacrilege and insanity flitted lightly through her brain but the caress of the sunny morning in August was profound.

"Archie," she called, trying not to shout, not willing to throw anything brittle at the good morning. Archie didn't respond. He stood in front of the caboose looking at the grass, the Queen Anne's lace and the bulrushes waving in the morning breeze. Juliette recognized his mood as one she would like to share. Victoria objected only a little to her meal being cut short. Juliette carried the baby to the side of the ditch next to Archie who barely acknowledged them. She found a part of the trance he was in. The grass undulated in low lustre gold when it caught the sun and then deep green as the blades of grass stood up to the breeze. The bulrushes waved slowly, having become heavy with big cattails. Queen Anne's lace jiggled in the breeze. The taller ones bowed and straightened up frantically in the little gusts; they still had flowers and were trying to be noticed by whatever pollinators might be out braving the zephyrs. Many of the stands had already gone to seed and were content to take the wind's help in spreading that seed. The light and the shadows got inside Juliette as more than sensual delights. She stared at the weeds. Her mind, lightly engaged and ticking over at idle speed, didn't dissect or name anything.

"Archie, have you got anything I can smoke?"

"A bit if you'd like. I smoked most of what I had left last night."

"No, no, I do not mean opium. A cigarette, tobacco. Can you roll the pipe tobacco?"

"You can if you've got papers. It's Sail and that's strong. If you roll a cigarette using Sail, it'll make your heart thump. You start up again?"

"Just had one but I seem to really want the next one. I hope that is the rattle of bulrushes I hear and not the sound of dominoes falling."

Archie smiled. The chipped front tooth always made the serious man look playful. "It's just the bulrushes. I hear them too. I've got chewing tobacco if you'd fancy that. I've never liked it but I buy a plug every year or so. And, sure enough, I still don't like it."

"I will try it, if you do not mind."

"Actually, it's on the table as you go in. I was looking for someone to give it to. Good morning, Juliette. Good morning to you. I'm in a lovely, morning-after opium haze and we have this day and now, you two beautiful ladies. Splendid."

Juliette took his hand and kissed his knuckles. Archie put his other hand on her shoulder, bent over a bit and blew lightly on Victoria's face. She was a delighted child.

"I'll take Victoria, if you want, so she doesn't have to watch you throw up if you react like some people do after their first chew of tobacco."

Juliette took an hour to chew the last bit of flavor from her first quid while the baby and the neighbor chewed and sniffed and laughed at each other. Archie suggested that Victoria should be fed and then he'd take her to the caboose for her afternoon nap. He had some fresh milk and a baby bottle so he could easily prepare formula for Victoria if she got hungry. "Go. I'll take care of her. You have a day."

Juliette had a day. She walked to town, bought some things at Percy's store and stopped at the library on the way back. She carried a light load but it was unwieldy because replacing the toilet paper in the outhouse was Juliette's responsibility. She also carried a William Faulkner novel, a Margaret Lawrence novel, the Fichte to Nietzsche volume of Coppleston's History of Philosophy, two baby books and two Vogue magazines. She worried about dropping some groceries or books. Juliette never worried about dropping Victoria, who often wormed and squiggled. Dropping the baby was inconceivable.

In the afternoon, she ate the smoked mackerel she bought. Juliette loved fresh spring mackerel but the summer catch made the best smoked fish. The big pungent flavors invited another chew of tobacco.

Up on the roof of the parcel car, she took off her clothes, lying on them in the sun. She rolled her head to spit tobacco juice to one side and watched it slide lazily down the slightly curved roof. Most of it evaporated on the hot metal before oozing over the edge. The Conroy kids from across the river came up the ladder sequentially to peak and giggle. Juliette pretended not to notice until fourteen-year-old Wayne came up. She didn't chance a tobacco-stained toothy smile but smile she did and Wayne didn't giggle. He came up another rung and lingered. One of the other children cried, "Wa…yne?" He climbed down the ladder, slowly.

/would I like that/ Juliette suspected that Wayne would masturbate as soon as a shroud of privacy allowed and she thought she might do the same. Only later did she wonder if Wayne's desire may have been tempered by a little trickle of blood coming from her vagina.

Victoria slipped from her mind and her own presence returned. She realized that her child had absorbed her life. Juliette felt an ebb and flow of two desirable spirits, hers and Victoria's

At eight o'clock, when Archie returned Victoria, he received profuse and genuine thanks. Juliette felt an unacknowledged anxiety drain away when she smelled Victoria. She released her breasts to the child's hunger. Victoria was ready to receive but Juliette knew that she and her baby had loved their day apart. Archie's satisfaction with the day pleased Juliette most. In the August evening he seemed lit up.

Juliette wanted to drink that night. She didn't have any liquor in her car and she wouldn't ask Archie. Lank's slop didn't appeal to her any more than going to see Winnie on Tillman Street, Sterling Reserve's only bootlegger when Ronnie wasn't around. She rapidly went from wanting it to craving it, to just letting it pass. In recognition that the salty fish, the sun and tobacco spitting made her thirsty she found the vacillation between craving and foregoing, a tickle rather than a torture. Juliette knew that the jiggles of one habit can feed the jumping of another. A glass of water, a glass of buttermilk, a few minutes watching Victoria sleep and a small resolve to resist another chew of tobacco, set her up to start worrying about money.

Juliette made her reputation as a fearless 'go get the fish no matter what' captain when she became The Slipper skipper. Slipper was her second boat and she made lots of money fishing. She and her crew put up with the boat's shortcomings because they got to the fish and got there fast. Juliette knew where the fish lived.

However, the present skipper refused to take Slipper out in any bad weather. Arnold Steele had a widely inclusive definition of bad weather. Most of the owner's share from the sale of Slipper's catches seemed to go to boat expenses. She and her father, who owned the fish plant, marveled at Arnold's ability to break gear while rarely leaving the dock.

Juliette's father or her mother would help her out financially but she didn't want to ask. In her years between being Glace Bay's high liner and arriving at The Tracks she spent money like a fisherman. Juliette was, however, self-congratulatory about having avoided debt. She liked money, liked having some in the bank and a bit tucked away in her home, in her purse or in her pocket.

She also liked spending. Juliette didn't skimp on food quality. A beautiful dress in her size was hard to resist, beautiful shoes were harder and seductive underclothes she simply did not resist. She sent for the clothes stored at a friend's house in Antigonish. It was a delight to get things she'd forgotten about. However, Juliette could no longer close her eyes to the pounds she gained while pregnant; too many of those pounds remained with her. Irma and Dr. Lawley said she looked great with the extra weight. Lank and Archie couldn't bring themselves to say she looked better with the few pounds she'd kept from her pregnancy. They liked skinny just as much as Juliette did. The chunky Nurse Marsh surprised her and advised losing the extra pounds. She said, "Most people who gain a bit in their twenties, gain a lot in their thirties."

The Antigonish clothes came from a period in her life when she bought a lot of pants because they weren't allowed at Mount St. Bernard, the ladies residence at St. FX. The girls from the Mount always had to wear dresses. They suffered lots of other restrictions. The nuns at the Mount acted as the female students' jailers. Juliette went to St. FX as a mature student and registered as a married woman so as to avoid the authority of the nuns. She got kicked out of here and there for improper dress or improper behavior. Her old house outside of Antigonish was a constant party. A lot of girls from the Mount who exuded piety and virginity in front of the nuns, got permission to visit a sick or dying relative. They spent the time at Juliette's doing things they weren't allowed to do in residence. The few girls from The Mount who could fit into Juliette's slacks borrowed them while they stayed at her house.

Juliette tried on some of the pants from Antigonish. They would go on but she looked like a woman wearing tight slacks. Back in Antigonish, the waistband of her slacks just marked the upper end of the garment. The fabric gathered in darts at the back, and falling seductively over her ass, kept Juliette's pants up. Even guys who didn't like skinny girls liked Juliette. She thought it was as much her behind as her face that caused the attraction. Finding the waistbands on her old clothes tight to the point of discomfort caused Juliette to give up using a baby carriage. She took her four-mile walk, on any day that the weather was reasonable, with Victoria on her hip. It was no longer a stroll but a brisk walk.

Juliette also wanted beautiful clothes for Victoria. A day in Halifax challenged her bank account. She made some of Victoria's clothes because she disliked the cute colors and cute styles of baby girls' clothes. Victoria often dressed in black, hounds-tooth, tweed, grey silk or deep purple Merino wool; anything but frilly, pale pink cotton.

Despite concerns about money, Juliette felt good. She never expected that caring for a baby would be a pleasure but, with help from Irma, Lorraine and Archie, she felt capable.

***

Feeling good pulled Juliette toward seeking more good feelings. The peace of mind she found being close to Victoria was a great pleasure. But it reminded her of what a great buffet of pleasures life presented. The tobacco didn't make her high but it kicked up the energy of desire. A habit gives a reason to live. Smoking, drinking, sex or betting, a habit keeps you looking forward, always an eye on the future.

"You need your next drink most when you are already drinking one." She said this to Archie when she was pregnant and trying, with the help of her tendency toward nausea, to not drink too much.

Archie replied, "Oh, I don't know. It doesn't apply to smoking. I used to give up the pipe. I mean tobacco not opium. The opium never bothers me like that because I don't use it often. Anyway, I quit smoking every June just to prove to myself I could do it. When I quit, the first few days, sometimes a week, I'd feel really empty. I figure a lot of people turn back to Jesus when they quit smoking. It takes a god to fill that empty space when you quit smoking. Perhaps religion is just a cheap cigarette."

Juliette laughed. "All of those images of suffering: carrying of the cross, the weeping Mary Magdalene, the agony in the garden; you empathize. I know what you went through Christ; I just quit smoking."

Victoria and her crib aged quickly in their first few months. Archie brought the white pine crib to Juliette a couple of months before Victoria's arrival. Its bars and railings were stark and smooth. The crib was a simple design, fastidiously built with Archie's methodical care in finish work. In less than six months, Victoria changed from a fascinating organism to a person with depth. Looking at Victoria asleep in her crib, watching them both age, stirred Juliette. The crib absorbed the world and became blonde. The crib arrived new and white and opaque but now she could see into the yellowing wood. Its progress toward what it became had a loose predictability. Victoria, also blonde, was not even loosely predictable to Juliette. Every change, every day, surprised her. Unbearable pleasure and intolerable anxiety can be difficult to distinguish, like definition and clarity. A notion closely defined shuts everything else out. It's opposite to clarity. But clarity and definition look the same.

Juliette drifted off with the day's sunshine and the sweet connection, with the child in the crib, inside her. Victoria breathed in the smell of the crib, which became more like her and less like raw unfinished pine every day. Juliette's peace of mind began to itch. She thought of pursuit. She thought of looking for a faster ride. Entering pre-sleep where plans and fantasies become dreams, her head was stuck outside the shelter of the wheelhouse on a boat slamming to windward on a purple sea with silver spray soaking her yellow party dress. She toasted the storm with a bottle of rum.

Perhaps Victoria dreamed about her day with Archie.

***

On a Saturday morning, Nurse Marsh arrived unexpectedly at the caboose. Archie welcomed her and made tea. The caboose was warm and bright, contrasting with the cold and cloudy early October morning. It had been a windy night and the stiff breeze continued to charge Archie's bank of batteries. The wind generator put out more power than the batteries could absorb. Archie had the radio and all the lights on when Lorraine arrived.

"I've got two things I want to talk to you about. I'm finished my training at the end of the month."

"Congratulations. I'm sure you'll enjoy your career. You are certainly good at it."

"Thank you. I wanted to stay here, in a way, and Dr. Lawley wanted to hire me back; however, I received a good offer from St. Rita's Hospital in Sydney. Of course I'd be closer to my family but also I'd be able to choose my specialty. I don't want to leave my patients here and I must admit that, foremost in my mind is Victoria Elizabeth. I wouldn't tell that to Miss Cameron. She would probably say that it didn't matter."

"Oh, she wouldn't say that. I know she appreciates your help." Archie had detected a prepared formality in Nurse Marsh and he thought it worked quite well. The diffidence was not evident. Archie expected that Nurse Marsh must use prepared speeches a lot in tricky situations. He would act predictably. Archie didn't want to put her off her game.

"The other issue is that I am quite sure that Miss Cameron is drinking again."

Archie knew Juliette started drinking, moderately and infrequently but he and Juliette believed she was on a downward slide and might at some time come to a point when she'd get too drunk to take care of an infant. He said to Nurse Marsh, "Oh is that right?"

"Yes. I'm quite sure of it. Of course, the worry is about the child."

"Yes yes, of course. Well, there is nothing to be done at this point. Juliette is, at the moment, perfectly capable and I know that George, Dr. Lawley, is keeping an eye open for danger signs. I do appreciate your concern and I will keep watch, too."

Nurse Marsh said, "I hope you don't think I'm being meddlesome. Perhaps I am."

"Well no, but perhaps you underestimate Juliette. She's careless I suppose… but Juliette will be all right, I would guess, as far as Victoria is concerned. Juliette may let herself go to the dogs but she'll give to Victoria or do for Victoria things that perhaps more conventional mothers would miss out on. If you know what I mean."

"I am perfectly aware of Miss Cameron's special qualities. I am perfectly aware that she loves her child but…"

Archie looked at her, a hard look. "You're miffed by what I said. You're mad at me for defending my friend."

Nurse Marsh did not flinch. The shy young woman was at work, doing her job. "Mr. MacKenzie, you might as well sit down. I know you're not going to throw me out or hit me. Would you please listen to my concerns?"

Archie was glad to relax again. He didn't like bristling. He sat down. "I wonder if a porcupine feels that uncomfortable when it gets its back up."

Nurse Marsh chuckled a bit. Mirth was not a frequent visitor to her face. "Not as uncomfortable as its victim. I got stuck one time. I was trying to save my friend's dog. The dog got a face full of quills and I got about a dozen of them on my hand and my ankle. They hurt."

"I'll bet they do."

"If Miss Cameron falls back into her old drinking habits, which I understand were severe, Victoria Elizabeth is in a risky position. I'm not talking about intention; I'm talking about safety. A child her age, any child, may need attention at any time. Just because Miss Cameron and I are so different doesn't mean that I cannot appreciate her unusual characteristics but if she's passed out drunk, which she probably will be by times, what about the baby? Babies need constant vigilance."

"Here at The Tracks, we are much more like family than the people who have lawns. Well, I have a lawn but that's just... Well I guess I don't know what that is. Anyway, we all watch out for each other and we tolerate a wider spread of differences than do the lawn people. Irma watches out for Juliette. Victoria is watched over. Juliette and I have discussed this very thing and she asked me to intervene if things get out of hand, and I will do that. I don't dismiss your caring about it, I don't think you're meddlesome but we've got it covered much better than you think."

"Well, that's great. I… That's great. I'm so glad. Yes, well that's great."

Archie could see Lorraine Marsh shrinking. While he said, "Well, I thank you. I know your concern is heartfelt." He realized she must be hearing, 'but, you've got a heart of gold'.

"Will you tell Miss Cameron I'm leaving? I won't be seeing her and Victoria Elizabeth until Tuesday and that will be my last visit. I expect that, at least for a while, the community nurse duties will come to an end. The hospital will be covered, though."

"I don't want to tell Juliette you're leaving. Why don't you do that?"

"She would say she didn't care."

"No, she won't say that and if she does it will give you practice in spotting a lie, because I know she does care. Let's just go over there together."

They did go together. Irma saw them and said they looked like a couple. Archie banged on Juliette's sliding door with the polished beach stone she hung there for that purpose. It hurt to rap on a steel railway car door with your knuckles. The stone hung by a small chain. Juliette had it drilled to accept the chain and engraved with the words 'BANG ME'. All of the old mining and assaying tools pilfered from the Sterling Reserve mines made it easy to get that sort of work done. Juliette slid the heavy steel door open right away. She and Lank built a simple spring mechanism, designed by Juliette, which stopped the door at three feet rather than letting it slide to the full nine-foot opening of the original parcel car. They estimated the weight of the door to be three hundred pounds. Despite Juliette having kept the runners and sheeves in good condition and well lubricated, overcoming all that inertia to get the door sliding took a lot of strength and it would stop with a bang. The door also closed with a bang. Juliette's mechanism with a spring above the door absorbed the energy that otherwise caused the bang. It stored that energy to be used for overcoming the inertia to get the door rolling again.

"I saw you coming, on a Saturday morning, almost arm in arm. It must be a sermon on drinking and a mother's duty."

"Juliette, you read minds. I thought of taking Miss Marsh's arm but I knew you'd be jealous. We are here to bring you to the Lord Jesus Christ our God and our Savior. You can have the loaves and fishes but stay the hell away from Canaan."

"Good morning, Miss Cameron. I just came to tell you I'm going."

It was the first time Juliette heard any attempt at wit from Lorraine Marsh. They smiled at each other. "I thought you would be leaving soon. Come in, you two, come in. You have graduated and you have gotten a job? Congratulations, Nurse Marsh, your proper title now."

"A week yet, well eight days actually, until I get my certificate. Thank you." She said the 'thank you' with her head lowered. Juliette always cringed when Lorraine did that but this time it struck her as honest humility that she could admire. /I am a cynical fool/I should not feel disdain for Lorraine's modesty/

"Where are you going to be practicing?"

"In Sydney."

Juliette asked, "St. Rita's?"

"Yes, thank you."

"That is wonderful. It is the best to be with the best. You will fit right in with that nursing staff. In six months, they will wonder how they ever got along without you. I do not know what Victoria and I would have done without you."

"Thank you, Miss Cameron."

"Oh, thank you for all your valuable time. What I mean is that your time was valuable to us. In addition to all you did and all the things you taught us, that I did not have a click or a clue about, you gave your time. You gave that to us and we drank it down because it was delicious."

Nurse Marsh convulsed lightly as with hiccoughs. Tears formed; she covered her mouth. For some seconds no one spoke. Juliette went to her and kissed the tears away on both sides of her nose. She gently took Nurse Marsh's hand from her mouth and kissed her.

"When we meet again, Victoria will not be your patient; therefore, I will not be your patient's mother and I hope you will call me Juliette and I can call you Lorraine without being presumptuous."

"Lori. My mother and my brothers call me Lori."

"Lori. Yes, that is lovely but please do not call me Julie. I would throw a fit."

***

Archie: You're darn tootin' it was an erotic kiss. I remember it as clear as day. The kiss lasted a long time and Lorraine was all flushed and I remember seeing a line of rosy pink fill in on your eyelid. Then you talked about meeting in the future. You were holding your arms around Lorraine's waist, kind of on her ass really.

Victoria: Whew. 'atta way to go, Mom.

Juliette: God, Archie, did you take photographs.

Archie: No. It's a movie in my head. I found the whole thing exciting and I actually felt a little horny toward her when she was at my place. I had seen this sort of thing before. Your mother really does seem to read minds. I would always try to determine a person's needs and accommodate those needs if it wasn't too much trouble but Juliette doesn't bother. She's polite and positive but she usually doesn't go out of her way to straighten up anyone's deficiencies. However, when she sees a need and decides to do something about it, she is an arrow to the heart of the matter. She can roar in with an attack of good intentions and patch up that hard to reach scintilla, a little thing but so deeply troubling it trips a person up.

Victoria: Is that the way it was? You saw where she hurt and kissed it to make it better.

Juliette: I was emboldened by my breath. I did not drink Friday night but, shortly after I got up on Saturday, I opened up a quart of Schooner. I just started on a little glass when I saw Lorraine coming across the bridge. I figured she was coming to see me so I hid the beer, gargled with salt water and had a quick Pepsodent brush up. I drank some tea before Archie and Lorraine got to me. I dislike lectures. I remember hugging Lorraine and saying something like, 'I am glad you are leaving because Victoria and I are falling in love with you.'

Archie: You said that? I didn't know you said that.

Juliette: Your radar ears and hawk eyes do not catch everything.

Archie: I guess not.

Victoria: Was that pure bullshit? You weren't falling in love with Nurse Marsh, were you?

Juliette: Oh love, I do not know the difference between bullshit and truth, you know that. I do not believe there is a real difference. It was something said that had no further consequences that I could foresee other than giving Lorraine what she wanted, to feel appreciated. Okay, it was bullshit but well-intentioned bullshit.

Victoria: Well, did you love her?

Juliette: No, but I did give her love for those few minutes; for half an hour. I do not know. Yes, I loved her for that time.

Victoria: Isn't that Juliette Cameron? Full speed love for half an hour. Isn't that my mom?

Juliette: I love you forever but perhaps I do not sustain that appearance all the time.

Victoria: Oh yes, I know. I didn't mean me. I wasn't thinking of me.

***

Nurse Marsh and her possessions went to the nurses' residence at St. Rita's in her uncle's panel truck. She and Juliette exchanged letters and birthday cards but the cards and letters trailed off in frequency and intimacy after a few years.

CHAPTER EIGHT

On a cold Monday morning in November, Archie woke up at eight o'clock to a dry mouth and a heavy blanket of too much alcohol over his mind and body. A glance out the port light in his bedroom showed the results of fall, the beginnings of winter. The grass sparkled with a gray white brushing of frost or light snow, he couldn't tell. But through the port light, through the walls of the caboose, he felt the crackle and promise of a cold, sunny morning. In seconds, a warm excitement filled his arms and shoulders up to his face. /*what a great day to do something with Victoria*/

Archie had an egg in a hole with two cups of tea for breakfast. He drank lots of water, sloshing around in the mouth and spitting out water, as well as good swallowing water that tickled his dehydrated esophagus.

A less attentive walker might have stepped in the vomit on Juliette's front step. He figured she threw up before entering because it was splattered on the top step to the right. Archie saw it often enough to know that Juliette turned to the right to throw up. If she stuck her head out the door to throw up, it would be on the other side. From that bit of evidence, he deduced that Juliette guzzled whisky before leaving the caboose the night before. Archie went to bed drunk enough for his taste, making no attempt to clear the temptation of an open bottle away from Juliette. He opened the sliding door. One of Juliette's shoes had vomit on it.

***

Juliette woke to her parcel car smelling bad and looking dismal. Bits of sunlight came in as splatters of garish litter on top of the mess. Her lips felt dry and brittle.

Juliette saw the matches and the outside part of the box lying in the crib. The box cover read, 'Eddy's Strike Anywhere Matches'. She remembered fumbling and dropping them there last night but didn't know if she dismissed the possible danger. Perhaps she hadn't thought of the risk or planned to clean it up but flaked out before she got to it. A piece of cardboard, carefully cut from the inside part of the large match box stood on her bed table supported by its own shape, like a dressing screen. It was the tidiest thing in her view. It held the words:

Juliette

Victoria has come to live with me.

Respectfully
Archie

He had printed the words neatly. She knew he took time to choose every one.

In the afternoon, Juliette went to Archie's to feed Victoria at her breasts. The idea of Victoria drinking secondhand whisky and beer sickened her. She remembered staying at Archie's to drink more after he went to bed but didn't remember walking home. She found Victoria awake. The child's crying drilled into her. These thoughts hung low in Juliette's body, her brain being in that overcooked, lifeless state that was alcohol's reward. Her failures crowded in her abdomen churning with the recurring need to defecate.

Juliette, still feeding Victoria, walked into the bathroom. One minute later, she reappeared hobbled with her pants at her ankles. Juliette cried quietly. She passed the baby to Archie and returned to the bathroom. Archie heard her sobbing, flushing the toilet. He put Victoria in the visitor's cradle he built for her and carried two buckets of water up from the river to refill the cistern mounted high on the back wall of his caboose. Juliette did not need the minor frustration of running out of water for flushing the toilet.

CHAPTER NINE

In April of nineteen fifty-five, Lewis Malay hit a patch of ice during an unexpected freeze up. Lewis and his one-year-old, red Fargo pickup truck went off the road. The truck looked okay; Lewis felt okay. Serious gunning of the engine and rocking back and forth from forward to reverse got him unstuck. Back on the road to Sterling Reserve, Lewis was a man with 'oh God, that was close' thoughts sending hot pepper feelings through his arms and chest. About half a mile from home, the Fargo died. Drops of oil stretched down the road from the back of his pickup truck. Lank told him those were the last drops, because the off-road excursion bashed in the Fargo's oil pan.

Lank gladly took the job. He enjoyed working on engines, and he knew Lewis would pay. Payment wasn't always made and rarely made on time for the work that Lank did to people's cars and trucks. If everyone who owed him money suddenly paid, he'd buy a good car for himself. As it stood, Lank put an old tire between the grill of his patched up Austin and the back bumper of the Fargo. He pushed it through Sterling Reserve over the rattling bridge to The Tracks with Irma at the wheel of the Fargo. As they got out of the vehicles in front of the dining car, Lank said, "She's a nice truck, isn't she?"

"Just fuckin' ducky. Real quiet truck. You get the creature from Juliette. I'm goin' for a walk."

Irma acted grumpy for weeks. He didn't know why. The first time he asked, she almost bit his head off. She had no time for Lank and no time for Lacie. Lank, on the other hand, felt something close to embarrassment by how much he liked spending hours with Lacie. He especially liked being alone with her. That way he wouldn't need to withstand anyone poking fun at him for extreme doting. Lacie dazzled him. If she smiled, giggled, picked her nose or said a new word, it blew him into a world of wonder. Lacie made work difficult but work didn't matter much when he took care of his daughter. Lank didn't drink as much when Lacie kept him company. He didn't think about drinking as much when they were together.

Lacie, Victoria and Juliette made a fine threesome. They always got up to something, which was not always Juliette's idea. The active and capable Victoria, who just turned three, deferred to Lacie and Juliette because she got lots of fun and affection from the two older women. Lank loved to spend time with the three of them. He wasn't really a part of the order, more like a very large plaything. Lacie and Victoria crawled all over him and a little girl could see a lot of world while getting a piggyback from Lank. Victoria usually got tired first but she was not always happy to be put to bed in the parcel car, preferring to go home to her room in the caboose. Lacie could frolic for twenty-four hours at any location.

The second time Lank tried to determine what ate up Irma's civility; he asked if she minded him spending so much time with Juliette and the girls. The word jealousy did not get spoken but it got in the room. Irma simply answered, "pfft". That became an element of conversation between Lank and Lacie when they played together.

"Pfft".

"And a big pfft to you, little girl. Pfft, pfft, pfft."

"Pfft." Lacie liked wiping the dribbles off her chin as much as the conversation.

Juliette kept the girls. Lank went to work on the Fargo. In three hours, he had it torn down enough to know that the engine functioned, except for two pistons seized to the cylinder sleeves. He walked to Lewis Malay's and described the alternative remedies for his injured truck. Lewis chose the cheapest, with the idea that he and Lank could look around for a good buy on a replacement engine to have on hand in case the cheap repair didn't last. With some heat, some pushing, pulling and banging, Lank freed up the pistons and determined that everything would work after he polished the cylinder walls. He sat on the floor patching the oil pan, in the dining car.

Irma came home at six o'clock. "How the hell can I keep this place clean when you drag in dirty old shit like that?"

"I got newspapers under it. Who's the letter from?"

"It's for me, from home."

"Is everything all right? Is everyone okay?"

"Everyone I know is just grand. Did you get your supper? Did you feed the baby?"

"Juliette still has Lacie. It's been a couple of hours since I checked but she was happy to keep her. I didn't eat yet but I can clean up and make supper for both of us."

"I know how to cook. It's goddamn cold in here. Will you get that greasy mess out of here?"

"It's more goddamn cold out there. That's why I'm workin' in here."

Irma put her hands on her hips. "Well now, ain't you the smart one."

Lank was a gentle man but he worked hard all day and didn't have a drop to drink. He felt tired and hungry. Lank rose from the floor, went to Irma and put his greasy hands on her shoulders. He looked down at her but could not think of anything to say so he folded himself up on the floor again to resume work on the oil pan. That was the closest they ever came to violence.

Irma stood there for a few minutes before she went to Juliette's to bring Lacie back. She also got a jar that contained a pint of moonshine. Irma got enough heat pumping out of the wood stove to boil potatoes. She made an instant stew with wilted carrots and deer meat that had been bottled in the fall. Lank cleaned up and they had a late supper.

"I got things on my mind. I ain't been the best, I know."

"Dear, my mind is as empty as ever. If you want to tell me your troubles, I got room up there for it."

"Mum's sick. She's dyin'."

"Is that the letter you got today?"

"No, it's from that one you got about a month ago. Remember that?"

"Yeah, I remember getting a letter addressed to you but that was from St. John's, wasn't it?"

"Yeah, St. John's. My cousin there first told me about Mum."

"Oh, that's too bad nobody from home told you about it."

"Yeah, too bad. You're right."

Lank liked to avoid fights. He knew that Irma often lied but he rarely brought it to her attention; therefore her manner of lying became familiar and easily identified. They quietly drank moonshine, quietly went to bed and slept as far away from each other as they could get in their little bed. Lank wondered why she lied and why she was upset. He hoped Irma was all right.

In the morning, Lank put the oil pan back on, filled the radiator and put oil in the engine with a little extra in the cylinders. The Fargo started up right away. After the extra oil burned out of the cylinders, no smoke came out and the engine ran quietly. He ran it for half an hour, torqued everything down. The gaskets held up. Lank went into the dining car to heat up water for tea and to wash the grease off his hands.

Irma said, "It works good, does it?"

"Perfect, like new."

"It's ready to go?"

"Yeah, and Lewis will probably pay me today. I think I'll charge him twenty-five dollars plus the cost of the head gasket. He won't mind. It's my oil I put in her."

"Yeah, great. Is there much gas in it?"

"I think there's half a tank. Why?"

"Oh nothin'."

Irma went into the bedroom, got a packed bag from under the bed, She put a note on the table and walked out. Lank heard the Fargo starting up. He watched his wife drive away. The note said, 'I am going to see my mother'. The red pickup turned left after crossing the bridge. She headed into Sterling Reserve. He thought about trying to get the Austin going but Lacie was up and around, bright-eyed and inquisitive. What would be the use? What could he do if he accomplished the almost impossible task of catching up to her?

That night, City told Lank that Richard Johnson made a complaint to the Mounties. Someone broke into his house, beat it up inside and stole some money, tobacco and rum. Two days later, City told Archie that people saw Irma driving the Red Fargo away from Richard Johnson's on the morning she left but no one told Richard or the Mounties. Five days after Irma left, Lank got a letter which said nothing but, 'The truck is at the ferry in North Sydney. The key is tied to the valve on the spare tire.' There was no salutation, no closing, no apologies, no 'I will love you forever', and no mention of their daughter.

Lank showed the letter to Juliette and Archie.

"She is gone, Lank. I would expect Irma to say a final goodbye just like that. She lies a lot but there is no bullshit to her. You will be getting reacquainted with your right-hand lover."

"What do you mean? What lover?"

Archie said, "Your right hand. Pretty soon you'll be jerking off like a fourteen-year-old." Lank felt embarrassed and looked around to make sure that the girls weren't listening.

Juliette said, "You will have another woman before you know it, before you want it."

"You two seem pretty sure Irma's gone for good. I don't think," Lank whispered, "I don't think she'd leave Lacie."

Juliette shot back, "She just did."

"Maybe she'll come back but you might be better off without her. If she comes back, I'm sorry man but I have to say, it will be because what she ran to was no good, not because she had a real change of heart about what she ran from. She never got the knack of being a mother."

"Some of us never get the knack of being a mother."

Archie said, "Don't sell yourself short. You've been a better mother to both Victoria and Lacie than Irma ever was to Lacie."

"Faint praise."

Lank rolled a cigarette. "I hope she comes back." Archie opened a window to get the cool morning air. "You want me to go outside to smoke this?"

"No, not necessarily. I just don't like the children to get too much smoke of any kind." Juliette looked at Archie's eyes. She stared at Archie. It appeared to Lank that his friend was getting fidgety, awkward.

Juliette put her hand on Archie's shoulder. "Always, always, always, thank you."

Archie put his hand over hers and looked straight back at her. "You're entirely welcome. Victoria means more to me than I mean to myself."

"I've got to get the truck. Poor Lewis has been pretty patient with me."

Archie asked, "Do you have enough money for the train for you and Lank?"

"You know me, the old miser woman. I always have a bit tucked away. Do you want to come too? We could take the girls."

"Not me. I'll stay and man the fort but the girls would love the train."

Lank said, "Be like their homes moving. I bet they would let them in the caboose since Victoria lives in one."

Archie asked, "Wouldn't it be the Railiner to Sydney?"

"Yes, I suppose you are right. Engine, caboose and cars all in one."

Lank said, "Sure, yes, we'll get drives to the train station easy enough with two kids in tow. The Austin's workin' good. I fixed it up for Lewis after my wife stole his truck but he didn't want to take it. You can use it when we're gone. Good tires and everything. You could drive to Toronto." Lank didn't expect Archie to drive to Toronto. He'd be surprised if Archie took the Austin to Brookfield. Archie thought of the Austin as a little wreck.

"Do you think we should put a sign on you saying, 'I am tall but I can sit in a Baby Austin'? Juliette and Lank quipped back and forth during the hour they waited by the roadside. They didn't see much traffic but three cars and a pickup truck passed them. Between Lank and Juliette, they knew all the drivers by name. It seemed rude. People they knew passed them by.

Lank said, "Perhaps they think we'll rob them. If Irma robbed Richard Johnson, The Tracks gets the bad reputation."

"It was just theft. Robbery, I think, is when people are there; like a holdup. It is just theft when there is no one there. Irma is just a thief not a robber."

"I was there when she took the truck."

"Hmm, good point. Let me clarify. Robbery involves force or the threat of force." A new Plymouth station wagon zipped by going fast and then stopped fast with tires squealing. The car backed up quickly, swaying all over the road and coming back under the driver's control again by a sudden application of the brakes. Juliette and Lank had the girls in their arms in seconds, ready to jump for safety.

"It's the nuns."

"What?"

A fine example of the Sisters of Charity opened the driver's door. "Good morning, I'm Sister Jeanne d'Arc." She rushed over, picked up their three bags and put them in the back of the station wagon.

"Sister, I am Juliette Cameron and this is Lank Graham." Juliette looked at her face and they both smiled, shaking hands, a light touch but enclosing and warm. Juliette felt something familiar and

130

realized it was a particular kind of welcome she had for another pretty woman. Sister Jeanne d'Arc seemed to have it too. /oh my/it only works if we both feel it/beats small talk/

Juliette got in the back seat carrying Victoria. Lank followed her. Lacie had enough of being carried; she dove into the station wagon. A new situation and Lacie gobbled it up. She was four and a half; it was her world. Victoria settled comfortably in Juliette's arms for now, willing to let Lacie open up all these new packages of life for their illumination.

An older nun, about sixty or sixty-five, scrunched herself up in the corner of the back seat. She was smiling; a grinning sort of smile. She seemed as excited to see things unfold as Lacie was to unfold them.

A young woman in slightly different garb sat in the front passenger seat. Sister Jeanne d'Arc made the introductions. "Our guests are Juliette Cameron and Lawrence Graham whose friends call him Lank if my sources are correct. And they've got a couple of kids with them. In the back with you, Juliette, is Sister Mary Ignatia, who is half crazy."

Sister Mary Ignatia, ignoring the fact that they were already above the speed limit, bounced her hand off the driver's head, almost causing her to hit the steering wheel. Sister Mary Ignatia said, "Oh, you gink."

Sister Jeanne d'Arc said, "Jesus… Mary and Joseph." The Plymouth swerved a bit but continued accelerating in third gear. The young woman in the front seat put both hands over her mouth to keep her heart from popping out.

"You old bag, you nearly knocked me out."

"Serve you right, Sister Soooooooperior." Sister Mary Ignatia giggled. The young woman put her hand over her mouth again. Lacie emerged from the back of the station wagon over the older nun's head and down onto her lap. Both of them had a great laugh about that.

Juliette put her hand on the young woman's shoulder. "Hello hon, we did not hear your name yet."

Sister Jeanne d'Arc said, "Oh, I'm so sorry, this is Sister Mary of the Angels."

Juliette spoke to the young nun. "Mary of the Angels, a beautiful name. You are a novitiate; what year are you in?"

"I just finished my postulant stage three months ago, so this is my first year."

"Your Sister Superior drives like a maniac. She has no sympathy for us poor sinners who are bound for hell."

"She's not my…" Sister Mary of the Angels put her hand over her mouth again.

Sister Mary Ignatia said, "Heaven for the climate, hell for the company," She giggled and then said solemnly, "Mark Twain."

Sister Jeanne d'Arc slowed down to moderately fast driving and said, "Maniac?"

Lank said, "Pretty close." Sister Mary Ignatia tapped the Sister Superior on the shoulder and overstated a laugh of triumphant at a little game.

"How can you see to drive with those blinders on?" Lank leaned against the passenger side door in the back but he could not see her face.

The driver pulled off her cap and veil. "You're right. I took my driver's test with a modified cap one of the Sisters made for me. I told the man it was our driving habit. Otherwise he wouldn't have passed me. Peripheral vision you know." Sister Jeanne d'Arc revealed medium-length dark brown hair. It was thick, rich hair slightly matted in damp curls. She removed the tight fitting coif from around her neck and tossed her hair around. Juliette thought she had never seen such a gesture of liberty.

Sr. Mary of the Angels screamed, "They're both drunk."

Lank didn't drink that morning so the smell of alcohol had puzzled Juliette. She leaned up next to the driver, her own hair brushing the Sister Superior's face, electric proximity. She whispered, "Exactly how much did you drink this morning, my sweet?"

Sister Jeanne d'Arc whispered in answer, "Just a bit of wine."

"That is not exact."

"Ah, who… why do you ask?"

"I think you had too much to be driving. Now please, do not act like a drunken shit brain. Ask Lank to drive. His legs are too long for the back seat anyway." Sister Jeanne d'Arc turned towards Juliette, breath on breath.

"Mr. Graham... Lank, your knees are up around your ears. Perhaps you would like to come up front and drive. There is much more leg room up here."

"Sure thing, Sister."

Lank drove and chatted with the young Sister Mary of the Angels. As often happened, Lank's apparent nervousness and his equally apparent comfort in his own nervousness put an anxious soul at ease. In the back seat, Sister Jeanne d'Arc might have headed for a peevish reaction at being displaced but Lacie would have none of that. She liked the Sister's hair; she sniffed and fiddled. She also liked Sister Jeanne d'Arc's cap on Juliette's head.

Victoria climbed up over the front seat to grab Sister Mary of the Angels' heart. She did this with exaggerated responses to the inane questions adults ask little kids. 'I don't know.' was accompanied by shrugged shoulders, upturned hands, elbows by her side and her big blue eyes cast up and to the right. "You're a smart girl, aren't you?" Victoria answered with giggles and buried her face in Lank's jacket. She stood up on the seat, stared at the nun's face and made a quarter-circle in front of her like a submariner at his periscope. "You're pretty." Juliette didn't know if Victoria was lying, just saying the words or she had somewhere misunderstood the meaning of 'pretty'. Sister Mary of the Angels' long face was not pretty. The large space between the bottom of her nose and the top of her upper lip made 'pretty' impossible.

The Sisters planned to go to Dartmouth but Juliette convinced them to drive into Halifax and take her and Lank and the girls to the train station where Juliette would buy them lunch. "You were heading for the convent in Dartmouth?"

"Yes, that's where we are going."

"If you have lunch with us, time and food will overwhelm the alcohol. You will be safe to drive, can freshen up at the station and you will not get the girls in the convent chattering about you."

"Yes, you're right. Thank you. Really, I feel like such a fool. Neither Sister nor I ever drank in the morning before. It felt delightful but..."

Sister Jeanne d'Arc and Juliette sat close together so their conversation could not be easily heard by the others but she put her mouth to Juliette's ear and whispered, "Our Sister Superior in Boston sent Sister Mary of the Angels to me, because she thought she was too serious and a pain in the arse. But I guess I went overboard showing her how informal it could be. It was mean, really. I think I scared the heck out of her."

"You scared the fuck out of me for a while there."

Sister Jeanne d'Arc took Juliette's arm and patted her hand. They smiled at each other, such smiles as could invite much more but Sister Jeanne d'Arc bent her head down shyly to put her cap and veil back on.

At the train station they ate a convivial lunch. Sisters of Charity taught Juliette as a child. She liked a lot of her teachers. Between Sister Jeanne d'Arc and Sister Mary Ignatia they knew all of Juliette's old teachers. Sister Mary Ignatia had something funny to say about most of them. Lank and Victoria managed to keep the younger nun smiling. Lacie and Sister Mary Ignatia went to the washroom, holding hands and skipping.

Juliette said, "You are unusually young to be Superior."

"Yes, the youngest. Sterling Reserve is our smallest convent in the province but the Sisters there didn't want to be annexed by a larger convent, say Dartmouth or Antigonish. It made sense because all of our other convents are far away and the point of it all is to teach at the school in Sterling Reserve. Anyway they appointed me Superior. I don't know why, really. It surprised me."

"How do you like it?"

"I like cities, which Sterling Reserve is not. I like being Sister Superior here… There, I should say. The nuns in Sterling Reserve, the character of the nuns there, allows me to be easy-going and maybe even irreverent. I could act like so many other sisters and just pretend to be completely absorbed with holiness but it is so much more comfortable not being bothered with that. We've heard a lot about you and the band of trackers."

"Is that what we are called?"

"Just by me and it's caught on at the convent. I've heard you called hobos too lazy to move, communist bums, and train flushings."

"I am learning to like Trackers."

"The Sisters generally think you're a great bunch. Sister Mary Ignatia and I know you better than any of the rest of the girls do. They'll want to know everything."

"No, we do not seem to travel in the same circles." Juliette turned from her low-volume conversation with Sister Jeanne d'Arc when Lacie got back from the bathroom. "Lank, girls, we have ten minutes to catch a train."

Lacie may have thought that catching a train involved some sort of trap or net or perhaps a large hook and line. She was ready. Juliette asked Victoria to say goodbye. She toddled around lifting the nuns' multilayered skirts and kissing their stockinged knees. Juliette paid the bill for everyone and went back to Sister Jeanne d'Arc. "Drive carefully, please. I would hate to lose you so soon."

"I am heartly sorry if I put your children in jeopardy. Please forgive."

"Yes, it is done and no harm done. You have all the forgiveness available to me but none is needed."

"I hope you enjoy your trip. God speed." Juliette hugged and tried to kiss her cheek but Sister Jeanne d'Arc presented her mouth. They kissed and she took Juliette's lower lip between her lips in a soft bite. Juliette responded by running her tongue along Sister Jeanne d'Arc's upper lip.

Getting on the train Lacie said, "Did you have a French kiss on the sisser?"

"No I did not. And it is sister not sisser. What you know about French kissing?"

Lacie shrugged and said, "I dunno."

***

"There's no fun on a train. The girls laughing and playing seems out of place here, like we should shush them up. In a car you can get bored or ya sing or play games or enjoy the scenery but it feels pretty good; not deep I guess but pretty good. It's like a party. You feel energetic like things are looking up. On a train it's all longing, like, I don't know. Your future goes to the back of your mind and the thing you're missing, that one thing, you don't even know what it is, circles all around you. What you've never been able to go towards because you don't know how and you don't know what it looks like, that's what comes to the front of your brain on a train."

Lank said these things looking out the dirty Railiner window. Juliette passed him the bottle of McKinley's orange pop filled two-thirds with moonshine. This train stopped everywhere. They pulled out of a tiny station twenty miles before New Glasgow. Nobody got off at the little station; nobody got on. No parcels left the train and none got placed on it. After eleven hours, the Railiner covered less than half the distance to their destination. The train stopped, waited ten minutes, and slowly left the little station. It followed that kind of a schedule, willfully slow.

Victoria drifted in and out of sleep across the aisle from them. She occasionally woke up because Lacie braided and re-braided her hair. Lacie didn't know how to make braids. They fell apart as soon as she let go of Victoria's hair. The falling-apart stage seemed particularly worthy of her attention and study. She looked on contemplatively as Victoria's blonde curls relaxed and unraveled. Juliette stared across the aisle, over the girls' heads, to the window above them. She played a game with her eyes focusing on the dirty windows and then on the slow-moving bushes and trees beyond the glass and back to the streaks on the window.

"I know that feeling Lank. When you are standing out between the cars on a real train, getting some air, it is so noisy and unstable but there is a peaceful, perhaps helpless, feeling. It pulls at you, a kind of painful peace. You are so right. I can sit here and say to myself, 'I wish I had… I wish I was…' But I cannot complete my own wishes. Is life a train trip?"

"I guess so. Should we have taken the express?"

"No, no this is good. We might not have had this conversation on the fast train."

"I kind of meant the life express."

"Right. Maybe we are on it, closer to our destination than we think."

"Right."

The time of evening and the type of forest they rode into conspired to make nighttime a sudden occurrence.

"Do you miss Irma?"

"I'm scared of bringing up Lacie alone but I was scared with Irma bringing her up too. Irma's idea of taking care of her was to do not very much and her tenderness toward the child, well, Irma didn't have any. And do I miss her for myself? No, not a fuck of a bit. I never really liked Irma. She just made me horny; I got her pregnant. You always have to second-guess her because she's always got something up her sleeve. Irma's very dishonest and tricky. She didn't fit at The Tracks, did she?"

"She did, because everyone on The Tracks is different and we all try to put up with everyone else's strangeness. I will miss her. She was the only other woman. Yes, dishonest but very straightforward and everything was about who is on top right now but still I liked her. Jesus, I really like that nun. She seems great."

Lank laughed, "I don't like her driving. I've driven with a lot of drunk people but I think she would be near as bad sober."

"Sister is a wild one."

When they stopped at Merrigomish, the four of them got out. The girls ran around and screamed in the small train station. They liked the echo. Lacie managed to get herself upstairs; the train had to wait for Lank to find her. The slow train seemed relieved at having another five-minutes rest. Juliette got two more bottles of orange at the canteen aboard the train. The night was warm and moist. As the train passed by ponds and marshes, the spring peepers stole the high notes from the clicking and clacking steel wheels on steel rails. The shrill little frogs' choral symphony of lust, in small bodies of cold water, rang in Juliette's ears. It sounded like the machinery in her brain.

Three self-propelled Railiners connected together, comprised their train. There was no bar car and passengers were not permitted to consume alcohol in the coaches; however, the railway staff tried hard not to see anybody drinking. If a passenger became troublesome, something got done about that passenger's drunkeness. As the Railiner moved along into the last hours of night the canteen attendants often volunteered paper cups with their soft drinks. Juliette poured half of the orange pop into the little cups, filled the bottle up again with moonshine and went back to the canteen. "You are here all night. Perhaps you would like a bottle of orange. I have opened it for you." The canteen man took the bottle with its noticeably paler than usual contents. Orange was always used for moonshine.

"Thank you. That's very nice of you." He took a drink and let out a small hiss in appreciation of the mixture's strength. "Ya can't beat McKinley's."

"Oh, it is good pop. I must get back to my friend and our children."

"Is Lucy yours?"

"Lacie. No, she belongs to my friend. The younger one, Victoria, is mine."

"I didn't meet her but that one…"

"Lacie. L.A.C.I.E."

"Lacie. Oh she's a firecracker. Real smart though."

"She is great. I am so lucky that she is Victoria's best friend." Juliette became quiet, distant and pensive. It would normally feel like an awkward silence but measures of time expanded on this train. She finally said, "I could not ask for better."

"Ask for better?"

"I mean I could not ask for a better friend than Lacie for my girl Victoria. Lacie is rambunctious and active but never harsh with Victoria. I hope they stay friends."

"Being a kid can be tough. A good friend is the best."

"Seems like you had one?"

"Yes, my friend, Lenny. Since nine years old, we were good friends and we still are. We're both forty-three now. Our wives don't care for each other but I'm pretty sure Lenny's boy, David, is sweet on my daughter Falda. I got no objections to that. David is a nice young man."

"That sounds wonderful. I do not keep in touch with my kidhood friends; it seems too far back for returning."

The canteen man took a swig of the fortified McKinley's and, a little bit breathless from the moonshine, said, "But you're just young."

"I am twenty-six but I think I took the express train to get here. I must get back to the girls." The canteen man laughed, thanked her for the McKinley's and bid her a pleasant evening.

Lank folded himself up into a small enough bundle to be able to sleep in the two seats he and Juliette had occupied. The girls both slept across from him. Juliette found an empty pair of seats in the same car. Already a little drunk, she decided on finishing off the remaining bottle of orange and moonshine.

Juliette started a new book on the train. East of Eden was easy reading and easy to get lost in. She curled up with Steinbeck's Salinas Valley slowly slipping by outside the train window. Sleep arrived in minutes. She had the McKinley's and shine propped up in the corner of her seat with a wine cork stuck in the top.

A good sleep, she thought, when daytime activity woke her. Her bladder raged against its fullness but Victoria pulled at her hem.

"I'm hungry. Mom, Mom I'm hungry."

"In a minute Victoria. I need to pee."

Victoria went back to where Lank and Lacie stared out the window like travelers condemned to ride the train forever. Juliette took her time in the washroom. She always did. Juliette felt herself to be quite arrogant in ignoring any rattling at the door, even in the outhouse at The Tracks. She particularly tried to discourage Victoria's attempts at intruding into her time alone within four close walls.

The day unraveled before it unfolded. Half the floor space of one of the three Railiner cars was set up as a dining area. Over breakfast, Lacie carelessly knocked a plate of toast on the floor. The thick, serviceable railroad china did not break but Lacie refused to clean up the toast at Juliette's request. Lank said, "I'll get that, don't worry." This rankled Juliette more than it should have. After a minute Lacie slid over toward her and said with a mixture of plea and apology, "Juls?"

"Go Away. Piss off, you little..."

As soon as it came out, she cursed herself as mean and silly but 'I am sorry' did not pass her lips. Lank said nothing but picked up Lacie and offered her his apple juice. Lacie shook her head. It may have been her first real effort to hold back tears. She was not completely successful. Victoria toddled around the table. She leaned against Lank and picked absently at Lacie's shoe. Victoria looked across at her mother with everything but words saying, 'I'm with Lacie.'

Juliette finished her breakfast, hiding the panic and pain. The regret at being mean to Lacie burned her but she quietly paid the bill and left the three of them together, walking out of the dining area like she had someplace to go.

CHAPTER TEN

Juliette's father picked them up at the train station in Sydney. He misunderstood who was who and began doting on Lacie but he shifted gears easily because Victoria was even cuter than Lacie. During the twelve-mile drive to Glace Bay, he cautioned Juliette several times about fighting with his mother. The last caution, as they pulled into the driveway, had something like a wink attached to it.

"Father, I will not fight with her. If she gets uppity I will knock her down. There will be no fight."

Jimmy smiled. He reveled in his daughter's capability at so many things. Her particular ability at reining in Mrs. Cameron, whose role in life was to make everyone afraid of her, dazzled Jimmy. Juliette, since nine years of age, could make her grandmother cower by cutting through, by exposing, by a straight gaze. Mrs. Cameron hated being bested but she was fascinated with how easily Juliette dissolved, deflected and exposed the tricks that worked to turn everyone else into malleable mush. Perhaps Mrs. Cameron wanted to learn Juliette's graceful, quiet power but she couldn't. Jimmy's mother was an attack dog, her teeth always bared. She snarled at everyone.

Things went well for half an hour. The girls didn't listen well enough to be bullied and Jimmy forewarned Lank. He looked no less uncomfortable than usual. Jimmy waited for the fireworks. Juliette did not take the bait and her grandmother's tone began to sound something like quitting. But the snarling dog, the hissing cat and the desperate need to provoke overwhelmed her.

"I'm a foolish old woman. Here I am putting out the good dishes for the filthy offspring of who knows who. The Lord knows it's not the little piglets' fault that they will smell like manure and fish offal all their miserable little lives." Mrs. Cameron straightened herself up with her nose in the air; she sniffed.

Juliette went to Lacie who shared an armchair with Victoria. "I am sorry, Lacie. I am very sorry for the way I spoke to you at breakfast. Will you forgive me, please?"

"We'll be friends, Juls?"

"I want to be your friend if you'll have me."

Lacie looked down at her lap and said, "I want to have you, Juls."

Juliette hugged her, picked her up and they twirled on the floor. They spun so fast Lacie's legs flew out. She giggled, as Juliette kissed her over and over and Victoria, seeing the familiar stunt sang out, "Spin top, spin top."

Jimmy's mother said, "The nerve, the utter nerve". She stomped out, making it clear that she knew they directed it all at her, a staged demonstration of triumph through humility.

Juliette and Lacie ended the spin top, staggering a bit before they regained equilibrium. They sat down in the big armchair with Victoria. The girls crawled all over Juliette. It was not the first time a beautiful residue of her Catholic childhood surprised her. /a state of grace/I am blessed/a prodigal daughter welcomed home/my sin is swept away by the grace of Lacie/

"Jimmy, where are we sleeping?"

"Two of ya can go in the little room on the plant side and two of ya in your old room."

"We could give Lank my room and the girls and I could take the big guestroom."

"I've been trying to find the time to tell ya but…well…I got a girlfriend."

"And you and she are sleeping together in this house?"

Jimmy grinned, "Yeah, you know she'd do anything to snub your mother. I didn't even ask. She got wind I was seeing my secretary from the plant so she suggested we take over the guestroom."

"Yes, she never wanted Mother to have that room. I am surprised Isobel let your girlfriend in at all; sin under her roof et cetera."

"Maybe it ain't her roof. I replaced it twice and it's due again. Seagull shit eats right through that cheap New Brunswick cedar. Karen thinks Ma had her checked out pretty good." Jimmy did a bad imitation of effete, "Making inquiries, you know."

"Father Jimmy, do I know this particular Karen."

"Yep. Now we come to the difficult part."

Juliette said calmly, "My old buddy Karen?"

"I'm afraid so. She's at work right now but she'll be home for supper."

"By the Jesus, Jimmy, I do not know how to feel about that."

"Well yeah, I dunno."

"Here, Father Jimmy, join me in my confusion." Juliette went to her father and whispered, "I had sex with her before you did."

***

Karen was tense for about two minutes but she and Juliette quickly fell into the rhythm of their old friendship. By nine PM everyone was drunk but Grandmother and the girls. The girls slept and Mrs. Cameron tried to make everyone feel bad in one way or another. Karen finally said, "Shut your Godamn mouth, you mean old bitch. Get to your room right now, or I'll kick your skinny arse."

"James, don't allow your whore to talk to me like that, in my own house no less."

"You asked for it Ma. You were a pain tonight, even for you." Juliette went to her grandmother. "Isobel, shall we get out of here. Perhaps you would like to kiss the girls good night."

Mrs. Cameron knew the drill. When Juliette called her by her first name, it meant that she had gone overboard and her granddaughter was taking control and that she attempted to do it kindly and with little fuss. Isobel Cameron knew Juliette was right in these situations. She knew that she had gone too far. She knew the anger would get out of control. But Mrs. Cameron was bold. She tried to antagonize until someone did something they regretted. She could get a string of venomous foul language directed at her but often a slap in the face or much worse. She walked with a limp exacerbated by arthritis but it began with a brutal beating her husband inflicted on her many years earlier. She would be willing to stand up to this crowd and whatever they delivered but 'Isobel' was a code word. If she didn't go with Juliette, she would be awakened after she slept an hour or two. She'd be captive in her bed as Juliette calmly explained to her grandmother the hows and whys of her personality. Juliette explained, 'you do this for this reason… You act that way because'. Mrs. Cameron could not withstand it.

She walked with Juliette, and kissed the girls good night, waking Victoria for a moment and not waking Lacie at all. Juliette wished her a good night. Jimmy was talking about the power she had over the old lady when Juliette came down the stairs. She said, "Father Jimmy, please, all of that should remain between Grandmother and me."

"Okay darlin'. I just don't know how you do it."

***

Victoria: It's kinda weird that Karen went to school with you.

Archie: Now, who is Karen? I forget.

Juliette: Karen Rudderham. She is Father Jimmy's girlfriend or mistress, whatever she is. But I expect that to fall apart pretty soon. It is weird, Victoria, when you consider that she was my girlfriend too.

Archie: Ah, what do you mean girlfriend?

Juliette: I mean we were adolescent lovers.

Victoria: Holy cow, Mom, you had sex with the woman who I thought was Granddad's wife? I thought that for years.

Juliette: Really, I did not know you thought that. We did it discreetly. God knows what would have become of us if anybody found out. Karen was also a damn good friend. I had problems back then. Karen treated me kindly. Things did not come to me naturally. Karen is partly responsible for my arched speech. I did not know how to speak. The diverse examples in my life confused me. My mother spoke Quebec French but sometimes went to Parisian French, as a conceit, really. All her relatives spoke with very local Cape Breton French accents but I felt okay with French. I adjusted to whoever I talked to as well as I could. All the English I heard seemed so different. My mother's accented English, Father Jimmy's Glace Bay talk, the way the nuns and priests spoke, Newfoundlanders fishing out of Glace Bay, and radio talk. I could not figure out how to talk. I took oblique paths to ordinary goals in those fucked-up days.

Karen suggested that I pick one individual and talk like that person. I liked Sister Joan Daniels' speech and that is what you hear today;

my approximation of a very proper teacher. It sounds stupid but I needed to solve that problem. Karen helped. Like a good friend, she helped.

***

Juliette and Jimmy borrowed her boat from her skipper, Arnold Steele. As usual, he wasn't using it. He never went out in bad weather and often had excuses to not go out in good conditions. "Arnold just doesn't like to go offshore. I don't think he can stand being out of sight of land. He's a nice guy but he's not a fisherman. Not by a mile."

"Would you have a job for him at the plant?" Juliette checked the oil and the belts on Slipper's diesel.

"No, that wouldn't work. I know you took him on partly because I wanted you to but he'd hate going to the plant. He wouldn't make enough money to support his family. Arnold would be no good in the plant. Tell Arnold he's got to catch fish or find another way to make a living."

"You are a hard old fucker, Jimmy Cameron."

"Got no patience paying anyone who don't do the work."

"I wonder how Arnold is going to like working in the pit."

"Yeah, like I says, he's a nice guy and he's got five kids now. His oldest boy is right fat."

"Who else could I get?"

"I steered you wrong once. Are you sure you want my advice?"

"Sure."

"Get that Newfy, Monte, back to be first mate. I got a guy in the plant, Kevin Murphy. He's young, maybe twenty-one, which is way older than you when you was first skipper. He don't have much experience on a boat."

"Kevin Murphy worked with Arnold on Slipper for a couple of months, right?"

"Same guy, yes."

Juliette and Jimmy got some mackerel trolling gear together and tidied up aboard Slipper. An early mackerel run made Juliette want to take everybody fishing. "How did he do when he went out with Arnold? Why did Arnold let him go?"

"Not enough work. Now Kevin never said that to me but I know that was it. He's single and he likes money. I'm offering you my best prospect for the future at the plant. Kevin works like a Trojan, and well now, I ain't given him a boss position at the plant but he's a leader. If he's on a shift that shift'll go better for it. Now, Kevin Murphy don't know fishin' or boats but he never got sick going out with Arnold, not that it says anything 'cause you could get rougher weather in your fuckin' bathtub than Arnold will go out in."

"That is good of you, Father. Thank you. I would keep Gerald on as crew and he could help show young Murphy how to find fish and how to operate the boat. I do not think he would resent that if he were mate but as crew showing the skipper how to fish. That might grate on him."

"Gerald don't wanna be mate. Gerald's good crew but he got no ambition. He can't read and pretty soon they'll have to get papers for this sort of thing. Gerald is good but you know he don't want no real responsibility."

"True. I will write Monte. You know I think he is a good man on a boat despite the look of him."

Jimmy said, "I never questioned that. You can sum up a person better in a minute than I can in a month. It's the likes of Arnold Steele that don't like Monte."

"It's too bad Lenny Ryan is not around. I could promote him, I guess."

"After that Christmas trip you took him on down your way, he realized just how bad Arnold was. That's why he went to Toronto. He's a backstabber though. None of the guys around the wharf trusted him 'cause of that."

"Between you and me he was fucking Irma, Lank's wife, on that trip we took."

"Oh, no doubt. He's ambitious. Is she gone for good, you think?"

"For good, and I think I will be the only one who misses her and I will not miss her much. She is also an ambitious backstabber."

***

Lank arrived with the girls. He had travelled on two types of boat: train ferries and car ferries. Lank and the girls fizzed with excitement.

"Father Jimmy is your captain."

"I am?"

"Yes, if you do not mind. Whatever Father Jimmy says, goes. You must listen to him. Do you understand, Lacie?"

"I unnersand."

"Victoria, you pay attention to Father Jimmy, okay?"

"Got it."

"Got it? Where did that come from?" Victoria stared at her mother with no comprehension. "Never mind. Just listen to Father Jimmy. He is the captain and the captain is the boss."

Jimmy put Lank at the wheel. He wasn't a natural. Awkward and jittery, he didn't understand the directions well. He oversteered and overcompensated but he grinned all the way. Lank knew that for today, he was one of the kids. "Look at that. Holy mackerel." He laughed. "Lacie, hold on, we're driving through a ditch. Vee, come back here with me and help me out." Jimmy had already taken to Lank who knew a lot about economics and had unusual, original views on politics, religion, child rearing, sex and cooking fish. Also, Jimmy was a sucker for anyone who could drink more than he did and stay pleasant. The night before, his girlfriend Karen and his daughter kept up with him but with Lank there, they drank so much rum, Jimmy ran out. That hadn't happened in years. After the taxi arrived with two bottles of bootleg rum, Lank just kept on going and showed no apparent ill effects in the morning.

They set out strings of mackerel hooks. Jimmy and Juliette continually felt the lines for tension and activity. Neither was pleased. They hauled the lines and got five good mackerel, some small ones and a few turd Pollock which they'd use for bait. Juliette said "Pretty good day for Santa Claus."

"You know there'll be a swell out there. Somebody might get sick."

"Now is a good time to find out who gets sick."

Jimmy went to the wheel, set a new course and told Lank to follow it on the compass. "When ya get the church there; ya see the church? When ya get just abeam of 'er, ya make a right turn fifty degrees." Lank took the wheel back. He was surprisingly good at holding a compass course.

"Two questions, captain. What's abeam of me mean and who's Santa Claus?"

Juliette explained, "Abeam of that church will be when you, facing squarely forward, can put out your left arm perpendicular to the boat and be pointing at the church. For example on the right side, starboard that is, that lone seagull sitting on the water is abeam of you right... now."

"Got it."

"Got it. She got it from you."

"What?"

"Oh nothing. Santa Claus is a little shelf. Father Jimmy and I call it that because we have good luck there. Do not tell anyone about Santa Claus."

"Of course not. We don't believe in Santa Claus, do we, girls?"

Lacie said, "Don't believe."

The girls went below crawling around, trying out the bunks, exploring. The engine on Slipper could be a screamer at full rpms but just jogging along, it ran quiet. They could hear the mackerel hooks 'pftt' as they hit the water with Lank steaming slowly over Santa Claus one knot too fast.

"Slow 'er up, Lank."

In another thirty seconds, Juliette said to Lank, "As slow as you can go and still keep moving." She held the line lightly, both hands touching it delicately. "Jimmy, we have cod or haddock."

Her father went to the other line and put his large, callused fingers under the line where it fell over the side of the boat. "Lank, let 'er drift. Take 'er out of gear. Help me get the tubs of line on deck." Juliette rapidly pulled in the mackerel line. They had no mackerel but several codfish hung on the mackerel hooks. She packed the lines away quickly in their tubs and moved them out of the way. She cut up the mackerel, pollock and the smaller cod. She put it aside for bait.

"Jimmy, can we set a little forward on the gunwales? I want the girls to be able to jig off the stern."

Jimmy responded, "We'll have to circle to stay over Santa Claus."

"I think the ground fish will be off the southwest a bit, too."

"What? You want to set two depths?"

"Yes, just let one hang off the shelf on the southwest."

"Hold on, girl. We're just out fishin' for fun. We're not gonna get rich today."

"Bless me, Father, for I have grinned."

Jimmy laughed, "Ah you." He pitched a small anchor over the port side with the long line attached.

As he readied to pitch out the starboard line, Juliette said, "Hold on, have Lank go fifty yards to starboard first, unless your throwing arm has gotten a lot better in the last thirty seconds."

Jimmy looked around at the shore and checked the sounder. "Fifty yards to your right, Lank, real slow. By the Jesus, Juliette, you remember the soundings better than I do and half the time I got traps out here."

"I remember this place. Slipper knows it too. Slipper knows where the fish are. You mark Santa Claus with lobster buoys?"

Jimmy chuckled, "I set 'em on a string. I only leave one marker; as close to crumble rock as I dared go. Nobody touched it yet."

Juliette laughed her big, spontaneous laugh. "Father Jimmy, bold as brass and tarnished by every imaginable sin."

Lank made a slow gradual turn while they baited the hooks and let the long lines fall into the water, one on either side of the boat. Setting two lines made inshore fishing tricky; few fishermen would ever consider setting them in a circle. Juliette dropped the buoys. She and Jimmy periodically looked out to check the bouys' position. They knew when the other had just checked even if they were busy doing something else. One never checked just after the other had checked. Juliette told the girls to go below when Jimmy pitched the anchors.

"Victoria, Lacie, all clear." They scrambled up to the stern with Juliette. "Be careful of these barbs, these hooks. They are dangerous. See Victoria; do not touch."

"Yes, Mom."

"Lacie, see that. This thing here looks like a little fish to the cod and sometimes they bite at it but you often just hook one of these barbs into them because they are hanging around. Codfish are curious."

"Why do they live in the water?"

"It is the nature of a fish to do that. They die when they leave the water. We take them out of the water to eat them."

"Poor fish."

"Yes, poor fish but everything we eat, we kill. It is the way we are. We kill a potato before we eat it."

"A potato's not alive."

"Oh yes. Not like us. The potato does not move around much on its own like we do but potatoes, beans, even a piece of toast, all come from living things. You drop this in the water. Do you see, Victoria? Oh, drop it in the water but hold onto the line right here. Pull the line up and let it fall back down. Pull it quite sharply. Yes jerk it up. If you are really good at it, you will feel a tug on your line. Then I will help you bring it in."

Lacie watched and listened to the instructions Juliette gave Victoria. Juliette hoped for the underdog, that being Victoria. Lacie was good at everything and she learned very quickly. Juliette could hear Jimmy giving Lank instructions about the turn towards the shore and watching the sounder and a rock he had to avoid. It seemed too complicated for Lank. She said, "Father Jimmy, it is almost dead low tide. Are you sure you want to do that?"

"It's your boat. We'll haul out if you want." Juliette checked the long line to starboard. She felt a lot of activity on it. She asked, "Do you have those instructions straight, Lank. When you make the turn it shallows up quickly just before that rock. Watch the sounder. You cannot afford to look up from it except to check your course towards those two trees. When you see twelve feet on the sounder, put her in reverse to stop her."

"Okay Juls."

"Well Jesus Christ, Juliette, I just told him all that."

"I know, I know but if he fucks up, we could have a hole in the boat so it bears repeating."

Jimmy said in a mocking singsong, "It bears repeating; la te fucking da."

Victoria screamed, "Who's doing that?"

"You have hooked a big codfish. Here, put these gloves on." Juliette passed over her best leather gloves. Victoria wore them like mittens with the fingers just flapping.

"Get a tea towel below. That'd work better." Jimmy was eying the buoy positions.

Juliette said, "Can you get it? I cannot leave them."

"They'll be okay for a second. I'll watch."

"Lank, please, get me a towel or a rag or something below. Just leave the throttle where it is and lock the wheel."

Jimmy said, "Jesus girl, don't be such a worrywart."

"For fuck sake, Jimmy, you got a jigger hook in your hand when I was a kid. You had already fished for years. You hardly ever jigged but you… I cut the fucking thing for you and pulled it out. It was right between tendons. Dumb luck for a fucking ninny like you, and you think I should leave them alone on the stern of…"

"All right, all right. You're right. I'm wrong. What's new?" Lank arrived with the towel. He looked awkward, somber.

"Lank, I am sorry. It is just the way Jimmy and I talk. We do not mean anything. Fishing talk. You resolve minor differences of opinion on a fishing boat by hurling hateful insults at each other."

"Well it seemed like a serious fight."

"No, I would never fight with Father Jimmy. If he made me mad, I would just throw him overboard."

Jimmy said, "Yeah, you and whose army?"

"There shall not be any necessity for military intervention. It would be an effortlessly accomplished independent task."

"I got friends, ya know."

"One would be surprised by that."

"You wanna foit. Do it here, roit now."

"You would be ineffectual at grappling a path through a wood-fiber sack."

Jimmy burst with a delighted laugh. He loved these exchanges when Juliette took the schoolyard clichés and couched them in her pompous speech. Jimmy loved to laugh. Juliette smiled at this man who lived so close to the present. Any worry he felt was merely a minor annoyance. He could plan ahead but, even without a plan, Jimmy would just go at the day. Jimmy caught her smile, their eyes met and they held each other's gaze for a moment before going back to their tasks. Both continued smiling. Jimmy, with his teeth showing a bit, his bright sharp eyes looking out at the buoys, was all here and now. She, with lips closed and her eyes calm and dreamy, was so far away, stretched out to the future and the past.

Juliette could see it but she waited for Victoria to spot the big cod, just feet from the boat. Lacie quietly said, "I hooked." Victoria looked over at her friend and let the line slip. Juliette had both girls' lines backstopped with her foot so Victoria only lost a few yards.

"Victoria, pay attention. I think you are about to land a big one. Pull in again." Victoria began pulling in her line hand over hand. The towel saved her hands from chafe and from getting a rope burn if the line got away from her but it slowed her progress. Juliette desperately wanted Victoria to land the big cod before Lacie pulled one in. /god/what difference/what difference does it make/ When the cod came back into view, Victoria appeared to suddenly understand fishing. She bent over the stern staring at the fish and pulling slowly with Juliette keeping back tension on the line. Victoria had its head out of the water, the jigger barb snagged firmly in its gills. Juliette got a gaff under the gills on the other side and swung the fish on deck.

Victoria knelt down in front of the big cod. She pouted and puckered, imitating the dying fish's mouth opening and closing. She didn't seem to share Lacie's sensitivity to killing things. Victoria landed the first big fish of the day. Juliette had big feelings for her daughter's triumph but for Victoria it was just play. Lacie landed her fish without much help, a smaller fish than Victoria's.

"Juls, if I put it back, will it die?"

"Not necessarily but probably."

Lacie stared at the codfish losing its life on the deck.

"Do you want to put it back in the water, Lacie?"

She shrugged and went back to her father at the wheel, climbed up on a shelf beside him and looked out the wheelhouse window. "What's wrong, honey?"

"The fish all die."

"Yeah, when we catch them they die." Lacie stared out the window, offshore where the gray sky and the ocean horizon blended.

Victoria had her jigger back in the water. Jimmy said, "Head in there now toward the two trees."

"Yes sir, captain sir. She's at five hundred rpm's."

Juliette gaffed another cod for Victoria. As soon as that one was off the line, Victoria had the jigger back in the water finding a good depth to jig with no help from Juliette.

Jimmy said, "Victoria, pull in your jigger. Things are gonna start happenin'."

"Why?"

Juliette didn't allow herself to get caught up in the endless 'whys' Victoria could use to delay or to avoid, so she pulled in the line herself. Victoria knew the futility of crying or protesting under such circumstances. She usually accepted what came to her, knowing that the next thing would be interesting enough. She was right.

Lank stopped the boat very quickly by getting it into reverse and gunning the engine. Other helmsman would have done this less effectively and with crashing of gears. Lank seemed to know an engine and transmission shortly after making its acquaintance. He had come upon the rock but had a good eye on the sounder. The sudden stop knocked Victoria over backwards and she slid up the slippery deck to the wheelhouse. Lacie got over her funk about fish dying. They both had a good laugh about Victoria's long slide.

Jimmy told Lank to head off ninety degrees to starboard. The buoys snaked behind them as they dropped the last one. Jimmy steamed along the shore and took some time to show the girls how to operate the boat. "Them first ones been soaking for an hour, Juliette. What do ya say, we start haulin' a line now? Maybe we'll make it home for supper."

"Sure, Father Jimmy, what are you making for supper?"

"Yeah right, corn flakes for everybody." Juliette and Jimmy began hauling. Jimmy sent the girls below while all the gear was flying around. They caught about as much fish as Arnold Steele caught on a good day, working all day with a full crew.

"We're payin' five and a half cents for good cod like this here. Me and the girls worked for free but you pay your wheelman. He didn't crash the boat. He could've but he didn't."

"I will pay Lank for sure and, if you will not take the skipper's share, I will pay your share, the crew share and the boat share to Arnold. He can have that or two weeks notice. I will get the Rankins to go over the boat to make sure the old girl is ready by the time I get my new crew. First though, why am I making a greenhorn the new Slipper skipper?

"Because your dear old dad says he's got the character of a good long liner skipper."

"Yes, that is why. What do you think? Is there a sixty percent chance he will work out?"

"Ninety percent he'll be better than Arnold; ninety-five percent."

CHAPTER ELEVEN

Juliette excused herself from the after-dinner chat to call a friend of Monte House in Port aux Basque, Newfoundland. Isle aux Morts didn't have telephone service. Early in the morning Monte returned the call. "No, Monte, he was not tormenting you. I want you as first mate aboard Slipper if you will accept it." Monte said he'd take the afternoon ferry to North Sydney. Juliette described the Fargo, told him where to find the key and asked him to drive it down to her father's place. It was ten thirty at night when Monte arrived with the pickup.

"There was a note on the steering wheel but I didn't have no money."

Lank said, "Could I see the note?"

"Yes my son, I got 'er right here."

The note said, 'She'll need gas.'

 "She's about bone dry now, I expect. I was wondering if I'd make it." Monte spoke slowly with a trace of a lisp. "I thank you for this, Juliette. I been outa work up solid, 'cept for a bit of fish plant work over home."

"It is no favor, Monte. I think you are a very good man on a boat. I have no idea how you are going to like your skipper. He is new to fishing but Father Jimmy thinks he will make a good captain."

"'Tis not of great importance if I likes him, I just hope he likes me good enough to keep me on."

"You are going to have to teach him some things. I will try to get time on the water with him, too." Jimmy invited Monte to stay at the Cameron's house but he wanted to sleep aboard. He missed Slipper. After a single drink of rum, Monte carried his kitbag aboard the first boat where he would be more than a deckhand.

Earlier in the day, Jimmy told Kevin Murphy that he no longer had a job at the fish plant and that he was skipper of Slipper. He and Jimmy went out on Slipper for a few hours setting out-of-season lobster traps. Kevin spent the rest of the day tidying up his new command. He was still aboard when Monte arrived at about midnight. They hit it off well and became comfortable enough with each other to act like they felt; like little kids on Christmas morning.

Arnold Steele was not happy. He railed at Juliette for hiring a skipper who wasn't even a fisherman. Arnold took the cash payment, put his house up for sale, packed up his family and headed for Toronto.

When Juliette met Kevin, she found him not particularly good-looking, nor did she find his personality sparkling. That felt good. Juliette didn't need the complications of having a skipper she liked. He took Slipper out, set some trawl, navigated and picked up some traps that he and Jimmy set the day before. Kevin surprised Julliette with his energy, his strength and his ability to learn quickly. He began to look more handsome. Juliette shook her head and surreptitiously loosened a connector to one of the injectors on the diesel. As soon as the engine started running rough, he went below. In five minutes the diesel purred, clacked and thumped like it was supposed to.

"The end of the fuel line musta shook loose. She was suckin' air."

Juliette said, "Okay Skipper, let us go home. Things rarely shake loose on this diesel. Slipper's motor is much better than your average piece of machinery as far as those niggling little annoyances go. I loosened the injector line to see if you would notice a problem and I had a wild hope that you might be able to locate the problem and perhaps fix it. There will be no more tests. I would like to come back and crew with you for a week after you get the hang of the basics. Do you want some of these to take home?"

"No, I don't like lobster."

"Well then, the Cameron household will be having a big, out-of-season lobster boil tonight. Father Jimmy set these because he can get away with anything in the Bay but you should not set traps until the season opens. I recommend you keep your nose clean until you know how to cheat and then only do it for a big payoff."

"That sounds like good advice. I hear that you are the best skipper ever around here."

"No, I was very good. The fact that I started as a girl made my accomplishments stand out more. It is in my blood though. My uncle Alphonse from Arichat might be the best fisherman on Cape Breton and he is in his sixties now. He loves it; he just loves it."

"Do you love it?"

"No. It gives me an obsessive appetite for success that I do not, otherwise, care about. I would guess that you have quite an appetite for success which will make money for both of us but it can steal your life away."

***

Lank tinkered with the Fargo, rebuilt an outboard for Jimmy and did little repair jobs around the Cameron's house. Both Jimmy and Isobel very quickly became fond of him, though Isobel rarely liked anyone. He took the girls on a tour around the area. They went in the cold water at Lingan Beach in their underwear, their first time swimming in the ocean. Lank made a mental note to take them to beaches in August.

On a Friday morning, Lank, Juliette, and the girls headed for home in the pickup. They stopped at Larry's River to see Lank's mother, a schoolteacher, still working at sixty-two. Lank's mother married a man dying of cancer while she was pregnant with her only child. She did this because an unwed mother could get fired from a teaching job for immorality. She dutifully nursed her husband through his last days and claimed she had learned to love him even though it was strictly a marriage built on necessity for both of them.

Juliette gained some insight into Lank's idiosyncrasies when she saw the tension between him and his mother. They seemed to be competitively unconventional. Lank's mother walked or rode a bicycle the five miles to her school every day. She only wore black or red, ate very simply and claimed to be a Buddhist. She maintained a calm appearance but spoke sharply, perhaps believing that gentle and diplomatic were dishonest. Lacie understood her right away. Victoria played with a small, tattered wicker basket. Lank's mother grabbed her by the arm, not very gently, and said, "Pick that up immediately before it gets broken."

Lacie stomped on the basket, "No worry now."

Mrs. Graham smiled, "No worry now."

The failures of the child appeared to be rectified in the grandchild. Lank's mother liked Victoria but fell headfirst in love with Lacie and Lacie responded with the straightforward affection that came so easily to her.

Lank and Juliette left the girls with Mrs. Graham and drove to Antigonish to sniff around the campus at St. F X looking for old acquaintances. Juliette found a former lover from her days at college. He still lived in Antigonish with his wife and a child about Victoria's age. A meeting and then to the tavern with some friends was the excuse he gave his wife as he left for the night. She thought that was a good idea because he didn't get out much.

Lank and Juliette rented a room just outside of town. She and her old boyfriend used it from seven to eleven. He talked about his wife and kid a lot at first and that he never cheated on her before and he loved her so much.

Juliette said, "You were the only man I ever knew who seemed to really love licking my vagina."

He stammered a bit, said he didn't do it much anymore, that it wasn't his wife's favorite. She thought it was a bit weird.

"Jensen, you talked about your wife since you arrived. I am going to take a quick bath and… take a bath with me." They were not dried off before he was on his knees with his mouth all over her. He was still good at that and he had an erection as Juliette had an orgasm.

She asked, "Does this soap smell different than what you use at home?"

"Well, yes I guess so."

"Are you usually clean at home? I mean do you bath often?"

He said, "We have a shower. I take a shower just about every day."

"Good. I am going to rinse off that soap."

She washed him down with water, dried him off and teased him until eleven o'clock but didn't let him climax. They got dressed before Lank arrived. Juliette gave him two quick drinks and told him to go home and fuck his wife.

"Juliette Cameron is the greatest. I'll always say that; just to myself, of course."

"Tell your wife you met an old friend, Lank Graham, who used to work at the college as a janitor. You went out drinking together. Do not feel guilty about this. It was sex medicine to pep up your marriage."

When Lank got back after dropping off Jensen, he asked, "Well, how did that go anyway?"

"Do you want to fuck?"

"Sure, I'd love to."

"God damn, Lank, do not get me pregnant. It is just this one time. Just one time."

"Got it. I'll pull out and squirt all over you. I can't wait."

She was surprised that Lank was dominant and assertive, even rough. He slapped her bottom and pinched her nipples. Lank held her face against his hard cock and she began to suck it. He pulled her hair with a lot of force. This sort of thing was not Juliette's preference and the roughness took her out of the mood. She squeezed his balls.

"Oh, ow. I don't know if..."

She stopped squeezing but twisted his pubic hair. It escalated until Juliette said, "Spank me. Make me cry."

Lank sat with Juliette across his long thighs. He came down hard on her ass with his right hand. She gasped, not knowing if she could take it. Another sharp slap. Unbearable but at the top of her vagina she felt more than a tingle; it was a fullness, a swelling. She steeled herself for the next blow. It came down hard. Lank's rough hand landed flat along the side of her left buttock. All her resolve collapsed. She cried out, a grotesque yelp, a sound she had never made before. The next slap came right away at least as hard as the others and Juliette felt like she was flowing out of herself through tears falling to the light blue carpet. Her nose ran and she sobbed without control. She relinquished all, as her loving friend beat her bum mercilessly.

Lank said, "You all right?"

"Yes…I guess. Do not hurt… injure me?"

They made love, passionate and sweet, with no hint of aggression. Lank kept his promise and didn't ejaculate inside her. When his breathing returned to normal he got up and poured a large glass of rum. "Do you want a drink, Juls?" Juliette mumbled a no thanks from her state of semi-sleep. The cheeks of her ass burned. Other than that, she was absolutely relaxed and comfortable. They heard a light, shy knock at the door. Juliette put her arms through the sleeves of a cardigan and folded it around herself. The sweater didn't go much below the waist but she opened the door a little. A young woman said that there had been complaints about the noise from this room.

"Do not worry dear; the noise is all over."

She crawled back in bed. Lank kissed her good night, a kiss like they'd often had before, a friendly kiss, the kind of kiss you would give your child.

In the morning, at breakfast, they discussed their unusual night. They talked with relish but without appetite. Lank said, "I don't want to do it again. It could change things at The Tracks. Archie would be secretly jealous."

"Yes he would. I think he gets his blood a bit fizzled when we cook together. In any event, we could never top last night. Do you carry on like that often?"

"Hell no. I never even think of that kind of stuff. My fantasies, like when I jerk off, can be a bit strange but that sort of violent shit never occurred to me. It must have come from you."

"From me? You started it, you sadistic woman-hating pig fucker."

Lank laughed, "I've never fantasized about a pig either. Be pretty nice after your skinny arse."

But Juliette knew where the rough sex came from. Lank had to protect himself from the seering love he felt for her. Far back in her mind, way back in her cautions, she thanked her friend because she also felt the dangers of love. Juliette smiled a faraway smile and looked into Lank's eyes.

"Why do you do that with your eyes, Juls? You look all dreamy and affectionate but your eyes keep bouncin' around."

"What do you mean?"

"I don't know. You're looking into my eyes all serious like and then all of a sudden your eyes flick back and forth."

"What do…Oh, at times I have wondered. I cannot look in both eyes at once. Can you? I mean, I go from one eye to the other, my focus I mean. Do I look funny doing it?"

"Yeah."

"Oh piss off; I do not. You are just razzing me because I did not spank your bottom."

"No Juls, I'm serious. It looks weird. Choose one eye and stare at that one. Do it; look into one of my eyes. Oh yeah, that looks normal."

"Jesus. That is a kick in the head. I feel like my slip has been showing for twenty years and no one told me."

"I like that look, when a slip is showing."

"Oh, so do I. It is naughty and dangerous-looking while still being… Ah, what, embarrassing, tenderly embarrassing."

"You like women. You had sex with women."

Juliette said, "Yes and yes. Do not ask me to explain it. I do not find anything contradictory about liking women but being, I guess, normal about men. I find fewer women attractive than men but there are women I want to go to bed with. It seems strange to me that anyone would not want to get close and horny with a beautiful woman."

"You don't have to explain to me, Juls. The way you act with women you like always seemed sweet and kind to me."

"That is lovely. It is wonderful of you to see it that way. You are sweet man. That is perhaps why I loved my spanking so much."

They spent the rest of the morning at a Catholic Women's League sale buying secondhand clothes for the girls. They started drinking at noon, talking about perhaps going their separate ways to look for new talent as bed-mates for Saturday night but instead they stuck together, played some pool and saw a movie, an advance copy of 'I Vitelloni' directed by Frederico Fellini. It had sloppy, add-on English subtitles, and it was, annoyingly, on three different reels. Despite all that, Juliette liked it, especially the music. Lank had a great time. He was the only one in the small classroom theatre who really laughed. Back in their hotel room they drank and talked about the movie.

"We are kind of like those poor sods. We're all self absorbed and crazy. Directionless pleasure seekers. I'm momma's boy and your daddy's girl."

"Yes but none of us at The Tracks is that funny and sad."

Lank said, "I saw an old friend there, at the movie. He pretended he didn't see me. Yeah right; everybody sees me. I'm always the tallest guy in the room."

"It could be anything. I think a lot of them did not recognize it as comedy. Maybe it was your enthusiastic laughter."

"Did that embarrass you?"

They sat across from each other at a small table. Juliette reached over and pinched his nose, "Do not be a twit."

"I guess he just didn't want to talk to me. The woman with him was sorta dumpy and not pretty. Maybe you scared him off."

Juliette said, "That happens, I am sure." She chuckled, "Karen and I used to discuss that endlessly; how horrible to be ugly or just not pretty. I remember a classmate, a girl who started hanging out with this guy. She was not ugly but a far cry from pretty. Now the guy, he was great-looking. We could not understand. It was the mystery of the year for us. Karen wanted the guy and kept trying to get him but he stuck with the non-pretty girl. She was sweet, kind of smart too and a really lovely human. They got married eventually."

"What's that got to do with Craig not talking to me?"

"Nothing, I guess."

"I'm not feeling good about it. We were good friends."

Juliette said, "Call him. Say you saw him but did not get a chance to talk to him because you and your friend had to leave."

"Yeah, I could do that. Better still, I'll say to hell with it and put it out of my mind."

"We are the spineless, dillydally jerks from the movie."

"Spineless! I'm not spineless. If it wasn't for my spine, I wouldn't be. There's only a few inches of meat around my spine."

"My god, Lank, you are skinny."

"That's not your preference, is it?"

"You mean in a lover?"

"Yeah, I guess."

"I like skinny. I like your body, your bag of bones. You are also great in the hard cock department."

"I think you are far and away the most beautiful woman I've seen naked… or clothed for that matter."

"You sound like a seducer."

Lank said, "No, I don't, at least at this time, want to make whoopee again. Amazing really, that I think that much of us as friends."

"I wonder if the difficulty in being easy-going about sex is societal or innate. Perhaps I should have been screwing with both you and Archie from the beginning, rather than abstaining from both."

"Abstinence makes the heart grow fonder. I would find it difficult if Archie and I were your lovers and I don't think Archie would be able to take it."

Juliette asked, "What about Richard Johnson; how did you handle that?"

"I didn't. I hated it. I think Irma hated it too. It was stupid really. I should've put my foot down for once."

"You are not a foot-down type of man. You, my friend are the quintessence of easy-going, at least on the outside."

"I get upset and stuff but when I look around at others, I think it's pretty easy for me on the inside. I don't have much pride on the inside."

Juliette was getting drunk. Her legs crossed, she jiggled her foot like a nervous person. Every few seconds she squeezed her thighs together. She said, "Do you want to screw? We could make it a weekend."

Lank said, "No I don't. Let's leave it at just one time. If we did it again it might get to be a thing. I'd be jealous and everything."

"Yes, you are right. It is different for me. Although I love sex, it is not a gateway to anything else; however, anything else can be a gateway to sex. Friendship, a total stranger, booze, a nun's outfit, it can all make me horny and I think it makes me happy."

"That's enviable."

"Okay, we are not going to screw so I am going to bed. I am bushed really. Thanks for a lovely day, Lank." She went to the bathroom, had a pee and came out wearing a modest nightgown. "I miss the kids."

Lank said, "Geez, I guess I hardly thought about them." Juliette was quietly lying in bed while Lank had another drink. She knew it would take a long time to get to sleep but she got started on what too often seemed like a task.

***

Lank wanted to spend very little time with his mother and it became clear that Lacie and, to a lesser extent, Victoria wanted to spend very little time with Lank's mother. But she was excited that Lacie and Victoria could do work that she would give to her grade two class. "These two young ladies are very intelligent. You must get started on their education early and they should go to a good school, not a country school." Juliette, Lank and the girls got out quickly. Lacie was uncharacteristically bitchy about the weekend. She had been drilled with arithmetic, geography, reading and science. Victoria said, "Lacie and Grandmother had fights."

Lank said, "She's not your grandmother, Victoria. You can be happy about that."

Juliette asked Lacie, "Did you like anything about your grandmother?"

"She'd get tired and fall asleep. Me and Vee could play."

"I hope you do not hate school that much."

"If it's like Grandmother, I won't go."

"Jesus, Lank, is she that bad?"

"My mother formed her personality at seven or eight years old and hasn't seen fit to make any adjustments. That's my theory. She always thinks her way is the right way. She's an intellectual of the worst kind, a child in an intelligent, adult mind. She's an intellectual but there's a willful little girl running the show."

"How will she view her weekend with the children?"

"She's done her part and if Lacie grows up and doesn't find a cure for cancer, that'll be my fault."

Lacie calmed down. The girls sat between Lank and Juliette, all a bit squished together in the cab with various parcels and snacks and luggage. Victoria, on her knees, stretched her neck to see over the dashboard. Lacie stared at Victoria's face like she was watching a movie. She took her little friend's hand. Victoria looked at Lacie, sat down and pulled her over toward her. Lacie's head rested on her lap. Victoria stroked her hair and pinched her ear. Lacie giggled.

Juliette said, "Lacie darling, I wish you didn't have a miserable weekend."

"It's okay, Juls."

***

When they got back to The Tracks, Juliette and Lank had a secret to conceal. Neither one of them liked it but Lank obsessed over it. He believed Archie and the girls knew because of the way he acted.

"What do you mean, the way you are acting?"

"I'm nervous and stuff, you know." Juliette laughed a big laugh at this. "It's not funny, Juls."

"Lank, it would be funny if you are not all nervous and stuff. You are not acting any different."

"Are you sure?"

"Positive."

"What if he asks me outright?"

"He will not. If he does you will pull it off and if you do not pull it off, Archie would deserve to know, to his own detriment, for being too nosy."

"I don't like this lying."

"Jesus, Lank, how Catholic can you get? Are you afraid you will go to hell for lying?"

"No pity from you. Ah, I'll get over it."

Juliette made another trip to Glace Bay at the beginning of summer. Father Jimmy's new Oldsmobile glided across the newly-built causeway to Cape Breton. Memories swarmed her. Juliette recalled images of car ferries, railcar ferries, the terminals at Mulgrave and Point Tupper and driving her old boat, My Cod Girl, through the

Strait of Canso. All these visions crowded her mind in a cloud of dark regret for their passing.

Jimmy was happy with his new car that Juliette picked up at a Halifax dealership. "Ah, Jesus girl, never mind that old stuff. Look, ya brung me my new Olds and no trace of salt spray on 'er from that fuckin' old ferry."

Juliette showed Kevin Murphy many things she forgot she knew. Owner, first-mate, skipper and Slipper had a great week of catches.

Juliette's uncle, Alphonse, arrived at the Camerons' house just before she got the bus back home to The Tracks. Uncle Alphonse was a small, handsome man, a very successful fisherman who made enough money to buy other boats and have other skippers work for him but he skippered his own boat. He considered himself a workingman, not a businessman.

Juliette bought Slipper from Uncle Alphonse. He contracted to have the boat built but he didn't like the results. She purchased it below the cost of construction so that Uncle Alphonse and the builder got out of a bad situation without any large losses. He was, along with Father Jimmy, a willing tutor in Juliette's fishing education.

Alphonse, a very shy man, arrived at the Cameron household saying he couldn't stay, which didn't surprise anyone. Alphonse never stayed. He drove Juliette to the Acadian Lines bus terminal in Sydney. "Pour vous." He passed her a small leather bag. She knew his handiwork. Uncle Alphonse spent his spare time making things, all sorts of semi-practical things of beauty. She opened the bag to find a knife in a wood and brass sheaf. The knife and sheaf were finely crafted and unusual.

He said, "J'ai eu un rêve. Y'a des mauvaises affaires qui va t'arriver. C'ta un gros rêve. Le couteau est pour s'battre."

"Why would I need a fighting knife?" Alphonse could not speak or understand English very well and being outside his local dialect of Acadian French made him uncomfortable. Juliette apologized. "Excusez-moi. S'battre? Pourquoi j'ai besoin d'un couteau pour m'battre?"

Her uncle replied, "C'ta dans l'rêve. Tu devrais l'avoir."

"Merci, oncl' Alphonse. C't'un beau couteau; un beau présent."

"Ça chindra un bon coin mais l'derrière du couteau est mou et c'est balancé pour tirer."

Juliette knew knives from fishing but she also had experience with hunting knives. She tested the balance and ran her finger along the back of the blade. It did feel like a softer metal and that surprised her. She hadn't realized you could tell the difference between hard steel and something like lead just by how it felt when you ran your finger over it. Perhaps she imagined the difference; and what about her uncle's imagination? Had it gone wild on him? The whole thing would have been more easily dismissed but she knew him to be an immensely capable and practical man. Juliette asked, "Tu crois ce rêve, ouai?"

"J'pense que t'auras besoin d'l'aide un jour et ça t'aidera."

/Jesus uncle/please do not invite me into your dreams/ She asked. "Que s'que tu veux dire? J'devrais t'y l'apporter avec moi?"

"Apporte la tout l'temps."

In the fall, she returned for two quick trips to sea, one on the Grand Banks and one on George's Bank. Jimmy had been right. Kevin Murphy made a fine skipper. The boat costs increased a little but, all told, Juliette went from making very little, after expenses, to making a good middle-class income. Although up there with the doctors and lawyers, Juliette had a tendency to save. She lived much the same as during the lean years.

She did buy a nice copper moonshine still and kept it in a sugar shack built of logs with the help of Lank and Archie. The shack was at the bottom of a hill covered with sugar maples. They had been collecting maple sap and evaporating it down to syrup over an open fire for years but it was much easier with a proper evaporator, which was a good cover for a proper still. The sugar shack stood on the bank of the river where Juliette got the water for making moonshine. She made the mash with molasses, sugar, river water and some maple sap. Evaporating the sap for maple syrup kept the moonshine mash warm. By the time the maple sap run came to a close in the spring of nineteen fifty-six, her mash was ready for the still. It took her five days to distill fifty-eight gallons of strong moonshine. Making beer was legal so she brewed that in her parcel car.

Many days and most Saturdays, Juliette made a big breakfast for her fellow Trackers. They all looked forward to breakfast at Juliette's car. She ended many nights drinking at Archie's but not to the extremes of the past. Juliette usually left Archie's on her own feet and got home to bed without incident. When Victoria stayed with her overnight, she remained almost sober.

Juliette made a point of visiting Sister Jeanne d'Arc. The nun had a crisis of faith. She wasn't sure about God and rejected just about all of the Catholic dogma but Sister Jeanne d'Arc also doubted herself. She no longer felt surefooted enough to be such a brazen troublemaker. She took her duties as Superior of the little convent more seriously.

Juliette realized that Sister was unwilling to step over the line to a romantic relationship with a woman. They did become good friends. The Sterling Reserve convent went without a cook because the Sister who had done that retired to the Mother House in Halifax. Juliette cooked for them and taught some of the young nuns how to cook. Rather than the basic food they were accustomed to, Juliette taught them how to cook French and Mediterranean dishes and some of her inventions. She made a meat pie like the ones from the Metegan area of Nova Scotia but with a Greek topping of nutmeg and garlic. Nuns visited from other convents just for the Greek Acadian meat pie.

The girls grew up frighteningly fast. Lacie would soon start school. Victoria grew taller. They were very different. Victoria was showy and dramatic but Lacie became reserved, confident and self-contained. They never fought and seemed to enter a comfortable zone together. Juliette would have prayed that didn't change as Lacie met new friends in school. But she left prayer behind at age twelve or thirteen along with any theism. Juliette, like Lank and Archie, did not believe in God and didn't encourage their daughters to believe in God, Santa Claus or the Easter Bunny.

Juliette said to Archie, "I act like I believe in luck, life force and spirits like the spirit of a tree or a human or the sun. These are useful metaphors for the mysteries. I love the mysteries but I guess I live by the metaphors."

"It would be difficult for you not to believe in those things at least as valid metaphors. You have luck, you have life force and you have spirit."

"Yes I have luck in my life. I have Victoria; I have the best friends; I am healthy and wealthy by any wide historical and geographical measure. I do not have luck in myself."

"What do you mean?"

"I am not easy for me to live with. My failures, my drinking and that tight grip I keep on myself, I wonder if it is any better than being stupid and ugly."

CHAPTER TWELVE

"I sold the Austin."

Juliette hacked out a trench with a pick and shovel, not much more than a foot deep and only inches wide in spots. She carefully placed the newly-dug soil on one side of the little trench. "Yes, I noticed we had no Austin but we still had you. My father said that when you sell a car that you owned for a time, you lose a parcel of memories. I certainly have memories from the Austin."

"Yeah, me too. A guy thought it was an antique, a guy from Halifax. He paid me three hundred and twenty-five dollars for the Austin."

"Hey, nice going. Great. You are a rich man, Lank."

"Yeah, I'm going without a car for a while, less trouble. You diggin' for silver?"

"No, just a project."

"What do you mean a project?"

"You'll find out soon enough. Lank, in my first cupboard there are four quart bottles of moonshine rum. I ran it off with my new super still. This may piss you off but I would like you to take one bottle at a time." She stood in the trench with her chin resting on her hands, supported by the shovel handle. Her head popped up and down a bit as she spoke. Juliette supposed that looked funny. She heard an odd staccato in her own voice. The weight of her head resting on her chin seemed to cause her mouth to close too quickly after forming words. Juliette didn't do this on purpose; she was tired. Supporting her head with a shovel provided one of those small efficiencies that mean so much when you're tired. However, looking and sounding a little ridiculous would perhaps make it easier on

Lank, who she was about to insult. "I should be able to provide you with a steady supply of shine and I have beer brewing. The beer will be ready in a month. Hopefully, I can keep up with the two of us for beer and shine. I figure if you take it, the moonshine, one bottle at a time and the beer maybe two or three quarts at a time, you would have an idea of how much you drink but you will always know it is not your last drink."

"It sounds like you're just gonna do this for me, no charge."

"Yes, that is right. If I run out of money, I may need help buying sugar or malt."

"Juls, that's a tremendous kindness but it's hard to take a lecture on drinking from somebody who sounds like Donald Duck. Lift your head up, girl."

Juliette collapsed to her knees laughing. She sat on the mound of dirt by the side of her trench. The relief of laughter and her exhaustion from the hard work penetrated Juliette, a delicious relaxation. She grabbed his ankle. "Get down here, you long skinny bugger." Lank folded himself up so he could sit on the clean bank, his big feet turned sideways to fit in the narrow trench. He stared at Juliette as her laughter subsided, he smiled. Juliette's laughing stopped; his smile went away. Lank bowed his head.

"Juls, it's hard to... It's hard to take that kind of help. You know what I mean."

"It is just me, Lank. It is only me."

"Could you take that kind of help for your drinking?"

"No, I could not. I would get mad and I would resist."

Lank said, "It'd be like you owned me." Juliette didn't speak. The trench was only as wide as the shovel's blade. They sat on opposite sides, trying to avoid the sight of each other.

"What are you thinkin'?"

"My love, I am thinking the drink owns you now. If you keep drinking that half-made swill, I should dig this hole deeper and wider because that shit is going to kill you." Juliette's back was curled forward. She spoke to her muddy knees. "I want to do it. Please Lank, let me."

"Is it good shine?"

"Good enough for the likes of you and me."

"Juls, my thankfulness is big. I'll try Juls. But you know how it is with booze. It can trip you up."

"I know. Is that a good plan, a bottle at a time?"

"I guess. It don't make sense to me but you probably know better. I want to try it your way."

Juliette continued to dig her trench. 'You will see,' was her answer to Archie's question about what she was doing but Archie said, "They say the frost went down four feet in February about ten years ago."

Juliette went through the full length of the trench digging deeper, mostly into hardpan. When she finished digging, a truck came with a load of pipe, all one-inch, thick-walled copper. Juliette had pilfered the pipe from the old washhouse at the silver mine. She bought all the fittings and reducers and borrowed Lank's blowtorch and plumbing tools. The pipeline, from the Tillman River to the outhouse sink, sparkled with well-soldered joints by the time the prize arrived.

Lank said, "Isn't that beautiful, an old Vacher water hammer." She got a lot of comments like that. 'Long time since I've seen one of them.' Or, 'I thought a ram pump would be good for here, although it'd be easy to run a power line from the other side and use an electric pump.' One older gentleman from Sterling Reserve said, "The only way to keep them old Vacher and Green pumps going is to put a balloon-tire bicycle inner tube in the pressure tank. Otherwise, the air gets dissolved in the water and she starts thumpin' like old hell. Liable to break herself apart."

All this was a great disappointment to Juliette. She thought a ram pump was a little-known miracle, almost a perpetual motion machine. She felt delight when her father found one, in good working order, at an old farm on the banks of the Margaree River in Cape Breton. It seemed like everyone around Sterling Reserve knew about them. However, all that local knowledge meant that she had it set up in jig time and pumping water to the outhouse sink. The ram pump operated on the strength of the river's flow with no other energy input. Water pressure at the outhouse sink was not great but they got a good flow rate. Juliette made provisions, in the pipes, for sending water lines to the cars. One line came off the main water line to a black tank on the south side of the outhouse. On a sunny day, warm water flowed from the hot water tap on the outhouse sink. Archie had one objection.

"It's a bit unfortunate, in a way. Building the outhouse was a Tracks affair, a kind of community project, whereas individual effort built the waterworks."

"I did not contribute to the building. This is my way of becoming a member of the community."

"Yes yes, that's right. That's right, yes."

"No dissonance for Archie?"

Archie, embarrassed but smiling said, "No dissonance for Archie."

Lank reported to Juliette if he drank less alcohol and apologized if he drank more. She told him that was not the point. The point was that he did not shit himself to death drinking Lank juice but he seemed to want a drinking confessor. She became that.

Archie wanted The Tracks on a sewer system with one large septic tank but the others didn't see the use in it. Lank and Juliette planned to bring running water to their cars but a flush toilet did not land high on their agenda. Lacie and Victoria liked walking up the kids' steps to the sink and turning the water on to wash their hands. Lacie tried to explain this running water in the outhouse phenomena to a little friend from Sterling Reserve. It took them a while to figure out that Lacie was talking about the same thing the Sterling Reserve girl had in her home. Lacie couldn't figure why it felt more special in the outhouse than in houses, the school or in Sterling Reserve's little library but it did.

Victoria didn't know any kids her age; she had one friend, Lacie. Victoria stuck to her like an only friend. Lank was a laissez-faire parent despite his extreme pleasure in his daughter's company. Archie leaned toward overprotective and Juliette made her decisions on the spot, acting differently toward the girls in different situations. She thought of herself as someone who did not need general guidelines or, perhaps, she couldn't form general guidelines. When she and Archie drank together, they had a wide range of conversations but the talk often returned to a basic difference between them. Archie needed to fit everything in an overall outlook, perhaps a theory of behavior, and Juliette was bereft of framework or systematic analysis. Archie had touchstones for everything and he admitted his dependence on those touchstones, whereas Juliette just floated. However, Archie and Juliette usually agreed on things.

The girls had this all figured out. Lacie often took Victoria's hand as they went places and did things around The Tracks. They stayed close to home with Archie supervising and went farther afield when Lank was in charge, perhaps because they knew he would join in if they had a particularly adventurous outing in mind. Some sort of fluctuating standard applied when Juliette was in charge. Victoria always seemed to be testing the limits with Juliette but Victoria and Lacie together knew where to go and how far to go. With Juliette as their watcher, they often went into the outhouse and locked the door. The girls spent a long time in there. Juliette thought it lovely that they hid out in the little building, breathing the muted smells of lime, hay and human waste. They had the half darkness, the sink, the taps and their sense of safe enclosure in their own little world with their own little friend.

***

Lacie found trouble early in grade primary. She would not stay in her seat. Juliette and Lank went to see Lacie's teacher, Sister Joseph Dorothy. It took Sister Joseph Dorothy some time to grasp the parentage situation. Her first assumption, that Lank and Juliette were a married couple and Lacie's parents, did not give way easily to the facts that Lank's wife had left him and her daughter, and that Juliette had a child of her own, father unknown. This woman in her late twenties seemed surprised that such possibilities existed.

Lank tried to keep his toes from tapping and his head from bobbing. He shifted in the straight-backed chair in front of Sister Joseph Dorothy's desk. Juliette, in a similar chair, sat relaxed and motionless but annoyed.

"Mr. Graham is the father of your student Lacie Graham and I am a friend. That is the only family structure you need to know in order to deal with our questions."

"Well, Mrs. Cameron, I may have questions of my own, such as why Lacie won't stay in her seat."

"She has muscle cramps. It is necessary for her to move in order to work out the cramps. If she stays in one position for any length of time, Lacie suffers severe pain from cramps due to her asthma, for which she may need to go outside for fresh air during school hours."

"Oh, I see."

"Dr. Lawley can send you a note to confirm all this if you wish. He is very busy these days so it may take a week or so to get the letter to you."

"I don't think that will be necessary but I'll ask Sister Superior. How often does she need to step outside?"

"That varies. Lacie says the air is not bad in your classroom, quite good she says but asthmatic responses are extremely unpredictable. She could become congested at any time for no apparent reason."

"Oh, the poor child."

"Sister, she is also embarrassed about it so it would be best, Dr. Lawley says, if it did not become a big issue with the other children. Dr. Lawley says that Lacie often puts up with quite severe pain, those cramps you know, rather than bringing attention to herself. She has a very strong spirit. However, as you well know any mental stress can exacerbate asthmatic congestion.

"Yes indeed. Perhaps you can tell her that she can get up from her seat when needed. She is not bad in…she's not…ah, disruptive. She doesn't bother the other children or anything."

"Yes, she suffers in silence."

"Poor thing."

Outside the school Lank asked, "When did you come up with all that bullshit, Juls?"

"On the spot. It will work. Do you think it will work?"

"We'll have to tell Lacie the whole thing."

"Oh yes. She will be amused, I would guess. I do not like silly nun nonsense. Most nuns are great but they put the silly ones in to teach the little children. Little ones are as big as any of us in passion and meaning. Do you know what I mean?"

"Oh yes, kids fill themselves up with themselves and the world, just like we do."

Lacie got on much better in school with her new permissions. Lank went to the monthly home and school meetings where parents talked to the teachers about how their children were doing. As the year progressed, Sister Joseph Dorothy's attitude of conspicuous kindness or pity for a sick child changed into something else. The Vice Principal, Sister Jeanne d'Arc, told him in January that Lacie's teacher was getting suspicious about her medical difficulties.

"It seems to worry Sister Joseph Dorothy but I have told her to never mind. When do you think Lacie's asthma or Miss Cameron's ruse will clear up?"

Lank felt unusually comfortable with Sister Jeanne d'Arc so he told her that Lacie could be over her asthma but she finds it difficult to sit still for five hours a day. The Vice Principal suggested that Lacie take the year off until June. She would provide Lank with the curriculum and an indication of what a child would need to master in order to get into grade one. "It will give her half a year off and perhaps she'll settle down a bit. Lacie could learn the grade primary stuff in a week but you'd have to teach her."

"But you would tell me what she needs to know?"

"Yes, I could do that."

"That would be very kind of you. I know that is beyond your duties."

 Sister Jeanne d'Arc laughed. "My duties are not demanding, boring really. I don't like to see a child like Lacie chafing at the bit because she is too advanced, too intelligent for the work that is presented to her. If I had my way there would be a different program for the smart kids but I'm neither the school board nor the Minister of

Education."

"I appreciate this. I'll ask Lacie if she wants to take the time off. She's pretty good with school since she is allowed to get up and go outside but Lacie dislikes not being honest."

"But Miss Cameron doesn't mind?"

"Oh yeah, she does mind. The asthma was her idea. She thought the sitting in the same spot business was ridiculous. Juls always thought that. It's kind of 'give to Caesar what is Caesar's' and the institution just needs a good excuse to do the right thing. But no, Juls don't often bullshit. Excuse my French."

"If you want Lacie to stay out until June, I will arrange a suitable excuse so that the principal can do the right thing."

***

"I don't know Daddy. Maybe I can just sit there like the other kids."

"Would you miss going to school?"

"No, I don't like it. It's right strict. Sister Joseph Dorothy yells at us."

"Okay honey, why don't you stay home. You can learn what you need to know from me and maybe Juls."

"Thank you, Daddy." Lacie and Victoria learned the alphabet with Juliette, even how to spell it, learned their colors and how to spell them and Lacie knew the range of wavelengths from red to blue. Lacie could do simple multiplication and division and she knew her numbers up to the millions. They drew and colored with wild imagination or with precision. In Victoria's case, it was almost draftsman's precision. The primary school readers were learned and discarded. Lacie read grade three books and she could struggle through parts of the newspaper. Lank and Archie helped but Juliette did most of the teaching. That was fine with Lacie. It became apparent to the Trackers that the girls were far ahead of the expectations for kids their age. Before Lacie started school, they had little frame of reference showing the girls as exceptional.

Juliette, Lacie and Victoria often walked over to Percy Donovan's store after their lessons. They called him Old Pricey behind his back but Mr. Donovan to his face. They bought chocolate bars, some with the price printed on the wrapper by the manufacturer, ten cents. Old Pricey charged twelve cents for all the bars. Lacie usually got a Cherry Blossom and Juliette a Jersey Milk and Victoria bought an Eatmore or a Macintosh Toffee. The Eatmore and the Toffee took a long time to eat but the Cherry Blossom, more like one big penny candy, was gone pretty quickly. Victoria always offered to share with Lacie after she finished her 'dumb Cherry Blossom'.

Being with Juls was being able. Everything Lacie wanted could be accomplished. She had room for error but no need for it. Things worked. At the end of the day in her own bed, Lacie slid down the dream river to sleep, with Victoria's little legs dancing in her eyes. Deep inside Lacie, Juls' soft, rich voice and the smell of Juls pulled her into the creamy whirlpool of sleep.

***

"Do you ever think of Custard Head, Juls?"

"Yes I do. It is an odd collection of thoughts I have about him. It would be nice to talk to you about it."

Lank looked at his glass of moonshine with the little bits of Salada tea in it. He loved the color and he found the drink satisfying. After one glass of moonshine tea, he could drink the second glass without constantly thinking about the third. Lank drank far too much alcohol but much less than before Irma left and before Juliette kept him away from the stuff he used to drink. He wanted to talk about Custard too. "I've been, not like Custard but you know, kind of torturing myself at times. I don't know where that comes from. I feel sorry for him."

Juliette said, "Do you feel sorry he is dead?"

"No. That was a matter of safety. He wasn't safe to have around."

"I actually killed him. He did not try to kill himself at my place. I punched him in the back because he was at Victoria and out of control. I suppose Custard rarely maintained self-control. He fell and looked like he lost the use of his legs. I do not know if I broke his spine or it was some temporary thing. Anyway, he tried to wail and he banged his head and I broke that head with a cast-iron skillet."

"That skillet?" Lank pointed to the big pan on the wall. Juliette went to the cupboard and took out a smaller frying pan.

"No, this one. It is much easier to handle for skull fracture. Good for fried eggs, too. I think of Custard often when I make breakfast."

"Do you feel guilty?"

"No."

"But what you said makes you a murderer."

"I never think of it in those terms. I never think of that word much but there would be a good legal case for me as a murderer."

"Do you look at it more like a mercy killing?"

"My my. I never thought of that phrase either. You sound like Archie; a need to classify."

"Well Jesus, if you don't classify the nature of the act of killing another person, then what? I guess I think it's pretty important to classify that."

"Yes it is for society's functionality and convenience. War, for example, allows us a lot of killing that we think is wonderful and heroic. It would be brutal murder otherwise. I did not make reference to societal norms before or after I killed Custard. It was strictly personal. Now if society found out, society would have something to say about it, and well society should."

"You're right, Juls. I've always had trouble with situational ethics if that's what this is."

"Yes, I understand that but I do not feel it. I rarely have trouble with situations. The whole weight of everything fucks me up."

"Shall we drink?"

Juliette said, "I will get Archie. We can put the girls to bed here."

"Yeah, actually, I still want to talk about Custard."

"Yes. Okay."

"It's almost like I miss him. It's not that, really but I feel melancholy when I think of him."

"Oh I know, yes, a sad case. He reminds me that horrible things can befall humans."

"Could we have helped him? I mean if we really wanted to?"

"Maybe someone could but is that the point? Custard was treacherous. Over and above his obnoxiousness, he could not be trusted. You can go on about right and wrong but you know we chose our children over Custard."

"You know… there's something owed or… I don't know, I don't know."

"I agree. I have taken on his soul in some way which I would never attempt to define but, you know, I am something close to sure and positive that I am a better custodian of that soul than Custard."

"Holy shit. That's weird Juls, a great way of looking at it but weird."

"Shall I get Archie and the girls? Custard is dead. If there is knowing in death I hope he knows peace. Peace evaded him in life."

***

The girls liked to hang out at Archie's caboose because of the radio. They both loved to hear music and Lacie danced. She mastered the big linear dial on the RCA radio to the extent that it took her only a second to change from the jazz show on CBC to a Halifax country or pop station. Lacie would stay on CBC for Sarah Vaughan or a big band like Count Basie and she'd leave the country station when Furlan Husky or Hank Snow came on.

They moved the night's drinking to the caboose so the girls could enjoy the radio. As Lacie danced, Victoria carefully drew vertical lines on a piece of lined scribbler paper. She divided the sheet into blocks a little bigger than a quarter inch. With equal care, she colored in the squares. Archie saw a pattern in the arrangement of colors, Juliette saw meaning and Lank thought it was random. They had corresponding differences of opinion on abstract art and classical music like Schoenberg and the new far-out jazz of Thelonious Monk or Shelley Mann. Juliette was the only one of the three who enjoyed it all. But the three of them enjoyed drinking together, talking and occasionally playing poker for pennies. Sexual tension wandered around the room like a friendly ghost. Juliette found both men attractive and they were both attracted to her. Archie had originally decided that he didn't want to be involved with a pregnant woman because he would be stuck with a child. Now he had the child but not the woman. They had openly discussed some kind of union, sexual and beyond, to living together or marriage. Archie said it would ruin everything. Juliette didn't know if he said that because he knew she wanted him to say it or because he meant it. After a few years, they realized they had a friendship too good to give up. Archie loved the fact that he could talk with Juliette about women and she felt a lovely, impious voyeurism at being that kind of confidant.

When Juliette arrived at The Tracks, Lank was married to Irma, not the ideal wife but she was there. Juliette did not want to couple with either of these men. It would be difficult finding a way out. She had no desire to have one man for a long time. It would interfere with having other men for a short time.

Lacie made the song selections until nine o'clock when Lank got the girls tucked in. Lacie could be heard singing softly and off key but they knew that when Victoria hit the bed, she slept. Archie said, "Sometimes I go in and look at her sleeping. It's so luxurious the way she sleeps. It's a devil of a time to wake her though before she's ready to get up. What about Lacie?"

"Yeah, she sleeps good but I let her go to bed when she's tired. One night last week, I drifted off in the chair and she woke me at quarter after twelve and said, "It's time for bed, Daddy.""

"She's smart for her age."

"Yeah, I guess so. That's what they tell me. I don't know myself. How do you get to know these things and how do you keep perspective? It's pretty easy to think your own child is as special as can be."

Archie smiled. "Yes yes, all guesswork. We're just here to make sure they stay alive till they're seventeen or so."

"What's that line at the end of A Tale of Two Cities? 'It's a better thing I have done'… I can't remember really."

"Yes 'it is...' No I forget too." Instead of trying to snare an elusive memory, Archie drained his glass.

Lank said, "Well anyway, it's a great thing you did by taking Victoria in. You know, Archie, I always thought a lot of you but I never would've expected you to do that. Can't beat it. You did a great thing, a great generosity."

Juliette sat up in the cupola. She looked out over a night lit by starlight, the few electric lights from Sterling Reserve and a faint aurora. She and Archie knew that sounds funneled out of the cupola like the small end of a megaphone but all noise from the rest of the world attenuated on its way to the cupola. It was part of its peculiarity. Juliette spoke in a husky alto with the breath of straight moonshine in it but not much louder than a whisper. "Why did you do it, Archie?"

Juliette saw Lank's startle. He jerked into a sudden keyed-up preparedness followed by a slightly more gradual slide back to embarrassed relaxation. At her best, in her favorite times, everything was a nebula. Her expectation, that Lank heard her voice in his head like a spirit or like a lover at his ear, melted into the nebula. She supposed that Archie looked for the best answer to her question and she expected that he would find something that he felt had enough truth in it to triumph and be spoken. Juliette's suppositions and expectations appeared and then emulsified in a diffuse awareness. Her knowledge that her affection for these two men came from the grand affection she felt for herself blended in a cloud that didn't reside anywhere. The nebula hung in her body, her head and all around. A few drinks made this formlessness the best part of Juliette's day.

"It wasn't as grand as Lank makes it out to be. I felt like a thief when I took her from your car. I saw Victoria and picked her up on her birth night. That kind of thing can make people believe in a benevolent God. I felt blessed and, from then on, I always schemed so I could be close to her without looking too obvious."

Juliette came down the steps from the cupola. "I am thankful that my circumstances did not allow me to choose Victoria's father at the time of conception and thankful for all the roads that lead me to you."

Lank said. "The Tracks is magic or something. It's good here."

Juliette took Archie's bottle of whisky, refilled his glass and added the touch of water he had recently become accustomed to. She poured moonshine into Lank's glass and added the generous amount of Seven-Up that seemed to agree with Lank's stomach. She dumped too much shine into her glass. When Juliette reached the stage of just drunk enough, she usually drank more. "To The Tracks, to we three and the two in the little room." The three raised and clinked their glasses. Juliette drained the four ounces of moonshine down her throat and said breathlessly, "I am going home before I get too drunk, maudlin and silly. Good night all."

"That water you poured in my glass came directly from the River to that pitcher."

Juliette's smile sparkled. "That is ram pump water?"

"Pumped by the river herself."

"How sweet. When did you connect?"

"Today. It's only a few inches below ground, no good for deep frost but great for right now."

Lank said, "Great right now."

Outside, the night fondled her in a cool shiny black embrace. Juliette could see the faint line where Archie had disturbed the soil to lay the water pipe and she remembered passively wondering about that mark on the earth while looking out from the cupola. A mild burn remained in her stomach from the last big gulp of shine.

Juliette wondered what they said about her when she left early. When one of them left early, she tried to avoid talk about the guy who left. Archie and Lank got the message that she disapproved of anything that smelled of gossip or backbiting. /a very conscious girl I am/conscious and conscientious/I mean to be straight/ I mean to be honest/must not be mean to be honest/

Juliette went to the outhouse but she did not walk to her parcel car when she finished. She marched toward City's car, her arms pumping. /slowdown hon/catch-up/catch your breath/ The response to her knock on City's door was his lamp being blown out. He seemed to have some trouble extinguishing it; the lamplight flickered before his car sucked in the night's darkness. She knocked again and felt him looking out at her. He lit a candle and came to the door in his dirty long johns with pee stains in front and she assumed shit stains in the rear.

"City, why not simply piss outside in the summer, or the winter, for that matter? Your pisser must be a wild thing if you cannot hold it steady enough to hit the big hole in the outhouse. At least clean it up afterwards. Nobody wants to sit on your mess."

"I'd rather go in the outhouse."

"Why, are you shy or something?"

"Nah, I don't get out of the car much. It's just good to get out. I ain't got no friends."

"What? Are you going to make friends at the outhouse?"

"You know, sometimes I bump into somebody, say hello anyway."

"Just try to hit the hole. Can you do that?"

"All right, Miss."

"And use the big hole for pissing, please."

What to do about City, Juliette wrestled with herself. /stay clear/it will waste time/he needs a break/it would take very little to help him out/ She chuckled a bit at her resolute, arm pumping march. Back at the caboose she said, "Hello, it is just me again. What about City? Should we all, well the three of us, get together and try to improve his lot or should we continue trying to keep him the fuck out of our lives?"

"Ten o'clock meeting at my place. I'll make breakfast. We can decide the fate of the City."

Archie said, "He is so goddamn boring, annoying, stinky and stupid. Why bother?"

"City reflects badly on the girls' neighborhood."

Archie laughed. "I might think like that privately, Juliette, but I never thought I'd hear you say it."

"Yes, well, there you go."

"Okay, ten it is. Can you make crepes?"

Lank said, "Who's got eggs?"

Juliette had eggs and blue cheese and Lank got excited about breakfast. They all stopped drinking and went to bed in their respective cars.

＊＊＊

Cheese crepes, sausage crepes and strawberry apple crepes were followed by a deliciously bitter concoction of tea, dark roasted sesame seeds, instant coffee and cream.

At one o'clock, City ate lunch with them. "I hoed into that, I did. My lord, don't I just love chicken."

They convinced City by threats and promises to change his ways. He was given clean underwear, a pair of pants, and shirts. Juliette scrounged a couple of sweaters from Dr. Lawley. She ransacked City's railcar throwing out almost everything, and then washed the car down with Javex.

When Archie and City arrived back from the bathing hole, a quiet, sheltered pool in the river, City wore his dirty clothes and Archie still carried the new ones. City barely moved, completely exhausted. The day had gotten warm and sunny. He flopped out on the shady grass by the caboose.

"Why the old clothes?" Juliette had just come out of City's car.

"Our friend is infested with body lice, head lice and crabs for all I know."

"Okay, I'll get some stuff from the hospital for that."

"I don't want none of that. I had that shampoo stuff when I was a little boy and I don't like it, no."

"Well City, you probably will not like it this time either but you will not have any more luck trying to get out of it than you had when you were a boy."

"Oh."

In two days he was clean-shaven, well-dressed and smelling good. Archie asked, "Those patches and mended spots on your old clothes, did you do that?"

"Oh yeah, who else? I can do a better job when these clothes wear out though. I just sewed them old ones like they was old ones."

"Yes yes, the work's not bad though but you can do better, can you?"

"Yes my man, I can sew good, so you hardly sees it. My aunt didn't have no girls so I did the sewing."

"Did you live with your aunt?"

"After I was nine and my mother died, I went with my daddy's sister, Aunt Joyce, cus they didn't want me livin' with my daddy."

"Why was that?"

"I don't know but my aunt taught me to sew because she had all boys and they were older than me and they all worked. Ralph helped on the pop truck and Scotty worked on the tram tracks off and on. Gregory and Damit worked in the pits." I think his name was Danny but we called him Damit. Now Pete the Brick, he worked on Labesky's truck sometimes but he was mostly too drunk to work. Nice fella though."

"Back to sewing, can you do other things or just patching?"

"No, I can mend and hem. If I got a pattern that's not too hard, I can make a dress or even a pair of pants. I can put zippers in. I learned that."

"Would you do sewing for money if we could get you some customers?"

"I don't want to jep'dize my income. I get thirty-five dollars a month allowance."

"Is that all the money you have?"

"That's the whole of 'er."

"It will not jeopardize your income and you will make more money than that. How long does it take you to hem a pair of pants?"

"Ten or fifteen minutes."

"Did you use a machine?"

"Oh yeah, Aunt Joyce had a good, good Singer. They said I was a natural sewer, like an old lady, they said."

Juliette took City to Dr. Lawley. It was his first time seeing a doctor. He very respectfully referred to George Lawley as Dr. Sir. City wanted Juliette there for the examination, his shyness with strangers trumping his shyness with females and Juliette was not a regular female. She had become his mother. Dr. Lawley found City in good health but for the fact that he was more overweight than the doctor himself. "Some people think that being this fat is bad for your health in lots of ways but some people think it's ok. The jury is out on that. It would be good for you to lose some pounds but not important enough to worry about."

As they walked back to The Tracks, "What did the doctor say, Juliette?"

"He did not say anything to me separately; nothing you did not hear."

"I mean, what he said, what did he mean?"

"Oh. Your tests will be back Thursday. If there is nothing bad in the tests, you are as healthy as a horse. Well, a fat horse."

Juliette found it difficult to keep her pace slow enough for City. She walked fifty feet, stopped and waited for him to catch up. As soon as she turned around, he slowed down and would be at a standstill after a few steps. When Juliette tried walking at his pace, he took the opportunity to go even slower. "I must get back to my kid. I will see you at The Tracks."

It turned out that City had mild diabetes but, for the most part, his poor diet seemed to cause the high blood sugars. With better quality food, introduction of more exercise and careful management of his life, City's health and energy levels improved. City didn't manage City's life. Juliette got his food, arranged customers for the sewing business they set up for him, purchased the sewing machine and materials and policed his eating habits.

Cleanliness was another thing. Juliette nagged him into slightly better habits but it became an onerous chore for her.

The sewing business didn't go well. City didn't do much. Juliette got the customers and he was good enough and fast enough that he could have made a close to normal income for Nova Scotia in the nineteen fifties but he wouldn't do it. Juliette had to take on most of the jobs. She did marginally better work than City but she was not nearly as fast. After eight months of picking up the slack from City's low motivation, Juliette began refusing most customers by eliminating the complainers, the always urgent and the ones who didn't pay. She made a few dollars for herself and a few dollars for City on about two hours a day for her and three hours a week for City. This kept City in cigarettes, food and the small amount of wine he drank. Juliette's fishing income was good and the money she earned from sewing never got to the bank.

Juliette and Lank connected up to The Tracks waterworks and winterized with a sluiceway to increase the flow pressure from the Tillman to the pump. They put the pump down a foot deeper to make it safe from winter ice. The flow rate and pressure into The Tracks waterworks increased to accommodate what had become ten taps and a toilet.

Lank and Juliette conspired to streamline his auto repair business. When the people who owed him money and the whiners wanted him to work on their cars, he told them to go see his manager, the lady living in the parcel car. Juliette had no trouble at all telling them that Lank wouldn't work on their cars anymore. He didn't get quite as much work but the work he did do, he got paid for and he didn't have to deal with annoying people. It was hell for Lank to deal with annoying people. He used time freed up by this arrangement to buy wrecked or run-down vehicles and fix them up for sale. He liked this work better than doing repairs for other people and he did a great job. Lank's rebuilt vehicles sold easily. In December of nineteen fifty-six, he had a Chevy truck and a Buick at the White Rose station and a Standard Vanguard in front of his dining car. The three of them sold on the same day. Lank remained rich for almost a week. Both girls got new clothes and shoes and everybody, including City, got skates. Lank never learned to skate and that was a good part of his motivation for buying blades for all The Trackers. He watched people skating and thought it beautiful, like awkward birds wobbling on the ground and taking flight into grace and easy speed. He wanted to learn and he wanted Lacie and Victoria to enjoy gliding on the stillwaters and the marshlands down river, where smooth, clear ice could extend for a mile.

The marsh froze hard in late January. They drove down there in a pickup truck Lank had just repaired. City, Juliette and Lacie rode in the back of the truck and they were happy to get in the heated cab to lace up their skates while the others put theirs on outside. City and Archie taught the girls the basics but, within minutes, Lacie learned enough to skate. She took the falls as part of the fun and Victoria followed her friend around, fifteen minutes behind in technique and daring. Archie watched them closely, correcting their methods at appropriate moments. City played with the girls for a while but, after an hour's practice, their short little legs took them across the ice faster than City was willing to move.

"God, Juliette, girl, I wish I was young again but livin' here, not with my aunt. Look how happy those children are. I wish I was like that."

Lank said, "I just wish I could skate." Juliette, his teacher, made slow progress. Archie disappeared, leaving the girls to their own fun. When he arrived back, gliding effortlessly from side to side with his hands behind his back, he took over Lank's training from Juliette. Lank's skill level took a sudden jump to the point where he had fun. Archie's first move was to tighten his friend's skate laces.

Juliette skated well, not as skilled as Archie but she skated beautifully. Lank and Archie's attraction to Juliette was well known among them but not often spoken. When she returned to their little encampment on some high ground where Lank had a fire going, Archie said, "Any man who has seen you skate would love you."

"Back home we skated in open rinks strung with a few light bulbs. It was more popular than the dances in the winter and it looked a great deal more innocent to parents and such other people who might make the morals of the youth their concern. However, it was attended by the twelve to twenty-two-year-olds, who make everything a sexual display. Skating is such a subtle and sort of mediated exposition of your wares. I absorbed all that and I will never get it out of my skating. I would never want to, even if I reach ninety."

"You're not ninety and neither am I. You look lovely skating but you always look lovely."

Juliette smiled just a little. "You too, Archie. You are lovely too, and you are attractive and I hope that you enjoy the attention as I do."

"Oh you're such a goddam nun, Juliette." She laughed as Archie set off on the marsh again, arms pumping, gathering speed until he disappeared behind some bushes poking up through the ice. Lank came back from another direction.

"That's so much fun but my legs are tired, boys oh boys."

"It uses different muscles. You did a lot in one day."

"Where are the girls?"

"I assumed with you or City, so that leaves City."

"I should get them back." Lank hobbled up to the truck for some birchbark and a rifle. Black smoke from the birch bark rose on the light wind. He fired the rifle. Lacie was supposed to skate towards the smoke when she heard the shot. In a few minutes, she arrived pulling a sapling over her shoulder with City five feet behind holding the other end. Victoria pushed lightly on his ass. City did not move his feet; he was dragged and pushed along by the girls.

Lank shook his head but Juliette fell on the snow next to the fire, laughing. The laugh took away any cares, concerns and reservations. It happened rarely but the occasional occurrence of this laughter took her completely away from herself.

"Girl, my feet are frozen stiff and I'm so tired I could die."

Lacie panted, bent over with her hands on her knees. Victoria did the same, more from imitation than exhaustion. A look passed from Juliette to Lacie that said, 'You are so beautiful. I want to hug you and squeeze you but my daughter would be jealous'. Lacie's return look showed understanding. Juliette came up delightfully unfastened by her own laughter at the comic picture of City being towed across the ice. Her memories of clear and true insights, while recovering from careless laughter, made Juliette sure that she correctly read Lacie's acknowledgment of her admiration and affection. How long did this understanding exist and could Victoria be picking up on it? But Victoria appeared to suffer hyperoxia, not jealousy, as she copied Lacie's breathing.

Lank stuck an iron pot full of water on the fire. He poured some of the boiling water into a pot of tea, some into mugs for the girls' hot chocolate and dumped some ingredients into the remaining water. In fifteen minutes, a pork and macaroni stew was ready. Archie obviously smelled Lank's cooking from half a mile away. He arrived just in time for stew and tea. Juliette had heavy dark bread made of wheat, rye, molasses and pork fat. Lacie put her large chunk of bread on a stick and toasted it. She shared with her little friend. Juliette busied herself so the way she felt about Lacie wouldn't show itself.

Victoria stuck to Lacie and imitated Lacie, who took it as it was given, naturally. With adults other than Lank and Juliette, Victoria became a star. Any talent is potentially a curse. Juliette worried about Victoria's ability to attract attention. Her cheek-pinching cuteness, her ingratiating tricks of snappy comments, pretty smiles, twirls and curls were her first response to almost anyone except Lacie. She didn't put on airs for Lacie. Juliette suspected that Lacie would have none of it anyway. Juliette tried to get the message to Victoria that the pretenses didn't work on her but Archie was the biggest fan of Victoria's antics. All the girlish, sweet and cute delighted Archie. He thought it was brilliant.

When Victoria got some black on her face from Lacie's smoky toast, Archie lit up with a smile of benign delight but Lacie got no credit for pulling a bit of her sweater sleeve out of her jacket so she could wipe Victoria's face. It all stumped Juliette. She thought that maybe her perception of her daughter got yellowed by Archie's pinked-up view.

Anybody can cook anything over an open fire by a frozen marsh and people who have been skating around on the marsh will love it. Lank concocted delicious soups and stews. He was a magic man in blending flavors. Juliette enjoyed arranging tastes, textures, flavors and colors and smells on two or three dishes contrasting and complementing each other but Lank always found a unity in his soups and stews that eluded her. The smoky stew by the marsh had a deep dark oneness about it but also bright surprises of the occasional whole peppercorns and the chewy sweet of dates thrown in for the last minute of cooking.

"Mom, I peed my pants. I'm cold."

"Okay dear, we will get something dry for you." Juliette whisked her off to the truck before Archie could declare it impossibly darling how she said 'peed'. They had no extra clothes in the truck to dress Victoria. Juliette put her pissed-on underwear and pants on the heater vent but little girl pee smells pretty bad blown out of a Chevy heater. She wrapped Victoria up in the blanket that lay across the seat, went back to the campfire and passed the sewing packet, little more than a couple of needles, some thread and a pair of tiny scissors, to City. She also passed him a towel.

"Make a warm skirt for her, with a waistband. Please."

She went back to the truck and got City's shoes and his zip-up black overshoes all warmed up under the truck heater. Juliette took his skates off and slipped on the warm shoes. City was a happy man with warm feet and a plan to make a skirt out of a towel. In twenty minutes he had an off-white skirt with darts just below a springy tight waist. He took advantage of the elasticity of the fabric with some tricky stitching. It had a single slit at the bottom. City went up to the truck to fit her.

"Is he all right with Victoria?"

Archie said, "What do you mean?"

"She is naked mostly. Memories of Custard, I guess."

Lank said "It's okay, Juls. Custard is gone. It's just City and we're here."

Lacie tilted her head a bit and looked up toward the truck.

Victoria got out of the truck wearing rubber boots, a snow jacket and an ankle-length straight skirt made out of the faded yellow towel. She walked with an overstated mincing stride, her arms out. The model stopped by the fire and did a couple of twirls. They all laughed. Juliette and Victoria caught and held each other's glance, both laughing. "Ah, Victoria, you can make an old towel look so beautiful."

CHAPTER THIRTEEN

Walking to school on the first Monday in June, Lacie felt invincible but, at the schoolyard, kids stared. An older boy said, "The Princess of The Tracks is back." A flash of practical understanding shocked Lacie. Her world had been small and protected. She had a few friends and she spent most of her life with Victoria and three adults. They weren't mean to her.

Two girls from primary and little Therese from grade one said hello. They seemed glad to see her. Lacie stuck to those three girls until the bell rang. She wanted to get back to a world controlled by adults with rules and expectations, where things went as planned. In the lineup to enter the school she thought kids criticized Therese for befriending her but Lacie wasn't sure. There were so many things to keep track of. In the classroom with Sr. Joseph Dorothy, the pain began.

"Well class, look who's back, the Princess of The Tracks herself. She is gracing us with her presence. Being a Princess, she got permission from the Queen to stay away from commoners like us for most of the year."

Some of the children laughed but others seemed to silently object. Lacie thought she got signals from some of them; signals that said, 'this isn't right. Sister Joseph Dorothy shouldn't do that'. But Sister Joseph Dorothy wanted to torture a child.

"Princess Lacie Graham, get to the front of the class this minute and show us what you know."

"I don't want to."

"What did you say? You just march right up here, you little snip."

"I can't say what I know. I don't know anything. Leave me alone. Don't you have work to do?"

"You are the sauciest little snip. You're a bad girl. There's nothing can be done for a bad girl. You can beat a bad boy but there's nothing can be done for a bad girl. You'll always be a bad girl and it's no wonder, the kind of things you come from. Children, I don't want you to talk to Lacie Graham."

The silent signals, the invisible, silent signals from some of the kids came to Lacie. 'She's not right. Sister Joseph Dorothy is mean. Sister Joseph Dorothy is off her nut.'

Lacie couldn't differentiate the feelings of anger, embarrassment, shame or defeat. She didn't know the concepts but she burned with something new and ugly. At recess, Sister Mary Ignatia came into the hall. "Oh, Miss Graham, I forgot your first name."

"It's Lacie, Sister."

"Oh yes, Lacie. I am Sister Mary Ignatia. I met you when you were little."

"But I'm still little. I'm just a child." Lacie's effort to not cry showed.

"What's the matter, darlin'?"

"Sister Joseph Dorothy said the other kids can't talk to me."

Sister Mary Ignatia's face stiffened. The benign, wrinkled kindness hardened. Lacie thought she had surely said the wrong thing.

"Just you wait a minute, dear. Colleen, come here to me, please." A little girl, who had not been kind, not been mean to Lacie, came over. "Colleen, dear, what happened between Lacie here and Sister Joseph Dorothy?" Little Colleen cast a glance toward Sister Joseph Dorothy who stood by her classroom door looking their way. "Don't mind her, Colleen. You just tell me what happened."

Colleen related it just about the way Lacie saw it. Colleen acted like Victoria, all gesticulations, drama and excitement. Sister Mary Ignatia walked over to the other nun. Lacie took Colleen's hand.

"Thank you." It looked like Colleen wasn't familiar with heartfelt thanks but she seemed to like it.

Words, at first intense whispers, passed between the women. Lacie caught 'my classroom' and 'as I like' and, then shockingly, 'mean-hearted stupid bitch'. The volume of their argument seemed to walk away with all propriety under its arm. A tall man with a booming voice trudged down the hall towards the arguing nuns.

"What's all this commotion here? Ah, what's this…?"

"You get out of here. I am taking care of this." Sister Mary Ignatia's faced glowed red under her white coif.

"Well I ..."

"Go or I'll get Sister Jeanne."

The large man mumbled loudly and incoherently as he walked away, finally saying to a boy who was heading outside, "You there, watch what you're doing, what you're doing there."

Sister Mary Ignatia backed Sister Joseph Dorothy into her classroom. No noise escaped from the classroom but after recess, Sister Joseph Dorothy treated Lacie the same as the other children and at one point, she sobbed.

At the noon bell, Lacie started toward home for lunch. The largest boy in her class, a fat kid, stopped her. "Goin' home to The Tracks for your dinner? You eat dirt, do ya?" The boy pushed her. Lacie turned away. The boy punched her back; Lacie spun around and punched his front repeatedly. The boy hit the ground crying loudly. She turned again for home, very surprised at how easy that was. About three minutes into her walk home, a big kid from grade three caught up to her. He was winded from running.

"You beat up my brother. I'm gonna knock your block off." He grabbed her arm; she kicked and punched. Lacie didn't flail at him; she kicked and punched with purpose. She didn't have the skills but she had purpose, which is all a kid needs to win a fight. Again, how easily she resisted the attack surprised her.

At home Lacie told her father about her first morning at school over a bowl of soup and a spring salmon crêpe. They walked to Juliette's. She looked hung over from a hard night's drinking.

"Well Lacie, you could quit and we will figure out something else for your education but I think you have…what? Yes, you have claimed your space and stood your ground. The school can be a violent place but people are not going to fuck with you. You are too tough, too smart and your friends will be good friends, true friends."

"Okay Juls, I wanna go back. Is that all right, Daddy?"

"Yes, you go along, girl. It can only get better. Lacie, if you can manage it, be kind to Sister Joseph Dorothy."

***

"Sister Joseph Dorothy?"

"Yes?"

"I'm sorry I was saucy. I'll try to do better."

"That's good. Now you go to your seat. The bell will ring in a minute."

"Yes, Sister."

At the end of school, Lacie found the older boy who tried to beat her. "Are you all right?"

The boy said, "Yeah, so?"

"I hit you and kicked you so much because I was scared of you. I'm sorry but you scared me." They ended up talking about the wild, nasty dogs up by the Currie's house.

During the next three weeks, it became apparent that Lacie knew the work a grade primary kid should know and that she had mastery of skills far beyond any of the kids her age. Lacie thought another kid in her class was just as smart but he didn't have the chances she had. She thought he had to act that smart. Most of the kids were afraid of something. It made them nasty or competitive or lazy but she believed it was the same thing that made them all afraid. She thought it might be God.

She told some of the kids that she didn't believe in God but just told the Sisters she was a Protestant so they would leave her alone and, for the most part, they did. On June twenty-sixth, she graded into grade one. Lacie had earned the right to keep doing this for twelve more years.

On her first summer vacation, she and Victoria could handle so much more freedom than ever before. Lacie had her friends from school and Victoria loved meeting new kids. She'd become a chatterbox and everyone liked her for the bright colors in her personality. They met other girls' parents and sometimes traveled with them to Brookfield and once to Halifax. They did very adventurous things outside but Lacie and Victoria often played at anything or nothing in her dining car, in Juls' parcel car or the caboose. Their friends were always eager to come to the rail cars. Sometimes parents discouraged their children's trips to The Tracks. Tommy Brian's parents and Terese Deveau's mother did not object to their children spending time at The Tracks. The girls liked the tiny, quiet Therese and they also liked Tommy Brian's cheerful exuberance. But Victoria and Lacie spent most of their time together, entirely by their own choice.

Lank made a plywood pram the kids could row around in the still waters of the Tillman River. The pram delighted the kids and worried parents. Lank added inner tubes to the bow and under the seat of the pram and told everyone that the inner tubes would hold up the boat and the kids even if they capsized. This caused parents to relax a bit. Victoria and Lacie swam well. Lacie taught three other kids how to swim. Juliette provided a little help which gave the learners the confidence of having an adult to supervise.

Lacie often read to Victoria but for Victoria a story usually became a play with instant rewrites to fit the props they found around them. One day, in the caboose, while they were being poor street vendors in nineteenth century England, Victoria passed a ceramic plate to Lacie, who let it slip. It broke on the foot of the stove. Lacie felt very bad. She hated to displease Archie. Victoria assured her that everything would be okay. They cleaned up the debris and slid down to the river and their little boat.

The girls saw a movie, a Western, at the Musquoboit Harbour drive-in. Lacie and Victoria traded being the good guy or the bad guy but they were frustrated that they had no black clothes to be the bad guy. Victoria had owned lots of black clothes as a baby and a little kid but they got passed on to a family in Sterling Reserve. The girls didn't even have a black cap or a black scarf. The acting sort of thing suited Victoria. Lacie's shooting was just a 'bang, bang' but Victoria made a sound in her throat like the word 'cur' but raspy and full of hostile energy. The movie was also a love story. There was some to-ing and fro-ing about who would be the woman and who would be the man but Victoria, being smaller, usually got the female role. They practiced kissing and hugging like a movie hug with the woman melting and going limp and the man getting bigger and stronger and more the boss as the hug went on.

Sometime during July, no one knew exactly when, a small man moved into the coal hopper car where her father said a man named Custard had lived for a while before he went to Saskatchewan.

Lacie and Victoria often played in the truck cab that served as the top part of the hopper car. The new man was unfriendly. No one saw him much and, when they did, he was always dressed in black. Lacie called him The Ghost. The name stuck and she began to believe she'd done the wrong thing by calling him that.

Lacie didn't look forward to school. The restrictions and the boredom, after a summer full of adventure days, made her nervous and she remembered more frightening things, mean teachers and mean kids. Two males worked at the school. The janitor didn't have much to do with the kids but the tall, sad, slow-moving principal, Mr. McLeod, seemed to enjoy exercising his big voice to make the children squirm.

August was bright and clear. Lank bought a Bedford delivery van that he offered for sale at an unreasonable price. He wanted to keep it for a while. Lank used the van for so many things, particularly loading up his daughter and her friends and taking them somewhere new. Slipper was making money for Juliette. Archie had as much work as he wanted from Cliff, his lawyer friend. Archie did research but also finish carpentry on Cliff 's real estate holdings in Halifax. The three adults and the kids went to beaches, spent the day fishing for mackerel or wandered about in Halifax. They went to the circus. The grounds, just outside of Dartmouth, were enormous. They went on rides and saw elephants and lions. All seven kids who crowded into the van won a prize for something or other.

Lacie wasn't so sure about the animals. Were they happy away from their jungle or wherever they used to live? It filled her up with something though, to be close to these wild, powerful animals. It felt like touching the moon. But she thought that having them here to look at, so close, was doing something wrong. That didn't apply to the monkeys who drove the noisy little cars around in a steeply banked circular pit. Staring down at them from the edge as they sped around the track, she couldn't imagine how the monkeys could have that much fun in the jungle. The attendant gave them a slice of banana between heats. Lacie wanted a little car like that.

It was probably too small for her but maybe Victoria could fit in. Victoria did not appreciate being volunteered as a competitor for the little monkeys.

On the way home from the circus, they had to drop off Tommy Brian Cross at his cousin's home in West Jeddore. People fished off the small wharves and from the rocky shore. They pulled in lots of mackerel which rarely came into those shallow waters. The mackerel chased small fish into the shallows. Juliette, who paid for the circus trip, had gotten a healthy owner's share from Slipper in July and, among other things, she bought a well-used old Cape Island boat and kept it at the Head of Jeddore. The boat finished up its days with an engine that came from a boat whose days were over and that boat had gotten the engine from a wrecked truck. Juliette's boat had a weak transom and was, overall, not worth rebuilding but she bought it for the licenses that came with it. As they dropped the kids off the night after the circus, Juliette told all the parents that she'd pick the kids up again at five in the morning if they wanted to go fishing for mackerel. "The kid's clothes will smell like fish but they will each have a load of mackerel."

The next day, Therese and another kid from Sterling Reserve went with Lank, Juliette and the girls. It was an overcast, misty morning two days before school started. But Tommy Brian and two of his cousins came along and they had buckets. Juliette had asked the man, she bought the boat from, to put a fish box aboard her boat. Mackerel rods, extra gas, a small filleting table and some kids' life jackets waited for them in the morning.

***

Jack Mosher limped over to Juliette from his truck. Jack, at seventy years old, was worn-out and arthritic and he carried remnants of old injuries from a life as a fisherman. Jack's one son drove a bus in Halifax and wanted nothing to do with fishing. The old fisherman was happy to sell his boat to a beautiful young woman who wanted the licenses. Fishing was a family affair in Nova Scotia. Jack Mosher and Juliette adopted each other while they haggled about the price of the boat and the licenses. He would have sold for less, she would have paid more and they both knew it. As adopted fishing family they had minimal rights and obligations, keep in touch, be fair and care about it.

"That is a large fish box, Jack."

"You'll be comin' in with 'er full up. You know that there mussel bank, the one before the west wharf?"

"Yes, I know the spot."

"You go east of that bank. Ain't nobody else gonna fish there but that's where the mackerel is. I seen it before. It's them little baitfish with the long fine tail that the mackerel is after and they likes the shallows. Don't get your lines snagged. I got three rods with three hooks each and two with five. The little ones probably won't be able to haul five. Them's big mackerel out there."

Jack's body got decrepit early but his eyes stayed as keen as when he was a teenager. He saw the care Juliette took in getting everyone on the boat. Being aware of the delicacy of the hull, she allowed no jumping into the boat. Jack could see her eyes gliding over everything while getting ready to shove off. She'd be taking in the weather, the wind and tide, the placement of everything and everybody on the boat. Juliette started the engine, listened and slipped it into gear. She turned around and smiled at Jack. He saw her lips, her teeth, her eyes. Jack bowed his head and waved a dismissive wave but his heart bounced. She heard the soft noises that a marinised old Chevy truck engine made when it was worn-out but well taken care of. Jack could see Juliette's appreciation for him spending half the night dragging his old bones around the boat making sure everything ran darn near as good as it could. He went back to his truck, lit up a cigarette, took two aspirin and washed them down with gulps of his morning fixer-upper, one third ginger ale, one third cold tea and one third Black Diamond rum. He carried the mixture around in a one-quart Iron Brew pop bottle and Iron Brew was exactly what it looked like, should the Mounties ever bother to check.

After an hour, Juliette signaled that she was coming in. She made other hand signals. He couldn't quite catch her meaning but he guessed right. When she made the dock, he had a fish box full of ice and bags of coarse salt.

"I seen you out there filleting. I never saw nothing like it. My Lord, you filled that box. They look nice, yes they do."

The kids formed a parade to the little outhouse at the end of the dock. They were tired and dragging themselves around except for Tommy Brian's cousins. The boy and girl, eight years old, were twins. The small scrawny Steele twins knew about fishing and this adventure energized them. They'd talk about this and teenagers would be impressed, their parents would be impressed and their uncle Ralph would want to hear about it again and he'd ask a lot of questions.

"Jack, could you make up a couple of troll lines for us."

"Got it just about done. Needs a dozen or so more hooks and lures and some bobbers. I got them here but my hands is stiff. I'm mighty slow tyin.'"

Juliette tied the hooks and floats that Jack prepared. She did this with alacrity that Jack couldn't have matched in his youth. Lank struggled with the hand- cranked crane, pulling the first of the loaded fish boxes out of the boat. Juliette asked him to help Jack with the ice and salt. Jack heard the crane going faster with Juliette at the crank handle.

A red International pickup truck pulled onto the wharf.

"Oh no."

Lank said, "What's that?"

Jack said, "I think we got trouble." Jack knew that Juliette hadn't met this man but Jack had warned her about him. She would know his truck. You identified men around Jeddore by their trucks. She would know his reputation, a bad one. He trundled from his truck, feet wide apart like he was still on a boat, his shoulders just as wide. He bristled with big man assurance.

"Where'd they get them fuckin' mackerel?"

"From the water." Jack sensed Juliette's inconspicuous attention to what was going on.

"You suck my cock again, you old bastard." He yelled down to the dock "You there, where'd you get them?"

"Leave her, Randall. It's none a' your business where she got 'em." He pushed Jack who would have fallen but for his truck behind him.

Juliette walked toward the big man in her usual gait. She looked deliberate but graceful and feminine even in rubber boots. "I know you are a liar." She walked past the man as she spoke so that he turned around, which put him between Juliette and the boat where the children had gathered. "I am a woman, a horny woman, and I know from the look of you that no one ever sucked your cock."

The big man was taken aback. He gathered himself up for some display of power but felt Juliette's odd filleting knife under his left eye making a tiny impression in his skin where the tip lay. Juliette held her hand in a twisted position like a hand about to make a circular cut. She stood between the road and the knife so the people who lived across the road couldn't see it and she kept the man between her and the boat so the kids couldn't see. The big man tried to pull his head back but the knife stayed in the same position just below his eye.

"Jack will not tell me but I will know, and the next time you show disrespect to Jack Mosher, I will remove this eyeball and perhaps the other one, depending on the severity of the offense." A trickle of blood ran down his cheek. "The children are fishing east of the muscle shoals. You can fish anywhere else." She put the knife back in its sheath after wiping the tip on the big man's shirt. Juliette stood where she was; he had to back off to walk around her. He must have realized that he sounded close to crying when he said, "No woman gonna tell me where to fish." He got to his truck and drove away in a spray of gravel.

"I seen 'em scared before and I seen 'em scared today."

Lank, who didn't see the knife asked, "What did you say to him?"

"Oh I suppose I said he was ugly."

Old Jack, who had seen the knife, laughed and coughed convulsively. He took a swig from the Iron Brew pop bottle, passed it to Juliette who drank and passed it to Lank. He took a large gulp, expecting Iron Brew. Lank's pleasant surprise was obvious. He took a tasting sip.

"That's good. Ginger and tea, is it?"

"Don't forget the rum."

"Yeah, the rum tops it off nicely. That's a nice drink."

Juliette said, "What is the deal, Jack? Ice for bait?"

"I wouldn't do that, girl. How much are you gonna catch for fillets?"

"We cannot handle what we already have for fresh and smoked and giving them away. I hoped you would take all but one of the boxes."

"Okay, that little bit of ice is free and I'll get a little more ice on the fillets and I'll drag it into the cool with the winch. How about twelve dollars a box for lobster bait?"

"That is generous, Jack."

"It's late in the year and there ain't been no herrin' anywhere close. People's gonna be short on bait. But you'll have to pay the Steele twins. They expect that."

"All my crew gets paid."

Jack said, "If I make money on the bait after buying the pickle and everything, I'll give you one-third."

"Great, thank you. We will take salt with us and layer the fish whole on the boat so you will not break your back lugging salt around." Juliette rolled a fifty-pound bag of salt from Jack's truck onto her shoulder and walked down to the boat.

Jack said to Lank, "I don't know if I'd want her to be my wife, my daughter or my son."

"I know which one I'd want but there's not a nibble." Jack smiled and helped Lank pick up a bag of salt. Lank carried it to the boat, holding it like a baby.

***

On the way back out to the mussel shoals, Juliette explained their crew shares.

"We make twelve dollars a box on the mackerel that Mr. Mosher is buying for lobster bait. There are nine of us and the boat gets a share. Now, do not expect this good a deal if you go out on a real fishing boat but there you have it. Mr. Mosher will pay me a bit more if he makes a profit and I will also divide that up ten ways. That may not come through so do not expect it. This all means that if we get three boxes of mackerel, each of us makes three dollars and sixty cents. If we get ten boxes each of us gets twelve dollars. The whooping and cheering was led by the Steele twins. Lacie felt a shift. This was an adventure but it wasn't pretend; it wasn't set up. She sensed something different. She didn't whoop it up. Lacie looked around the boat for things that needed doing. She passed the rods to the other kids.

"What's in the bags, Juls?"

"Salt. You and Therese make sure a scoop, this scoop here, of salt is spread over each layer of mackerel and also make sure the mackerel are spread out in even layers." She told them to call on Susan, the girl from Sterling Reserve who came with Therese, if they started to fall behind.

Lacie listened intently to the different jobs assigned and realized Victoria had no special job. She went to Juliette at the wheel and spoke softly. "Vee is good at taking the fish off the hooks. She's really fast. She helped Tommy Brian before. Maybe she could take them off the whatcha call it."

"The troll lines. Yes, good, yes thank you, Lacie."

Lacie saw Juls swallow, look down at the wheel and touch the lever that made the boat go faster. She didn't make it go faster or slower; she just rested her hand on it for a few seconds. Lacie knew she made Juls feel bad by reminding her she forgot Vee. But what about Vee? She'd be the only one without a special job. Lacie stood there next to Juls feeling bad, because she made Juls feel bad. Then a hand on her shoulder, "Lacie, thank you. Thank you, sweet, you are a gem." Juliette shouted back, "Victoria, would you take the wheel, please. I have to show Lacie and Therese what to do with the salt." Victoria came up from the stern with a little yelp and an 'oh my god' as she balanced in the boat. She flipped her hair once but, when she put her hands on the wheel, she was all business.

"Drive just like you drive the truck standing on Lank's lap."

"I can't see over very good."

"Tiptoes."

"Juliette showed Lacie and Therese how to scoop out the salt from the bag she had split with her knife. The kids caught a few fish even at the five knots they motored on the way to their trolling spot. They salted the mackerel down and started to spread them out. Therese held Lacie's legs as she bent over into the box, which wasn't much shorter than she was.

"Lacie, you can jump right in until it gets half full. Your boots are clean and it is just lobster bait."

The mackerel were running. The troll line filled up every ten or fifteen minutes and everyone who wasn't doing something else held their rods way out, the hooks barely in the shallow water, trying not to snag the bottom, each other, the trolling lines or the propeller. By noon, they had four boxes completely filled. The old boat rode low in the water. Victoria steered to within twenty feet of the dock when Juliette took over. Jack had pop, milk, tea and sandwiches prepared by his neighbor's daughter. He also had a small bait box for Victoria to stand on. Juliette said to her crew, "Lank and I will unload so you folks have your sandwiches that Mr. Mosher brought."

Lacie saw her father putting everything into the heavy work, keeping up with Juls. She didn't look like she put everything into it but when she stopped pulling on the winch to guide the fish boxes onto the dock, Lank barely kept the winch going. Mr. Mosher hooked on to one of the boxes and dragged it with his truck. The box scraped over the concrete wharf, sounding like loud radio static, until it was beside the building that he called 'the cool'. Mr. Mosher hooked on a chain from inside the building and turned a crank to slide the big box in. Juls always got there to slide the door closed as soon as the fish box went inside. They got the boat unloaded in fifteen minutes. One fish box remained on the dock and another by the cool house door. Jack took a breather. Lacie went to him with the cardboard box and the empty bottles. "Thank you, Mr. Mosher for the sandwiches."

"Are there some left for Lank and Juliette?"

"Yes, in the boat, and the tea, too. Will I put these in the back of your truck?"

"No dear, put them in the van. You can get the money for them."

"Thank you."

The big man in the red truck drove by again. He slowed down and stared at them. Mr. Mosher bent down to Lacie, put his hand on her shoulder and pointed at the man in the truck. /he wants the man to see this/like when the teacher tells some kid to do something and wants the whole class to know/

"That's Randall French. He's not a nice man. If you ever see him around, you tell your mother, I mean Juliette. You tell Juliette."

Lacie repeated, "Randall French." Randall French roared off in his red truck.

Victoria called, "All aboard.Wooo Wooo." The Steele twins cast off the lines and climbed aboard after Gloria kicked out the bow and Gary pulled in the stern to get the boat pointed out. Victoria stood at the helm on her bait box.

Juliette said, "This is one and a half knots. That is the speed you go when we get the gear out."

"What gear?"

"Get the gear out means when we have the troll lines in the water. Look here now, where I have the throttle. This is for five knots. That is how fast you go to get out there and back. Got that?"

"Yes sir." Lacie had been watching Victoria steer. She thought

222

the throttle might be too much for her but, as before, Juliette sometimes left what she was doing to give Victoria instructions. Victoria took them somewhere different, farther out at more than six knots now. Juliette looked around.

"No, let's head back to our old spot. We'll still find mackerel left there but go that way, dear, on the other side of that little island."

"What island, Mom?"

"Right there; it is an island. You will see that as we start to go by. Stay off it the same distance as from the Ghost's car to the coal mine."

Gary Steele told them to take their lines out of the water because they were going too fast. Lacie wasn't sure what he meant by too fast. Victoria turned the boat sharply to head back; it skipped sideways a bit over the waves coming up in the afternoon breeze. Lacie looked around the boat. Her father was ill at ease but he often seemed ill at ease. Tommy Brian and Susan held onto the gunwales for dear life but the Steele twins and Juls calmly continued what they did and paid little attention to what Victoria did. /she's so good at this/I'll never get to drive the boat/

Juliette said, "Over there, Victoria, slow down. Go over there close to the bank where that little white house is, slower than two knots."

"Stop Vee! Put 'er in neutral. There's a big rock right where you're headin'." Gloria Steele dropped her mackerel rod in the bottom of the boat and began moving quickly toward the bow. Victoria didn't wait for her or for Juliette to confirm. She put it in neutral as the old boat ground up to a ledge and slid back into the water. It was a soft grounding but Juliette and Gary looked in the bottom of the boat for water coming in.

"My father hit it once. That's how I know. Can't see it 'cause the water's right dark here 'cause of the swamp flowing in."

Juliette said, "Put your lines in. There are lots of mackerel here."

They caught fish, working hard, always pulling in mackerel. Victoria steamed back and forth by the big rock at about one and a half knots, fully confident, fully competent. Victoria had been stopping the boat to help take the fish off the hooks. But now she stayed at the helm, carefully trolling in the shallows close to the big rock. Lacie filled in for Vee taking the mackerel off the troll hooks. She couldn't do it as fast as Vee.

Lacie worked hard and tried to think of everything. You had to be carefull on a boat. But something better than excitement, better than fun, slipped into her. The boat's motion and the afternoon breeze pressing and tickling her face felt sweet as sleep. The sun made jewelry of every little wavelet. Lacie smelled sea air, fumes from the old engine, mackerel and the late summer perfume of the woods on the little island. Gloria Steele smelled of a small house where a large family lived a modest life. Eveyone was in place, at work on the boat. The muted thrum of the old engine running slow, the muted voices of the boat's crew, now tired and familier with their days work, and the light swish of the water pushed away by the hull played a concert. All of Lacie's sensations slid into their perfect place within the day like the rollers her father dropped into the cage of a large bearing he found at the silver mine. He had no use for it but Lank loved such things. The bearing became Lacie's. Three years ago, her father made a stand for it so Lacie could spin the outer race. How long the outer race turned, after she overcame the inertia became Lacie's measure of her own growing up. With the race spinning, she sent her mind to the rollers whose existence was to offer no resistance. She remembered her father slipping them into the bearing cage where they found perfect belonging.

At seven in the evening, they came in for the last time. The kids were exhausted except Victoria who had the least physically demanding job. They all got together to lift one box of fillets into the van without mechanical help. Lacie heard Gloria Steele say to Victoria, "Nice job at the helm. Couldn't a done better myself."

Juliette apologized for leaving Jack stacking fish boxes using the cable crane in the cool shed. "Jack, I must get the children home before their parents think I drowned them."

"That's good, dear. Everything in the cool will be done tonight and, if not, it can wait. One hundred and ninety-two dollars. Darn good day's work for a bunch of kids, wouldn't you say?" He counted out the cash into her hand. Little Therese, tired and hungry, with mackerel scales sticking to her hands and hair and clothes, stood watching them in stunned amazement.

"Juls, you're rich."

"Therese, we are all one-tenth rich."

Even the Steele twins, accustomed to the boom and bust of fishing, stood wide-eyed when they got a twenty dollar-bill. The bills were soft, almost wilted. Jack would've had them in his pocket for some time. Like many people in the fishing industry, he liked to have cash available. A chance to purchase fish, or bait, or a motor, or a boat at a good price might come up anytime, anywhere.

On the drive home, the kids talked about what they would do with the small fortune they earned. Lacie didn't know what she'd spend it on but Victoria wanted a schoolbag. Lacie thought she would get Victoria to delay that for a few days, because grade primary kids didn't really need a schoolbag, especially early on when they didn't have any books.

Lacie watched her best friend talking easily with the others but not making herself the center of attention. Lacie had expected her to crow about operating the boat and Lacie expected to get mad at that but there was none of it. Victoria acted like she did when it was just the two of them. She didn't show off. Juls went around to where Victoria sat. She put her arm around her. Victoria leaned into her mother, glancing up at her face occasionally. Lank pulled into the gravel parking lot at Ship Harbor where the chip wagon was parked. Somebody said, "No fish, no fish please, just chips."

Lacie said, "Lots of chips and I'm paying." Six large boxes of French fries at fifteen cents a box, two hotdogs at ten cents each, and six bottles of pop at eight to twelve cents a bottle including the bottles, took a shockingly large bite out of her twenty dollars. She had expected greater loyalty from the money she worked hard for.

***

The next morning Juliette fried mackerel outside over the fire pit. She filled up her large frying pan three times to cook up about twenty pounds of fish. She also boiled corn on the cob and made tea and coffee for everyone. Lacie delivered the breakfasts.

 The Ghost lived at The Tracks for a month and a half but Lacie never spoke to him and saw him only twice. The first time, Victoria said, "What's that over there?" Lacie turned to look and saw nothing more than a dark shadow on a sunny day. Lacie got no answer when she rapped on the door of the old truck cab that sat atop The Ghost's boxcar. She tried the door. It opened. She called out, and heard a weak groan down below. Lacie went down the makeshift stairs into the dark hopper car. The Ghost lay under a dirty blanket and a winter overcoat. He was so thin. It just looked like a pile of clothes on the bed. He appeared to be quite ill. "Bert, are you all right?" The Ghost moaned again. That was the end of the conversation. The Ghost spent five days in Dr. Lawley's care at the hospital. He had a cut on his leg that became ulcerated and caused a general infection. The Tracks people thought he should be looked in on occasionally. Lacie volunteered to do it.

When Juliette or Lank made breakfast for the people at The Tracks, The Ghost would not join in the gathering but Lacie brought the meal to his car. Sometimes she left right away and came back for the dishes later but this made her feel like she skipped out on something. She stayed and talked to or at least listened to Bert as he had his breakfast and drank tea. He never wanted anyone else to stay and talk but he liked Lacie and she did her best to pretend

226

she enjoyed listening to him. She did like it when he talked about hunting or the motorcycle that he used to own but every story seemed to have some sort of thing at the end which was supposed to make The Ghost look smart or tough or mean. He was like the teachers at the front of the classroom, giving away more about themselves than they wanted to, talking to themselves and listening to themselves. They forgot about the people watching them and listening with nothing more on their boredom-filled agenda than picking out lies and character flaws.

"He talks like some of the boys in grade two."

Victoria asked, "What do ya mean?"

"I don't know, he doesn't seem to have many words and he sort of brags a lot. It's stupid really and the only time he's interested in listening to me is when I talk about Juls."

"Did ya tell her that?"

"Yeah, she said don't worry about it. But he says stuff, I don't know, stuff that makes me wonder. He said, well, the first thing is he always calls her Juliette Cameron. He said her voice is so soft but you can hear it from far away and he said one time we were all playing together and Juls got grass stains on her knees. Once he said, just out of the blue, that Juls was wearing a certain skirt and her slip was white. You never see him around but I think he watches us a lot. I told him about that guy, Randall French, and what Mr. Mosher said about him. I told him how Tommy Brian said he saw Juls face off with the guy and put her knife back in its holder. He asked me a lot of questions about that. That kind of stuff really seems to interest him."

"What kind of stuff, Lacie?"

"Tough stuff, like fights and stuff. He's so sick looking. Remember that old man I told you about in Halifax, the man who was dying? Bert looks the same."

Lacie and her father met the old man on a street in Halifax during
the summer. The man knew her father but didn't call him Lank; it
was Mr. Graham. He had one clear blue eye but the other eye had
no real color. It looked injured. The old man spoke in a clear loud
voice. Lank made introductions, speaking like Lacie would speak
to an adult. "Mr. Dempsey, this is my daughter Lacie. Lacie, Mr.
Dempsey used to be a priest but he left the church. Father Dempsey
married your mother and me. I mean, he was the priest at our
wedding."

"Good morning, Mr. Dempsey."

He said she was beautiful and he stared at her. He apologized for
staring and told her father that he was a lucky man. "I can tell by
the way you hold Lacie's hand that you two are fortunate to have
each other."

Her father looked down at their hands. She wondered if he forgot
that they held hands. Lacie always knew when she held someone's
hand, her father's, Juls', Victoria or some friend at school. City loved
to hold her hand.

Her father said, "Do you have any regrets about leaving the
church?"

"None whatsoever. As you know, it was about thirty-five years
overdue."

"Do any of the church people make note that you got ill right after
quitting?"

"Oh, no. No, Mr. Graham. You misunderstand that. My friends

from the church are still my friends. Most, well, all of my friends have doubts about dogma, catechetics and God but it's their job. Not many other jobs require belief in some certain proscribed thing. A lot of jobs require a dedication to an aim but not belief. By the time you met me, I had customized my job to the degree that my aims and the church's aims were so different as to be contrary. No, thankfully my friends in the church are still, well, I suppose they are still my refuge."

"I'm glad to hear that. That's glorious. I'm surprised but I guess that's because I was ignorant of the facts. Perhaps I'm cynical."

"No, Mr. Graham, cynicism could never touch you. Well, I'll say goodbye. I am overdue for death, my doctor tells me. I won't be seeing you again. I know you must miss your mother Lacie but your father is really such a wonderful man that you've got more love than most children."

"I don't miss her, Mr.Dempsey. Juls is better."

Lank said, "That's Juliette, Lacie's best friend's mother. She lives at The Tracks."

"Ah yes, the beautiful Juliette. I met her once with Archie. So Victoria is your friend?"

"Yes sir. She's my best friend."

"Goodbye to both of you."

Lacie said, "I hope you don't die."

"I'm happy to die. There is a time for everything. Toodle loo."

***

Juliette's community breakfasts were usually a Saturday affair. For Lacie, after breakfast with Bert, it was bottle searches with Victoria. A little beer bottle got them one cent at the store in Sterling Reserve. A big beer bottle was worth two cents. A little pop bottle got two cents and a big pop bottle three cents. It was among the many things Lacie and Victoria did not understand about the world, that the rum and wine bottles, which could be great big things, were worth nothing. It was a sad Saturday when the girls didn't make fifty cents on bottles and it got better over time. They had two wagons. Lacie filled her's up first. She was stronger and didn't mind pulling a loaded cart. Sometimes people saw them coming and gave them bottles. They thanked the people, and soon learned that the easy 'thank yous' brought good business. People smiled at them with a tilt or a bob of their heads; 'you are very welcome, girls.' The smilers and head bobbers asked them to come back for bottles each week. One Saturday on their way home from the store, their empty wagons no effort to pull, Lacie talked about all the trading of bottles for money and then trading money for other things that sometimes came in bottles. Victoria said, "People trade bottles for thank you and we trade thank you for you're welcome."

It happened to Lacie more and more. Something came about, someone said something or she just thought something and a big wave passed over, like the big breakers at the beach. Everything looked different after the wave.

Juls told her to be a little careful with her eyes. She said Lacie's eyes sometimes scared people who did not know her. She said, 'intense'. Lacie knew the word 'tense' from her grammar lessons with Juls but what it meant to be 'in tense' she wasn't sure. But she always asked questions of Juls when she didn't understand. Juls told her what 'intense' meant. For a while she became frightened of her own eyes. 'Strong and powerful' brought a lot of responsibility. Her father said it differently. "Your eyes are clear and brave. People are just surprised to find bravery in a little girl."

It felt like a wave. To Lacie, a scare felt like a tingle. She didn't mind it much and it didn't happen often. Being in the woods scared her, especially if she was alone or with just Vee. She could feel it in her bum, like she needed to use the toilet but she loved the woods. She liked walking alone in the woods. Scared was okay. People didn't scare her, even the principal with his big voice. He didn't scare her.

"Juls, was… I mean, is my mother brave, too?"

"There is a word 'brazen'. Brazen describes your mother perfectly. She would stare anybody down; tell anybody to fuck off. Irma responds to any challenge. I do not think of Irma as brave. Bravery is a long-run sort of thing. You must stick to it. Irma does not stick."

"Dr. Lawley said I was predotious."

"Was that predatious or precocious?"

"Precocious."

"Yes, that means advanced for your age. In the brains department, you and Victoria are both precocious. You are smarter than other kids your age."

Unlike Victoria, Lacie didn't hurry to grow up. She didn't know if she wanted to be like big people, all loaded up with troublesome and nothing new. She noticed things that gave her a toppy, bump-up feeling in the past didn't matter much anymore. When she first started frying eggs for herself and her father, watching the eggs turn white around the yellow part and flipping them over to see the hardened-up part on the bottom, that gave her the bump-up feeling. Later, frying eggs became a reminder that she didn't get that feeling from cooking eggs anymore.

Juliette knew this about her more than anybody. They played at things that Victoria said were silly even though she was a year and a half younger than Lacie. Juls got old newspapers and crayons. "Let's draw rings." Juls and Lacie drew endless coiling rings and laughed until Victoria joined them first with the laughter, then with the rings. Juls could keep old things fun but that was Juls.

Lacie felt lucky. She enjoyed the passage of a day but was sad to see it go. She looked forward to the next day if they had something good planned but anything beyond tomorrow seemed like the very top of a big tree. You could climb up but never touched the very, very tiptop leaves because the flimsy branches couldn't hold you.

Lacie liked cats; Victoria liked dogs. They had no pets of their own but their Saturday bottle collection took them well past noon because they petted every dog and cat they came across. They often had treats for different animals each week so that none of them felt left out. It didn't go smoothly with the Curries' dogs. A lot of people lived in that house and they had four dogs. An old, furry dog limped around the yard. It came over to the girls to sniff. They patted the old dog, scratched behind its ears and talked to it. The other three dogs, chained and unfriendly, looked like German Shepherds. On a cold November Saturday, they had lots of deer bones because Lacie's father butchered two deer given to him by The Ghost. The girls approached the dogs. A boy of about eight years old stood in the yard wearing a skimpy jacket and ragged pants, the cuffs falling under his torn rubber boots. They never saw him at school.

"Is your dog cross?" The boy didn't say anything. He looked at Victoria and Lacie like they were very far away. The Curries built their house on a mound of pit rock up about three feet higher than the other houses on The Rows and set back about twenty feet more than all the company houses. The company houses, built by Glover Metals and rented out to the mine workers, stood in a straight row, all identical. The Currie's never worked at the mine. The Curries built their home out of salvaged creosoted timbers stacked up to make walls. One side had begun to collapse. They propped it up with two by sixes.

The dogs' chains snagged up on rocks and the tortured bushes that grew among the rocks. Victoria said they would be nicer dogs if they were treated nicer. Lacie said, "We've got bones for them." The boy did not respond. Lacie gave a small piece of gristly meat to the furry old dog, the only Currie dog not tied up. She approached a black dog, the most docile of the chained dogs. They all barked, growled and snarled. Lacie tossed a large bone. One of the other dogs took it from the black dog. The door of the Currie's house burst open and a young man with bushy blonde hair and a reddish beard yelled at them, "You fuckin' little whores, leave them dogs alone. Get away. Fuck off home."

Victoria took some particularly meaty bones from the waxed paper bread wrapper Lacie carried. She gave the bone to the dog that didn't get one up until that point and then gave one to the black dog. Victoria petted that dog and scratched behind its ears. She petted the other dog she had given the bone to and tried to pet the one with the stolen bone. It snarled and snapped. Victoria let it settle down and she tossed a small piece of meat to it. Two men at the front of the house yelled at the girls. The Tracks was rich in the vernacular but, 'cock tease', 'arse fuckin' whore' and 'cunt baby' were new expressions to the girls. A slight lull in the yelling allowed Victoria to say, "We'll be back next week to pet your dogs." The cursing resumed.

"You're so bold sometimes, Vee."

"Mom says that people with mean dogs are afraid of people."

"Yeah, ah well, okay."

The next Saturday they fed the dogs, not as well as the first week because they didn't have bones but the dogs ate some old wieners and bread that Lacie soaked in the liquid she got from a pan used to fry up deer steaks. The dogs appreciated it and the young men came out yelling when Victoria petted the yellow brown dog, the mean one. He, they could see it was very much a he, enjoyed being tickled behind the ears. Lacie knew enough to expect that if the chain was a bit longer, he'd be humping Victoria. The dogs were quiet when the girls walked away with their carts. The Currie boys yelled curses.

Victoria talked. Lacie didn't like her telling people about what they did; however, Victoria talked about how much money they made. During Christmas holidays, three grade three boys began collecting bottles. They got all the stuff from the roadsides but Lacie and Victoria's donors didn't give bottles to the boys. They saved their bottles for the girls' 'thank you's'.

Christmas wasn't a big event at The Tracks. They didn't exchange gifts except one item for Victoria and one for Lacie that they picked out from the catalog. The gift had to be less than ten dollars. Lacie picked a blonde doll with a bit of wardrobe. She picked it as much for Victoria as for herself. Victoria got a huge box of fancy chocolates and shared it with everyone. City brought a big surprise, a skirt and blouse for Lacie and a dress for Victoria in the latest style. He didn't use a pattern. They were well-executed copies of items he saw and examined at an expensive store in Halifax.

Archie worked for a week, off and on, building a sled for the girls. It was a good downhill sled that could accommodate both of them but it had a place to attach a box so they could use it for bottle collection. When school started again after Christmas vacation, Lacie and Victoria got up early on Saturday and hit the road. She told the Ghost that Juls would bring breakfast to him. The girls scooped up all the roadside bottles on the way out except a few obvious ones. They left them so that the grade-three boys would think it was just slim pickings. That was Lacie's father's idea. On the way back, the girls called at their regular spots and sold their bottles at the store by the time the grade three boys got on the road.

The grade nine boys posed a different problem. Most of the school, students and teachers, could hardly wait until next year when Lorne Oliver and his crew, Paul Mailman and Christopher Aucoin, finished school in Sterling Reserve. They would go to Brookfield for the higher grades and become the school bullies there. Lorne had been a bully since grade primary. He played rough but it wasn't his roughness that scared the other kids; Lorne was mean. He often got a kid down, kicked and stomped on him. He warned the kids that, if they told, they'd get it again. He had severely hurt Lacie's arm in what he called an 'Indian burn'. Lorne held both hands tight around her wrist and twisted in opposite directions. He did this to impress on her that she shouldn't tell anyone that he had knocked a boy down and pissed on him. His buddies, Paul and Christopher, pretty tough and mean themselves, were also afraid of Lorne.

Lorne Oliver and his two sidemen got up early enough on Saturday. Lacie saw them coming while they fed the Curries' dogs. The Currie boys hadn't yelled at them for several weeks but occasionally one came halfway down to the road saying the same nasty things but almost in a whisper, glancing nervously back at the house. Lacie cut it short so they could get to the other side of the road to avoid Oliver and his boys. The bullies crossed over, too.

"Give us them bottles."

Victoria said no but with a rise in her voice that made the 'no' a tentative question. Paul Mailman pushed her over on the sled full of bottles. Victoria got up. He pushed her again, harder this time so she tumbled over the other side of the sled. Lorne Oliver began to walk around to Victoria. Lacie felt a quick desperation. She smashed a quart pop bottle on the edge of the pavement, breaking the bottom off. She sprung over to Lorne, thrusting the bottle toward his face. He backed off but tried to catch Lacie's hand as she made her stabs at him. Christopher Aucoin and Paul Mailman closed in behind her. She swung around. Lorne cried out. Lacie swung back toward him. The black dog had him by the leg and was not letting go. In the Curries' yard, an old woman with fat legs stood halfway down to the road holding the yellow brown dog's chain. The yellow brown dog lunged, snarling. The old woman had the chain wrapped around her big buttocks but she struggled to hold the dog.

"Come on, Topee. That's enough. Come here, boy." She called out, "Just so yous know, Topee's our nice dog. This one here don't have no name 'cause it'd be no good to call the boy. He don't know no words like 'that's enough'. He'll eat you till you're all gone. Now you boys don't ever walk this road on a Saturday. If you gotta go by here on a Saturday, you'd better get a ride. And if you boys, you there Aucoin and Oliver, I knows yous all. If you boys do anything to harm them little girls, the dogs is gonna hear about it.

CHAPTER FOURTEEN

Archie slid the door open. "Take your kid back. I'm finished."

Juliette was eating fricot for breakfast. "What do you mean, take her back?"

"I mean you can stuff her back in the shit house for all I care. Just get her out of my place."

Juliette felt the bottom drop out of everything. A hard, cold panic struck her. "Just for today though, Archie, just for now you mean, right?" Archie stomped off toward the old farms and his cathedral of birches. "What do you..?" Juliette stopped in mid-holler. She read Archie's back, his gait, and the vapors all around him which said, 'Piss off. Leave me alone!' Archie stayed in the woods all night. In the morning, Juliette asked Lank to look for him.

"Oh sure and who's gonna look for me? Jesus? If you need to find somebody in the woods, don't send me, don't send Jesus; send Archie."

"I am worried about him. He was really pissed off. Victoria told me that she broke something. She denied it to Archie. He got furious when she kept lying about it."

"Man, he's got to get that together. Kids lie. That's how it is."

"He said I had to take her back; that I could stick her back...That I had to take her back."

"Archie said that?"

"He was extremely angry. He did not even look like Archie."

"This is great. The rest of us down here piss our pants every day and Archie never has anything to be ashamed of. I'm never going to let him forget this."

"This is serious, Lank. I hope I can take care of her."

"Serious but temporary, Victoria will sleep at Archie's tonight."

"You think?"

"I'm sure. Looks like recess is out in hell."

"Pardon me?"

"Across the bridge, that noisy old Ford, that's the Curries."

"Who?"

"The family in that creosote beam house. They supply Sterling Reserve with successive generations of morons. They're musclely little fuckers though. The Curries like to fight but they'd rather just beat up people who can't fight back. That won't happen here but, unfortunately, they have no capacity for learning."

"We can fight back, can we?"

"The Ghost already saw them. He's got his door open and he's ready, I'm sure. Let's go and meet them so we can set them up better for Bert."

"Well, okay." They met the gang of young men. Juliette said, "Hello Mr. Currie, is it? Have you come to split wood?"

The man in his twenties with a reddish face covered in redder splotches stood ten feet from Lank and Juliette. The ruddy man carried an axe. The thin lips of his wide mouth opened to show decayed teeth and to say, "Whaa?" It was a wide-open 'Whaa' that accurately expressed a deep level of incomprehension.

Lank said, "No, he's not a Currie, Juls. He's an in-law, sort of. He looks like the others because the Currie girls are used to having sex with their brothers and fathers."

The rest of the group, five in all, had arrived. They all carried things that could serve as weapons. They carried a peavy, a pan shovel, about six feet of rusty three-quarter inch chain, a very fancy small caliber rifle and the in-law's axe. Some of them had knives in sheaves. One had his hand on his knife; the other hand swung the chain in the most menacing fashion he could manage. The menacing look failed. He tried to swing the chain around on a horizontal axis but the chain kept hitting the ground because it was too long. The group reached a confrontation line in the gravel where two of them moved their weight one foot to the other like dull troopers marking time while the in-law scraped the gravel like an angry cartoon bull. They didn't look at Juliette and Lank.

"Excuse my friend, please. His manner is not sufficiently solicitous for such a potentially pugilistic, perhaps bellicose, occasion."

There was no 'Whaa?' They looked at The Ghost. He had come up behind Juliette and stood close to her. The Ghost wore black pants and a long black overcoat, no shirt, no shoes. He had both hands behind his back, under his coat. Bert was no taller than the Curries but thin and feline.

"Hello Bert, these are the Curries and attachments. They seem to have come prepared for some sort of work."

"You people leave or I'll kill you."

"You's a fuckin' fruit." The in-law seemed to be the spokesperson. The Ghost took two guns from behind his back, from under his coat. A lightweight deer rifle hung in his right hand. In his left hand was a short, double-barreled shotgun pointing at the in-law's crotch. The shotgun fired with more of a fooff than a bang and the in-law screamed. The Ghost raised the deer rifle to his shoulder. It fit perfectly, his right arm at a relaxed extension, the butt resting firmly against his shoulder. The shotgun was held just above his waist. It looked like The Ghost had practiced this in front of a mirror.

"That was just salt. The other barrel," he raised the shotgun slightly, "has birdshot. The rifle is a 30-30 and I'll shoot that through your heads. I'll drop the shotgun and I can shoot two rounds in a second with the rifle. I hit what I shoot at."

Lank said, "You know, you fellas are lucky. If my wife was around, most of you would be dead and she'd be halfway through the butcherin' process. Go back to The Rows and don't come back, ever."

The in-law cried. He opened his pants which were shredded in front, and pulled them down to look at the damage. Everything was there but all somewhere between highly inflamed and bleeding as Dr. Lawley later described it. Lawley said that the in-law must have experienced extreme pain from the salt. Dr. Lawley gave him a good shot of morphine and some codeine to take home. He came back many times looking for more codeine because he liked it. The in-law and the Curries went back to their truck but it was not a decisive retreat. They seemed unsure. Perhaps they were supposed to stay around and get killed. The Ghost walked back to his hopper car like a movie hero. Lank smiled and chuckled while berating the Curries.

"Please stop, Lank. You do not speak like that. You are scared. We both got a scare and we acted badly. One or all of those poor fuckers could have been killed."

"Yeah, well they could have killed us, or the kids. They're so stupid. They could've done it."

"I know, I know but it is not… it is sad. We should not be acting like we won something. They are what they are but we should know better. I acted like an idiot. A sad stupid incident that we should have defused, rather than counting on that crazy Bert to be our shining hero."

"We didn't need him. I could have gotten a gun quick enough."

"You have guns, too? And Irma, what you said about Irma, would she shoot them, too?"

"I overstated that. But Irma hates those kind of people."

"What kind of people?"

Lank thought about it for a few seconds, "Stupid and violent, I guess."

"A lot of people hate our kind, drunk and lazy, but we hope that shooting us is not in the cards."

"Yes, dear child, there is hatred in the world and yes, it is driven by fear. So what? That's the way it is. It's a fact of human existence. Like physical injury is a fact of human existence. If you get cut and start to bleed, you stop the bleeding any way you can. When someone arrives at your home carrying weapons and you believe they'll use them, you respond any way you can. You respond fast. You should."

"Yes, I know but we jumped on them too soon. I made fun of them straightaway and then that crazy fucker shot one of them. He would have shot them all."

"Yeah, he would've killed them."

"Jesus."

They sat in the dining car with two glasses of moonshine. Lank mixed his with 7 Up; Juliette had a beer on the side. Lank's drink was almost empty but Juliette hadn't touched hers. If she did drink, it may have brought the 'whew' that comes with turning away from a difficult moment and brings about reflection on that moment. Juliette remained in the bad moment. Lank was reflective. "Do you have any tea?" Juliette sat by a window. She looked toward the bridge every two minutes.

"Yeah, I can make tea. It's Morse's."

"Good, yes, thank you. Did you want me to make it? "

"No, I'll get it. I have to light a burner; the woodstove's almost out. It'll take eleven minutes from start to steeped." Lank got the stove going. He measured out 1 teaspoon of tea for the pot and one per cup. "Are you gonna have more than one cup?"

"Yes. I will drink tea until I piss my pants. I would like to be sober when Archie arrives. Maybe I will try and stay undrunk so he will have an alternative. I have to be able to take Victoria, if he will not keep her. It is the thing I should do anyway, I guess."

"Archie's best for Vee. He knows that, you know that and so does Vee. Where is she anyway? She didn't go to school with Lacie and I guess Archie didn't take her."

"I walked her up. Walking alone is okay with her anyway. You make better tea than booze."

"Yep. I really got to thank you for getting me off that muck I used to drink."

"How do you like being a drunk?"

"I don't like it."

"This is good." Juliette sipped from a fancy little teacup. Her hands crowded around the cup for warmth.

Lank stared at the almost empty glass, swallowed the dregs and picked up the glass of straight shine and the beer he poured for Juliette. He took a substantial drink of moonshine and grabbed the beer quickly. "Whew, I forgot how strong that stuff is straight. You always drink it straight, don't you?"

"It is about a hundred proof, maybe a little more; stronger than rum anyway. I like the feeling of strong drink in my mouth and going down my throat but not so much in the stomach. My stomach demands the beer chaser."

"Yeah, you inhale too, right?"

"You mean tobacco or moonshine?"

"Moonshine, rum, whisky."

"Yes, I figure breathing in the bits of alcohol that evaporate on your tongue gets to your brain faster."

"I hope I'm not out cold when everybody gets back. It's early for me to drink like this."

***

Archie always seemed to know where everybody was. He knocked on the dining car door as Lank started on his third glass of shine and Juliette poured her second cup of tea. "I'm sorry. I was an idiot over nothing. All the way back, I tried to come up with a better way of putting it, explaining it, but that's the best I can do."

"Welcome back, Archie. You scared me into drinking tea."

"Oh my, I'd like to have a cup of tea."

"Comin' right up. I've got smoked herring and bread. I'll make toast and I got butter, too. You must be starved."

"Yes yes, I'm hungry."

"I will have a piece of fish too, Lank, if you have extra."

"Yep, got lots. I meant to take fish to both of you. I got a bunch from Joe Drane when I fixed the heat exchanger on the old Chevy engine he uses in his boat."

"Was Victoria very upset this morning?"

"Yes, she was desolate. I didn't get her green scarf from the caboose and she had to wear the blue."

Archie smiled, "The little twit."

"Actually, Victoria does feel like she fucked something up very badly."

"She broke a plate, that's all. It was a favorite plate, a prewar Japanese thing."

"Was it that thin bit of pottery, a beautiful burnt orange?"

"Yes. It was a favorite of mine but I really don't care about plates. When she said she didn't do it, I got all wound up. I turned into an old nun or something. I think I actually used the phrase 'bare-faced lie'. God, kids tell lies. It's to be expected. I don't know where I got my ideas."

Lank asked, "Is there any chance she didn't do it?"

"No, she looked guilty and it was in her room in a bag with some dust where she swept it up. I don't know how long ago she broke it but I didn't miss it until I found it when I cleaned under her bed. Anyway, I acted like a spoiled four-year-old and Victoria acted like a five-year-old, which she is."

"Bert shot an in-law of the Curries."

"What!?"

"The Ghost, he shot an attachment to the Currie clan. They came down en masse this morning carrying weapons. The Ghost shot one of them with, what was it Lank, rock salt?"

"I think just table salt or I guess coarse salt like you use for fish. One of them had a gun. They had knives and they looked like they got up on the wrong side of the bed. Juliette thinks that the Ghost shouldn'ta done it but I say it was necessary."

Archie shook his head and swallowed some tea. "Necessary or not, this is going to get very bad. Only old Elizabeth kept this from blowing up. She's dead a week now, maybe ten days."

Juliette asked, "That earlier incident, about some underage girl or something, was that the Curries."

Lank said, "Yeah, a woman named Mary had a kid eight years old and one of the Curries, an adolescent, started having sex with her."

Archie buttered his toast more rapidly than he did most things. "I injured the guy, not fully intentionally but the Currie boys wanted revenge. Old Elizabeth held them back. She figured I was looking out for them as well as the people here. The rest of the Curries didn't agree."

"How did you injure him, Archie?"

"I kicked him in the ass but he fell out of the boxcar because his pants were down around his ankles. That was before City moved into the boxcar."

"Okay, I remember hearing about this but it seemed like stories from the distant past. The Tracks, as a place to live, has no distant past, does it?"

"I'm The Tracks' distant past."

Juliette poured the dregs of the teapot into their cups. "You persuaded the old woman to keep the dogs off?"

Lank said, "Everyone knows Archie is honest and it's easy to be persuaded by someone you trust."

"I'm not trusted now. Old Elizabeth trusted me; the dogs don't."

Juliette said, "There is a problem with the girls and the Curries' dogs too."

"Our girls?"

"Yes, get Lacie and Victoria to tell you about it. They both thought that you two would get upset. They did not know if they should tell you. I guess they fed and petted the Currie dogs and the boys yelled at them and cursed at them. Some of their invectives I never heard before. Anyway, a fat older woman protected them from the Currie clan and also from some particularly mean grade nine boys."

"Well, the girls are right. That does make me upset. You try to be so protective of children. But the world they live in, it's cruel on kids, isn't it? The fat lady was old Elizabeth; the old doll returned the favor, I guess. A reasonable woman really. She ruled the Curries and if there is anything can be said about them, it is that they are unruly."

Lank said, "They trusted her. Could you use that?"

"You mean bring it up directly that old Elizabeth trusted me to look out for their welfare?"

"Oh no Arch, don't be direct. Use metaphor, subtle hints, clever allusions to classical literature, quote Shakespeare. They really look like Shakespeare kind of guys."

Juliette had a good laugh. Archie said, "I should've stayed in the woods. Anyway, I'd get killed if I went to the creosote house now. They're just mad dogs who own mad dogs."

Lank suggested he take The Ghost with him.

"There are police. This is not the Wild West. Archie, if you do not want to go there, that is how it will be. You understand the dynamics. We should contact the Mounties; tell them that the Curries are on the rampage but got discouraged by shotgun salt. Lank, I will write out what happened in the half minute before Bert shot up the genitalia of that guy so it will be more directly self-defense. You, Bert and I can go over what I wrote and that is what we will tell the Mounties."

Lank said, "Archie, if you'll meet the mad dogs, when and if they come back, Bert and I will back you up with guns. We certainly can't count on the Mounties being here when it happens."

"Sounds good; yes yes, that's the best we can do. We have to keep a constant watch for them. They'll be back soon. Ah, maybe leave the shooting out of the story when you tell the cops. Nobody but us and George Lawley knows that The Ghost exists."

"Mmm, scary. Okay that is good."

Lank reached a level of drunkenness where he sipped rather than guzzled. Archie suggested, "We should remain reasonably sober for the next few days. Why don't you have a snooze, Lank? You'll be in better shape when Lacie gets home."

"Yeah, you're right, Arch. She disapproves of me getting drunk early in the day."

"I have a task ahead of me. I must apologize to Victoria for being an ass."

Juliette said, "Really? She did lie to you."

"She's got to know that I'll never run out on her again. My God, I missed her."

CHAPTER FIFTEEN

The next day was Saturday. The girls returned from bottle collecting early and headed to the caboose. Twenty minutes later, Archie walked slowly to Lank's railcar.

"They're coming this morning but there'll probably be police, too. How close would the Curries need to be for you to be able to shoot them?"

"Two hundred feet. If I got a place to nest the barrel of my rifle, I could hit them on the other side of the bridge."

"They'll probably be on this side of the bridge. Find a way to prop up your gun in here so you can shoot through an open window but the police won't see you. I'm going to get The Ghost set up somewhere so the police can't see him." Archie looked out the window. "Okay, he's already got an old door by that ash tree. They won't see him. I gotta see Juliette. Don't drink, Lank. Nothing, okay?"

"Yeah, I won't drink."

Juliette arrived at the dining car. "Lacie and Victoria told me what Mrs. MacKay said. The gang could be here soon. I told Bert. I told him the police will be here"

"Okay, I guess we're ready."

Lank asked, "So Archie, what's the plan?"

"I'm going to meet them. No other plan really."

"I will keep the girls in the caboose, if that is okay."

"Yes, thank you, Juliette. That would be great. Did either of you tell Victoria and Lacie to tell me about the plate?"

Lank said, "What plate? Oh, the broken thing."

"How about you, Juliette, did you tell them?"

"Ah, that is between me and the girls but no, I did not tell them in so many words."

Lank asked, "Did Lacie break the plate?"

"Yes."

"I thought maybe that was it. Did she do it some time ago?"

"Yes yes, months, I guess. So Juliette, you didn't tell them what to do?"

"No, Archie. I did not know what they should do." Juliette munched on a piece of Lank's oatmeal bread.

"Here they come." Lank opened a window for shooting. "Juls, here, take this." Lank passed her a large handgun. It looked like a leftover from the old West."

"No 'hank you, 'ank. 'ere wi' be p'enty of guns." Her mouth was stuffed with oatmeal bread.

Some of the Curries already reached the bridge on foot when a truck arrived with the rest. The ones from the truck took the lead, walking quickly and purposefully across the bridge.

Archie went out to meet them. He moved slowly, trying to bring the scruffy gang in close to allow Lank a shot. He offered a handshake to each of them but few responded. Archie asked their names. Saying their names seemed difficult for a few of the men who answered. They looked back to the bridge when a police car pulled up. Archie mingled, introducing himself. Another car with two Mounties arrived. Mrs. Mackay had called the police and told them she heard Ray Currie say that they would 'teach them little bitches that ruined our dogs'. Archie glanced up at the ash tree where The Ghost hid from the police. The Curries also saw The Ghost, bristling with armaments.

"Old Elizabeth told you that I was for your welfare as much as our own. Old Elizabeth was right."

"The old woman's dead and good riddance." It was Ray who spoke. He hadn't shaken Archie's hand but he did tell Archie his name. Ray showed a glimmer of intelligence but he was clearly a nasty man. When Archie introduced himself, he looked directly into their eyes. It frightened many of them but not Ray.

Archie felt excited, not afraid. He saw a collection of unfortunate mutts caught between snarling and cowering. He also saw his own dishonesty. Their welfare didn't concern him. He cared only about the people of The Tracks. Most of the Curries were afraid. They looked for the dominant animal to emerge. Archie figured that Ray ran a very poor second place.

"How many of you think good riddance to old Elizabeth? I don't guess she was always easy. She was smart. Most of you aren't smart. None of you are anywhere near being smart like Old Elizabeth. She was smart in a deep way. Old Elizabeth could look into things and she could tell how it would turn out. So this guy here, Ray, has spoken against the old woman. I bet he thinks he's smarter than Old Elizabeth. Ray thinks he's tough enough to handle everything. Ray is dead wrong. Anyone else who thinks Ray is right, just come up front and go with Ray who thinks he's smarter than Old Elizabeth. You come forward and follow Ray because he's going over there to beat up The Ghost. The Ghost is what you see over in the trees. The ghost has all the guns. We call him The Ghost because we never see him until we need him. He's our protector."

"You see where he is in the trees? The cops can't see him from there.

After you're all dead, the cops will think you shot each other. If the shooting starts, there'll be shots from other places, too. You'll never know where the shot came from. Nobody's ever going to find The Ghost. And when you're dead, maybe you'll have to explain to Old Elizabeth, out there in the afterlife, how you fucked this up."

Most of the Curries got upset at the mention of Old Elizabeth in the afterlife. They weren't good at stoically faking indifference.

"So who is ready to go over there and fight The Ghost? Who is ready to so much as raise his hand against me and die for it? The Ghost doesn't have any salt today and no birdshot. It's all buckshot and bullets."

"Ray and Marta killed Old Lizbet."

"Yeah, dem two smoddered da ole woman wid a pillow."

Ray had an eighteen-inch square cut spike and a sickle. He swung wildly at his accusers. They defended themselves with their own crude weapons and their forearms. Ray dropped. He had a hole that went all the way through his thigh. The police revealed later that it was a hard-nosed 303 shell of the type used by Canadian soldiers in the two big wars that marred the first half of the century. Those shells didn't mushroom when they hit the victim. A mushrooming bullet of that weight did a lot of damage; the hard-nosed shell injured but rarely killed. It could go right through an enemy soldier and on to hit another. Injured soldiers were a greater liability to the enemy than dead soldiers on those battlefields. The police found the shell halfway through a baseball bat that one of the Curries carried. He thought that magic or some sort of Old Elizabeth presence ripped the bat out of his hands.

The Ghost disappeared as ghosts generally do when it comes time for inspection and accountability. Archie convinced the authorities that there was no such entity as the Ghost and that the Curries probably got the idea because he had mentioned Old Elizabeth in the afterlife and the ghost of Old Elizabeth. The Mounties were not terribly interested in where the shot came from. The crown attorney said that shooting Ray was self-defense or defense of others because the police had clearly seen Ray trying to bludgeon his brothers with that oversized railway spike. Given the circumstances, the shooting of Ray was not a crime so why bother expending a lot of effort trying to find out who did it.

Old Elizabeth's trust was misplaced. In the end, the Curries didn't count for much. Some of them became institutionalized, two went to prison, one girl went to a mental hospital and several went to Poor Farms. Some of them fell by the wayside and some just fell.

The Mounties said ten of them were at The Tracks that day and twenty-two lived in that house. The roof leaked badly. The Curries and their attachments dispersed as the roof began to collapse.

***

Archie: Of all those men here that day, I didn't see one who had a half decent chance in this world. If I accepted the responsibility that Old Elizabeth would have me take on, it would be no fun at all trying to help them through life. I am nowhere near being that generous. It is much more pleasant to be rid of such a maggoty pack of inbreds.

Juliette: They are, or were, an unfortunate group but it is good to have the lot of them out of our lives.

Archie: The old girl bore up that huge responsibility when she was alive but it killed her.

Victoria: Yeah, and we got stuck with crazy Bert. Like Lank said, the day you broke Bert's ghostly little heart, those kinds of people find each other.

Juliette: I think we absorb some of what they are, because…well, just because they entered our lives, I guess. At the very least, we get their shit on our shoes.

CHAPTER SIXTEEN

In late October nineteen-fifty-seven, the Ghost asked Lank to look for a one-ton truck. He wanted to buy it on credit. Juliette assured Lank that she'd make up his losses if Bert didn't pay. None of the Trackers enjoyed feeling indebted to this strange little man for having shot people.

Lank found a heavy-duty Chevy one-ton with stake pockets on a flatbed. It was only three years old, in good shape, but bashed in on the passenger side. Lank and Juliette fixed it up in two days with a replacement door, a new windshield, and a lot of work with two hydraulic jacks to straighten it. Lank smoothed out the bumps and wrinkles with a hammer and dolly. It got painted a bright red with green lettering that said:

Albert Ballanger

Christmas Trees

Bert worked hard through November and December cutting and hauling balsam fir trees from various locations between Sterling Reserve and Halifax. He got permission to cut from only one of those properties but, for the most part, nobody bothered him. He cut small trees growing wild but, if they grew in a sunny spot, they could be the perfect shape for Christmas trees. Bert sold them from a parking lot in downtown Halifax and did quite well.

A few days before Christmas, Archie arrived at Juliette's parcel car. "What's wrong with Victoria? She seems jumpy or something; have you noticed?"

"Yes, in a way. I think she has been avoiding me. What do you think is wrong?"

"At first, I suspected a secret Christmas gift so I just left it alone but this morning I asked her what was wrong. Her denials looked suspicious."

"Ah yes, it could be Christmas gifts. Lacie also looks a bit shifty."

Archie said, "No, I'm sure it's something serious but I have no idea what."

"I can tell them both that, if there is something wrong, they can feel comfortable in talking to you or me or Lank. Do you think that will suffice?"

"Best we can do, I guess."

There were no secret gifts at Christmas and the girls continued to act strange but less so every day. On the last day of December, Juliette stopped in at Jack Mosher's. She had a gallon of Jack's favorite rum, smuggled from St. Pierre.

"I guess you heard about the late Mr. French."

Juliette said, "No. No, tell me."

"Well, two days after Christmas, Randall French went out the harbour checkin' his traps. Everybody got a good price for lobster around Christmas and everybody was hopin' for a good price at New Year's. That's the last anybody seen Randall. Somebody said his boat just drifted out with the wind but they didn't think much about it because he could've been down below usin' the toilet or somethin'. Any other day, he likely woulda went aground. God knows you got lots of places to go aground in these waters but the wind was blowin' straight out that day. Some other people saw him drift by Harpell Pond and they didn't think much about it, either. Then some fellows from up along Country Harbor were headin' home from fishin' after dark and they heard an engine idlin' but it passed by. They thought enough of it to shut down and listen but they couldn't locate it although one guy said he still heard it. They was four miles out at the time. They hailed it and got nothin' so they continued steamin' home. Nobody seen Randall French since, so he's a goner. Must've had a heart attack or something."

When Juliette got back out to the Monarch, she'd parked in Jack's driveway, snow filled the trunk. Lank bought the car to fix up and sell. He removed the trunk lid so that Juliette could put an engine in there and take it back to The Tracks. Lank wanted to replace the smoking monster V-8. Juliette thought she probably looked like a nineteen-thirties hillbilly heading to California. /*I will have an extra engine sticking out of the trunk coming home/why the hell am I doing this/he should have gotten Bert to pick up the engine with his truck/* She started up the Monarch. A plume of blue smoke came out the tailpipe. Juliette turned the car off and went back in to see Jack.

"Jack, did you see a red one-ton around here after Christmas, a flatbed Chevy with a rack?"

"Yeah, I saw that truck with the Christmas tree sign but the sign was gone that day, the day after Christmas. I saw 'er goin' out t'wards West Jeddore."

"Was that the day before Randall French drifted away?"

"Yep, that's right."

"Did you see it the next day, the day Randall French disappeared?"

"No I didn't see it that day but I wasn't lookin'. What are ya thinkin', Juliette?"

"I am not sure Jack; not anything good. Our talk about the red truck, could you keep it under your hat. Maybe, do not mention to anyone that you saw it."

Juliette didn't go to the Harbour to get the engine; she drove back to The Tracks where she saw Lacie's footprints in the snow heading down towards the Tillman. Juliette followed the tracks and found Lacie sitting on her mittens by the river.

"Where is Victoria?"

"She's home."

"Okay Lacie, we will get her; we are going to have a talk."

Lacie seemed relieved. She held Juliette's hand as they walked up to the caboose.

"Hello Archie, Hello Victoria. Archie and I want to know what's going on with you two."

Victoria said nervously, "What do you mean?" But Lacie opened right up.

"Randall French came to Sterling Reserve before Christmas. He grabbed Vee's hair and said for her to wish you a Merry Christmas because you weren't going to live to see another one after this year. I went to The Ghost because I figured if I went to you about it, you'd go after him and get hurt or something. Bert agreed with that, said I shouldn't tell anybody else and that he would take care of it. He said we shouldn't worry, that Randall French wouldn't bother us again. I told Vee not to tell. She wanted to tell you but I was afraid to. I mean, what you would do and what could happen to you."

"Oh Lacie, you made a bad decision. I can say to you that you can always trust your father and me and Archie but that is up to you to sort out. I wish you had not done this. I know what you tried to accomplish and I understand but it was a bad decision."

"Sorry Juls. Vee wanted to tell you."

Juliette suggested that they all go to the dining car to see Lank.

"The gang's all here."

Juliette said, "Randall French is dead."

Three of them spoke simultaneously. Lank said, "Is that that guy from Head of Jeddore?" Archie said, "What?" Victoria said, "Holy shit." Lacie didn't say anything; she didn't look surprised.

"Were you expecting this, Lacie?"

"I guess, kind of."

Archie picked up Victoria and held her, stroked her hair and said things like, 'It's okay now… Don't worry, it's all right.'

Juliette explained, "No one knows at this time what happened to Mr. French. He may have taken a heart attack; any number of accidents can happen aboard a boat."

Archie said, "Well, what's the plan?"

"Lacie, you did not do anything really wrong, except make a bad decision. Randall French was just a blowhard. He would never kill me. He is a cowardly… he was a cowardly man. However, it is clear that Bert likes to shoot people. I will investigate that further but I do not see any reason why I should tell anybody else what I find. It would be best if no one spoke of this. Did you tell anyone that Randall French accosted Victoria?"

"Just Bert."

"Best to leave it at that, would you think?" They all agreed to assume that Mr. French got his leg caught in a lobster trap line and went overboard or had a heart attack or something.

Juliette went to The Ghost's rail car. He wasn't at home so she opened the locked door of the pickup-truck cab. Juliette was good with locks. She looked for guns. He walked down behind her and asked what she was doing. "I am sniffing, Bert." She picked up a handgun from under a tattered, dirty pillow and sniffed the barrel.

"Ya shoulda asked to come in before you go nosing around somebody's house." Juliette did not respond. She ran her hand along the gap at the top of the makeshift wall covering the cold steel of the car. She felt the leather case and pulled it out from behind the wall. The case contained a long-barreled Mauser with a scope. She smelled the barrel but couldn't detect any recent firing.

"I clean my guns after I use them."

"Did you shoot Randall French?"

"Yeah, I did. I did it to save your life."

"Fuck off, Bert. You did it because you like to shoot people. He is dead, you know."

"I know. I got him in the head. It only takes one shot from that sniper rifle. I got him in the head. I was hopin' he'd just blow out to sea in his boat. I guess that didn't happen, eh?"

"He did blow out to sea but people saw your truck out at West Jeddore the day before he went missing. Bert, just get in your truck and get out of here. If he is ever found, and it is my experience that fishing boats out on the sea with nobody alive aboard, stay afloat for a long time. A body with a hole in its head will get the interest of various authorities. There would be an investigation and the best strategy for the guilty party is to not be around for an investigation."

Bert sat on the bottom stair. He braced himself on the stair above him and held the other hand to his chest. Head raised, chin stuck out, Bert said, "I ain't scared."

"Oh, for fuck sake. Look, you little shit; I am scared, scared for your next victim and scared for the girls. Lacie went to you for help because you shoot people. None of us here want Lacie to think like that. You are not welcome here. We do not want a killer in our midst. Do you understand? "

"I was just tryin' to help out but I guess maybe I helped the wrong person. I guess I thought you'd be thankful. I guess I didn't know you very well." Bert's pose fell apart.

"You have money; you have your truck, so please go. If you need more money I can give you whatever you need. You can be certain of this, Bert. I do not appreciate you killing someone on my behalf or on behalf of Victoria. We can take care of ourselves. When a person finds it easy to shoot people, they will see opportunities to do so. It is rarely necessary to kill someone. It is the wrong thing to do. Randall French would never have killed me. He was not that sort of person. He was just a bigmouth bully. I warned him not to bother us and I had a plan of action if he did. I step too easily into violence and I consider that violence a sign of some kind of cowardice within me. You, Bert, you were glad to get the opportunity to skulk along the shore and put a bullet hole from a sniper rifle in a man's head. I prefer that you moved far away. I prefer that you do it very soon. Today would be great."

The Ghost stammered and appeared to be trembling as Juliette stepped around him to climb the stairs out of his car. The fresh air and the sweet innocence of new snow flushed through her. /we should burn that fucking old car/Custard and The Ghost/fuck a duck/

They waited for Juliette in the dining car. "I spoke to Bert. He is leaving soon, I expect. Does anyone need to know more than that?"

"I certainly don't want to know any more, Juliette."

Lank said, "I'm fine, Juls. And you girls should not talk about what you do know about it and please don't inquire about anything else having to do with Randall French."

"I know I did the wrong thing. Now, I wish I told you about it. I guess I kind of knew that The Ghost would do something far-fetched. Maybe I even thought he would kill the guy. I was sure of myself at the time but not now. Sometimes I just don't know what to do."

"That's a part of growing up." From where he sat in one of the dining chairs, Archie pulled Lacie toward him for a close-up hug.

Lank said, "It's a part of living, hon. Most of the time, most of us don't know what to do."

"Amen to that." Seeing Lacie and Archie holding on to each other in grand comfort and affection brought a sweet gratitude to Juliette. She felt a little unhinged. "Lacie, it is not your fault that Randall French got killed. Wait now…just a second; I am trying to get this right. He appeared to be mean and nasty but Bert had no right, no reason to kill him. This is not a simple mistake on your part. You made a very consequential error. I do not want you to feel worse than you do already, love, but… I am getting this all wrong. Somebody help."

Archie said, "I don't know if Lacie did do the wrong thing. The guy apparently grabbed Victoria by the hair and threatened to kill her mother within a year. Is that about how it went, dear?"

"Yes, he said Mom wouldn't make it till next Christmas."

"I feel like I'd want to kill him, too. He also assaulted Jack Mosher, didn't he?"

Juliette said, "Yes, but that was not serious and I suspect that my response at that time also amounted to a bad decision. I thought a show of dominant force would make a man like him back off but instead he visited my family. I fucked that up."

Archie asked, "In what way did that dominant force manifest itself?"

Lacie said, "Juls stuck her knife right under his eye."

Juliette said, "I did not realize anyone but Jack saw that. I am more to blame than anybody. You suffered a bad example, Lacie. I am sorry."

They sat around in the dining car, more or less in a circle. Lank suddenly stood up. The tall man became a commanding presence in the morose gathering. "No sense blaming ourselves or blaming each other. These are two violent men. They always find each other; those kinds of people always find each other and they go too far. French and The Ghost both went too far so one of 'em's dead. Whether or not he died at the hands of The Ghost don't really matter much. Who the hell's gonna miss the fucker?"

Juliette said, "Good point. Apparently his wife left him because he beat her up too much. They had no children. I am pretty sure The Ghost will be gone this time tomorrow night, another sad case. He said he did it for me. I suppose he did."

Archie said, "I hope you two girls realize that we don't have this sorted out. Just because something is important, in this case vitally important, that doesn't mean we have answers. I suppose there are always more questions than answers. You're both too smart for us to make rules when we don't even know what we're talking about."

Lank said, "I think we're done. Let's get on with it."

"Sure. Yes, all right, girls?"

Lacie nodded her head and Victoria said, "Yes Archie. Lacie and I are okay."

Lacie asked, "What do we do now?"

"It is New Year's Eve and I have treats in the parcel car for you two lovely ladies. We could cuddle up on the couch and watch a movie."

"Watch a movie?!" Victoria sprung up from her slouch against Lacie and Archie.

"Sister Jeanne d'Arc loaned the school's movie projector to us for the holidays. I also borrowed a gasoline electric generator from Jimmy Fox. We have three films from the National Film Board; one of them is strictly for girls. Maybe you boys can watch the other films with us tomorrow."

Archie said, "I'll call Cliff and tell him we won't get to his New Year's Eve party. A visit to The Grumpy's, oh joy." The Grumpy's lived just across the river from The Tracks. The Trackers used their phone and paid them for it but The Grumpy's and the house they lived in were dirty, stinky and unpleasant.

The girls watched the film with Juliette. It was good but only a half an hour long so they watched it three times. In the morning, Juliette woke to the sound of Bert's truck rattling across the bridge to Sterling Reserve. The Ghost's footprints led to her door. New snow falling in the windless morning painted The Tracks into a Christmas card. Juliette opened the door to her front step. The faint sound of Bert's truck faded on the road out of Sterling Reserve. The arm on her Something or Nothing box was turned up to Something. Barefoot, on her snow-covered doorstep, she picked the note out of the Something or Nothing box. Back in her warm car, the early morning chatter of the girls came from the little bedroom. The note said, 'Dear Juliette   I tried to do something good for you but you just do not understand. I did it because of love. Albert Balanger.'

Juliette mumbled "stupid little fucker" as she threw the note in the stove.

***

Archie arrived at Juliette's car in time for breakfast. "Cliff was sorry to hear that we couldn't come to his party. I told him we had a little trouble with the girls; I said it wasn't serious. Cliff said that if he could be of help with anything to just give him a call. What do you think?"

"Yes, perhaps that would be a good thing. I will call him in a few days."

"He's going to the Lieutenant Governor's levy tomorrow and I wouldn't mind going to that. You could get the ball rolling tomorrow."

Cliff, Archie, and Juliette listened to Lieutenant Governor Fraser's speech and then mingled about in the crowd. Cliff knew everyone and he introduced Archie and Juliette to the Lieutenant Governor who seemed quite taken with Juliette. However, they got in an argument about the value of the Canso Causeway, the new land link between the mainland of Nova Scotia and Cape Breton Island. Fraser thought the causeway was the best thing since the Garden of Eden but Juliette argued that it would bring porcupines, skunks and other mainlanders to Cape Breton. She was only half-kidding. She strolled the gardens around Government House with Cliff and outlined the Randall French incidents. He told Juliette not to worry but they set up a meeting at his office for a few days later.

When Juliette got back to The Tracks, Victoria said, "Mom, The Grumpys said you got a call from Granddaddy and he wants you to call right back."

"Hello, Jimmy. Is there anything wrong?"

"Wrong or right the doctor says mother is dying but I'll believe it when she's gone. He says she's got a liver problem but Jesus, you and me drink more in one night than she ever drank.

"A lot of things can happen to the liver that do not involve alcohol."

"Yes, I suppose but she don't seem that sick."

"I guess I should come and see her."

"I think you should, dear. I'd appreciate it even if she don't." Juliette cancelled her appointment with Cliff and headed to Cape Breton. Jimmy picked up his daughter at the Sydney airport the next afternoon. "Mother's not looking good today. I guess Doctor Erickson is right. She looks like a dyin' woman today."

A hired nurse sat downstairs eating pie and drinking tea. Upstairs Isobel lay in her bed. "Juliette. I'm glad...to see you." Isobel spoke in short bursts, inhaled a noisy breath and spoke again. "Will you fire that... that lazy bitch...that MacPhee girl? Put a thing like ...like that in a ...nurse's uniform and she'll...she'll sit on her arse...and do nothin' all day."

Juliette said, "She is not doing nothing. She is eating pie."

Isobel hacked out a laugh. "That old apple pie... I made that...four days ago...before I got sick... Too lazy to...to put some jam on a piece of bread. Juliette, my girl... I wet the bed...hours ago. I told her... She don't care."

Juliette pulled down the covers. Some of the urine had already dried. "Grandmother, I will get you and the bed changed, then fire her."

Isobel nodded her head slowly. She put her thin yellowed hand on Juliette's arm and whispered, "Juliette... Good."

Juliette politely dismissed the lazy nurse and made tea for Isobel. "I have biscuits baking but you probably did not have tea for some time."

"Not since this morning. Just because I'm dying...they needn't deny me...my tea. Would you cook something...for your father?"

"I have potatoes on and I will fry up some pork chops. Would you like a meal for yourself?"

"No, dear...the smell of food...would do me. Ah but I... I'll have a biscuit...with butter and jam."

"In about six minutes."

Downstairs, Juliette slid biscuits out of the oven of Isobel's new electric stove. "Did Doctor Erickson tell Grandmother she was dying?" she asked as she tended to the boiling potatoes.

"That's damn unlikely. He's afraid to tell her anything. Why?"

"She said, 'Just because I am dying there is no need to deny me my tea but perhaps she was just kidding." Juliette later recalled to Cliff, "The old girl savored that biscuit with butter and jam and the cup of tea just like it was her last. She enjoyed that last bit of life."

Isobel sat propped up by two pillows with the biscuit plate resting on her chest. Juliette brought the fancy gray and red tea cup to her lips. She drank her second cup of tea after a day of forced abstinence. "Juliette, you have to take care of everything. I left it all up to you because, well, because you can." She spoke clearly in complete sentences. "I'm glad you're here to see me off. You got more guts than ten men from the Bay. You make good biscuits, too. They tasted like heaven just hot from bakin'."

"You know you are dying?"

"Willy Erickson couldn't keep a thing like that from me. I knew it before he did. Willie's just a little fruit, anyway. Ah, your smile, dear, why don't you smile for me?"

Juliette thought a forced smile at such a time would be a miserable experience. But the smile came easily and she could feel meaning coming from her face and much more affection than she thought she had for her crotchety old grandmother. Isobel closed her eyes and licked butter and jam from her fingers.

Juliette went downstairs, took the potatoes off the stove and put the pork chops on low heat in a covered pan with a little water, oregano and onion slices. She went back upstairs to sit with Isobel who slept, breathing loudly through a wide-open mouth. Juliette didn't know when the breathing stopped; she just noticed it wasn't there anymore.

"Father Jimmy, are you ready for supper?"

"I'm starved, Juliette."

They talked about fishing and boats while they ate pork chops. Jimmy praised the food as only a person who can't cook praises someone else's cooking, a supplicant at the feet of a saint. They were drinking their tea when Juliette said, "Would you like rum?"

"Yeah, sure thing. Should you check on Mother?"

"She died half an hour ago."

"Oh. I'll get the rum."

Son and grandaughter sat at the kitchen table with rum in front of them and a quart of beer between them. "Jesus, I should call Erickson, I guess."

"Yes, he should pronounce her dead. She said he is a fruit."

"He's got his ways; that he has."

Juliette expected Isobel to have her Glace Bay lawyer write the will but she hired a lawyer from a Halifax firm. She hadn't named a proctor so Juliette transferred probate to Cliff. Isobel named Juliette as executrix and a beneficiary. Juliette also held the house property and the one-quarter of Cameron Fisheries in trust for Jimmy. Isobel had owned half and Jimmy owned the other half of the company. Isobel gave half of her share to Juliette out-right and half to Juliette in trust for Jimmy. A letter for Juliette accompanied the will. It said among other things, "I want to save James from gold diggers like your friend, Karen Rudderham. Your father doesn't have much sense where his dick is involved."

**

Cliff agreed with Juliette's handling of The Ghost. He said a small chance existed that somebody might try to make something of a case for accessory after the fact, if it was a fact that Bert murdered Mr. French but Cliff would get her a good criminal lawyer. It wouldn't even get to preliminary inquiry. Juliette knew that idle boasting was not part of Cliff 's behavioral repertoire. She placed a large folder on his desk which contained Isobel's will, deeds and incorporation documents, as well as other documents she thought might be relevant. "Cliff, I would appreciate you sorting this out for me and tell me what I have to do. I am in no rush if the law is not in a rush."

"Who is Isobel Cameron?"

"She was my grandmother, my father's mother."

"Oh yes, old Isobel."

***

In those days Juliette had one female confidant, Sister Jeanne d'Arc. Juliette called her Neala, her name before she joined the Sisters of Charity. "Neala, you should get used to the name. I expect that you will leave the convent in the next few years." They spoke openly about many things and Juliette began to question why she had kept herself so insulated. The area of 'my own business' had wide meaning for Juliette but her talks with Neala caused her to re-examine her poker-player reserve. In her teens, she figured out what to tell and what not to tell and then went on automatic. After revealing to Neala so many things that she'd kept as her own secrets, the useful borders of privacy blurred. It involved making more day-to-day decisions when she spoke with people but Juliette felt a release in opening up.

Neala removed her cap and veil. Juliette took that as an invitation to go around the Sister Superior's little desk to at least play with Neala's hair. "No, Juliette, you stay there. I like having a desk between us. You make me too fluffy when you're close."

"You take your cap off like a stripper."

"You don't get enough man loving. You're too horny. What about Cliff? He's made it clear that he wants you."

"I find Cliff… marginally attractive, I suppose. He said he would be patient. Perhaps the lack of urgency makes him not my type."

"Following your type never worked. Certainly you got sex but really not much else. A woman in her thirties needs a regular man for sex and friendship. I don't know Cliff very well but he seems like a great guy, a sexy guy. I wouldn't mind having his shoes under my bed, if I wasn't a nun."

***

Juliette made the phone call from the post office. The discreet postmistress, Jane Christie, ducked into the back room when people made calls. "Could I speak to Cliff, please?"

"Mr. McLellan is with a client. Could I take a message, please?"

"It is Juliette Cameron. I will have to call back. I am using someone else's phone."

"Just a moment, Miss Cameron, I'll see if he can talk to you."

"Hi Juliette, can you wait a minute? I'll excuse myself and take your call in another room."

"No need, Cliff, it is just one question which needs only a yes or no and we can sort out the details later. Would you like to spend the weekend together?"

"Yes, oh yes."

"Shall I call you at home tonight?"

"Yes, or I could pick you up in two hours and the details will follow."

"As Victoria would say, 'splendid.'"

"I will see you at six."

"Bye"

Cliff arrived at the parcel car with lots of tentative plans and alternate plans for a weekend beginning on a Thursday evening but Juliette suggested that they get to sex first thing.

Juliette was relaxed about initial sexual encounters; she had been through a lot of them and she had confidence in her own desirability, despite a night two months before her date with Cliff. She found a college boy in downtown Halifax. They were drunk when they sneaked back to his room at Kings College. His roommate got out of the room and Juliette took off her clothes.

"Jesus, you're skinny. Your tits are so small." She got dressed and left the room. The college boy followed her down the hall. "Look, nobody's perfect. I'm sorry, come back. You look great. I don't know why I said that. I'm sorry."

"You should stop talking and go back to your room or your friends will know you did not fuck me."

She saw the half-second of consideration he gave this before he whispered, "Good night".

Cliff didn't have wide interests but he enjoyed life. He listened to light classical music, pop music, and two jazz singers, Rosemary Clooney and Nat King Cole. Cliff read Shakespeare's plays and often went to see Shakespearean productions but that was it for literature. He read nonfiction related to his work and little else. His secretaries had a standing task each week to get two or three newspaper clippings which might be good icebreakers for clients. Otherwise, he avoided newspapers, television and radio except the classical music stations. Cliff was a satisfied man.

Cliff delighted in clever conversation. Irony, good puns, and playing with language and meaning caused, in his eyes, what Juliette referred to as a twiggle. She had never used that word to describe anyone else's ocular reaction. When she saw it in Cliff, she could feel something within herself that was a kind of twiggle.

They made love in Juliette's bedroom. She often set the agenda in lovemaking but not with Cliff. His relaxed pace and complete lack of hurry made having sex more of an indulgence than an event. At ten o'clock, they got to dinner, which they cooked together. They talked through what they expected from each other. Both liked their lives as single people and planned to stay single. Juliette would probably have more other men in her life than Cliff would have women. They asked only that they make efforts to not share in unpleasantries like gonorrhea or jealous lovers.

Cliff felt okay that Juliette didn't have a phone and therefore, she would be the one to initiate most contacts. "I would probably ruin the whole thing by calling too much and eventually begging for your hand in marriage and we both know that a boy should be able to get on with his own hand."

Juliette said, "I speak more frankly and openly with several people of late. Perhaps you should set the boundaries on where my new blabbermoutheism should end and your privacy begin."

"Well, I wouldn't want the specifics of our sex being discussed."

"Okay."

"Ah no. Hell, I don't care. Well, if we get into anything weird, run it by me again. Also, if I ever discuss anything about my clients which is unlikely, that should never get out."

"Okay, good. We can talk about the anything weird later. It sounds like fun."

But they never got to the weird. Their love affair, which is what they both called it, was characterized by comfort. It lacked challenges. They acknowledged that and they both liked it. Cliff ran a solo law practice with three support staff. He focused on corporate and commercial law and his few clients paid him well. He charged at least as much as the senior partners in the big law firms but his clients liked him better and, in most cases, he was better. Cliff emphasized that one business fighting with another business rarely amounted to a good idea. It tends to take away your choice of who you can deal with in the future. He became known as a lawyer who did not fan the flames and he thought it silly to go to court unless he knew he would win. Two of his best corporate clients went with Cliff after their previous lawyers told them they would win. But Cliff beat them. The justices of the Supreme Court of Nova Scotia also liked Cliff because he kept a lot of things out of the courtroom. When they did hear one of his cases, he presented no bullshit and few motions. Cliff allowed opposing lawyers to go through all the play-acting and posturing for their clients' entertainment but he remained straightforward. A judge nicknamed him 'Clarity Cliff'. The name stuck.

Cliff and Juliette considered each other admirable. "Acceptance of your limitations as a mother and accepting that someone else does a better job raising your child is an act of love that very few women could make. Most parents are near psychosis in their belief that they are doing the best for their children, women especially. They can be all wrong, completely selfish, and stupid but they believe motherhood has sainted them."

"My kind man, being aware of one's failures is sometimes a triumph but failure is failure."

"Right enough. My point remains that you've done way better than the vast majority of mothers."

Juliette said, "I hope it is not us who are psychotic about Archie being a stellar guy."

"Be careful with that word. On Thursday, Victoria called it a stellar afternoon."

Juliette laughed, "Only my beautiful daughter would come up with such a superlative, hyperbolic malapropism."

"Hey, you're not doing badly yourself." The comment got him a light punch on the shoulder and an embarrassed smile.

"You know, she believes you like her better than Lacie."

"Speak clearly, woman. Do I like her better than Lacie likes her or do I like her more than I like Lacie?"

"The latter."

"And what was the question?"

"Fuck off, you evasive prick."

"Well, my sweet, some questions do not need answering. An answer to a question can sometimes solidify what should remain liquid."

"You are a smart cookie, Clifford. It is lucky for the world that you are a good man."

"But didn't I just hear someone call me a prick?"

Juliette spoke softly, looking at her lap, "Restraint, in your hands, has a sweet smell. Your restraint is nourishing."

CHAPTER SEVENTEEN

"It's too dirty to work on a Buick." Lank stared out at light rain bouncing off the hood of Gary Webber's six-year-old Roadmaster. Gary bought it cheap because the transmission broke. Lank didn't have much experience with automatics and none with General Motors automatics but he believed that mechanical things made sense. Even badly designed or badly built machines followed some logic, an inevitability. He had the Buick up on blocks, railway ties under the axles. Lank towed the monster Roadmaster a mile and a half with his little Hillman Minx in low gear all the way. Getting it to The Tracks without burning out the little car's clutch surprised him. City steered the Buick. Lank wanted to celebrate the journey from downtown Sterling Reserve to The Tracks with a drink but City drove him crazy.

City challenged Lank's patience. He recounted the ride in the Buick like a combat mission. The mission climaxed on the Tillman River railroad bridge. "When we was comin' over the bridge an' you was slowin' up a tad, 'member?"

"Yes, City I remember."

"Well the Buick was goin' at a good clip an' she's heavy. Boy, she's a heavy car. Must weigh a ton, eh Lank, eh?"

"Yes City, I guess the Buick weighs more than a ton."

"More than a ton. My Lord, yes, more than a ton and I was headin' for the back bumper of the little car at a good clip, you know. Had to put on the brakes fast, I tell you Mister, or I woulda' run right into ya."

"Well, thanks for doing that City; I'm sure we all would've died."

"Ya think? Ah no. You're makin' fun 'a me, ain't ya?"

Lank hesitated, "No, just kiddin' City, just kiddin."

 But he did make fun of City. He got so bored and annoyed with him that unkind things just slipped out of his mouth like his brain was specially lubricated for jabs at the defenseless City. Lank knew better but he made the same old mistake. He'd feel sorry and spend hours with the man to make up for some small slight. Lank explained this to Juliette who could tell you things about people.

"Yes, Lank, I often think City is not as dumb as he looks. We know that his present goal in life is someone to talk to. He feels blessed because he can afford to live here at The Tracks and he thinks that you and Archie and I are brain gods. Mark at the White Rose Station told me that City brags about talking to us, particularly Archie, it seems. He told them he talks about communism and the atmosphere and 'ball o gee'. Perhaps City sets us up to slight him so we will give him a few drinks and grace him with our presence. Am I being incredibly mean?" Lank accepted, as a valid conclusion, what Juliette offered as speculation.

The Hillman and the Buick still roped together and the black flies biting, City ruthlessly inflicted the dull pain of boredom. Lank just wanted to have a drink and get to work. He knew City wouldn't hang around if a risk of real work threatened.

"Well, City, I gotta get the Roadmaster up on blocks and that's going to take hours of jacking her up, wheel by wheel, and shinnin' and pryin."

"Ah, yeah, well Lank, I wish I could help but I gotta be goin."

"That's all right, man. It's dirty work. Thanks a lot for drivin."

"Yes, bye, it was quite a drive, I tell ya, with that…"

"Yeah, could you pull up on the bumper to get some weight off the springs?"

"Look, I gotta go, Lank. Glad to help ya there, eh, like with the drivin'."

Lank took out the jack. City waddled off to his boxcar to hide from work for the rest of the day. Amidst the black flies, Lank got under the car to properly place the jack. He didn't feel bad about City. They had guilt reduction in the works. He and Juliette and Archie made a plan to cut a hole in City's dismal boxcar. They expected to get it done in two hours, leaving a brand-new window behind to bring some light to the poor man's life.

In twenty minutes, he blocked up the Buick on railway ties. It wasn't nearly as difficult as he led City to believe. Lank didn't want to start work on the transmission. He wanted a drink. Juliette provided him with her homebrewed beer and moonshine. Juliette would go without, rather than see him drink stuff that would make him sick. He did things for her but could never fully repay. His life and Lacie's life improved because that continuing act of kindness saved him from the desperate urgency of running out of liquor. A few drops of rain came out of a darkening sky. It was June and the tiny black flies seized possession of The Tracks. They became particularly obnoxious with a little moisture in the air. He did want to get the Buick fixed and he did want to avoid attracting City to the dining car; however, he got out of the black flies and into the beer.

***

"It's too dirty to work on a Buick."

"What's that?"

"Oh Lacie, hi, I didn't know you were home. How was your day in the education factory?"

"Good, nice actually. I saw you working on that big car but you were busy cursing so I didn't want to disturb you."

Lank laughed and squeezed her wrist with his thumb and little finger. "I'm all dirty and greasy. But, you know that one smile from you can blow away any anger and frustration like a hurricane blowing out a match."

"Jeez, Daddy, that is so sweet. I just wasn't dressed for rain and I wanted to get inside. God, it's really starting now. Listen. Those drops are like hard knuckles rapping on the roof."

Lank got a beer, which meant a quart of beer because Juliette bottled it in quarts. "Holy Lord, it's pouring. Vee is out there in the rain! It's thunder and lightning like blazes."

"Where is she, Daddy?"

"Just out front, in the rain."

Lacie put on her boots, her yellow raincoat and a cap. Victoria wore no cap or raincoat. Her hair and face were drenched. "What are you doing, Vee?"

"Lacie."

She saw that it wasn't just rain on Vee's face; she cried. "Are you scared? Did you have a fight with Archie?" A flash brightened up the dull afternoon sky. A loud thunderclap made Lacie jump.

"No Lacie. It's alright. I just like it so much. It makes me cry."

"Like what?"

"The thunder, lightning, the rain, I like it so much."

Another flash and a tremendous crack came together, no brooding roar but a crack loud enough, to Lacie's ears, to split everything just by the size of the sound. "Vee, let's go in. It's bad out."

"Why?"

"We could get struck."

"I'm staying out."

"Me too, then." Another crisp flash and bang rattled Lacie and made Vee look enraptured. This was new to Lacie. She never saw it in anybody and never suspected anything like this lay inside her often times affected friend. Another flash and a loud rumble overflowed with power but without the immediacy of the crack that shook Lacie a few seconds earlier.

The big heavy raindrops changed to a normal rain. In a minute, it got warmer and the wind flattened out. Vee looked spent or fulfilled. Lacie didn't understand but she was glad for Vee. Vee had this thing and Lacie was glad. Vee walked toward the dining car without saying anything. Lacie caught up with her. She looked normal. "Can I dry off in your car?"

"Yup."

***

Lank made hot apple juice and honey for them. Victoria's jacket hadn't kept her dry so Lank got her to take her clothes off, toweled her dry and wrapped her in a flannelette sheet. He wrapped a thin towel around her head as a turban. Vee wore it like a princess. He said to her, "Beautiful thunderstorm wasn't it?" She looked at him, nodded and sipped the hot drink.

"I didn't like it." Lacie knew it was the wrong thing to say but there, she said it.

Lank said, "Most people don't like thunder."

"I'm not most people."

"Of course, honey, I know."

"I'm sorry, Daddy. I know what you mean."

"Okay sweetie, okay."

Vee's electrification from the thunderstorm wore off and she settled back to her old self, a little too gabby but good company. At first, Lacie was glad, partly just to have her friend back acting like she expected. Vee standing in the rain, brave as anything in some kind of other, some kind of knowledge, made Lacie uneasy. Did she want her friend to be like that? But, as Vee came back around to her normal manner, that disappointed Lacie, too. Vee started to talk about the thunder, how loud it was and the brightness of the flashes. "… weren't they, Lacie, really bright." Lacie didn't want Vee to brag about it and get all frivvy and showy.

Lank must have felt the same as Lacie. He said, "Listen Vee, honey. I saw you out in the rain and you found something… something special. It's yours alone. You keep that. It's yours alone. You can't explain that kind of thing to other people."

"Hope I don't catch cold. This is nice." Victoria raised her mug of hot juice a few inches, smiled a little smile and took a little sip. "Thanks."

***

Two weeks later, Archie mounted an anemometer on the caboose roof, twelve feet above the cupola. He mounted the readout in the cupola along with a short wave radio. Victoria started keeping weather records. She didn't take observations at standard times but she always got two a day and, if the weather became interesting, she might fill a scribbler page with one day's observations. Archie bought her a rain gauge and Juliette bought her a wind direction indicator which also had a readout in the cupola. Lank, the best scrounger of the bunch, found a hydrometer and a barometer in a junk shop and bought them for Victoria. She didn't jump at learning to use these instruments but got to them gradually, on her own time. The weather was her interest. She didn't talk a lot about it and didn't make a big thing of it. Listening to forecasts on the short wave and recording her observations took her about fifteen minutes each time. She spent most of that time looking out the cupola windows, sometimes checking a book on clouds or looking back at past records. Afterwards she might say to Archie, "Fine day tomorrow." or "Rain comin' overnight or by noon at least." Archie found her to be slightly more accurate than the radio forecasts which covered a wide area but he also saw that she continually improved her local knowledge. Archie talked about Victoria as the weather girl much more than she did.

Vee told Lacie to take a raincoat on a sunny Monday morning. The kids at school poked fun at them for carrying a raincoat on a sunny day but it's a powerful thing to see a school full of kids, at dismissal time, yelping and running and trying not to get soaked except for two girls who calmly put on their raincoats.

The two of them walked to school together every day and they usually walked home together. Lacie often went with Vee to the cupola during weather observations. You could see far in all directions. Lacie didn't like the way her friend looked when she did the weather stuff but she didn't say anything because Vee never looked like that in school as far as Lacie knew. Vee held her lips together loosely and blew air to the front of her mouth creating a bulge in front of her teeth. She'd occasionally let the bubble pop with a little pissht that Lacie could hardly hear. Vee looked stupid when she did that but Lacie let it go. Her friend wasn't thinking of herself when she did the weather, she wasn't thinking of Lacie either. She wasn't thinking of anybody. If Lacie spoke during the weather time, it took a minute or two for Vee to respond with "Whadja say?"

Gary Webber got a chance for a job in Ontario before Lank had the Buick fixed. He asked Lank to buy the car for a hundred and seventy-five dollars. Lank beat him down to ninety dollars and Gary took the train to his new job. Lank worked dawn till dark to repair the Buick. Juliette was in Halifax during the week when this transpired.

Juliette often made excursions to Halifax to see Cliff and get some work done on Isobel's estate, the trust, and selling fish. Selling became lucrative. Cameron Fisheries, like most other fish plants in Nova Scotia, had regular markets in New England and the Caribbean. Juliette and Jimmy sought out new markets. Sometimes it took a lot of work but, when they got a good one going, they made much more money than simply shipping fish to New York or shipping salt fish to Jamaica. Jimmy and Juliette brokered fish for other plants, particularly a select few Newfoundland outfits. They paid premium prices for top quality, very fresh fish and shellfish at the Gander airport, ready to be packed on a chartered plane going to Europe. It was tricky at first but, after some expensive losses, they learned how to do it well.

Juliette also took trips to Halifax in order to get drunker than she got at The Tracks and to fuck around a bit.

Lank got word to Juliette that he'd pick her up. He worked feverishly on the Roadmaster. He replaced the transmission and fixed, cleaned, and polished everything else. When Lank arrived to pick her up, the light blue, two-door hardtop gleamed.

"My soul, Lank, what a car. Who owns this boat?"

"She's got a hundred and seventy-five horsepower fireball engine. Quiet as a moonbeam." Lank wore an exceedingly wide grin.

Juliette chuckled, "That is mighty quiet."

"She cost over four thousand dollars new." Juliette looked at the car and ran her hand along the fake portholes on the front fender.

"Ooo, maybe I should not be touching."

"You'll have to touch it. She's yours." His voice trembled. "I was gonna fix it up for Gary Webber but he left for a new job so he sold it to me and I had him sign the registration over to you and then I fixed her up perfect for you. You're probably the reason Lacie's still got a father. I'd be dead from that old swill I used to drink."

"How are you getting home, Lank?"

"Huh?"

"Hell, I'm not going to let just anybody ride in my Buick."

"Oh yeah. You move up in the world and your old friends get left behind. Do you like her?"

"Oh yes, Lank. It is a beauty. Thank you so much, Lank. Only you would do this. You are such a wonder." Juliette hugged and kissed him which required tiptoes for her and bending down for him.

"Have the girls gone for a ride yet?"

"I took her out for the first time today. Nobody knows it's yours. Nobody knows I bought her."

"It must have cost a small fortune."

"I could afford what I paid. It was mostly work. I put everything into it this week. I kept thinkin' of all you did for me."

"Are you saying you did not get drunk all week?"

"I had some drinks but didn't get nowhere near drunk all week."

"You did that so you could wrap this beautiful gift for me?"

Lank could not speak. He was overwhelmed. Juliette snuggled against his side, her arm around his waist; Lank's arm went over her shoulder. They stood looking at the Roadmaster. Juliette's head nestled against Lank's shoulder. He was so tall but he felt insubstantial, like spider legs. Juliette didn't kill spiders but she didn't want them in her parcel car. Their legs were so delicate. She carried the spiders outside so carefully to avoid breaking off one of their legs. She felt that squeezing Lank tightly might break him. Juliette leaned down to look along the side of the car. "It is so swoopy but very substantial."

"She's a beauty. Even the ostentation is somehow endearing."

Juliette said, "Yes, you are right. It does not say conspicuous consumption the way that a Cadillac or Rolls-Royce does." She turned to face him, hugged him tightly and held on, squeezing despite Lank's spideriness. "You have an erection; how sweet. You need a girlfriend. It will not be me. We are too good at being friends to fuck it up, literally."

"I know, I know. Don't shit where you eat, right?"

"Right, but I hate that expression." Juliette took him by the wrists and leaned back in a crotch-to-crotch position which was more like her belly against Lank's hard on, given the difference in their height and his cock being quite stuck up. "I am a tease. Some of that is just the way it is but some of it is intentional. Do you object? I feel a pleasurable discomfort to get horny and not get satisfied."

"You're a tease all right but nothin' wrong with that, and you're right, we shouldn't be lovers. I'd fall in love with you. I'd just act ridiculous."

"It is still the fattest part of you. It is a nice penis you carry around."

Lank swallowed hard.

"Okay. Shall we drive?" They did drive. Juliette remarked on how she always loved the sound of those Buick straight eights. Lank said he knew that; heard her say that once or twice. She looked at him, took his hand and said, "It is a fine love between us."

"It's a fine line between us."

They drove to Spring Garden Road to pick up a gallon of good olive oil and a big jar of salty black olives from a little Greek store on the corner and then to Queen Street for rice noodles and spicy sauces in jars with no English writing on them and some stinky little dried fishes in a bag. They bought an Elvis Presley record for Victoria and the latest Daphne Du Maurier book for Archie. At a pawnshop, they got a non-working transistor radio. Lank spotted the problem with the Raytheon radio and he had the battery leads fixed before they reached the Midtown Tavern. They ate porkchops and cabbage and drank lots of beer. Driving out of Halifax, Lank said, "Who did we get the transistor radio for?"

"Gee, Lacie I guess. Does this car have a bathroom? Draft beer leaves me quicker than I can drink it."

"Stop at the gas station on St. Margaret's Bay Road. I'll need to pee by then too. Are you too drunk for driving?"

"Sure."

"You got money left?"

"Yes. I guess. Look in my sachel."

"How's the gas situation?"

Juliette looked at the dashboard and then tapped the gas gauge. "Does it work?"

"I'm afraid so. Are we empty?"

"Yes."

"Happens a lot with a car like this. Maybe give the radio to Lacie and Vee both. All Vee got was a record."

Juliette said, "Jesus, why is it that everyone gives Victoria so much slack. She will get a gift and a half and Lacie will get half a gift."

"Lacie will understand."

"Fucking right she will. Lacie will understand perfectly that the spoiled little princess gets more because she will whine if she gets anything less than more. Fuck, I hate gifts. They are too complicated."

"Do you hate getting the Roadmaster?"

"A Buick is a different thing; oh piss off, I know what you mean. Is it easier to receive than to give?" But she lied. A Buick was not different. It wasn't easier to receive. Juliette felt the dance of gifting reach an uncomfortable pace as soon as she saw the Buick. Lank had carefully arranged to pick her up; this cue and that clue and the rate of Lank's head bobbing told her it was a gift. But the necessity of surprise remained.

Cliff avoided gifts. If someone could spy on them together, the voyeur would think Juliette and Cliff disliked each other. They acted a little rude, insensitive. Juliette wanted a convenient bed partner and friend in Cliff. He realized that he could succumb to a 'for better or worse' relationship but Juliette would chafe against it. So would he. They shared more of themselves than most long-term married couples do but they worked at keeping their distance. They worked at staying free of each other.

Juliette said, "Anyway we should give the radio to Lacie. Victoria has electricity and Archie's radio and her short wave."

"Okay, but she won't like it."

"Let her pretend she does, although she will not do that either, will she?"

"Nope, not a bit of it. You know, she went through a thing last week. Vee stood out in a super boom-boom lightening storm. She was transfixed, ecstatic, in a rapture. She never mentioned it since."

Juliette didn't speak for minutes. She pulled the big Buick up to a liquor store a few minutes before closing time. "What does that mean, do you think, Lank? About the thunderstorm."

"Don't know. It's good, I'm sure but I don't know what it means. Never happened to me."

Juliette came out of the liquor store with a large bottle of Black Diamond rum and a case of Molson in quarts.

"You have any money at all?"

Lank looked like a snake climbing a rope as he checked all his pockets. "I got a quarter."

Juliette chuckled, "That is more than I have. I counted out change at the liquor store. Will forty-one cents worth of gas get us home?"

"Most likely not."

They stopped at a gas station. Juliette went in to try exchanging rum for gas. Lank sat in the Buick polishing the dash board with his sleeve. Juliette called out the door, "Will you pump gas for anyone who comes…ah, arrives. The price is on the pump."

He pumped gas. Lank became agitated by the thoughts racing around his brain. The big clock on the top of the gas pump told him that nineteen and a half minutes past before Juliette got back to the car. She filled up the Buick's big gas tank while Lank brought the twelve dollars he had collected for gas in to the attendant who looked to be about seventeen years old, tired but happy. They got underway again. "Did you fuck for him for a tank of gas?"

"No. He masturbated while looking at me in iny bra and panties. Then he gave me a tank of gas. What a gentleman, eh. Oh, I kept my shoes on, too"

Lank looked disappointed, jealous, insulted or something. Juliette thought perhaps he wanted apology or explanation. "What is wrong, Lank? Do you feel tainted? Would you rather walk so you will not be driving off the avails of a prostitute?"

Lank did not respond. She had used the angriest tone that ever passed between them. At Lake Echo, Juliette turned on the radio. The car filled with Country and Western music which she disliked but she turned up the volume anyway. At Brookfield she stopped the car, turned off Ray Price and faced Lank. "What!?"

"Nothin'. I don't care. Not as much as you do anyway. I don't care."

"Oh, this is me is it?"

"Yeah, Juls. It don't matter to me. I felt shitty about it for a little while but I got over it. It's already done so you should try to get over it, too, rather than being hateful about it."

"Hmm, maybe I am feeling guilty; new for me. I am sure that rum will alleviate that sickness." Juliette crawled over the seat to get at the rum. She got up on the back of the seat, grabbed the rum and two quarts of beer. With her ass stuck out, she felt Lank's stare, as she pivoted on the back of the front seat. Flipping herself around with three bottles in her hands she caught Lank's eye and said, "You need a girlfriend."

"Yes. I suppose you're right."

They set out again. The big Buick glided over what had been a rattley old road for the other vehicles they drove. Juliette unscrewed the top of the rum bottle and Lank opened the beers with his pocketknife. She took a big swallow of rum, a throat burning-drink that landed in her stomach with a welcome hot pain. Lank took the rum and handed her a beer. She chased away the stomach pain and resisted a beer burp until she could let it out unobtrusively between her teeth. Lights flashed behind them.

"Do you think we can outrun the cops?"

"Yeah, but it's not like they won't recognize the car later."

Juliette pulled over. Bob Hoskins came up to the car. "Juliette, where the heck did you get this bomb?"

"Hi, Bob. It was a gift from a friend." She pointed at Lank.

"Hello Lank. Is this the car that Gary sold you so he could get to Kitchener?"

"God, Mounties are nosy. I thought it was a secret that I bought this. I fixed her up for Juliette because she keeps me out of trouble."

"Don't want to hear about how she keeps you out of trouble. Juliette, for Christ's sake, give me a break, will ya? You can't drive with a bottle of Molson, and you just a guzzlin'."

"Sorry Bob. I did not know you were there. But I guess it is your job, to not let us know where you are."

"You know I should charge you with drinking and driving."

"Yes, but we just pulled over and opened the bottles. The beer will not even be digested by the time we get home."

"Yeah, okay Juliette but don't be so god damn obvious."

"I do apologize for putting you in an awkward position. It will not happen again."

"Okay you two. Happy motoring. Great car."

"Thanks, Bob, bye." They rumbled off in the Buick. Juliette asked, "Do you think he saw the rum bottle?"

"Can you see it?"

"No. Where is it? Oh, in your shirt. There is a lot of room for extra stuff in your shirt." When they had gone a couple of miles, Lank had a swig of rum and passed it back to Juliette who said, "Perhaps we should slow down. We can get drunker later. It would be nice to show the kids the car first. Maybe they would like to go for a spin."

"Okay, I'll just sip on my beer."

"Lank, I'm sorry I got a bit bitchy. Juliette's bitchy bits. Thanks for the car. My only shot at prostitution felt very innocent and easy at the time. I am getting over thinking that it was anything but innocent. It was innocent. Thanks for the car, my love."

Archie put both girls to bed at his place by the time they arrived, so Juliette, Archie and Lank went for a drive around Sterling Reserve, listening to classical music on CBC and drinking Molson. The tour of Sterling Reserve was well over before they had finished their quarts so they did it three times. Lank said, "Nothin' much seems to have changed since the last time we came through here."

"Not so fast, buddy. I'm sure Libby's cat was on the lawn when we last passed by and she's on the doorstep now."

They rolled across the bridge to The Tracks, checked on the girls and went to Juliette's to drink. Lank strummed a guitar while Juliette played an old autoharp and sang St. James Infirmary and some plaintiff sea shanties. Nothing was perfectly in tune and Juliette sang with a limited range but her voice was sweet and cool and fair. Archie said, "We really should move the outhouse. It would be nice to move it back behind the old sites."

Juliette suggested that she could push it back up the slight incline with the Buick. When Lank brought it to her attention that after two feet of progress the front of the Buick would land in a shit hole, Juliette decided she was drunk enough and went to bed. She swirled in and out of fitful sleep with the rumble of men's voices in the other room reminding her of childhood sleeplessness.

***

Except for the girls getting off to school, the day did not start on The Tracks until eleven. Archie and Lank finished off most of the rum and all but two quarts of Molson. They drank Juliette's moonshine and went on to Lank's, to drink some of the beer Juliette made for him. Archie woke up at Lank's. It was six AM and he worried about the girls alone in the caboose. He arrived home to find Juliette sleeping on his couch. A note told the girls where to find juice and the porridge which 'should still be warm when you get up'. Archie looked over at the double boiler on the stove. A low fire, fueled by a piece of gnarled beech and two lumps of coal, kept it warm.

Archie and Victoria often woke up to Juliette's porridge in the double boiler. The oatmeal could have various bits of fruit and berries in it. Sometimes it went in another direction with pieces of bacon or ham, pepper and summer savory. Through Archie's drunkenness, a realization formed in his muddled brain. He and Victoria ran an unacknowledged race to get to the double boiler first; to be the one to lift the cover and see the heavy drops of water fall off the cover into the porridge from where it had risen as steam over the hours. An aromatic burst from the slowly cooked mixture rewarded the first to open the lid. The rich smell of Juliette's intentions piqued a truly righteous breakfast hunger.

Archie resisted the temptation to open the pot. It seemed wrong to sneak ahead of Victoria and get the first smell by arriving home drunk at six in the morning. There was already some stirring in

Victoria's room so Archie quietly slipped off to bed. He'd rather not deal with Lacie and Victoria in a drunken state. He drifted off to sleep wondering if the unspoken, unhurried race to first smell the porridge would be run between the girls.

***

Victoria and Lacie tried to be quiet but Juliette woke anyway, feeling good with no hangover, no leftover. She watched them and listened to their sparse chatter as they ate porridge and got dressed. Lacie looked out the caboose window at a misty morning.

"The blue bomb is still here. The guy who owns it must have found something else wrong. Maybe Daddy didn't fix it right."

"Good morning, Victoria and Lacie."

"Hi, Mom. You're awake. How was your trip?" Victoria went over to the sofa and sat on the end where her mother was propped up on one arm. Juliette held Victoria and kissed her back in the little gap between her sweater and her skirt. Victoria giggled, "Don't, Mom." She turned around. In the morning light coming through the windows and coming down from the cupola, she looked radiant and happy. Juliette could not recall what she thought was becoming less pretty about Victoria.

"Victoria, you are beautiful."

"Thank you, Mom. Did you get me anything?"

"We will see, maybe after school. May I pick you two up for lunch, at five to twelve?"

"Are you sure, Mom?"

Juliette knew Victoria's ambivalence about her mother picking her up, especially at lunchtime. Staying around the school gave Victoria the opportunity for lightweight talk with casual friends. She had a large appetite for that. Juliette speculated that Victoria had ambiguous feelings about the attention that her mother got. Juliette grew accustomed to being attractive; she'd always been that way but Victoria told her that so-and-so said she looked like this movie star or that movie star. Juliette didn't see much similarity between herself and those stars but those stars were recognized symbols of beauty. A lady from Sterling Reserve told Juliette she looked just like Arlene Dahl. Juliette didn't know who that was until a month later she saw Arlene Dahl's picture on a magazine cover. She complained to Archie. "I look more like Winston Churchill than fucking Arlene Dahl."

Archie said, "I bet, if you surveyed those people who say you look like a model or an actress, the one they chose would be their favorite."

Victoria seemed to be disturbed by the attention her mother got when she appeared at the school but what her friends thought of the rickety old cars that Juliette borrowed from Lank probably bothered her more. He usually had one barely operating vehicle. Lacie however, never seemed to care about the opinions of authorities or casual friends. To Juliette, it seemed that Lacie had no useless thoughts.

"Yes, Victoria, I am sure. I will pick you up at five to twelve or as soon as you are available. You too, Lacie."

"Okay, Juls. We'll be ready."

The girls skipped off to school and Juliette lazed around counting her undeserved good fortune that Victoria was her daughter and Lacie, Victoria's close friend. For the first time in her life, Juliette washed a car.

***

Lacie spied her first. "Juls got the blue car." They ran over to the shining Buick where Juliette stood, looking unreasonably beautiful. She held the big wide passenger door open with one hand and held two popsicles in the other hand. Lacie took the chocolate and Victoria the strawberry as they scrambled in the front seat. By the time Juliette got behind the wheel, they were licking their popsicles and chattering. "Daddy never let me in this car before because he said the owner was somebody special."

Juliette smiled, "Lank said that?"

"Yup. And you let us eat popsicles in the front seat."

"I am the owner. Your father gave this car to me. He bought it and fixed it up and gave it to me.

"Are you and Daddy going to get married?"

"No, Lacie. Nothing like that but I think your father and I will always be good friends."

Victoria said, "Like me and Lacie?"

"Yes, like you and Lacie."

"Me and Vee would be sisters if you and Daddy got married."

"Better to be friends, do you agree Victoria?"

"Yeah, look at Jane and Beverly, they're always fighting."

"This car is so big. It's all shiny stuff everywhere. Look Vee, look at the radio."

Victoria said, "Turn it on, Lacie."

"Better not, sticky fingers."

Juliette told them to go ahead and push the buttons down below to get a station. They drove to Brookfield in a swish. Juliette went to the bank while the girls ate fish fritters and French fries at the Seagull restaurant.

On the way home, Lacie asked, "Are you and Daddy... Does Daddy screw you?"

"No sweetie, we do not screw. We never have and very likely never will."

"What is screw, Mom? How do you do it?"

"A man or boy puts his penis, which is also called a cock, a bird and I cannot think of all the other names right now but you know what I mean. What do you call it?"

Victoria said, "A pee pee or a cock."

Lacie said, "Don't call it a pee pee. That's baby talk."

"Okay, so a guy's cock gets hard when he is horny. Horny is when he is excited by someome he finds sexy. It gets bigger and harder. That is what is called an erection or a hard-on. Most boys your age do not get erections. That usually happens when they are about twelve or thirteen, somewhere around there."

Juliette pulled the Roadmaster up in front of the school. "You girls have to go. We can finish this later." Victoria looked at her wristwatch. "We got seven minutes."

"Oh, seven minutes. Have I talked to you about this stuff before?"

"No."

Juliette tried to describe sexual intercourse accurately and completely.

"Why?"

"Ah, because it feels very good, if it is done right. How much time do we have?"

"Three minutes."

"You two should go in and do not let me get away with not telling you about screwing when you are too young, about orgasm and about getting pregnant. That is three things. Maybe tonight we can talk."

"Okay, Juls, we'll make you do it."

"Thanks, Lacie. How do you like my new car?"

"It's nice. Bye. Thanks for lunch."

Victoria kissed her mother, out of the blue, she kissed her on the cheek. It was a rare occurrence. "See ya."

"I will see you. Thanks for the kiss."

After school, the girls got their presents, a record for Victoria from her mother and a radio for Lacie from Lank. Victoria seemed to be all right with it. "Elvis is superb. We can play it on the school's record player as long as some certain nuns aren't around. I could play it at Janine's too. Her mom likes Elvis." She asked a lot of questions about the car; would they be able to go places, would she be able to drive it when she was sixteen, could she and Lacie sleep in it sometimes.

***

Juliette planned to take them for a drive after supper and continue their talk about sex. Archie and Lank were grateful that they didn't have to do it. It puzzled Juliette that she dreaded the job.

She planned to jump into it feet first because nothing else came to mind. Juliette felt apprehensive but she had no strategy. They finished dinner and headed for Brookfield, the only choice for a drive unless you wanted to go back and forth on the rutted roads of Sterling Reserve. Juliette thought of her life like that, always needing to leave herself to get anywhere. It did not matter if she started a conversation, or got up in the morning, or told her daughter and friend about sex. Juliette traversed the same bumpy road in the beginning of everything. She hated the viewpoint, wished it never occurred to her and wished she hadn't played with the notion until it started to play back. It skulked around, haunting all her beginnings. It didn't actually make sense but it held some tiresome truth.

"Girls, you wanted to talk about sex but I do not want to do all the talking. People have a lot of different opinions about sex, when you should do it and things like that. Some of that is tied up with religion. Different religions have different rules, about everything I guess, including sex."

"Juls, what about religion? Most of the kids at school… well, their parents, go to church or they believe in God."

Victoria rode in the backseat with a doll in her lap. The doll had wiry reddish-blond hair and a big rubber face. "All the parents believe in God. Why don't we?"

"Just give me a minute, girls. I did not expect to have to deal with sex and religion." Juliette started out on the bumpy road to a new topic. Over five miles of driving, she explained religion from her viewpoint as a complete skeptic. "Did I lose you completely?"

"Kinda."

"I understand what you're saying, Juls. Besides, they don't agree. There's five or ten different religions, not just the Catholics but the Protestants and the Arabs and the pistol palans and Buddhists; they all got different gods."

"So your father has talked to you about this?"

"No, not really. Not about them disagreeing. You can just see that."

"Okay. Now, the religious people claim that they have faith and those of us who do not believe, do not have faith. They say, I guess, that faith is a gift from their particular brand of god. Some people get it and some people do not get it."

"Will I get it?"

"I hope not, Victoria."

Victoria pulled herself up to the back of Juliette's seat. "But if it's a gift, like a present."

"That is what they call it but I call it fooling yourself. You talk to Jiki like she is a real person but you know she is just your doll. The people with faith cannot get back to reality. They keep talking to god like he is real."

"How come you curse?"

"Just a habit, Lacie, no good reason except that it serves some sort of notice."

"Huh?"

"Perhaps we have enough to talk about without getting into that."

"Yeah, Mom, never mind God; let's talk about that other stuff."

"What stuff?"

Victoria said "Oh you know."

"Sex, Juls, screwing, cocks."

"Okay, Lacie, I got it."

"How do babies get born?"

Juliette went into it headlong from the beginning to the end, being as straightforward and explicit as she could manage. Victoria asked why.

"No idea, dear. It seems awkward and inconvenient to me. Now, the people who believe in God would say that it is God's plan. I say that it is just the way it is. Can we stop, now?"

"Do we know it all?"

"I hope not. There would be no fun left if you knew it all."

"What do you mean?"

"If you knew it all, there would be nothing to wonder about. I suppose I would not trade wonderment, I mean, sometimes I would rather wonder than know. Can we stop now?"

"Yeah sure, Juls, you're off the hook."

"Mom, can we tell our friends this stuff?"

"Oh shit. I guess I would rather you did not. Some of their parents are surely religious and the religious ones can be a nasty bit of business."

"I don't think Sister Jeanne d'Arc believes in God."

"Why do you say that, Lacie?"

"I dunno. Something she said once. One of the other nuns said something, something about religion, and Sister Jeanne d'Arc said, 'that may be' or something like that. She's awfully nice; I mean Sister Jeanne d'Arc."

They had driven to Tangier, turned around and headed home. Between Brookfield and Sterling Reserve, Juliette could see her daughter in the backseat sleeping. The doll was probably on the floor. Lacie spoke occasionally, commenting on roadside things, the car and school. She asked some questions about various things. One of the questions was for clarification of some points about sex. Juliette encouraged her to ask any questions like that or to talk about anything that bothered her but they were mostly silent, following the high beams up the road to home.

Victoria hardly woke up to get ready for bed and Lacie left for the dining car tired and sleepy. Archie said to Juliette, "You must be ready for a drink?"

"Yes. Shall we get Lank and go to my place? I bought some nice cheese and other goodies in Halifax. There is not much rum left but the moonshine is good."

"Is that the moonshine you aged in the barrels?"

"Yes. That is all I have now; Lank takes all of my raw moonshine."

"You know he's as proud as a peacock about giving you that car."

"I like it more than I thought I would. It just floats along. It is more fun driving one of his beat-up little English cars but this is a comfortable thing. When they built it, they did not miss any opportunity to overstate. However, as you might expect, that kind of talk is for your ears only. The lovely Lank will only hear the good side and there is a good side. It is like a soft motorized couch that screams to everyone it passes, 'I am of consequence'. The girls love it. It will be great for trips."

"Good for hauling coal."

"Now, you piss off. Do not get us started. Seriously, I really appreciate the gift and that is all. Okay, Mr. Mac."

"Yes yes, I'll be good."

They gathered up Lank who already started drinking. They set out for drunkenness and enjoyed every drink along the way. Juliette bragged up the Buick, how it floated over roads that other cars crashed and banged over.

"Thanks, Juls, for taking Lacie on the facts of life tour. I wasn't looking forward to that."

"It was okay with the two of them but not easy. I am not shy about sex but I felt awkward explaining things to them. I wonder why."

"I'll drink to you doing it rather than me."

Juliette put out cheese and bread and some little treats from the Greek store and some from the Chinese store. A lazy wood fire burned in her stove. Lank tossed half a dozen potatoes directly onto the fire and went about mixing up something greasy and spicy to go inside the potatoes when they baked.

"Lank, if I were to choose a female from around here to pal around with, it would be the same one Victoria chose. If I wanted to go for a drive or go to an art gallery or just sit on the beach with a female, Lacie or Sister Jeanne d'Arc would be my choices. Probably if I wanted to talk to someone, it would be her. Jesus, she's only eight."

"What about Victoria?" The question snapped out of Archie, spring loaded.

"Unfortunately, despite my feelings about motherhood, we get along like mother and daughter, which is to say, not very well. Victoria and I always wish that the other had said something different or not done a thing the way she did. We seem to be trapped in something. We disappoint each other. Lacie and I do not disappoint one another. We seem to be just like the other one wants us to be. Victoria and Lacie do not disappoint one another."

Archie said, "Well that's all very nice and clever but isn't it your responsibility to fix that?"

Juliette was silent. Lank filled in the lull with some talk about there being a lot of coal in the old mine, just strewn around the place. He said you could probably get a ton of it pretty easily. Juliette spoke, "It is my responsibility and I am failing at that but I do not think I am shirking it. I try but it does not seem to work for Victoria and me; we seem to be displeased with each other."

"Displeased? How can you be displeased with Victoria? How come you think you have the right to be displeased with your daughter? Jesus. And then you say Lacie could be your buddy, your girlfriend."

"Come on, Archie, Juls is just trying to say the bitter truth to us. It's hard to tell the truth when somebody is jumping on you, blaming you for everything."

"Well, maybe the blame should fall on whoever deserves it."

Juliette checked in on Victoria. She slept soundly. Juliette got her jacket and walked to the river. She took the canoe out for a paddle in the moonlight. She worked up to the beaver lodge, down to the falls and then back home. At her car, six potatoes waited for her with a note from Lank saying they might need a little more cooking. Archie and Lank must have left in desultory moods. In the days following, Archie and Juliette resumed their usual behavior. They didn't talk about Juliette's difficulties with Victoria.

CHAPTER EIGHTEEN

In the summer of nineteen fifty-nine, the Roadmaster rolled. During a week when Lacie suffered headaches and extreme fatigue, Archie and Victoria went to Yarmouth and Moncton and to Halifax. They stayed in hotels and one of those new creations, a motel. He returned from that trip melancholy and apprehensive about transportation of humans replacing humanity. "People get eaten by their cars and the roads eat up the land. When you stop for gas or to get something to eat, you're not seen as a traveler anymore. Nobody is a wayfaring stranger. We're all just passengers from cars."

Lank drove the big Buick just to drive the big Buick. He usually washed it before he took it out. Sterling Reserve had no taxi and Lank drove a few customers to Brookfield, Dartmouth or Halifax. Three ladies from Sterling Reserve occasionally got together to hire Lank and the Buick for the day. He dropped them off on Barrington Street in Halifax and picked them up an hour later to take them somewhere else.

"It keeps me sober all day. Maybe I should get a job, stay sober, make a living."

Cameron Fisheries became very profitable for Jimmy and Juliette. Slipper had no serious breakdowns and she made money but she was an odd boat. Juliette got a new one built. A more comfortable boat for the crew, it had greater capacity, greater range and better gear. She ran almost as fast as Slipper empty and just as fast loaded with fish. Kevin Murphy proved to be a good skipper who could find fish and keep his crew productive and harmonious. No one had a permanent job with Kevin. You worked on his crew as long as you did it well. Slipper sold for a good price to a young guy who knew the boat's reputation. He wanted to fish hard and make good money.

Kevin and the crew chose the name Our Pet for Juliette's new boat. A television show that followed the Saturday night hockey game was headlined by an attractive and constantly smiling blond singer whose television name was simply Juliette. Each week the show opened with, 'and here's Our Pet, Juliette.' Juliette Cameron did not have a television and did not like to watch television. She didn't catch the reference. Cliff explained it to her after 'Our Pet' was already painted on the stern. Juliette didn't have strong objections to the name but she thought it was silly.

Archie said, "Well, Slipper was silly, too."

"Perhaps but it did not come from the fucking television."

Kevin, Monte, and crew had Our Pet making money right away. Fish prices were up and she had comprehensive licenses so they caught anything they could sell. The boat ran fast and reliably. The new boat payments looked pretty small compared to earnings. Juliette paid it off in a lump sum eight months after launching Our Pet.

A few days after school finished, Lacie became ill. She had a mild fever and felt tired. Lank reported that she slept well the first night but awoke with damp sheets. By noon, Lacie had headaches; she didn't want to move or eat. That night she sweated profusely and the headaches seemed agonizing. Lank and Juliette took her to the hospital where Dr. Lawley told them that she had an infection and perhaps, she should stay in the hospital for observation but they chose to take her home.

Lank said, "Kids get sick. She'll get over it." Archie said something similar as did George Lawley. These pronouncements made Juliette a little more relaxed. She had never been physically sick and this was the first illness for either Lacie or Victoria. Archie and Victoria had plans for a long drive in the Buick and they set off. Juliette gave them money to stay in hotels rather than sleep in the car but, after they pulled away, she asked Lank, "Are they being callous?"

"How do you mean?"

"Lacie is deathly ill and Victoria, supposedly her best friend, goes off to have a good time. It does not seem right."

"Well, they can't do Lacie no more good here than if they're on the road. I told Lacie they were goin'. She seemed glad. Anyway, don't you disapprove of loyalty?"

"Okay, I guess."

Lank had a short-term job as a plumber's helper. Juliette took Lacie to her car. Juliette talked to George Lawley at least once a day reporting Lacie's condition and looking for advice. She got the same advice each day. "Watch her temperature, try to get food and liquids in her and wait it out."

Everyone seemed cavalier about Lacie being sick but it spooled Juliette up tight. Lacie's mouth was very dry but she objected to the liquids: water, juice, and soup that Juliette insisted she take. Lacie didn't complain but she obviously suffered severely from the headaches. A few times, when Juliette entered the room, she found the girl whimpering or quietly crying. Lacie held it back while Juliette was with her. She spoke very little. When she did say something, Juliette knew that Lacie thought it through so she could communicate in one or two syllables. Anything else required too much effort. It took too much effort to move, too much effort to suck liquid through a straw. Juliette didn't force liquids on her that could just lie in her mouth. Lacie needed to marshal her energies in order to accomplish simple tasks like moving her arm.

Lank, at Juliette's request, made a potty chair for Lacie but, watching her get up, sit on the side of the bed for two minutes or so, then stand and wait two minutes before she made her way to the potty chair, right next to the bed, prompted Juliette to pick her up and carry her. She also took Lacie's piss pot to the outhouse and noted that the small amount of urine was quite dark. Dr. Lawley set up an I.V. to rehydrate the patient. The day after he started the

I.V., the headaches went away. It seemed to take an enormous effort for Lacie to say "pee" or "drink" or "thanks". On the day that the headaches stopped, she said three times, "The pain's gone. Thanks, Juls".

Archie and Victoria got back as Lacie began to move around. She had the I.V. at night but ate and drank during the day. The next day, she got to the outhouse on her own. She talked much less than normal but a lot more than she had for a week.

Archie said to Juliette and Lank, "Nobody can be that tired. I think Lacie is puttin' on the dog a bit." Juliette stood close to Archie. She took his hand in her small feminine hand. Archie knew that Juliette was twice as strong as she appeared to be and he knew the uncanny strength of her grip.

"Lacie does not put on the dog."

Archie winced. "You're crushing my hand."

Juliette squeezed harder for a second and let go. Archie told her some weeks later while they drank together at a bar in Boston that he felt beat up and overpowered. "It wasn't so much the vicious monster grip as the anger. You were burning."

"I guess I am sorry about that incident. I am not entirely sure though, about the being sorry part. You said she put on an act but I saw what that child went through. Do you know she waited until I left the room to cry? Lacie just does not cry."

"Well Victoria doesn't cry much; very rarely."

"This is not about Victoria. Giving Lacie credit for her... for her straightforwardness has nothing to do with Victoria. I do not choose Lacie over Victoria. Okay, this is it. If I had the choice of saving one of them from sure death, I would choose Victoria without thought. It would be automatic. She is my daughter."

"Hmm, I never thought like that. I guess that is some sort of acid test. That's good to know, actually. But Victoria knows you'd rather spend time with Lacie."

"That is not entirely true but I guess it is mostly true. I hope you do not try to deal with that problem. Victoria and I need to find our way out of the shithouse."

"I just wish you two were better together."

"I bet you a nickel I wish that more than you do. Probably Victoria wishes it more than both of us put together."

"Yes, I believe so."

It took Lacie all of July to get fully back to her old self. Lank, Lacie, Archie, Victoria and Juliette set out in the Roadmaster the first week in August. Juliette paid for everything but, by the time they got back, she hoped Our Pet had made some money during her absence.

They drove to Fredericton, New Brunswick, and stayed for two days. They looked around the university campus, went to the museum and rented a speedboat to spend a day on the river. The girls both loved hotel living. Not picking up after herself appealed most to Victoria.

They spent three days in Montréal. Lacie had come into her own and Victoria went along with anything Lacie had up her sleeve. Juliette, Lank and Archie never told the girls not to talk to strangers. They did talk to strangers, the stranger the better for Lacie and Victoria. French would not be a school subject for them until grade seven but the three days in Montréal gave Lacie some rudimentary French communication skills and Victoria got quite good at it.

She walked up to a pretty girl who looked to be about her own age. The girl sat alone at a sidewalk café table. "Bonjour Mademoiselle,

Je m'appelle Victoria."

"Je ne parle pas francais but je m'appelle Colleen. I'm not from here. I'm from Boston."

"That's where we're going next."

Colleen's mother, Bonnie, returned after about five minutes and by then Victoria, Lacie and Colleen were old friends, foreigners in a foreign land. Juliette and Bonnie conversed while the children conversed. Bonnie asked what hotel they stayed in. It seemed suitably upscale so she invited them to stay at her house in Boston. "Thank you, Bonnie. That is very kind but we are five."

"You have two other children? Oh no, what am I thinking? One of them is your husband, I'm sure. I've been divorced for two years and I sometimes forget there are such creatures as husbands."

Juliette laughed, "No husband but the other two are men."

"Oh. Is there a good-looking one for me? Cover your ears, girls."

Colleen rolled her eyes and tisked. Victoria looked quizzically at Colleen. Juliette asked her about it later.

"Oh Mom, Colleen's mother is sublime. And she's divorced. That's really something. Colleen shouldn't act like that."

"Victoria, that is sweet that you think that way. Thank you for not ever treating me like that."

Victoria smiled and said, "You're welcome."

Bonnie said, "Juliette, surely you don't need two men."

"We are best friends and neighbors, not lovers."

"Girls, you really have to cover your ears. Well, Colleen and your girls get along so well; perhaps they could have a sleepover at my home. It's in Newton Center, just enough out of the city." They arranged for the girls to stay over at Bonnie's when they got to Boston.

Juliette took Lank out and bought him new clothes; linen pants, a summer sport coat, a sport shirt, a dress shirt and new shoes, socks and underwear. She told Archie that he and Lank should be on an equal footing when they met the slightly plump but attractive divorcee. When they did meet, Archie thought Bonnie was annoying and fat. Bonnie and Lank found each other attractive. Colleen and Bonnie got a late start for home the next day. Bonnie handed her daughter over to Juliette and the girls. She and Lank spent the morning in her hotel room. After lunch, Lank glowed.

"I thought I might have forgotten how to do it. It's been two years now since I had a woman and that was Amy."

Archie laughed. Amy was a strange young woman who often said inappropriate things. Amy flexed and shivered like firecrackers exploded inside her. Archie called her Shellshock Amy.

Juliette said, "What happened to Amy, Lank? I really liked that sardonic wit."

"I don't know. I think she lives in Dartmouth."

Archie said, "No doubt." Many Nova Scotians knew Dartmouth as the location of the province's largest mental hospital. Dartmouth became a euphemism for all those other euphemisms like loony bin, the mental, nuthouse and bedlam. Juliette figured that Archie had an unusually short list of the ways people were supposed to behave.

In Boston, Lacie and Victoria spent most of their time with Colleen at Bonnie's house in Newton Center. Both Colleen and Bonnie became enthralled by these sensitive, attractive, intelligent people. Lacie's ability to get to the heart of the matter and her lack of concern for very much other than the heart of the matter made Colleen say, years later, "I was in the presence of greatness." But Victoria's unique flair charmed Bonnie and Colleen.

"Oh yes, I know, she can overdramatize a smidgen at times but she does it so well. Very original and there's a certain sweetness and sincerity, sort of like Judy Garland."

Juliette said, "Judy Garland is sincere?"

"Oh, you know what I mean."

"Fuck no, Bonnie. I have no idea."

Bonnie laughed, "Oh, you people."

Eight years later, Colleen joined the youth movement, the summer of love, the hippies. Bonnie felt good about that. They had been seduced by these dropouts from The Tracks. Colleen used her mother's money to allow her to be poor from July to October nineteen-sixty-seven. New York to Toronto and Montréal to San Francisco and back to her mother's arms where she arrived disillusioned, jaded and carrying a taste for amphetamines.

The group from Nova Scotia left Boston for New York City. Bonnie and Colleen didn't want them to go but the Roadmaster called. They booked a downtown hotel. Juliette drove into the city on a busy afternoon. It couldn't be called a traffic jam; everything moved fast. The frantic pace intimidated Archie but Lank and the girls had faith in their driver and the pace got Juliette charged up. She challenged other cars, particularly taxis. If she saw an opening big enough for the Buick or if it looked like an opening could develop, she charged for it. Juliette cut off cabdrivers and bounced a couple of wheels up on the sidewalk to pass on the inside. Her inclination to standup for the little guy emerged. A hot dog vendor couldn't get across the street. No one gave him a break even though he tried to wheel his cart on a crosswalk. Juliette stopped and backed up onto the intersection in front of the crosswalk, daring other drivers.

The vendor passing by Juliette's open window said, "Thanks, lady. Woohoo, you got the look."

At their hotel, Juliette simply double parked until the attendant took the Buick to the car park. The fun before caution theme continued. They walked everywhere in the city, stopping into bars with Lacie and Victoria. Lacie enjoyed getting kicked out of bars but Juliette could talk most bartenders into allowing the girls to stay. They heard some live music: jazz, rock 'n roll and pop. Their rooms were not the best but not the worst. They saw cockroaches; the first time for all but Archie. Victoria said, "They're sooo cute." Juliette watched for sincerity in Victoria's overdramatization but she couldn't see it. She decided instead to simply assume that she was wrong about the whole issue. Juliette tried to think of herself as just too tight and not demonstrative enough. It didn't work very well and, during a late-night of drinking with Lank while Archie looked after the girls, she explained her approach.

"My God, Juls, you might as well pretend you're Santa Claus and Vee is Dumbo the Elephant. Your kid exaggerates every move, every everything. The breathlessness over nothing just drives me nuts. On any kind of trip, there's always somebody who ends up being an annoyance and Vee gets the prize this time around."

Anger grabbed Juliette. Anger made her run cool. She didn't shout or threaten with empty noise. "I do not like what you said. I do not believe that Victoria is making this a miserable trip for anyone. Perhaps we could…"

"Oh Juls, I didn't mean she was making us miserable, just that, you know, sometimes I find her annoying."

Juliette looked at his mouth, a look too cold to be a stare. "As I began to say; perhaps we could ask Archie and Lacie if Victoria is, 'driving them nuts'. It is not usually the case that one person annoys the others in a small group activity but often one person becomes a bully and attempts to enlist allies against the individual in the group who appears most vulnerable, in this case the smallest and youngest of the group."

"Hold it, Juls. Don't be pullin' that hateful shit on me. You know God damn well I wasn't trying to be mean to Victoria."

"Yes, you were."

Lank raised his voice close to shouting. He was shrill. "You fuck right off, Juls. I seen you turn hard bitch before and I don't fuckin' like it."

A large man, in his mid-twenties, walked toward them. He made each step as intimidating as he could manage. "Hey you, buddy. Who taught you to speak to a lady like that?"

Lank stood up. "Do you have a position here or are you a customer?"

"That doesn't matter a lot, does it? If I hit you, you're going down hard."

"You will hit me, will you?"

"That's right, buddy. I'll hit you." Juliette figured that Lank planned to hit the guy first and he just set it up to be a case of self-defense because of the direct threat but instead, he just looked at the man and sat down. The young man nodded and said, "All right then." He went back to his seat. Juliette resumed the conversation as if a waiter simply asked if they wanted another drink. "Having my child insulted does, I suppose, turn me into a hard bitch."

"Can I just erase what I originally said and phrase it with more care? I'm right drunk, Juls."

"Sure, rephrase."

"I guess I don't have much patience with kids. I don't think I ever really wanted one."

"Who am I talking to, just you?"

"Just me, Juls. You never carry stories and neither do I."

"Victoria annoys the shit out of me, too. So, can we just drop the topic and treat her like we were mature adults even if we cannot seem to manage that with each other right now?" Lank leaned over the table and kissed her. Juliette kept her hand on his face as he sat down. The young man, still looking on, said, "Oh brother." Lank and Juliette laughed. Lank said, "Thank's, buddy. You saved our marriage."

Juliette bought a flask of rum and two bottles of beer from the bartender, wondering if they broke the law buying from a bartender. They carried on with as much caution and discretion as could be expected from two drunken people. Lank and Juliette developed a way of keeping each other under the limit so they rarely got too drunk together. The two walked arm in arm for hours, stopping into bars for a beer or a Coke and a piss. Back on the street, Juliette took the bottle of rum from her shoulder bag and they drank as lightly and surreptitiously as they could manage. Lank noted with satisfaction the small amount of rum they had consumed. Manhattan closed down around them. The open bars thinned out. At an ambiguously closed bar, someone said, "Yeah we closed an hour ago but come on in. No harm to it."

Lank and Juliette enjoyed each other's company. Sitting at the bar, they touched and patted each other. On the street, Juliette leaned into him to create mutual support. A young couple from California asked for directions which Lank was able to give them. They chatted for a while and when they parted, Lank and Juliette talked about them.

"Did you find her pretty, Juls?"

"Oh yes, she is pretty. I like that kind of body, too, not wide. She is probably thicker than she is wide." Juliette demonstrated. "If you put your hands under her armpits and ran them down both sides of her, your hands would not be far apart and they would touch her tits on the way down; her breasts are not big but they are as wide as the rest of her. Do you know what I mean? The rib cage does not widen much from the waist to the shoulders."

Yeah, yeah, you're right. She was like that, yeah."

"Same with her hips. They are not broad but she has a beautiful bum that sticks out nicely in the back and her tits stick out nicely in the front. Thicker than wide, right?"

"Yeah, I'd like to see her without her clothes on."

Juliette said, "I would like to touch her without her clothes on. How was Bonnie?"

"I don't like to talk a lot about how things went with a woman."

"Fair enough but it is just me."

Lank went quiet for a minute and then said, "She stroked my dick and massaged my balls for a long time. She wasn't at all interested in me touching her. When I put my hand on her vagina or her breasts or kissed her breasts, I felt sort of unwelcome. When we screwed, she seemed to want me to come quickly and didn't care about herself. I kind of thought I should pay her. I've never been with a prostitute but I guess it would be like that. However, it felt wonderful to shoot my load inside a woman and she's nice. Bonnie's nice. I think I hope I never see her again."

"You were glad though that you had sex with Bonnie?"

"Yeah it was good, 'twas good."

"I am glad you got your rocks off."

"Yeah, I mean I jerk off lots. It's not the same but it keeps me sane."

"Sanity is a desirable state."

Back at the hotel, they didn't really want their evening to end but exhaustion settled over Lank and Juliette's feet hurt. They reluctantly gave up the night. Archie and the girls slept in the room Juliette had shared with Lacie and Victoria so Lank and Juliette took the other room. They slept in separate beds, Lank soundly and peacefully while Juliette, not being drunk enough to pass out, took whatever sleep she could get. She found her usual: about one quarter awake, one quarter in a restful sleep and half the night spent on the uneven edge of sleep.

***

Juliette connived to get a day alone with Victoria. She wanted to make some progress in liking her daughter and believed it would be easier if she didn't have Lacie around to compare.

They went to the zoo; the first time either of them went to a zoo. It filled Juliette with ambivalence about the captured animals but she was thrilled to see those wonderful creatures. She remembered Lacie's reaction at the circus in Dartmouth, the same as her reaction to the zoo. Juliette quickly put that memory out of her mind. The tiger stirred up things in her, so large, a fully qualified carnivore, a sleek and efficiently predacious body of great beauty. Victoria did some ooing and ahhing but didn't seem impressed. They went to a restaurant for lunch. Victoria ate her first pizza. She liked it but picked off the green peppers, which were "awful slimy." Juliette had oysters and did not find them slimy at all. Victoria's pizza meant she couldn't complain about Juliette's garlic breath. Victoria wanted to shop for gifts.

She chose a pair of casual shoes for City. She knew his size and the eight and a half she chose seemed about right to Juliette. The leather felt supple, like living flesh. The store clerk said the shoes could be mailed back for a full refund if they weren't right. They cost sixty-five dollars, the most Juliette ever paid for shoes and she loved shoes. "Victoria, that is an expensive gift. They cannot all cost that much. I am sorry but we have gotten a bit short on money, sweetie."

"I can get little things for everyone else, except I'd like to get some expensive socks for Archie. He don't get socks from Cliff."

Juliette knelt in front of Victoria and hugged her. Victoria's well-considered gift gave Juliette a deep something, in her shoulders and thighs and chest; the feeling had no cognitive co-relate, no name. It might be named later but Juliette knew that naming the feeling would be a lie, just something to satisfy the mind because the mind gets jealous when it's not included.

The socks Victoria chose were not particularly expensive or of very high quality but, worst of all, they were far too bright and colorful for the subdued suits worn by Cliff and re-worn by Archie. "Victoria, the socks do not go with any of Archie's suits. The thing is, Archie finds Cliff 's suits a bit drab sometimes but he wears them because they are good quality, comfortable, and they do not cost him anything. So why not buy him a sportcoat and pants and perhaps a sport shirt that would match the socks better?"

"I thought you didn't have money."

"We will be okay. You can pay me back when you grow up."

"What's a sportcoat?"

"Oh, it is like the suit coats he wears but more casual. That means it is not as stiff, more easy-going. That jacket I bought for Lank in Montreal is a sports coat."

Victoria looked down at her shoes. "He'll know it's not from me."

"Yes, sweetie, you are right. The socks are beautiful. Archie will love them."

"But are they the wrong color?"

Juliette avoided lying to Victoria and she didn't like to hedge but often careful selection of words seemed to be called for. If she dealt with Lacie in the same situation, she'd simply say, 'Archie would not want argyle socks of acid yellow and royal blue.' Lacie would look at the socks, consider the options available to her and then make a decision. Victoria required delicacy.

"They are the right color. His suits are too drab." The socks were in a small tan shopping bag with little woven paper handles. Victoria looked at the brown boxes inside which contained the three pairs of socks. Without speaking or looking at Juliette, she walked to the mailbox, reached up on her tiptoes, to pull down the handle of the chute, and dropped the bag in the mail. She said, "Mrs. Christie can have them."

Juliette did not know how to react. She thought of scolding Victoria for wasting something of value but instead she just turned sad. Victoria had been introduced to the complexities of giving gifts. It is a stern and dishonest business. Juliette's spirit failed, slipping from the top of her. It would have gone all the way down and out her ass but her mind interfered. The mind put forward the sort of senselessness that passes for wisdom as she told herself everything is everything, everything is nothing. A few minutes earlier she felt grateful at the reprieve from thought as the uncomplicated beauty of Victoria's desire to give to Archie filled her with a sudden unrequested joy. After Juliette fucked it all up, she gladly allowed her mind to invent mechanisms to buffer the blow.

At the hotel, Juliette tucked City's shoes away in the trunk of the Buick and then went back to their rooms. Victoria talked about the zoo with such animation that Juliette found it necessary to explain that the lions lived in cages and didn't attack them. The girls realized how sarcastic this was. Juliette felt mean about it.

That night, she trudged through the ordeal of trying to get a good night's sleep. The resentment she often felt towards this child of hers chewed her up. She resolved to act better and try harder but Juliette smelled the sickly weakness of such resolve, an empty prayer to her future.

They got an early start for the Canadian border. The air conditioning in the Buick was a Lank add-on, from a later model year. It provided some cool air but not enough to make up for sunshine pouring into a closed-up car. Archie drove out of New York with all the windows open. Juliette sat by the back window. Victoria leaned against her watching the upper part of the world slide by. To see everything, she would have to stand up on the seat. Getting into Connecticut, Juliette raised her arm, showing a streak of sweat on Victoria's blouse. Their sweat blended on the front of Juliette's sundress and Victoria's back. Victoria stood up to face her mother. Her blonde hair flew about wildly in the buffeting window breeze and mingled with Juliette's. The wind tossed them together. Victoria laughed and shook her head around to exaggerate the effect.

"Please do not let this moment stop."

"What, Mom?"

"You are my sweet love."

Lacie heard them talking in the back seat and said, "It's nice to be going home but maybe we missed something." Nighttime arrived as they found what they missed, the State Fair in Skowhegan, Maine. Lank said, "Maybe deciding to stay before you find a place to do that stayin' is a bad idea."

Archie said, "You don't mind this, do you?"

"Naw, it's kind of fun except for the flies." The urgent whine of mosquitoes filled the night. Juliette or Lank started up the car and drove for two minutes, then parked until the mosquitoes got too desperate and the Roadmaster rolled out again. They had rooms booked for the next night at a hotel with a pool. But they found refuge from mosquitoes by the roar of the Kennebec River falls. Archie and Lacie slept on the riverbank while the others found some sleep in the car.

They had to wait until noon to check in. Juliette, accustomed to fractured sleep, took the girls to the fair while Archie and Lank snoozed through the afternoon. At around five, they found Juliette and the girls in the pool. Lacie swam well. Mother and daughter looked like they belonged in the water. Juliette spent much of her time underwater. The three of them got out of the pool and toweled dry. Juliette became aware of the eyes following her movements. She liked it. She liked her sleek coral swimsuit. She liked that men made comments about busty, voluptuous women but her thin, proportioned self drew the narrowed eyes, dreamy or ready for action. The curiosity about which one of these two handsome men was the lucky one piqued a naughty desire. She kissed them both, not just friendly kisses but lovers' kisses. An audible tisk came from a woman in a print sundress as she creaked out of a lounge chair and stomped off. Juliette turned to Archie. "Why did I want to make that woman angry?"

"If she's mad, that's an automatic affirmation that she was judging you."

"Hmm, yes precisely, yes. The fair is great. They have harness racing tonight. Do you gentlemen want to go and lose some money?"

"That sounds wonderful."

The adults broke even at the racetrack. Both girls loved the races and Lacie made her own two-dollar bet on a horse she liked. She asked questions about racing, horses and what chance meant. The adults were humorously baffled at her questions. Archie did most of the explaining about chance, dredging up memories of statistical methods studied at St.F.X.U. Juliette, the midnight reader and a fright for librarians because she ordered books from any place libraries could get them, corrected Archie on some aspects of chance. Juliette elaborated on others points but, as often happened,

Lank provided the answer. "Chance is what you get sometimes, dear."

Lacie bet on the least attractive-looking horse, sulky, and driver to place. She won twelve dollars and gave six to Victoria. After too much fair food and just enough fun for everyone, the girls went to bed. Archie, Lank and Juliette went to the lounge with four other hotel guests. The hotel did not sell alcohol but they didn't mind people bringing their own to the lounge. They had a fine quality record player and everyone took turns playing records. They listened to Elvis Presley, Benny Goodman, Victoria de Los Angeles, the Mississippi Sheiks and the Everly Brothers. They danced and got to know new friends.

Lank said, "The way Victoria accepted half of Lacie's winnings; she was grateful but only in the way you're grateful for getting what's yours. Such a friendship they have. I wish we had friendships like that when we were little kids."

"I am surprised every day it continues. I cannot help waiting and expecting it to come to shit."

"Piss off, Juliette. Oh sorry. I didn't mean to yell." Archie offered his apologies all around. "Juliette, you're so pessimistic. They will be fast friends forever."

"I hope you're right."

Lank said, "They are true friends to each other right now. That's the important thing, isn't it?"

Juliette nodded. She learned so much from the tall thin man who often found what she lost. She filled herself with complications and contradictions but Lank took things as he saw them. He saw the obvious.

Rich smells of a late summer night combined with tobacco smoke and the elusively complex odor of people drinking together through a comfortably warm evening. The warmth of rum in Juliette's veins enhanced her fondness for the congenial company. Victoria's hair blowing in her face the day before transformed Juliette's memory into a garden of grace.

Juliette and the girls swam and played at the fairground in the afternoon where Victoria and Lacie dickered successfully with a woman selling handmade jewelry. They bought a beautiful, tasteful bracelet for Therese. It surprised Juliette that such a thing could be purchased at a state fair. The next morning, they did some sightseeing and headed for home. Fully satisfied, they felt unequivocally glad to be going home.

Juliette arrived at The Tracks completely broke and late summer was not a productive time for Our Pet. Boat and gear repairs planned for September required a loan. The fish plant backstopped credit for the independent boats. It was not exactly free. The boat would be bound to sell to Cameron Fisheries until the owner paid the debt but fishermen usually didn't have extra cash for big expenses. Jimmy avoided squeezing anyone. It worked, except for fishermen who whine about anything or fuck up everything.

Both Cliff and Jimmy realized that the New York trip, paid for almost exclusively by Juliette, left her a bit below penniless. They wanted to give or loan money to her but she looked forward to the austerity. Archie and Lank weren't in much better shape. However, Archie made some money doing research. Cliff's client faced a major dispute over large woodland holdings. Archie did a lot of library research but also field trips. He talked to woods workers and managers and just looked at the land and assessed the machinery and procedures. These field trips became the Roadmaster excursions. The girls, Juliette, and Lank often accompanied him. By mid-September, the girls got tired of seeing trees and trucks and bulldozers so Archie dropped them off in the nearest community. Juliette always took chalk. Hopscotch squares decorated the two-lane roads they visited in rural Nova Scotia. They also left three drawings of the Empire State building, obviously by different artists, and poetry, obviously by different authors, and odd sketches of train cars with porches, fences and flowerbeds.

City was never healthy and particularly unwell during the summers. He went on one of the Roadmaster trips but bad knees, bad back, and breathing problems brought on a whining exhaustion after half an hour of physical activity. Strenuous physical activity for City included standing up. City usually found a reason to stay seated in his boxcar. "Ah jeez wiz, Juls I…I…I just can't, you know. Oh my God, girl, the pains I've got."

The girls missed a lot of school because they had better things to do. A few kids and a few teachers resented Lacie and Victoria. They were the top students in their respective classes despite missing more school than anyone except Therese. She missed school because of illness. Therese was in Lacie's grade but looked destined to spend next year in Victoria's class. The girls had other friends but no close ones. Therese was one of the other friends. Lank said, "It is one of the best things to see that the girls are kind to Therese." Therese received little kindness in the schoolyard. Kids pushed her around and mocked her. Lacie got in trouble at school because she beat up a grade-five boy who had put a handful of mud in Therese's hair. Lacie asked Juliette, "What's a grand gesture?"

"A large sweeping movement a person makes. It depends on the usage. Why do you ask?"

"Sister Jeanne d'Arc called it a grand gesture when I beat up Arnie Doucet for what he did to Therese."

"Ah, Sister Jeanne d'Arc, she is a smart woman. She meant that you did the right thing. Your teacher did not see that but Sister Jeanne d'Arc did."

"No, my teacher yelled at me. Sister Jeanne d'Arc said that was a small price to pay."

"Yes, smart woman."

Victoria taught Therese how to keep her runny nose from being so disgusting. She provided her with Kleenex every morning and showed her how to use them, store them and dispose of them. It took Lank to determine that Therese was deaf in one ear. Therese tried to avoid intruding on Victoria and Lacie but it made her happy to be with the girls. When Lacie put her arm around Therese's skinny shoulder, the little girl leaned into her, looking happy and at peace. The girls didn't do it as a charity. They liked her. Therese made no demands. It didn't take much to please her. The scraggly-haired, snotty-nosed, sick little girl gained many benefits from her friendship with Victoria and Lacie. They helped her with schoolwork. Her status and her chances of making other friends improved. Victoria and Lacie were the most admired little kids in the school. Victoria's sparkle and Lacie's ability to do almost anything well meant other kids looked up to them. Some of this rubbed off on the tiny, sweet Therese. She hung around with the two coolest kids. The other kids became curious. They got rewarded with a placid and patient companion. Lank, Juliette and Lacie provided her with tasty, nutritious food. Her friendship with the girls didn't make Therese's life beautiful but her life improved.

CHAPTER NINETEEN

"Leave her alone, Juls. It's the way she is."

Juliette certainly stopped talking. Victoria and her mother fought about all sorts of things but Lacie never had a bad word for Juliette. Victoria blurted out, "Yeah, you'd never say anything like that to Lacie."

Juliette looked at the floor. Victoria didn't like this. Everything turned over into something new. It felt bad. "We gotta go, Mom." She kissed her mother where the bottom of her jaw became her neck. She smelled of Palmolive soap.

"Thank you, dear. Thank you for the kiss." Lacie slid the door open. She didn't say goodbye to Juliette. Outside, Victoria reached for her friend's arm, ran her hand down Lacie's forearm until she got to Lacie's hand, which closed gently around her own. /this is good/ her hand isn't angry/and I kissed Mom/she thanked me/okay/what's going to happen/

"You shouldn't have said that to her." Lacie's head turned like a spring-loaded trap. /that's what people see in her eyes/that look scares them/ Victoria heard a noise. She looked back. Her mother scrabbled over to Archie's. She walked like Tommy Brian when he got shot playing cowboys, when he ran for cover; a little hunched, shoulders curved in toward each other. Juliette walked almost sideways, facing the tracks, on her way to Archie's. When Victoria turned back to her friend, the stare was gone, their hands remained clasped, relaxed.

Lacie said, "I don't know. She's always harping at you about something."

"But you and her, you get along so good."

"I can't think. I made myself mad. I can't think."

"Are you mad at me?"

Lacie quickly said, "No, not you."

"But Mom and you are…"

"That's why I'm mad. Juls and I never say boo to each other but she's always at you."

Some cat jumped out of some bag; some balloon, puffed up with bad smells, burst. Victoria needed instructions. There must be instructions about this kind of situation. "But you and Mom are the greatest."

On the bridge, Lacie bent over the railing and looked down at the river. Victoria stood beside her. The springtime water swirled, jumped and thumped. Victoria pointed at the frothy pool by the ram pump. "It's like a washing machine."

"Do you think there's trout?"

Victoria felt good saying, "Yeah, fuck school. Let's find out if there's trout."

***

Lacie had Sister Jeanne d'Arc that year. Victoria's teacher was new. Mrs. Knickle's husband didn't live with her in the little house they bought in Brookfield. People in Sterling Reserve, including the school kids, both girls and boys, speculated about where her husband lived. Did he have another woman? Did she leave him? She wore clothes that were kind of sexy for a married woman, for a teacher. Nothing too revealing, just clothes that hugged her shape, a very nice shape. Anything could be going on with a woman like her. Some people said that.

Victoria liked Mrs. Knickle although she seemed sad and far away. When her mother suggested that she invite her teacher for dinner some night, Victoria said, "That would be splendid." She couldn't describe exactly what she saw but it showed that her mom didn't like her to say 'splendid'. She could say 'fuck' but she couldn't say 'splendid'.

Mrs. Knickle accepted the invitation. She came to the parcel car for dinner with Juliette, Victoria, Archie, Lank and Lacie. No one asked, 'Where's your husband?' Juliette made beef roll-ups, thin slices of beef rolled around pickles or asparagus or pepperoni or bread crumbs with garlic and stinky cheese. They were dredged in flour, fried in pork fat and served with potatoes and string beans, smothered in butter-fried chanterelles. Victoria's teacher ate it all, had seconds and a third serving of salad. Mrs. Knickle scavenged the chanterelles that Victoria thought were gross. She drank Juliette's beer and some of the wine she brought. When Juliette suggested that she stay over so they could drink rum, Mrs.Knickle said, "Oh I don't know. It doesn't strike me as proper to have Victoria see her teacher drinking rum." She gave Victoria a sweet smile but a hint of wanting to be bad trickled through the smile.

Juliette said, "Victoria sees her mother occasionally drinking rum although I have a preference for moonshine these days."

"Your offer is very generous. I ate more tonight than I had all week, perhaps longer than that. I wouldn't want to drink to excess."

"Well Laura, tomorrow is Saturday and I will try to keep you from doing yourself serious harm."

"Thank you. I would enjoy a glass of rum."

People stayed late. Victoria and Lacie waited for somebody to say something about their bedtime. Mrs. Knickle sat on the couch with Archie for a while. They smiled a lot and laughed some and tilted their heads at the same time. When Lank went home, Victoria and Lacie went with him and slept together in Lacie's little room. She liked the soft smell of Lacie's room and of Lacie herself. She liked the smell of her own room but it was bright and noticeable. The girls woke up later than usual for a Saturday. As they ran off to their bottle rounds, Juliette called, "Did you have breakfast?" Lacie said no. They had to go back and Juliette gave them cereal and an egg. It only took a few minutes but that was long enough to see that Mrs. Knickle sipped her tea, staring at nothing. Juliette seemed to have absorbed some of her sadness.

The bottle rounds went smoothly but they were tired of collecting bottles. They got tired of the competition when it sporadically turned up and the money they collected, a fortune for a six or seven year-old, didn't amount to much for a nine and a ten-year-old.

The girls bought a few chickens with their bottle money. The chickens made money for them after only a few months. They sometimes didn't have enough eggs for their own households because the people who gave them bottles also bought their eggs. They had endeared themselves to many in Sterling Reserve; these two girls, so pretty, so different and who for years had done their Saturday rounds and could often be seen holding hands. Mrs. O'Leary, who lived on the rows, referred to them as the dark beauty and the bright beauty.

After bottle rounds, Juliette asked them to come for lunch. Mrs. Knickle had gone. "What is she like in school, Victoria?"

"Oh, she's outstanding." Victoria was going to say 'splendid' but caught herself in time. Perhaps 'outstanding' wasn't any better.

"Ask her to come over again, soon. Ask her on Monday, please. Let her know she is welcome at any time. Be good to her, hon."

When her mother said, 'Be good to her, hon,' Victoria realized suddenly that Mrs. Knickle got smaller. She'd lost weight since she came to the school and her perfect figure diminished toward too thin, and all of the eating she did at dinner seemed strange.

Victoria asked her to come back for dinner but Mrs. Knickle wasn't right. The sadness had grown. The next Monday in early June, she didn't show up to teach. The story came out by Wednesday. Mrs. Knickle's husband of two years spent almost six months in a Halifax hospital. On the weekend, he died of throat cancer.

She came back to work for the last week of June. She didn't talk much in class and not at all out of class. She came back to watch over students as they wrote their exams. At the end of school, Mrs. Knickle left. Victoria never saw her again. It wasn't the sadness that made her so memorable to Victoria. Except for her mother, Mrs. Knickle was the only sexy woman she knew. Victoria often wondered during class what her teacher would look like without clothes. She wondered about this with all of her teachers but usually in a simple curiosity about skin color and the shape of this and that part of their body. With Mrs. Knickle it wasn't curiosity. It was desire. When Victoria stood close to Mrs. Knickle she felt an excitement. Standing next to her while she sat at her desk, Victoria glanced down her scoop-necked blouse one time and saw the top of both breasts, and a lacy bra. Mrs. Knickle's skin had a shine. Victoria felt a small tickle; so pleasant, like spinning on something between her legs. She wanted to touch her teacher's breasts. She knew that Mrs. Knickle saw her staring because, when she looked at her eyes, they looked straight into hers. Victoria couldn't help it; she looked down at the beautiful breasts again. The teacher's arm went around Victoria's waist. "Perhaps you should go back to your seat. Miss Cameron." Mrs. Knickle's arm turned her, directing her toward her seat. Victoria, so shaken by an overwhelming something, was surprised the students didn't stare at her. As Mrs. Knickle's arm turned her toward her seat, it also pulled her in close, bringing Victoria the warmth and pressure of her teacher's body. As she took the first steps back toward the class, her legs wobbled a bit and she felt a light pat on her bum as Mrs. Knickle's arm fell away.

Victoria didn't tell anyone about this. She didn't feel embarrassed but she could find no reason for sharing it. Sharing could diminish. Telling others about her sweet desire to be close to this woman didn't seem like a good idea. After the dinner party when Mrs.

Knickle drank too much to drive home and spent the night with Juliette, Victoria wondered if her mother knew that sweetness.

Mrs. Knickle left the school with few goodbyes, none to Victoria. She wanted to grow up like Mrs. Knickle. She wanted to become a woman like her. The sad occurrence in her beautiful teacher's life made it more powerful.

Victoria hinted at what happened to her in the presence of her teacher to Lacie but her best friend did not understand and did not ask for details or elaborations. That was fine with Victoria. It was hers alone.

The summer turned into a blur of sunshine and confusion, warm days with clear cool nights. Lacie stayed at her aunt's place in New Glasgow for most of the summer. From the second week in July until the last week in August, her best friend was missing from her life and Victoria didn't like it.

During the first week of Lacie's absence, Juliette spent a bit of time with her daughter but a herring run in Musquodoboit Harbour took her away. The big Buick Roadmaster had worn out. The Tracks didn't have a car for almost a year. Juliette bought two trucks, lots of gear and she rented a bigger boat and a skiff on a weekly basis. With her sense for fish behavior and her, up until then, useless herring trap license, Juliette went to work. Victoria crewed with her mother but they worked an endless cycle of steaming out to the herring traps, loading tons of glistening fish into crates, steaming back, unloading on the docks and then back out. Victoria ran the boat in clear water but Juliette set a herring trap near the shore. The Musquodoboit Harbour dock required tricky maneuvers and they always ran at full speed. Juliette really didn't want Victoria aboard. It got dangerously hectic on deck. Archie drove a five-ton truck full of fish to various fish plants, sometimes a hundred miles away. Victoria went with him a few times but Archie drove very attentively. He concentrated on driving because he always ran overweight and usually well above the speed limit. Twice when she went with him, other truck drivers waved him down and said, 'The weighers are out.' They used a headlight flashing code to tell other truck drivers the RCMP were around. Sporadic meals and lack of sleep left Archie tired all the time. Lank worked on the docks icing down herring, running a forklift, and spelling Archie on the five tons. He also fixed anything that broke. Juliette just worked. She did everything all day and all night. They talked about sending Victoria to Lacie's aunt's place but that didn't materialize. Nobody said it to Victoria but she figured the aunt didn't want her. During the summer, Victoria did not feel wanted by anyone except Lacie. They wrote each other every day.

Victoria stayed with a friend, Judy, for a week but never felt welcome. Judy was also an only child and having 'another kid underfoot' as Judy's mother put it, seemed too much for her. Her husband said, "It's beyond me that you can't look after a perfectly sweet child for a few weeks. If I make sixty dollars a week after gas that's a damn good week and you can't do this little thing for forty-five dollars a week. It's beyond me, woman."

He said this in front of Judy and Victoria. The next time she saw her mother, Victoria told her about it. Juliette took two days off to stay at home with her daughter. Juliette got up at least once a night to pee. Both nights, Victoria heard her on the way back to bed and called out, "Mom". Juliette came into her room, crawled into bed with her, cuddled and kissed. Both nights after the cuddling, Victoria watched her mother drift off with a peaceful smile on her beautiful lips. As Juliette fell asleep, the smile turned to light twitching and Victoria also drifted off. That her presence caused her mother to smile, so innocently and uncalled for, reassured her in that tristful summer. They spent some time together during those two days but Juliette kept busy with bookkeeping and hours of phone calls using The Grumpies's phone. Victoria heard her say to them that she expected the bill to be more than a hundred and fifty dollars for the long distance calls.

"Mom, forty-five dollars to Judy's mom, a hundred and fifty dollar phone bill, that's a lot of money, Mom. And the trucks must be expensive."

"Yes, Victoria, it is a lot of money but we make a lot of money on herring. I had hoped that the herring license would come through for me. Mr. Mosher told me to be patient. He was right but the huge quantity of herring surprised both of us. It may never happen again. That is why we have to work so hard, probably for another three weeks or a month. Then I will be home again. I am sorry it is so hard on you."

"I wish Lacie was around."

"I know dear, your best friend."

"She hates it in New Glasgow."

"It is the same thing with her father as with me. He has to work hard at this, too. I will pay Lank more for these two months' work than he made in the last two years."

"Do the three of you drink a lot?"

"Archie hardly at all because he drives all the time but Lank and I drink around the end of the day. We have a rule that I am not on the boat drunk and he is not on the dock drunk. We all keep safety rules in mind and we have been safe. I appreciate your concern. Thank you for that."

Victoria often tried to puzzle through what her mother appreciated from her and what she didn't. When she really tried to please, it didn't usually work. "I could visit Granddaddy, so you could get back to your boat."

"Are you sure? By yourself?"

"Yeah, sure."

"Oh, he would love that."

And love that he did. For the last two weeks in August, Jimmy entertained Victoria in any way she asked for and he added a lot she hadn't thought of. They went to the Bill Lynch Shows in Sydney. It was a carnival and circus. They both laughed until they had pains when they saw just how much an elephant can piss.

Jimmy and Karen, his girlfriend, had extended fights. In the summer of nineteen sixty-one, he lived alone except for a housekeeper who came every day to clean and cook. Victoria could cook better than her grandfather and she knew very well that she was not a good cook, even for a nine-year-old.

The second week in Glace Bay was the best. Juliette made phone calls and arrangements. Lacie arrived at the Glace Bay bus station. Victoria knew that her grandfather felt left out on the first day Lacie arrived, because she and her friend talked to each other without any let up. Victoria told this to Lacie and they made plans to include him. Together, Victoria and Lacie could figure out what to do in most situations.

Two nights before they left Glace Bay, after a day of tooling around in Jimmy's Oldsmobile and swimming at Ben Eoin beach with a lobster boil afterwards, Jimmy stopped at the Midtown Tavern on the way home. It was okay for a while. They had the car keys. They listened to the radio and put the power windows up and down a lot. Lacie said maybe they would wear out the battery so they started the car and after a while began revving the engine. Some man came to the window and said, "What the hell do you think you're celebrating?" Victoria said, "Christmas." and rolled up the windows. After two hours in the parking lot, they went into the tavern.

"Hey, you girls ain't allowed in here."

"I came in for Grandfather." She walked over to Jimmy who sat with a bunch of men talking intently. She heard Lacie say to the man who tried to stop them, "Get your fucking hands off me. She's going to get her grandfather and we need to pee." Victoria spun around and said, "Lacie, calm down; don't hurt him." The waiter looked up at Victoria, then back to Lacie. She must have had those eyes because he turned around and went about his business picking up empty beer bottles. They both peed in the bathroom that smelled even more like beer and cigarettes than the rest of the tavern did. They could tell that Jimmy felt just as proud of their boldness as they did.

The girls were in bed for an hour when Jimmy woke them. "The caplin are runnin' on Number Two beach."

The girls didn't quite know what that meant but it sounded exciting and it was the middle of the night. They bounced out of bed. Jimmy loaded the shiny Oldsmobile with buckets and small nets with handles. They also took rubber boots but the boots hardly got to the beach before the girls took off their boots and pants in favor of bare feet and legs. The trick was to pick up the silver caplin as they washed up on the beach and before the next wave took them out again. Getting wet was inevitable. They picked the caplin by hand; the nets proved useless.

Jimmy wasn't his gregarious self. When he spoke to people, he faced away from them. Jimmy didn't stay at the beach long. He told the girls not to go out too far, and then walked back to the car.

"I wonder if he's sick or something."

Lacie said, "He's drunk and feels out of place."

Victoria let the place seep into her. Two dozen people picked and scooped the sleek, chined-bodied little caplin from the moonlit beach. She heard talking and a few cries when somebody got a new part of their body or their clothes wet but it was not boisterous. It wasn't gruff like fishermen on the dock. Nobody drank and nobody swore. The water felt warmer than the late August air and the company acted more subdued and gentle than a kid could expect from an after-midnight gathering of adults. Two boys, loud and pleading and running, scrambled down the rocks to the beach with their mother behind them reciting a litany of cautions and, "Wait up, Davie". A young man, there with his girlfriend, said to one of the boys, "Oh, look here. There's a good patch of 'em here. Come on." The first boy shyly went to the area the young man indicated, the second boy ran to it when he saw his brother holding a little fish in each hand. The boys settled into the quiet rhythm of the caplin moondance.

In forty-five minutes of picking caplin, Lacie and Victoria filled three buckets and their two nets which slumped over in the sand trying to contain the piles of fish in them. The caplin stayed in when the girls lifted the nets but the fish flopped over the edges when they put the nets down. One of the boys cut his toe on a rock or a piece of glass in the surf. The boys hadn't caught a lot of fish but their mother wanted to leave in order attend to the cut. "Mommy, let's stay." Even the boy with the cut didn't want to leave but their mother insisted. Lacie picked up the two nets of fish and poured them into the boys' buckets. She filled the buckets and still had some caplin left in one net.

Victoria said, "Let me see your foot." The boy lifted his foot. There was a small trickle of blood coming from a fine cut on his big toe. She brushed away some sand, kissed the toe and looked up at the speechless boy.

"Ahem, say thank you for the fish, David and Leonard." A weak, tentative thank you came out of both boys. They went up the rocky hill. Their mother carried one full bucket and supported the injured boy as he limped along. The other boy carried a bucket of fish. Both boys turned around several times saying, "See ya", "G' night", "Bye".

Grandfather Jimmy sat in the backseat, passed out. He had a pint of Anne Bonnie rum between his legs, close to his crotch, and a quart of Schooner beer a bit farther down. The wider beer bottle and the flask of rum stood safely wedged so they didn't spill even though he was completely unconscious. Victoria found the cap for the rum bottle. Half a quart of beer remained so they each had a good slug of it before leaving it by a rock. They drove home with Jimmy sleeping in the back. Lacie worked the pedals, only two on the Oldsmobile, and Victoria stood on the seat and steered. Driving the automatic was a breeze. Victoria even waved at a couple of people. As they headed down Commercial Street, a police car followed behind them right to Jimmy's paved driveway.

"Your name is Vicky, isn't it?"

"Yes sir, Victoria is my name."

"You tell your grandfather to see the sergeant in the morning. I know your mother and I never saw it but I'd be surprised if she never done this when she was your age."

"Yes, sir. Would you like some caplin?"

"Now, don't you be tryin' to bribe a policeman."

"Yes sir, ah, no sir."

"I'm just kiddin'. Just kiddin'. Yeah sure, I'd like a dozen caplin. I'll have that ready for my wife's breakfast when she gets up." Victoria scooted into the house with a bucket of caplin. The policeman said to Lacie, "I don't like fresh caplin but the wife loves them. If you got some smoked though, I'd love to have a few."

Lacie grinned at him, "I didn't see any smoked fish of any kind washing up on the beach."

"Now, you're a smart little thing aren't you?"

"My apologies but I couldn't resist it." The policeman had missing teeth at both edges of his wide smile. Lacie said, "I've smoked fish at home with my father and Juls, I mean Juliette, Vee's mum, I mean Victoria, but I don't think we'll have time here. We're leaving in a day or two. Now, Jimmy's idea of food preparation comes to an end when he gets the fish on board a boat."

The policeman said, "Well, my God, I would've said it was you who was Juliette's daughter. I can just hear her sayin' them same words."

Victoria, bare legs, bare feet, and her underwear still wet from the surf, returned with a waxed paper bag. "I got them in tinfoil with some ice cubes. I could take their heads off and clean them if you like."

"Thanks Victoria, thanks. No need to clean them; she eats the whole thing. I'll get them home to the Frigidaire right now and cook 'em up when I get off shift." Then he said to Lacie, "You can put pepper on them before the flour or while they're cookin'. The wife likes the pepper on late, just before they're out of the pan. She says black pepper is the most underrated spice. You can do a lot with pepper, you know."

It took Lacie an almost awkwardly long time to answer. She looked like she was trying to add up a bunch of big numbers. "I never thought of it but yes, it's not just hot, is it?"

"No, girl, a rich warm flavor it's got."

"Does Jimmy like caplin in the morning, do you know?"

"Jimmy Cameron will eat any fish that's goin' any time of the day."

Victoria said, "Should we try to get him to bed?"

"Nah. He sleeps in his car lots; sittin' up just like that. I'll come around about five o'clock and get him up and bring him into the house if he's still here."

"Thank you, sir."

"Thank you, Victoria. The wife will love these. You tell your grandfather to see the Sergeant." The policeman laughed as he got back in his car.

The next day, Jimmy took the girls with him to the police station.

"Did they tell you how ya got home?"

"Well no, Victor. I never thought to ask."

"The little one was steerin', so George says, and the other one pushin' the pedals. The little one stood up on the seat, drove perfect, so George says." Jimmy and the sergeant laughed until they both had a coughing fit. Before the coughing ended, Jimmy took out his cigarettes and offered one to Victor. "No, no, I can't do them Sweet Caporal." He pulled an "Export A" from the open pack on the desk. The type hammers of a typewriter swatted mercilessly hard on a piece of paper somewhere in the police station. Victoria picked out the intention behind the sound; someone did something badly and hated it. The angry, halting type would surely leave holes in the paper.

"Now, Jimmy, two little girls drivin' the car and you passed out drunk. Jesus, Jimmy."

Jimmy did his best to look somewhat repentant, "Ah yes, I know, I know. 'Jesus, Jimmy' is right."

"My God, man, what are ya, sixty-two, now?"

"Yes, Victor, you're as right as rain, bye. Should know better, eh?"

"I know ya drove home after drinkin' at the Midtown."

"I guess you would know. Ralph Connors was sittin' right with me. The town crier himself."

"Now this stuff happens too much, Jimmy."

Victoria saw her grandfather in a sorry position. He said 'sorry' in so many ways but he looked at her with a grin and he winked. This meant some kind of fun.

"Jimmy, bye, it's got to stop. You know that, man."

"Victor, do you remember the time at the Mira River, we…"

"Nah, now there'll be none of that now. You get your fat arse out of my chair. I got work to do."

"So long, Victor."

Both girls said goodbye to the sergeant. Walking out they heard somebody say, "Hey sarge, tell us about the Mira." The next night, the night before they had to leave Glace Bay and two nights before the first day of school, Jimmy took them out in the car. He asked them to drive. He was sober. He just wanted to see it. At first he laughed and found it all quite amusing but then watched them and watched the car's progress. Victoria thought he was serious, not making a joke when he said, "Yeah, well ya drive better than I do but ya should because there's two of ya, and I usually got half a brain and just one eye open."

On the last morning, Lacie fried caplin and made pancakes. Everyone ate a lot, including the housekeeper who happily arrived to a breakfast already cooked. They had fresh blueberries and tea for Jimmy and the housekeeper. The four of them walked to the bus station carrying the girls' bags. When the bus pulled away and everyone waved goodbye, Victoria saw Jimmy patting the housekeeper's bum. She thought perhaps he winked at her.

***

"How did you like Glace Bay?"

"Fabulous. Granddaddy is the greatest."

Juliette carried their bags from the Acadian Lines bus station to a new looking Dodge.

"Who owns this, Mom?

"We do. I traded the blue five-ton. The herring are still running about half what they were but the price flopped out. We got the best of it. All of us made a lot of hard-work money and we want to thank you two for putting up with it. There's a party for you and Lacie on the weekend in Halifax. Invite whoever you want. We're going to rent a bus and a whole floor of a hotel. Does that sound like fun?"

"Yeah, superb fun."

The party was fun, perhaps not superb but better than okay. The adults didn't drink at all. From her hotel room bed, Victoria said, "Granddaddy woke us up because the caplin were running."

Juliette said, "Great, how did that go?"

"It was great, yeah great. Nobody curses on the beach."

"Oh, really. I never noticed that. Did you like that; nobody cursing?"

"It was all nice. People acted nice. We were good to each other. Lacie and I gave two boys a bucket of caplin because one of them cut his toe and had to go home."

"That was very kind of you."

Victoria looked up at her mother from the hotel room bed with Lacie already asleep in the other double bed. Juliette stroked back her child's hair and ran her fingers over her forehead. Those fingers, usually fine and warm, felt rough, dry and cracked from the abuse Juliette put them through all summer on the herring boat.

"If I tell you this, you won't get mad at granddaddy, will you?"

"Well, how could I know if I will get mad? It depends on what you tell me."

"I don't want you to get mad at him."

"Well, this is difficult because you do not want to tell me until you know I will not get mad but I cannot guarantee that, unless I know what I am not getting mad about. Perhaps you can keep it to yourself. I have known Father Jimmy all my life. Jimmy has always been Jimmy and I never got mad at him yet."

"Okay, I'll tell. We went down to the beach but we had to take off our boots and slacks so we only had our panties and granddaddy was kind of drunk and he went back to the car." Victoria saw the faint smile disappear with whatever else it was on her mother's face that she loved to look at during times like this. It's hard to tell what changes in a face to take away the all-good look, and make it something else. Even the position of her mother's mouth and lips didn't change that much. "Maybe I shouldn't tell you."

"No, go on. Tell me what happened."

"Don't get mad. The police already got mad at him."

"Tell me, sweetie, what happened?"

"Well, okay. We picked caplin and got wet and gave some away and I kissed the boy's toe so it would get better and we went back to the car and Granddaddy was asleep in the back. We put the cap on his rum and poured out the beer and then… then we drove home. I stood on the seat and Lacie did the pedals and the policeman followed us and said we drove good and I gave him caplin for his wife and he told Lacie how to cook them and Lacie made caplin breakfast two days in a row and Granddaddy had to go see the sergeant and we went with him."

Victoria saw all the worry and darkness drain from her mother's face, replaced by a big smile. Her teeth picked up the reflected city light through the hotel window. Victoria felt just right.

"Well, you can pretty much count on Jimmy getting drunk. You know that you and Lacie are too young to drive."

"We're almost twenty between us."

"True; you got me there."

"What happened at Mira?"

"I have no idea. Why do you ask?"

"Granddaddy made Seargent Victor stop scolding him when he talked about Mira."

"Oh yes, Victor Mumbercat. One time, so I was told, they convinced Victor that he could play the bagpipes. Victor was very drunk and he marched right off the end of the wharf into the Mira River. They say the bagpipes were still squealing when Victor went under."

"That's funny."

"Victor is a sweetie. And good night to you, my sweetheart."

"Good night, Mom. Thank you for the big party."

"You are welcome Victoria. Manufactured fun is not as good as the real stuff is it."

"Huh, I don't know." Victoria did know. She knew that her mother meant you can't set up fun that's as good as fun that just happens. She thought her mother was probably right about that and she would mull it over in her mind and compare the just-happened fun to the put-in-place fun and then decide for herself. But tonight she would like Juliette to think that the party was the greatest.

CHAPTER TWENTY

Cliff, in his late thirties, became a moderately wealthy man. His legal practice exposed him to various money-making opportunities. He chose real estate and did well. Failing enterprises often got an infusion of cash from Cliff when he bought an option to purchase or a right of first refusal. The business had another chance to make it. Cliff would sell the option back to them if the establishment became viable again but his predictions of eventual failure were always correct. He acquired all of the optioned properties and a few of the first refusals. After that, his real estate management team found new tenants.

A nasty and difficult lady worked for him. She had a nose for the areas of town on the verge of rising status either as housing rentals or commercial properties. Cliff rarely spoke to her but often took her advice. She received a salary from him but had no real job except to live in Halifax and tell him where to buy next. She took other jobs for extra income but mostly to poke around and determine which commercial tides flowed and which tides ebbed. She joined clubs and churches and did volunteer work for the same reason. Cliff wanted to distance himself from her methods and he felt ambivalent about paying her to be manipulative and devious. However, he made the compromise for money.

Cliff suggested that The Tracks move itself to Halifax. He owned a building in the South end of the city that needed work. He could guarantee very low rent for three years with an opportunity for Archie, Lank, and Juliette to work on the place in lieu of rent and for pay. Archie knew the building as beautiful and historic with lots of potential for being eased into the modern age while keeping its character.

The Trackers wondered what their decisions to retire in their twenties would mean for their fifties. They might need to get a not-so-great job when they were older and perhaps less capable and less willing. They talked about schooling, culture and various opportunities for the girls in the vibrant little city. Victoria and Lacie participated in these conversations.

One year maximum, they told Cliff. The Trackers moved to Halifax in late summer of nineteen-sixty-two. City stayed and took charge of the chickens and kept an eye on the railcars. It didn't involve much work. Tommy Brian fed the chickens and delivered eggs to customers. If anything needed doing at The Tracks, City told Tommy Brian, Tommy told his Uncle Bill, and the doing got done. But the responsibility weighed heavily on City. They had a phone in Halifax but didn't give City the number. He'd call ten times a day. City eventually fell into the rhythm and felt good supervising twenty-three chickens.

Victoria went into grade five and Lacie into grade six at the same school. They made friends easily and, as had been the case at Sterling Reserve, they got the highest marks with little effort. The adults enjoyed the libraries, the universities, live music, plays, museums and bars. They found two after-hours, illegal bars they liked. One of the underground bars booked surprisingly high profile rhythm and blues bands from New York, Boston and Detroit. Cliff and his friends from The Tracks were often the only white faces in the bar. The management worried about publicity in the wrong places so they didn't usually admit strangers, particularly white ones, but as often happened in Halifax, Cliff had an arrangement. In exchange for admission, the club got free informal legal advice on this and that, mostly on the difficulties of becoming a legal drinking establishment.

His value to the rhythm and blues bar became apparent only a month before The Tracks crowd arrived in Halifax. Cliff had a talent for picking discrete informants. He got wind of an impending raid. The police arrived to find just Cliff and a lot of well-dressed black people drinking coffee and learning the tango from a Uruguayan couple. The next day, a secretary from the police station called him, "Nice work, Mr. McLellan. Nobody else will say it to you but just about everybody here is happy about how the raid went. It's a nice quiet bar for the Negroes. There's never any trouble there, you know, they take care of their own. We had a complaint, you know, from some hoity-toity. Everybody here, well damn near everybody, is glad it was clean."

Lank met a nurse, a young married woman, who came to the house to have sex on her lunch break any time Lank wanted. Juliette had Cliff and occasional couplings with near strangers and Archie had adjusted his standards. He didn't know why but a woman did not need to be perfectly gorgeous before he noticed her.

"Yes yes, it's equivalent to becoming much more desirable to women. I now have a wider choice. It's convenient as hell."

They worked on renovating the building they lived in. At the end of October, they had one small apartment ready. Juliette and the girls moved in. A problem became clear to all of them by the beginning of December. They preferred living at The Tracks. By Christmas, they concentrated on getting the work finished. Over the Christmas break, even Lacie put in a forty-hour week. Victoria managed about fifteen hours but in January, she designed a kid's room. They executed her design. The apartment with the Victoria-designed room rented in April. Victoria's room was a big selling point for the first apartment to start making money for Cliff.

It reinforced Juliette's belief that she did not understand her daughter. She felt happy that her child achieved this triumph but Victoria genuinely thought nothing of it. Her overly dramatic behavior didn't apply to her actual accomplishments. Victoria's self-consciousness was, Juliette thought, fed by some lack of confidence but not alleviated by success. However, it could be replaced by success. Victoria didn't brag or exaggerate her abilities nor did she display false modesty. It seemed to Juliette that Victoria expected to do things very well. Anything less made her awkward.

This knowledge did not help mother or daughter deal with the attention seeking when it came around. Juliette had a hierarchy of the types of people she disliked. The mean, nasty and violent people stood squarely on top of her dislike list, then came the know-nothing know-it-all's and, right behind them the flitty and overly demonstrative. Victoria's loud sighs and exaggerated gesticulations inflamed, like needles in nerves.

They finished the building in September, nineteen sixty-three, with the last group of tenants waiting for the last apartment. Archie's fastidiousness ruled their workdays and they did a good job on the renovations. Cliff's spy lady made a good call on the location. Fully occupied with five renters, it gave Cliff great leverage in buying other promising buildings. The Trackers received good pay for good work but all felt reasonably sure that they didn't need to do that, again.

Cliff talked to Archie and Juliette about it. "That wasn't a very good test to see if you liked living in the city. If you both had decent jobs and places to live, it would be different. I know I could get each of you a proper house that will go up in value. You've both got some money and you both have earning potential. Fuck, you're wasting away out here on The Tracks. I'm sure it was fun for a while but you're squatters in old railcars, for God's sake."

"Do you think we're stupid and don't know what we want?"

"No Arch, but living in a building under construction when you're the ones doing the constructing can really get to you. I know; I've done it."

Juliette said, "What your lawyerly brain cannot comprehend is that Archie and I and Victoria like living here, a crowbar could not pry Lank out of here and Lacie loves the woods. We like Halifax but prefer living here.

"Okay, okay. I guess I can understand that but if you change your minds, I'll put something together."

"He's a foreign power looking for a defector, isn't he?"

"Yes sir, that's what I am."

Victoria came into the caboose, "Oh hi, Cliff." She hugged him. She hugged Archie and said, "Mmm."

Juliette asked her about her school day.

"It was monstrously boring. Cliff, to what do we owe your illustrious presence?"

"I don't know how to answer that."

"I know you're going to whisk Mom off to places unknown. Did Lacie get back yet?"

Juliette said, "She is probably at home or on her way."

"I'm going to Lacie's. Toodle loo."

Archie asked, "Are you coming back for supper?"

"I don't know. It depends on what Mr. Graham or Miss Graham has on the menu."

"Right, would you let me know by five?"

"I'll think about it." Victoria left with a big smile and a dismissive wave.

"Even me; sometimes she pisses me off."

"Steady now, Arch. She's eleven. You've still got twelve, thirteen, fourteen and fifteen to go through and by sixteen you'll be so worried about her, you'll forget she's a pain in the ass."

Archie said, "Lacie is almost thirteen, she's never been a pain in the ass."

Juliette went to him and put her hand on his shoulder. Archie covered her hand with his. "It's all right, love, just a little lapse on my part."

"I wish I could offer relief but she has to have you."

"I know, I know, and my life would be hollow without Victoria. Does she ever hug you?"

"Oh, is that it?" Archie didn't answer. "Victoria returns hugs, sometimes warmly but she does not initiate. I am not a huggable sort although I certainly embrace you two and the bag of bones down the tracks and Sister Jeanne d'Arc."

Archie said, "You hug Sister Jeanne d'Arc?"

"Yes, you should try it, a warm sexy body. We make each other excited, just hugging."

Archie headed for the liquor cupboard. "Jesus, Juliette, you're a nasty whore sort of girl."

Cliff laughed, glad that homeostasis reasserted itself; the normal tease-and-be-teased banter returned.

"Cliff, you have hired members of the oldest profession. If Sister Jeanne d'Arc and I became tagteam hookers, do you think we would do all right?"

"If you decide to do that, I could give up law, be your representative and live better on the crumbs that fall from your table."

Archie said, "I didn't know that you visited prostitutes."

"Oh, sorry, Cliff. I thought Archie knew that. I am so sorry, Cliff."

"Does it feel weird to pay for sex?"

Juliette said, "You do not pay for the sex, Archie. You pay to have them leave afterwards."

"Well, sometimes, particularly with one regular girl in Halifax, I used to get her for the whole evening and she'd stay for breakfast."

"Oh, lucky girl, hard fried eggs, dried up bacon and pale toast."

"Juliette, you know I can cook cream of wheat."

"Oh yes, I am sure the lumpy cream of wheat kept them coming back."

"Now I'm hurt."

Archie said, "I like Sister Jeanne d'Arc. Seriously, I do. She's fun and, dare I say, sexy in some kind of way. I don't know how that can happen with that garb they have to wear."

Juliette said, "Sex exudes. It does not need exposure."

"So my past is with whores and your future is with nuns." Cliff turned to Juliette. "Do you think you might have chosen the wrong old buddy?"

"No, fuck that. I do not want to compete with the virgin in the cool threads."

***

"She's intimidated by you. She thinks of you as some sort of goddess or movie star. She'd want nothing, nothing more than to be just like you. She gets stuck in that saucy, strutty showing off. Can't shake it. It's like a fear response."

"Holy shit, Lank, I hope you are wrong. I know she has… Well we have a problem with each other but, afraid of me? I sincerely hope you are not right but I suspect you are."

"Not afraid, like of the dark or danger but you're what she wants to be but she knows, or believes, that she'll never reach it."

"What do you think I should do? I am lost here, Lank." Juliette had eggs out, some onions, and wilted celery. She pondered what to cook. Juliette loved the dining car kitchen.

"Well now, maybe there's unconscious meanness going on here. Vee might think that keeping you believing you're failing her is the only way to cut you down to her size."

"Lank, do you have any positive insights, perhaps something nice or at least promising? There is a Siamese dish, I guess Thailandese. It is something like chow mein but spicy. Do you know anything about that?"

"Thai noodles. You need bean curd for it though. What I've said is pure speculation. I don't know Vee at all. She's all complication and kind of enigmatic. I mean, Lacie can be unpredictable but it's easy to know her." Lank bent over one of the dining car tables repairing a carburetor.

"How right you are. Lacie is right there in front of you. She will have secrets but she is straightforward. It is funny. Lacie could be more unpredictable than Victoria as to what trouble she might get into but she stands right in front of you, clear and clean. Stewed deer meat is exactly like bean curd, is it not?"

"Yes, it is not. Yeah, Lacie's easy. It's a good thing for me because I don't know a damn thing about raising a daughter."

"Knowledge has fuck all to do with it; it is a failing of the heart that I have. Railroad Thai noodles it is." She chuckled and dug out a bottle of stewed venison from the icebox.

CHAPTER TWENTY- ONE

On her way back from the hospital, Victoria met City. He made a display of trudging off for groceries. "Oh my, it's some slippery underfoot, eh Victoria? It's a long way to the store."

"Do you have a list?"

"That I do."

"I'll get your groceries. I'll get Mom to go with me if she's not busy."

"Victoria, you're an angel, my dear. Here's the money and here's the list. I hope it's enough money."

"Okay. I'll see you in an hour or so."

"Hi, Mom." She kissed Juliette on the cheek. Her mother smiled; she looked shy. /oh god/I don't kiss her enough/she likes my kisses/ "Ah, Lacie says Hi and thanks for the little rice things. What are they called?"

"Sushi."

"Sushi, yeah, she knew what they were."

"Did you give some to Dr. Lawley?"

"He wasn't there and Mrs. Ingram didn't want them so Lacie and I ate them all. They're nice. Weird tastes though. The black stuff was good."

"That is a soy sauce mixture."

"Anyway, City found it slippery underfoot. I always feel like saying something like, 'is it supposed to be slippery overfoot'. It wouldn't hurt him to fall on that fat ass. Anyway, I'm doing his grocery shopping."

"Did he complain about his bones, dragging them to town, et cetera?"

"No. You think maybe he's finally realized that it's all the lard around his old bones that's the problem?"

Juliette laughed, "City always gives us a chance to act mercifully to an unfortunate."

"I helped turn Lacie's bed. She had to shit when I was there. I hate that. Mrs. Ingram said that in about three weeks or a month, she'll be able to use a bedpan. I mean, Lacie is waiting and looking forward to being able to use a fucking bedpan. Jesus Jesus Jesus fuckin' Jesus it's not fair. Lacie stuck there like that… like the filling in a sandwich and City won't even walk to the store. He's got two good legs."

Juliette pulled Victoria toward her and held on. Victoria saw the glistening tears forming as her own eyes clouded up. She had ranted and made her mother cry. They held each other and couldn't escape weeping. Her mother's voice, right in her ear, resonated with gentle strength.

"City never asked for the curse of fat and lazy but he must accommodate that curse."

"Yeah, I know." They both wiped tears away. Juliette's hair stuck to the side of her face. She used two fingers to unstick her mother's hair, sliding her fingers along the smooth, damp skin of Juliette's cheek under the strand of hair. Juliette closed her eyes and touched Victoria's hand. *Mom feels this too/she feels like I do/me and her feel the same/oh Mom/*.

"Oh Mom, it's not City; it's Lacie. It's so hard for her, and what if she doesn't get better?"

CHAPTER TWENTY-TWO

Tommy Brian Cross and Therese Deveau hung out with Victoria and Lacie. The Tracks girls preferred each other's company when they weren't doing things with their parents or with Archie but next in line, they enjoyed Tommy Brian and Therese.

Therese, almost two years older than Victoria, looked two years younger but acted like a quiet little old lady.

Lacie and Victoria walked Therese home. She invited them in and gave each of them a cookie from what appeared to be her own cookie tin. Therese kept the cookie tin in her small bedroom, separated from the rest of the house by a curtain and two sheets of a flimsy pressed-wood paneling called beaverboard. She gave Victoria and Lacie each a teacup of water with their stale cookie. Lacie worked at getting the thanks right. /let her know we appreciate/don't overdo it/she's not stupid/ Lacie had a sneezing fit. The hand she held over her mouth got covered with cookie crumbs, water, and mucus. She wiped it on the inside of her skirt, smiled, and shrugged her shoulders. They heard a yelp from Mrs. Deveau. /good to know she's alive/sometimes you can barely tell/. The three girls scrambled to the kitchen.

"The cat brought it in. Look in the corner. It's not a mouse."

Lacie said, "Ooh...oh look; it's a flying squirrel, isn't it?"

Mrs. Deveau sniveled, "Will it get in my hair?"

"No, Momma. That's a bat and it's not true, anyway."

"Oh."

Lacie bent down in the corner. The flying squirrel didn't move. She picked it up and blew a ball of dust off its tail. The squirrel's eyes were enormous. Lacie held it in her palm. The flying squirrel didn't move.

"Vee, Therese, look! It's as light as a feather. Here, hold it, Therese."

"No. It's scared of you; it would be scared of me. All it knows is that we're even bigger than the cat. Put it out in a bush or something, please Lacie. It's so scared."

Lacie could tell that Vee would love to touch it but that couldn't happen now. Mild-mannered Therese spoke with the authority of kindness. Lacie went outside holding the flying squirrel in her open palm. It made no effort to escape until she got to the big ash tree behind the house. The tree made the Deveau's small house look even smaller. Lacie placed the squirrel in the ash tree where the huge trunk became two thick branches. The flying squirrel stood still for two seconds before scrambling up the tree.

Therese said, "Oh wasn't it sweet? Those eyes, did he feel as soft as he looked?"

"It was so light in my hand. Almost not there."

"You're so lucky, Lacie. You'll remember that forever. You saved him."

***

Tommy Brian was thirteen. Early in December, he told Lacie that sometimes his bird swelled up. It didn't hurt but it made him feel funny. Lacie explained to Tommy Brian that he got a hard-on and that's how you screwed. He didn't seem convinced until Lacie opened up his pants and started rubbing his cock. It began to swell up. As he got hard, Lacie got more interested. She knelt down in the wet snow in front of Tommy Brian. Juliette had told her and Victoria all about that stuff. Lacie's head flung back. She spit and said, "TB, do you ever wash?"

He lived in an old farmhouse with his mother. They had a cold-water hand-pump in the kitchen and personal cleanliness didn't have high priority in the family. "It's right big; it swells up."

"You gotta wash. You smell bad and you taste awful."

Tommy Brian did stink. Tommy Brian got clean only in summer when they swam in the river but his clothes always smelled. It wasn't unusual in that time and place for kids to be stinky. On a rainy day in Sterling Reserve or Brookfield, a pungent atmosphere hung in most classrooms; however, nobody considered stinky a good way to be.

Between Lacie and Victoria, they had three dwellings available to them, always an empty car to play in. Juliette's was best with a large open space, curtains, blinds and water. Juliette had hooked up to the ram pump. When she got running water, she purchased a bathtub and an old hand-cranked ringer washer. With the wood-fired cook stove on, she had running hot water.

Little Therese didn't want to have anything to do with that swelling cock business. She thought it was all kind of dirty.

Juliette went to Halifax for three days. Victoria and Lacie took advantage of her absence. They gave Tommy Brian a bath and cleaned the clothes he wore and some clothes he took with him. The clothes didn't dry quickly enough. Tommy Brian sat by the woodstove in Lacie's pajamas. They decided that he could wear his damp clothes home with Lacie's pajamas underneath so he wouldn't freeze. He could pick up his other pants, two shirts, one pair of socks and one pair of underwear in the morning when they dried. Tommy Brian felt better with a plan in place so the three of them explored the hard-on phenomena.

Victoria asked her mother, "What can you do without getting pregnant?" Juliette answered, "Sit on your ass." She and her mother did have a talk. Victoria told Lacie and Tommy Brian she knew all that stuff anyway but it was a good review.

Lacie said, "Daddy talks to me about sex but Juls does it best."

"Yeah. Anyway, Mom explained the best way to do stuff. I'll give you a hand job." In three minutes, the job was done.

"That's the stuff that comes out in my underwear sometimes when I'm asleep."

Lacie said, "If you jerk off, do a hand job on yourself, that won't happen at night and you'll have more fun."

"Mummy noticed that I ain't been to communion."

Victoria asked what that had to do with jerking off.

"You can't go to communion if you got a mortal sin on your soul."

"Oh yeah, that shit."

"I don't wanna go to confession. Our priest gets right mad if you got sins, especially with girls."

"Maybe it's time to give up religion. You're almost fourteen."

"Then, I'll go to hell."

Victoria asked, "Does your religion say that I'll go to hell?"

"No. You don't know no better 'cause your mother's a heathen."

"Well, that's good."

"I'll go to hell if I die with a mortal sin on my soul and Mummy is watching me 'cause I'm not goin' to communion. Ya can't go to communion with a mortal sin on your soul. It'd be a sacrilege."

Lacie asked, "What happens if you get a sacrilege? Is that double hell?"

"I don't know. Somethin' like that."

Tommy Brian got to confession and communion. Mrs. Cross relaxed and Tommy Brian's brief affair with Victoria ended. The priest called it a severe sin to do it with non-Catholic girls and that those girls created occasions of sin. Tommy Brian still hung around with The Tracks girls but Therese joined in again. Just between themselves, Victoria and Lacie called Tommy Brian 'Sinbad' and Therese, 'Mother Therese'.

"Let's not tell Juls about the names. She'd find it too funny."

"What is it about Mom finding things funny?"

"We shouldn't tell anybody about the names."

"Why not tell Mom? She won't tell anybody else. You know that."

"They're our friends and we're mocking them. It's bad enough between us."

It was true though, that Lacie had a problem with things Juliette found funny. The conversations among the adults, the smart adults, thrilled Lacie, particularly with Juliette involved. To Lacie, she was clearly the smartest. She told this to Juliette who answered simply, "Yes, I am."

It bothered Lacie that Juliette came up with something, a new way of looking at how people acted. It could be about all people, or the people at The Tracks, church people, white people or just herself. She'd find things nobody noticed and before you knew it, that little thing would show up stuff people didn't want to see, things that embarrassed them, made them edgy. So many times, Lacie saw Juliette with two or three of the men and she'd start on one of these things. She'd be smiling, laughing a bit, being kind of happy but the men, there were rarely any other women involved; the men looked like they were in a battle. They walked into a town full of snipers. Lacie's father saved himself by admitting the funny fault right away.

"Yeah, I do that." Archie fought her and always lost. Sometimes Archie got surly and it looked like he was in the wrong but Lacie knew better. She knew it was Juliette's fault. She was too strong. She should let up.

Cliff could handle it. He moved like the littlest guy who played on the Peanut Line for the Glace Bay Miners' hockey team. Whenever some guy from the other team tried to check him, he'd either pass the puck real quick or make some slippery little move so that the player from the Halifax team crashed into the boards alone.

Lacie thought Juliette got kind of mean when she latched on to one of these things, often just before she got real drunk. She figured Juliette didn't intend to be mean because she never tried to nail Cliff. She never tried to nail anybody. She just talked about people and what a joke we all were and she didn't realize it hurt to hear that.

Doctor Lawley suffered most from Juliette's enjoyment of her own cleverness. He encouraged it and pretended to like it. He called Juliette's cynical tirades a great learning experience. But when she got going strong and fast, he'd raise his glass to his mouth but stop, not take a drink, and lower it again. He made moves to get up but then settled uneasily in his chair. Geoge Lawley's eyes flicked around looking for a way out and he stammered when he tried to get a quick comment out there on that battlefield. George hid behind his glass again. None of the men except Cliff seemed to know they got caught in a war.

When Juliette went off to Halifax for the three days that gave the girls a chance to clean up Tommy Brian's body and get his soul dirty, Lacie and Victoria walked her to the bus stop. Mrs. Reynolds met them by the bridge on the Sterling Reserve side. She said hello and talked with them for two minutes.

Juliette said, "She wore brand, new leather gloves?" Then she started in on hand movements and how one person would try to make a chance encounter into a big event and how the manufactured eventfulness became contagious and everybody's hands would start to do this and that. Lacie said, "Don't push that cynical trade on me and Vee."

She meant to say 'cynical tirade' but 'cynical trade' came out and she didn't know why she said 'push' rather than 'pull' or 'try' or 'use'. Juliette looked rent. Lacie knew she spoke harshly but could she take it back? /could I say I meant to say tirade /I'd look stupid/I don't care about stupid/maybe it's best to hit Juls hard/any easier and she'd just play along/it would be to and fro/

Juliette didn't hide her distress. She walked quietly to the bus stop. While they waited, she said a few things, about the stove and where Lacie could find the raisins if she wanted to make the apple raisin crunch. Juliette found the recipe in Redbook and Lacie wanted to try it. The bus came and she hugged both girls. Juliette said she loved them. Then she was gone.

Lacie recalled hearing Juliette say she loved them but it seemed that she was too shy or something to make it sound true. This time it came from way inside her. Lacie knew that. She felt her neck and throat stiffen up, a sickness formed just above her stomach. A hot, dripping apprehension scalded her insides. Did she start something she shouldn't have fucked with?

When Juliette got back, Lacie met her as she walked toward the parcel car, "Was what I said mean? I wish…I don't know."

"Ah, was it mean? I cannot imagine you trying to act mean but you kicked the shit out of me. I got flattened underneath what you said."

"Vee is mad at me. She said I was saucy and mean. She says you just found it funny and that there's nothing wrong with that."

"Do you think Victoria knows what I did wrong?"

"Yes."

That answer startled Juliette. "Is it obvious, my aggressiveness?"

"Everybody knows but they're scared of you."

"Lacie, please."

"When you get started, you're so pleased with yourself. You're never that smart when you say good things about people."

"I do not say good things?"

"You do but you just say it. It's almost like you begrudge the good things."

"Lacie, please, go easy. You are hurting me."

"I'm sorry, Juls. I should…" Lacie opened her eyes and saw her feet, the ground and Juls' legs; all of it blurred by tears.

"I am an arrogant woman, Lacie. If anyone else said these things to me, I would have effectively dismissed them. From the time you first spoke about this the other day, I knew that I would come to thank you for it. I know, have known for years that you are true. Thank you, Lacie. I got terribly lazy. I did not keep track of myself."

Lacie got a whispered smell of the expensive soap Cliff bought for Juliette. Lacie felt Juliette's strong, thin arms lift her up. They leaned back, almost fell backwards onto the hood of the old black Ford that Lank kept for parts. Everyone wanted him to get rid of it. They knew he'd turn The Tracks into a junkyard if they let him. Lacie avoided the expression of strong feelings. She had them all the time. Holding down the strong feelings she had for Juliette often absorbed her attention but she drew her head back when Juliette lifted her up by her bum like a baby. Lacie looked into those dark eyes.

She kissed Juliette on the mouth, pressing their lips together. They tilted heads to get their noses out of the way and they kissed. Lacie didn't know how long they kissed but it was way too long and way too strong to be innocent child and best friend's mother.

"We should not do that or anything like that, Lacie."

"Can you tell me why?"

"No, not precisely. You know it is a legal rule. I suppose people have found it worthwhile enough to reinforce it with a lot of vigor. Adults are not supposed to have sex with children."

"Was that sex?"

Juliette hesitated. "Maybe not sex but it was sexy. I guess you know the difference as well as I do. I suppose, for sex there would have to be tits or vagina or ... involved, I guess."

"Thank you Juls, for the kiss. It felt better than anything yet for me. Our secret. Just us."

"You are ... well, everybody says amazing or something. I think of you more highly than amazing. That is our big secret. Cliff says you are smarter than me. He said you told me off about my verbal battery because you saw my big flaw and I had not seen it. You knew I did not see it."

"Did Cliff see it?"

Juliette began laughing, "I cannot get out of this position without dropping you, no metaphor intended."

"Just let go my ass, Juls; it's only a few inches to the ground." Juliette let go. Lacie's rubber boots hit the ground with a thump. She slipped on a patch of hard-packed snow. "Well, maybe a foot or so."

Juliette slid off the hood of the Ford and they stood side-by-side, shoulder to shoulder. Lacie felt every contact and every separation; she tasted hunger for everything Juliette.

"Did Cliff see it? I asked him that, too. He answered like a lawyer. He said he saw it but did not crystallize. He did not crystallize his understanding."

"Do you have sex with Cliff?"

"Yes."

"What do you do?"

"Ah ... we screw. I feel okay telling you what we do but Cliff might want more privacy. Sex is usually very private."

"Why is that?"

"Why, indeed. Everybody shrouds sex in secrecy. If you ask people to talk about it, some will be insulted, some will make up extravagant lies and some will get a little grin like they just stole your wallet. A private place to do it is more important than a comfortable place. Maybe they are wor..."

 Lacie took Juliette's hand, "Are you doing it, now?"

"What...you mean being cynical?"

"If there was a group, would you make somebody feel bad?"

"Holy fuck, Lacie! I guess probably it might make people feel bad. But that is what I do, how I think, I think. God, how much of myself would I need to excise? This is much harder than I thought."

"You'll do it right. It won't be that hard. Pfft, what am I saying? You'll just make it look easy to the rest of us. Is sex with Cliff enjoyable?"

"Yes, it is good. Not like our kiss but good."

On the first day of Christmas holidays, Tommy Brian wanted to go somewhere private. He had masturbated at home. He already put sins on his soul and would go to hell if he died before his next confession so he might as well enjoy himself. Victoria told him to fuck off.

"Lacie, gimme me a hand job."

"Sounds boring, TB. Let's find Therese and tell her we're done playing dirty with TB."

Stirling Reserve lay in a snow belt. Brookfield, along the shore just fifteen miles away, might be open, perhaps foggy and rainy, but Sterling Reserve lay under a cozy blanket of snow. In early December of nineteen sixty-three, The Tracks got a big snowfall. Every day or two for the rest of the month, fresh snow renewed the brilliant white and the sparkling excitement that comes with it.

All of the Trackers except Lank liked snow. Juliette said he didn't like it because he was a car man. Cars dislike snow. City loved to look out at the fresh clean white of it all and the others, including Archie, liked playing in it. He or Victoria announced 'good snow' and started a snowball fight. The snow had to be packy enough to make a ball but not so compressible that it hurt when you got hit. Even Lacie's father joined in sometimes. Lacie loved to bring down her beanpole father and give him a good ducking. She couldn't manage it by herself but with help from Victoria and Tommy Brian or Therese, she'd stick him down into the sharp, alarming pain of snow in his face. The kids' sense of immunity in this sort of combat gave them a big advantage. Sharp, alarming little pains drove up the fun level for Lacie and her allies. Lank hated snow but he loved to play.

The principal dismissed school early on the day before Christmas holidays because of a cold snowstorm. The first day of vacation, the shortest daylight of the year, came blinding white. The sun shone but the air and the snow were cold; no good for snowballs but great for sliding down the pit bank behind the coal mine. They got Tommy Brian and Therese. Tommy Brian didn't have a sleigh. Therese liked that. She had plenty of room for two on hers. Pulling the big, heavy sleigh up the hill just once would drain her limited reserve of energy but it was no trouble for Tommy Brian. He hauled her and the sleigh up the hill. Her sleigh flew down the hill with two aboard which thrilled Tommy Brian and stirred Therese to ecstasy. Her path through the world usually progressed slowly. They had a good time. They ignored the discomforts of cold, near exhaustion and snow crawling into any little opening in their clothing.

It started with Victoria. "I skidded sideways in a big snowdrift halfway down the pit bank."

Lacie was right behind. She tried to avoid Victoria but did a somersault when her runners dug into the snow under Victoria's sled. Then Tommy Brian and Therese came whooping and screaming into the whole mess. Therese flew off the big sled, landing on top of Victoria. Tommy Brian and the sled drove straight toward Lacie. They all laughed except Lacie; she wasn't sure why. Tommy Brian pushed cold snow into her face. It felt good, a different kind of good.

Tommy Brian said, "What's wrong?" Lacie didn't know how to answer. He brushed the snow off her face. "What's wrong, Lacie? Are ya knocked out?"

"Can't move my legs. Can't feel my feet. No feeling in my legs." Lacie couldn't find a reason to say any more.

Victoria snapped out orders like an army sergeant. "Tommy, go get someone. No, go get Archie. Get Mom and Lank, too. But go for Archie first. Therese, don't touch her. Here, put my coat over her. Lacie, please don't try to move. Lie still. Help is coming. Therese, brush some snow off Lacie before you put my coat over her. Don't move or bump her."

Lacie felt the extreme delicacy of sweet Therese brushing snow from her clothes and hair but below the waist she felt nothing. "Vee, I think you're right. My back's broken. I think you're right."

"Hold on. Don't try to move. They'll know what to do."

Tommy Brian raced back through the snow. "Archie's coming. Lank too."

Within twenty minutes, Lacie felt cold deep inside but she didn't say anything because adults surrounded her saying things like 'careful', 'take our time', and most frightening, 'delicate operation'.

Juliette arrived. She and Victoria spoke calmly, like nothing important happened. Everyone else got excited. Archie took charge. He moved and spoke with urgency. Juliette and Victoria talked to each other; they were thinking and remembering. Lacie could see the bottom of the pit bank. She said, "The doctor can't get up the hill. He's slipping."

Juliette looked down. "TB, come on." She held the rope on the big sleigh. Lacie remembered her pulling it up on the snow like she wanted to go sledding. Juliette ran down the hill, leaping through the deep snow, dragging the big sleigh. Tommy Brian ran right behind her. Doctor Lawley wore regular shoes; his coat was open. They helped him onto the sleigh. Tommy Brian pulled and Juliette pushed, talking into the doctor's ear as they got the sled up the hill. When Doctor Lawley got up to her, Victoria let go of Lacie's wrist and gave the doctor a number. She backed out of the way and passed a wristwatch back to Juliette.

Lacie remembered a night over a year ago. Doctor Lawley, Archie and Juliette drank and exchanged stories in the caboose. She and Victoria kept the radio on good music while Doctor Lawley told about a mine accident in the silver days. A man broke his back in a fall down a ventilation shaft. His rescuers fucked up any possibility of recovery by the way they handled him. Juliette asked lots of questions and, as it usually happened, Lacie and Victoria paid attention.

They wrapped her up on the hard ambulance stretcher. Four men carried her so slowly and carefully. Down at the rail cars, five people shoveled snow. They made a path for the hearse waiting on the other side of the bridge. Forsyth's ambulance was temporarily out of commission. Nurse Ingram explained to Lacie, in words widely spaced and carefully pronounced, why she'd ride to the hospital in a hearse.

Lacie said, "It's okay. I know I'm not dead."

The hearse drove slowly all the way to Halifax and just crept along on the bumpy road from Brookfield to Porters Lake. Her father curled up his long body in the back of the hearse. His breath smelled like beer. Juliette was there, too, and Victoria. Nobody said, 'It's going to be all right.' Lacie knew it might not be all right. Still, she'd like to hear it. She almost asked someone to say it.

The doctor in Halifax said it. He said a lot of things. He poked and felt all along her back causing flashes of pain. "That's good, that's good. Lie completely still. Don't move, not even an inch. Pain there, that's a good sign. You felt that, right?"

Lacie said, "Yeth." She lay face down on a stretcher, someone's hands held her head. Many hands had transferred her from the first stretcher to this one and they turned her onto her stomach. The doctor told everyone else what to do.

The doctor was a jolly, talkative man with younger doctors and nurses fluttering around him. A serious young doctor, who spoke very fast, brought in the x-ray films. The jolly doctor said, "Wonderful. Just as I thought."

He said some words Lacie didn't understand but showed her the x-ray. "Don't move your head, just your eyes." The large, dark film made loud cracks as it bent and straightened out.

"My beautiful Miss Graham, see right here. Your back is broken here but we're going to fix it and you will be as good as gold again."

He said 'back' louder than the other words and sudden like the crack of the x-ray film. "The people who took care of you after the accident did a marvelous job. It would have been easy for them to ruin your chances for getting better. Now, it's all up to you and me. I am going to operate on your back and fuse these two vertebrae together. That's the easy part. You have the hard part. You will need to lie on your back or stomach for a long time. Months."

The doctor kneeled on the floor, crouched. He looked up at Lacie. "We'll have you on a bed called a Stryker bed. When you're lying on your back, we put another mattress on top of you, squeeze them together a bit and then turn the whole thing over so you're lying on your tummy. We squeeze you between the two parts of the Stryker bed so your spine won't twist when we turn you. You can use your arms and hands but only in the way we show you. You'll have to be still and calm, especially right after the operation. Even a cough can hurt your back."

"I can suppress a cough. I will keep as much control as the mind can have over the body."

The doctor looked over at the nurse bent down on Lacie's other side. Lacie turned her eyes towards the nurse who looked back at her with a faint smile on her placid face. /a sweet smile/ The nurse shook her head two slow sweeps back and forth. /is she saying yes or saying no/

The doctor said, "I believe you will control your body."

They did things to her, needles and things. She felt people at her back but couldn't tell what they did. Many hands turned her over, face up again. She lay naked and wondering if anybody cared about that. The placid-faced nurse asked her questions with such a gentle voice and washed her with such gentle hands that Lacie wanted to say, 'Therese, is that you. Have you grown up?' but nobody would get the reference and they might think she was a little off. Lacie wanted them to believe she was completely on. It would give them confidence. She remained still and answered questions with minimum movement of her chin. She smiled a little where appropriate.

Within the limits of their exchange, Lacie and the nurse communicated. Lacie thought /*she knows me*/*she knows what I'm like*/. The nurse placed a small white sheet over her.

"Lacie, you're going to the operating room now. I'll drop in and see you tonight."

"Thanks for the dance. It was lovely."

She didn't see the nurse's reaction. Her stretcher moved on down through the corridors where she could feel the bumps in the floor. The bumps felt good. Lacie understood the bumps; how the hard wheels of the stretcher came up against the small ridges in the floor and fell into the small crevices. As the lights of the ceiling passed by, Lacie wondered about the floor. What color was it?

In the operating room, she got her first taste of life on a Stryker bed. They put a wide board wrapped in sheets on her stomach. It reached from just above her feet to under her chin. A nurse strapped it to the part of the stretcher she lay on and they turned her like a pig roasting on a spit but it seemed to Lacie that the room turned. Her forehead rested on a strip of lamb's wool. Everything was so clean and medicinal in the room but she could smell the lamb's wool. It came from a different world, from Mr. Grafton's farm where she helped with haying in the summer, from the outhouse at The Tracks, fishing boats, snuggling with a dog. The smell of living was too dirty to allow in this room except for the lamb's wool. Someone busily did things to her back. It seemed like the doctor wrote on it.

Lacie thought of her mother. She didn't know if she held a real memory of her mother or Juls description of Irma Graham, all glowing in arrogant, animal beauty. She hoped Irma would not hear about her daughter dying in an operating room. Lacie saw a small explosion of liquid on the floor. It was a tear. /*feels different when it doesn't trickle down your face/.*

A nurse said, "Don't be afraid. Doctor Tobias is a marvelous surgeon. You'll be just fine."

Lacie wondered why so many nurses sang their words. Did they think sick people turned into babies? The half melodies in the sentences annoyed Lacie. She felt like saying so but, */just doing her job/her way/who am I to say/.* "I'm not afraid. It's my mother."

"Your mother is sweet."

"Oh, no...she's not here. That's Juls."

"Lacie, dear, I'm going to put this mask over your face. You'll be able to breathe through all these little holes."

"What does the outside look like?"

"The ... oh, yes."

The nurse seemed to smile under her white cotton mask. She turned the brown breathing mask around. It had no features, no eyes or mouth drawn on the outside, just some things connected to it and a small metal frame. Lacie hadn't expected a Halloween mask but it would be a good joke. She began to nod her head to acknowledge that she was okay with the mask but the sheep's skin made her think of stillness. She said, "Thank you."

"I'm going to put this up to your face now. Just breathe normally. Count to ten slowly and you'll go to sleep slowly."

"Like this, one, two, three?"

"Yes, that's good. A little slower, if you want."

The mask came up to Lacie's face. Two gentle hands steadied her head. At the count of two, she smelled the ether. At the count of four, she got smaller or the mask got bigger. She swung in great circles attached to the brown mask which stretched and contracted like elastic. She swung wildly out in one direction and then got flung back toward the center but around again. She heard the doctor say, 'a hand job, please, Miss Nurse'.

Next, Lacie heard quiet voices and someone crying. She opened her eyes to a different colored floor. It was half dark. Somebody said, "Lie still now, Lacie." And then, a bit louder, "Little Lacie's back." Someone farther away said, "The Graham girl is conscious." Right at her ear, a man's voice said, "Lie perfectly still, sweetie. Just breathe easy. That's right. Nice easy breathing. Don't move at all; just lie there and breathe easy."

She started to drift off but that made her afraid. She woke up with a jolt.

"It's okay. You're all right. Everything is fine but you must stay still. You'll feel a little prick in your arm."

Lacie thought about a smart remark, some pun on prick but she couldn't come up with anything. A nurse came to the other side of the bed.

"Hi, Miss Graham. Can we see if you can wiggle your toes, just your toes?"

Lacie felt the effort and felt the results.

"God be praised." The man's voice said.

The nurse said, "Lacie, your toes work. That means your operation was successful. Now, you must do your part and lie as still as you can."

***

People put their hands on her. She became something to touch. It happened more when she lay on her stomach. She made a secret game of determining what a touch meant. Lacie usually knew who touched her because everyone announced themselves with their voices. 'Good morning, Lacie', 'Hi, Kiddo', 'How are we, today?', 'Hi' or 'good afternoon, Miss Graham'

"Vee, do they tell you to say hello or something and then touch me?"

"No." Victoria sounded insulted.

"Ah, Vee, I don't mean anything. I asked 'cause everybody touches me."

Victoria didn't put her hand on Lacie when she left. She just said, "Bye. I'll see ya tomorrow." The next day, Victoria came with Archie who put his hand on Lacie's shoulder, fiddled with her hair a bit as he spoke to her, and kissed her on the cheek before they left.

Victoria said, "See ya later, gator."

Lacie heard her own voice like a little child or a cat pleading, "Vee – ee." She held out her hand, perhaps beyond the range of movement recommended by the doctor. Victoria came back and took her hand. Lacie pulled Victoria toward her.

"I don't mind people touching me, putting their hands on me, especially you."

She pulled Victoria down to her and kissed her on the nose which was the part of Victoria which came closest to the lips. They both laughed. Lacie laughed with restraint.

"Can't laugh much; a giggle makes me jiggle."

"You're a poetess on a mattress."

"You're a rose with a kissed nose." It was a game they often played.

***

On the way to the car, a Rambler that Lank bought and repaired so they could all drive back and forth to the hospital, Archie asked, "Did you and Lacie have a fight?"

"No, not us, we're not fighting friends. We never fight. She asked me if the nurses told us all to touch her when we came into the room and I thought she didn't like it but she does so she kissed me on the nose."

"Ok, so everything's fine?"

"Well no, Lacie's still stuck in there."

***

Juliette got the touching right from the beginning. She stayed at Cliff's for the time Lacie was in the Halifax hospital and spent most of her days with Lacie. Juliette learned all about handling her from the physiotherapist. She washed her and cleaned her after she had bowel movements. She talked the doctors into removing the catheter and allowing Lacie to pee into a slipper pan which could be whisked away quickly. She also learned how to turn the Stryker bed. Juliette rubbed Lacie's legs and arms and brushed her hair and her teeth. She convinced the doctors to leave the body cast off for a day after they cut it away to inspect the incision. Lacie's progress pleased Doctor Tobias and the x-rays showed no disturbance to the spinal fusion.

CHAPTER TWENTY-THREE

Doctor Tobias agreed to discharge Lacie early. At the Sterling Reserve Hospital, they had a room prepared for her. Lacie's new cast, lower on the chest and higher on the bottom, gave her more freedom to move and it didn't pinch her bum. The old cast chafed her bottom. Lacie had little breasts. A few months before, she had no breasts at all. Everyone chose to ignore the small bumps beneath her nipples until Tommy Brian came in with Victoria. Before he said hello, Tommy Brian said, "You got tits. They're nice." Victoria put a hand towel over Lacie's chest but Lacie wasn't so sure about that. When Juliette and Cliff arrived she said, "Tommy Brian said I have nice tits. Does that mean I have to cover them up all the time?"

Juliette said, "It seems strange that you have to cover up something for being pretty but that seems to be the rule for breasts in this country. So my suggestion is to show them off as long as they let you."

She took the hand towel away and Cliff said, "Yes, you are forming breasts. TB is just too sensitive to such things. Like Juliette says, you'll have lots of time to hide them in the future."

"I guess I'll have to keep the covers pulled up to the bottom of the cast. When it's just Juls or Nurse Trent, they take the sheets off. It gets hot in here."

"Oh, it must be excruciatingly hot in that cast." Victoria lifted the sheet at the bottom of the bed and flapped it to give Lacie a breeze. "But you can't show your pussy with Tommy Brian here. The priest would be shocked if TB confessed that he jerked off because he saw a non-Catholic girl in a body cast."

Lacie thought this might be too dirty for Cliff but he managed to soothe Tommy Brian who looked like he wanted to die and be forgotten.

"TB, a study proved that ninety-six percent of guys under sixty and over twelve masturbate. A second study proved that four percent of the guys in the first study lied."

Everybody laughed. Tommy Brian seemed skeptical about the statistics but perhaps he'd like to be convinced. "But God says it's a sin."

Juliette liked to bring down God a notch in the presence of children. "About one in six people of the world believe God inspired the bible, which has a rule against spilling your seed. The church decided to say this meant 'you go to hell if you jerk off'. The Bible, which contained some practical advice, probably referred to turnip seeds or something."

"But Mommy and the priest say it's true."

"Yes, but remember they told you Santa Claus came down your chimney with presents."

Tommy Brian turned his attention away from sex and catechetics to the guy carrying Chinese food into the room. Cliff invited all the staff on the orthopedics floor for Chinese food and dessert. Most of the staff arrived, including doctors and a couple of nurses who were not working that day. Lacie was a favorite at the hospital and her room had become a gathering place.

After lunch and goodbyes, Cliff drove Tommy Brian and Victoria to The Tracks. An attendant and Juliette went with Lacie in the ambulance on the slow drive to Sterling Reserve.

"Daddy didn't come?"

"No, sweetie. He probably figured there would be a crowd, anyway."

"Yes, I guess." Lacie knew her father worked hard getting cars fixed up to sell and buying others to work on. He expected considerable medical expenses. Lank visited her only twice in the hospital and he stayed in the background, hardly talking at all.

"I think he is scared, love. It is unfair of me to say. We did not talk about it. I should have made a trip to The Tracks to see him about this. I do not have his permission …well…to talk about him. But here goes, anyway."

"Lank is terrified that you will not get better and he hates seeing you like this. He, I think this is it; he cannot bring himself to visit. The last time he came to see you, they turned the bed and you told them your head was not right. Remember that? We had to tape your head in place halfway through the turn. It always looks bad when they turn the bed. That day, it looked terrible with your face all taped up. I got them to turn you in the other direction after that."

"Yeah, thanks for that, Juls. It meant I could see out the window for seventeen seconds."

"Whoa, you timed it?"

"Yeah, Nurse Wood was always up to something like that."

"Archie said your father did not speak all the way back in the car that day they turned you with your head taped to the bed. He was stricken."

"I'm scared, too."

"I know. I know."

She heard the helpless anguish in Juliette's voice. Lacie hated to do this to Juls but she couldn't hold it back.

"Daddy should be brave. They all said at the hospital what a brave girl I was. Daddy should be brave too."

"Oh, my love."

Lacie didn't know if Juliette had absolutely no answer or perhaps her mind churned, trying to find some grip, some way to make it right. "Are they bull-shitting me when they say my chances are good?"

"Excellent, Lacie. The last time I talked to Tobias he said excellent. If they are bull-shitting you, they are lying to me."

"Excellent. I didn't hear that."

"He said he could not ask for a better patient. You are unusually brave, Lacie. Do not expect that of everyone."

"Vee is brave. I think she wishes it happened to her, instead."

"Lacie, I guarantee that your father would take your place if he could. I can say that truthfully and without doubt. It is not for lack of love he did not visit, just the opposite. Sometimes a father's love paralyzes him. Do you know what I mean?"

"I know, Juls, but I could have used him. He can be just the right amount of funny. It's easier when Daddy's around. I'm kind of mad at him. I hate that. I shouldn't feel that."

"Can I tell him you miss him and he should visit?"

"Is he drinking a lot?"

"No. Archie said he works all day and all night. Maybe he really does feel that is the best way for him to contribute."

Lacie considered this. She had no arguments one way or the other. What she wanted and what she believed were the same

"Daddy should be with me."

"I will tell him you miss him."

"I miss him a lot."

***

When Lacie got hurt, many medical costs remained in a gray area. The government paid for hospital stays and diagnostic services but not drugs. The system paid for Lacie's casts, her surgery and the medication she received in the hospital. Juliette paid for the private room. If Lank had to worry about money, it would be long-term expenses for his invalid daughter. Lacie knew this. His lack of faith in her recovery felt like betrayal. The trick in her head was that she felt guilty about getting injured while playing. She became a burden. /maybe kids play too much/I should get grown up/.

"Juls, will Daddy have to pay rent on the Stryker bed I'll be on in our hospital?"

"That is not a worry."

"The province pays for that?"

"Eh… you will know in about an hour."

"What do you mean?"

"Wait an hour."

At the Sterling Reserve Hospital, the cool air assailed her face and arms and she felt the late winter sun on her neck. Uncountable scents piqued uncountable memories. Lacie remembered the sensual extravagance of life beyond hospital walls. /I'm glad I didn't think of this in there/ I'd have tunneled out/ She saw Juliette talking to Victoria who scooted off. Her father showed up at the hospital a few minutes later while they wheeled Lacie into the lobby. His clothes were dirty, his hands looked recently scrubbed and he carried a tired, defeated look. Doctor Lawley and Nurse Ingram tried to make a cheery welcome. Lacie, still lying facedown, twisted her head around as much as she dared.

"Hi, Daddy. You're too tall. I can't see your head from here."

Lank grabbed a chair and sat by her, bent over with his hands on his knees. They talked like old friends catching up until Lacie said, "The Doctor told Juls that my chances of full recovery are excellent."

"Well honey, that's great but we'll be ready for anything and we'll make the best of it."

"No, Daddy. I won't be making the best of it. I'll get better. That's what it is, Daddy. I'll make a full recovery."

"Okay, dear. All right. That's great news; excellent chances."

"Daddy, there's no need to prepare for anything else. I will be well."

Her words dazed Lank. He looked dumbfounded and Lacie didn't know what to say. Everyone except Victoria had let them have their time to talk together. Lacie could see that Vee pretended to not listen. Victoria said, "Let's get down to the circus tent." She started to wheel Lacie's stretcher by herself.

Nurse Ingram intervened, "Perhaps I should do that, dear." Victoria ignored her.

She wheeled her into the room at the end of the corridor. Lacie saw a blue floor with all sorts of animal prints painted on the floor in green, brown, and yellow. The carefully detailed painting was clearly Victoria's work.

"Ta da. You've got your own Ferris wheel."

Lacie said, "Oh wow, that's a circular electric bed."

"That's 'Circo-Lectric', my dear."

"Jesus, they don't even have… Oh sorry, Nurse Ingram. The language I mean. Yeah, they don't even have them in Halifax, yet."

"They will as soon as you're done with this one. Mom bought it for you and it's going to be donated to the orthopedics department when you don't need it anymore. Can you see the whole thing?"

"Not from here."

Victoria pressed a button and the bed rotated so Lacie could see the sandwich board above the horizontal bed. She said, "There are numerous advantages over the Stryker bed."

"Yeah, the same guy designed it, Doctor Stryker."

"Yeah, isn't that the coolest?"

"God, Vee, you got beautiful famous paintings on the wall."

"They're prints. The ceiling is all Dutch painters for when you're on your back. It's mostly French on the walls, Impressionists and some Canadian, too."

"I can tell you did the floor."

"Yeah, d'ya like it?"

"It's unbelievably beautiful. The bed must have cost a fortune."

"Eh, Mom's rich. She just doesn't spend it until there's a good reason." Victoria wheeled and turned Lacie's stretcher around the small room, being careful not to bump anything.

"Yeah, this is fun. Will you have a wheelchair any time during this?

That would be cool. We could race around and cause a disturbance."

"We already are." The room filled up but everybody crowded together to avoid Victoria's back and forth and turning of the stretcher.

Doctor Lawley said, "Let's get Lacie in her new super bed before Victoria cracks her head."

"You're a poet, so I'll go sit."

They put Lacie in the new bed on her back and Doctor Lawley got everyone to leave the room so he could examine her.

"We've got instructions from Dr. Tobias on physiotherapy for you. Next week, you'll be bending your knees a bit, one at a time. If all goes well, back to Halifax in a month to get the cast off, then another month in the bed. This bed allows us to gradually get you upright without sudden compression of the spine. Those muscles around your spine have not been used in a long time and they'll be pretty weak. After that, we'll probably start you walking with a small cast or maybe just a brace."

"But I will start walking, right?" Dr. Lawley cocked his head. His face looked like a question mark. He said, "You'll start walking. Yes, that's right. What do you mean?"

"Well, I don't know. Is it a sure thing that I'll walk, again?"

"Yes, absolutely sure, yes. I don't know where you got the doubts. When you got hurt, there was a lot of risk but, after the operation, almost all that risk disappeared. You can get up and walk right now but that would be foolhardy. We're looking for a perfect repair so you won't get arthritis at that spot when you're old and decrepit like me.

"Can you put that all in one sentence so my father can understand?"

"My dear girl, Lank can understand anything I can tell him. He's no dumber than I."

"No, I don't mean that. He doesn't believe I'll get better. Juls says he's scared and can't think straight."

"You can usually assume Juliette is right about such things. So what..."

Lacie interrupted, "She doesn't mean to insult people or hurt anyone when she goes on a tirade. She gets, I think, so thrilled by what she's seeing and able to explain that she doesn't notice everybody has to take it seriously. Like, she can apply those criticisms to herself with no problem but, well, you know. It makes everyone else edgy to see the ridiculousness in themselves. And you know, I never said this to Juls but I will. I think it's all wrong, too. She turns things around backwards, things about people, not anyone in particular but about humanity. With everything all backwards, you're bound to see a lot of asses." Lacie laughed but caught herself before she jiggled too much. "An unplanned pun on asses, it's nice, huh?"

Lawley looked out the window of Lacie's new room, the hospital's best view. He could see the banks of the river. White pine and red maple interspersed on hillsides through the village. He saw the tops of railcars at The Tracks and the snow-covered pit bank behind the old coalmine. The woods behind the coalmine, an ancient old-growth Acadian forest, had never been logged.

"Intelligent and insightful, that's what one of the Sisters said about you people at The Tracks. What makes you all like that?"

"Archie. Archie created The Tracks in his own image and likeness. That's actually Juls' line."

"You know you did the same thing Juliette does. By looking through things as they appear, you went on a tirade as you call it but it was against Juliette. Maybe if someone is made uncomfortable by such things, it's the uncomfortable one who needs to correct something."

"Oh, come on, Doctor, I've seen you and Archie and Daddy squirm while Cliff sidestepped. It can't be harmless if it gets to everybody like that."

"Jesus Lord, I'll squirm if you're in the room. I thought of you as a harmless little girl playing with dolls."

"Am I like Juls, too aggressive? Hell, I'm sure she'd tell me."

"They must be waiting outside."

"I guess so."

"Okay. Very interesting, Lacie. I'll tell Lank you'll be walking soon if your brain doesn't get too heavy."

He left the room and returned with Nurse Ingram, Juliette, Victoria, Lank, Cliff, and Archie. "Lacie, I'm going to explain your condition and diagnosis. There's a girl out there, Therese Deveau. Should I have her come in?"

"Yes. Please. Hi Archie, where are you? I know you're here."

"Right above your head, Lacie." Archie came around to the side of the bed so she could see him. "Hi. How goes the battle?"

"Good, and you? You must be thinking about spring things." / *why don't I ever have anything to say to Archie/he's interesting and interested in everything/*. She said, "The promise of spring is summer."

"Winter's not over. Maybe I'll do some sledding."

"Right. I've given sledding a bad name, haven't I?"

Archie laughed. "I think George wants to address the crowd."

"Therese! Hi, Therese, I'll talk to you later."

The little voice said, "Hello Lacie." and the bold smells of a dry cleaned suit, mild remnants of shaving cream and tobacco were replaced with the soft, pungent smells of a child who wore the same dress for two weeks. Therese took Lacie's hand, such a light touch. Therese hardly existed until she coughed, a deep, loud cough, too big for her body.

Doctor Lawley got underway, explaining what Lacie went through and what she could expect. Lacie learned something she didn't know. The thoracic fracture probably occurred because she got twisted in her own fall and the runner on the big sled with Tommy Brian aboard hit her right in the spine. Two smashed vertebrae pinched her spine. Doctor Tobias cleaned up the broken bits, took pieces of bone from Lacie's pelvis and they clicked together so nicely that he didn't need to use any metal to keep it all in place.

Dr. Lawley said that the healing process for this surgery took six to twelve months. "I'd say there's a ninety-five percent chance that Lacie would be fine if she got out of the fancy new bed right now and continued as if nothing happened. Her x-rays look great; however, a violent twist or bump might cause damage and she'd have to go through some of this all over again. I expect to keep her here for two more months on this bed but gradually doing more activities. This particular bed, as you can see, is new and it is a great innovation which will allow a more thorough recovery. Oh, this cast she has on now should be going in a few more weeks. The major cost will be the ambulance trips. Any questions?"

Therese asked, "Will Lacie still be able to play?"

"Good question. Yes. The part of the spine, right around here in the middle of her back, is where the fusion was done." Lacie felt a tap at the side of the cast but couldn't tell where he was tapping. "These vertebrae don't move very much. They don't flex like the lower back

or like the ones up here in the neck. These ones move like crazy."
She felt his thumb and index finger under her neck, pointing for
the benefit of the audience but moving in a light massage. Lacie
thought maybe she should keep those newly forming-breasts
covered.

"So, Doctor Tobias made one disc out of two. Lacie will be able
to do anything she did before. Her back will actually be stronger
in that spot. The small loss of flexibility won't matter unless she
decides to become a master of the East Indian practice called yoga.
No, I take that back. Lacie could be a yoga master if she wanted."

Lacie saw Juls move closer to her father like they would kiss but
Juls whispered in his ear. /Juls/ make him believe/. Doctor Lawley
and Juliette demonstrated the new bed. Juliette told Lacie to use her
knees to put a little pressure on her bum so as to stabilize better.
One person could operate the bed. Lacie could even move the
position herself.

People trickled away but Therese, Victoria, and Lank remained. It
was lively because of Victoria but, while Lank talked to Therese,
Lacie whispered, "We gotta get a new dress and new stockings for
Therese. Do we have money left?"

Victoria snapped around, putting her hands behind her, resting
on Lacie's bed, a movie star pose from any angle. She turned back
to Lacie. "We've got eighteen dollars and tomorrow is Saturday.
I'll make two or three dollars. She gets half if she comes with me."
Victoria whispered, "I'll pick some slacks out from when we were
little. She should wear slacks after school."

Lacie said, "Right, but stockings for school."

"Really, I know, and those shoes; God she wears them in the snow.
No wonder she's always got a cold. Did we give her boots last year?"

"Yes, last year, I had them from when I was nine."

"I'll see if I can find shoes and boots. If I don't have anything, I'll buy them on credit if I have to. Fuck, I was so busy. Poor Therese. I wasn't paying attention. Fuck."

"It's okay, Vee."

"I gotta go."

She took Lacie's hand and kissed her fingers and then bent down and kissed her cheek. "You're the best, Lacie."

Lacie didn't have any words; tears started. She held onto Victoria's hand but turned toward the window. She knew, from the silence of the room, that Therese and her father watched them. Lying on her back in a body cast, she felt so lucky in her life and the thing she called 'thankfulness' took over.

Victoria said, "Do you want me to stay?"

"No Vee, no. Thank you."

"For what?"

"Oh God, the room is unbelievable. You're unbelievable. Our friendship is all in the world I could ask for. Thank you, Vee."

"You know that goes double for me. I gotta go. I'll see you tomorrow after bottles."

Victoria left the room with a lighthearted smile, a wave, and "bye" to Lank and Therese. Victoria's attempt at nonchalance didn't work very well. They stayed and the conversation came in small bursts, talk made for comfort. It was comfortable. Before Therese went home, Lacie asked, "Is anyone pushing you around at school?"

"Naw. It's all right."

"Therese, you don't lie very well. You're an honest girl; tell me."

"It's Melvin and Gary."

"Gary Thorne?"

Therese dabbed her nose with a Kleenex, "Yeah, Vee tried to stop them but they sorta beat her up."

"Are they a team? Do they pal around together?"

"Yeah, they're the new tuffys in school now."

"Pass me my notebook and my pen. I think Juls put them in the little drawer. I wrote all kinds of stuff in Halifax, not school stuff but just things I wrote. Daddy, could you please get some Scotch tape from the nurse's station?"

"Sure, I'll see."

Lacie wrote:

Melvin and Gary, I have a broken back right now so you got away with picking on Therese and I guess Vee, too. If that happens again, I will write it down so I remember to make you eat each other's nuts when I get better.

Lacie Graham.

Lank returned with the dispenser of Scotch tape. Lacie taped the note shut and told her to give it to Gary or Melvin. Therese took the note and said her soft, reserved goodbye.

"Vee and I were at her place once. You know what it's like?"

"Yeah."

"We looked at the dump where they throw their cans and everything. It's only ten feet from the house. Therese said she sees that stuff, all those cans and bottles, and she thinks there's so much that her mother does for her and Rory; buying all the cans of milk and beans and everything."

"Geez, isn't that something?" Lank ran his hand over his forhead, over his hair and all the way to the back of his neck. She never saw him do that before.

"How are you, Daddy?"

"Me, I'm good. Life goes on."

"You know I'm okay? I don't mind this as much as everybody thinks. I'd rather be up and about but, this way, I can listen to the world, see things differently."

"You were always good at that. Juls has been, not telling me but hinting that I'm all wired up wrong about your accident. I think she's saying that I shouldn't take it so seriously and I guess I now see you put her up to that."

"I really want you with me through this."

"I will be, honey. I do have work to do though."

"Don't worry that my back is going to make us poor. You and Juls and Archie have kind of chosen to be poor, anyway. God, Juls could squeeze a hundred dollars from a dishrag. Cliff always says to just say the word and he would get you a good job in Halifax and he said Archie could be making ten thousand a year in no time."

"You want me to get a job in Halifax?"

"No, no. I don't mean that. I'm saying… I mean you're the father, I'm the kid. You have to make all the decisions. I know that but I think we should go on the way we use to rather than you working so hard. How hard are you working?"

"Oh, I don't know."

"Come on, Daddy, tell me."

"I get up about eight, work till about eleven at night. I have a few starting around nine at night but I haven't been drinkin' much. I keep the fire on and grab a bite to eat."

"What are you working on?"

"I got six cars and two trucks at an auction. One truck is a three-ton with a closed-in box. I run a car in there to work on it when it's cold. I just leave the truck engine on and run a duct from the heater to the box. That gives me lights, too, with the engine on. No fun working outside on a cold dark night with just a flashlight."

"Daddy, that's crazy. You're out of your mind. You gotta stop. Take a breather so you can see what you're doing."

"I got a car and a truck left to fix and two cars left to sell."

"The Rambler Archie takes to Halifax, did you do that?"

"Yeah , that's one of mine."

"They say it's nice."

"Yeah, that's a nice car."

"Where do you sell them?"

"I sold a Studebaker here to Tom Marshall and I sold a car in Brookfield, one at the Harbour, and there's the Rambler. I can sell that, now you're home. I got customer cars, too. That Rambler was smashed, took a new windshield, hood, grill and a lot of straightening and welding, all used parts. The grill is a mismatch but it looks good."

"Sounds like you kind of enjoyed the ordeal, in a way."

"Can't say I enjoyed it. I don't know. You matured so much."

"Juls thinks you were scared for me."

"Ain't that the truth?"

"Daddy, I'm going to be fine. All the doctors say so and there won't be any big expense."

"Yeah, isn't it amazing? You healed up so well. You had a broken back and you're going to be all right. I can't believe it."

"Believe it, please. I think even if we didn't know what was going to happen, to believe it is better, don't you think?"

"Lacie, I don't know what I did to deserve you. I just picked up the best lookin' woman I could find in Halifax, married her, and took her to The Tracks. I'm just an old drunkard. I don't deserve the likes of you."

"Well if I'm so damn great, will you do me a favor?"

"Anything in the world."

"Go home, cook something nice, get a little drunk maybe with Archie and Juls and sleep in tomorrow."

"Yes, Mother, and I'll remember to brush my teeth."

"Hey hey. I still hold back on laughing. I probably don't need to, now. I hope that goes away."

***

When Lank went home to cook a meal for himself, Lacie felt the day's joy evaporating. She went through a trial and became stronger but she had to lift her father out of it. She knew he couldn't handle some things. But she had too many cares. Would she have to act like his big sister, his mother? /*I'm only thirteen*/ Her thoughts turned sour.

Juliette said she'd arrive at ten o'clock to show the night nurse how the Circo-Lectric bed worked. She got there at ten forty-five more than a little tipsy. She got the job done all right, showing Nurse Mc Auley how to do things and giving her tips on Lacie's care. Lacie wanted to communicate her real gratitude to Juls for buying the expensive bed but sincerity to someone wearing a silly drunken grin, what would that mean? Juls gave Lacie an alcohol breath kiss on the cheek, said, "Sleep tight." Then she left. /*who are these people/my people/Daddy Juls Archie/none of them has a job/no plan for anything/living in train cars*/. She lay face down looking at the floor where Vee painted in black and white, a piano keyboard of twenty-four notes. Above it was a guitar fret board. Vee labeled the notes on the piano and the guitar. Only she and Vee had regular jobs. Vee would be out collecting bottles tomorrow like she did every Saturday. She fed the chickens, gathered eggs, and cleaned the chicken house every day. None of the adults did anything every day; none of them did anything every Saturday or every Thursday. They had nothing scheduled for the rest of their lives.

She wondered where her mother lived and who surrounded her. Lacie hadn't heard from Irma in more than a year and her mother gave up the pretense of taking care of the old and infirm. No more letters, not letters really, just notes. Three sentences that said fuck all. /*well look Mother/I'm infirm*/.

Nurse Mc Auley tiptoed in on squeaky shoes. /*like that wouldn't wake me if I was asleep*/.

"Hello there, you're wide awake, are ya?"

"Yes, I am."

"I'm going to sit and have a smoke with you. It's so boring here on the back shift."

"You just started working here?"

"Yes, apparently the day after you busted your back. There's just you and old Mr. Frisson down at the other end. I guess you don't hear him coughing, do you?"

"Sometimes, very faintly."

"They put you way down here so you could rest good. I tell you, if I was in your position, I'd like to be in the thick of things but I guess there's no thick of things here. No thick of things anywhere around here if you asks me."

Lacie asks, "Where are you from?"

"Same place as your mother."

"Isle aux Morts?!"

"Well now, I know she's from Glace Bay. I saw her when I was a girl. It was like she was famous in the Bay."

"Juliette's not my mother. She's Victoria's mother. Victoria is the pretty girl with the blondish hair."

"Oh, do you all live together in some sort of group or something?"

"No, my father and I live together, Juliette lives alone, and her daughter lives with Archie Mackenzie."

"What? She's just a little thing, isn't she?"

"She doesn't live with Archie like that. He is... he's like her foster father."

"Why don't she live with her own mother?"

"That's their business, I guess."

"Well."

"Are you an RN?"

"No, I'm a nurse's aide. By rights, there should be an RN on duty. This place calls itself a hospital. I'm glad to get a job though because work's hard to come by. I got someone looking for something for me in Kitchener, a factory job. Better money and you don't have to clean bedpans."

"You won't have to clean my bedpan because I can't use one except the slipper pan for peeing. Of course, I guess my bed pot is the same thing."

The nurse's aide said, "Yes girl, pooping through a hole in the bed, that must be the worst, I say."

"I don't know; it beats having shit come out your ears."

"Mmm, yes, I guess it beats that."

Miss Mc Auley lit up a second cigarette. Lacie wondered if she planned to stay all night.

"No girl, I can't see this hospital lastin'. Nobody wants to waste hospital taxes on the likes of this. Sterling Reserve, by God, what is it? A mine town without a mine."

"Sort of like Glace Bay."

"Well, we got the mines at number twenty-six and number two working just about full tilt."

"I wonder how people like wasting our tax dollars on keeping them open?"

"Well, you're the smart one, smart-assed one, I'd say."

"Say what you like. I don't care."

Lacie turned her head to get a look at Miss Mc Auley. She was older than her voice. She looked big and made of that hard fat you sometimes see on the edge of a poor cut of beef. Lacie put her foul mood aside. /it's not her fault/I treated her mean/   Miss Mc Auley was a rough, unpretty woman who should have a raspy note in her voice but she sounded squeaky and young. The phrase 'who would have her' came to Lacie. She felt shriveled with guilt thinking that. Their lines of sight connected. "Hi, I'm Lacie Graham." She put on her best smile.

"I'm Freda Mc Auley; pleased to meet you." Freda dipped her head. Lacie saw something sweet and gracious in the movement.

"It looks like I'm going to be staying in your fine establishment for a while."

"Well, be nice to me. You look pretty helpless there. Just kiddin'. Don't mind me, dear."

"You be nice to me, too. I'm a vengeful little witch."

Freda Mc Auley laughed. The cute giggle didn't go with her appearance any more than her voice did. She said, "I don't wanna hear your hard talk. Are you really a witch?"

"No, I'm pretty nice, they tell me."

Freda said, "No, no, I mean a real witch. I knew two of them. Did my training with them. They called it Wicca, W I C C A, and they said it wasn't like a religion. It was the science of the day back in the Middle Ages. Well, I thought they were nuts until they cured a man who had a heart attack and the doctor, well, he was an arsehole, anyway. Don't mind if I curse do ya? I guess you heard it before."

"Fucking right."

"Oh now you."

"But don't let Nurse Ingram hear you swearing. She's really okay but straightlaced. Can I call you Freda, I mean, when there's no one else around?"

"Sure thing. Anyway, those two girls, Evelyn and Betty, they lit candles and had water and salt and burned some stinky stuff. We had to leave the windows open all night; the man near froze to death. Like I said, the doctor wasn't givin' him drugs or nothing. Thought he was a goner, about to die, so he kept him in his bed to do so. The girls gave the fella a dark, shiny little stone to put over his heart and then, one night, I guess three days after they started the spells, the moon was right. Like in the right phase and they said incan…"

"Incantations?"

"Exactly. You're some smart. Anyway they said those and we made sure the Sisters weren't around. I did my training at St. Joseph's and the nuns would've burned us at the stake. Boys oh boys, the fella was up and walking in a week. He signed himself out and he's still goin', as far as I know. Drinks like a fish, too."

"You say it was science. What do you mean?"

"The way she, that would be Evelyn, explained it was like this, and it's true. If we didn't invent a way to use radio waves, like radios are the machines we use to pick up those waves but, if we hadn't invented the radio, we'd never believe those waves existed. She says it's the same with a spell or talisman. They affect other things. We don't know how it works but we can use it.

"What's a talisman?"

"Talisman, now let me get this straight because I always mix them up. A talisman brings good to you and the amulet wards off evil or bad luck. They're both things, like the little polished stone they gave the fella to put over his heart."

"Do you believe in magic?"

"Sure do, always did. I just gave up the Catholic magic for a more general kind that at least works once in a while. I'm not no witch. I didn't study it or nothin' but I call television magic. You're watching some guy talking or singing or chasing after somebody in a speed boat but the guy's thousands of miles away. That's magic. Like your back healin'. They don't know how that happens. They say the capillaries do this and that and this does that but why?"

"All new stuff to me,"

"I hear a yawn in your voice, dear. I could talk the leg off a table but I should let you sleep."

"I really liked the conversation but, yeah, I should get to sleep. If I snooze during the day, I think I squirm a bit and that's not good for my back."

"I'll come around later to check you're sleeping good."

"Your shoes squeak, Freda. They'll wake me."

"Oh yeah, okay, I'd rather walk around in my stocking feet anyway. Good night, my dear."

"Good night, my nurse."

Freda giggled.

***

Nurse Ingram arrived in Lacie's room before seven.

"Oh, my my, the smell of tobacco smoke in here. Your visitors must've smoked up a storm. I'll get nurse's aide Mc Auley to air out the room overnight. That might mean you'll need a blanket. And how are you, Lacie? It's so good to see you back and feeling so good. I just looked at your chart and it is simply marvelous how well you're doing."

"Yes, it's like magic."

"Yes, indeed."

Nurse Ingram separated the 'in' from the 'deed' of 'indeed'. /*in deed*/ *that's what it means/different from in fact/*more alive.

"I expect Doctor Lawley will come by soon." She tidied and tucked and fussed.

"He works on weekends, does he?"

"Doctor Lawley works every day. If it weren't for him, we wouldn't be able to have a hospital. He's marvelous. I don't know how he manages with his wife sick and all, you know."

"Multiple sclerosis, isn't it?"

"Fifteen years since her first diagnosis and she's bedridden now, poor thing. He has a woman come in to do the cooking and cleaning but still." Nurse Ingram stepped closer to Lacie, bent down to her ear but spoke in the same volume to say, "It's a burden." She moved her mouth in the style of a stage whisper. "Do you mind waiting till he comes before we turn you?" She said, "Sometimes he's a little late" with the same exaggerated facial movements. Nurse Ingram walked out of the room with the efficiency of direction.

Frank rolled in. Lacie could see up to his waist and could tell that Frank was fat and she could tell from the front of him that his ass had a little wiggle.

"Good morning, my lady, breakfast time." Lacie barely managed a 'good morning'. She really needed to pee.

CHAPTER TWENTY-FOUR

"Indomitable." Neila had asked Archie what he thought of Lacie on her first day out of the hospital.

"Oh yes, I suppose she is tough as a nail but she's so sweet. I just love her."

"Everyone loves Lacie."

"Yes, I suppose."

"Has Juliette talked about my difficulties with Lacie's near perfection as a child?"

Neila said, "No. Juliette wouldn't talk to me about you."

"Right. Juliette would be nearly perfect, too, except for her glaring character flaws. God bless drunkenness."

"So are you going to tell me? About your difficulties with Lacie, I mean."

"She… she used to be, I guess, head and shoulders superior to Victoria, who is both headstrong and flimsy. Victoria always goes for the latest expressions and makes a big thing out of nothing. Between you and me, I'm surprised Lacie remained her best friend but you'd see them together and Victoria wouldn't be waving her arms around or… Well, there was one period when she'd put her right hand on the side of her face and say "really", at just about anything. All I could ever think of was Jack Benny. Anyway, somebody accused me of acting standoffish with Lacie. I appeared jealous or protective because Victoria was this quirky, difficult child and Lacie was, as Victoria would say…"outa sight.""

"Were you standoffish?"

"At least standoffish, maybe worse. Juliette always reacted when Victoria got overly dramatic. She didn't want to but she couldn't help herself. It just grated on her. So I just took it all in stride and, like most strangers Victoria met, I enjoyed it. She's an odd duck, no doubt but charmingly odd."

Neila said, "I really like her now but, early on, I hated to see her work so hard at the little Miss Princess act. I almost felt like saying, "just be, don't pretend".

"All kids pretend."

"No, they don't. Many of them are quite straightforward within the bounds of propriety."

Archie said, "I don't know. Actually, here comes Victoria now, back from the hospital, I expect."

Neila said very quickly, "If I stayed over, would Victoria be here?"

"What?!"

Victoria came in the caboose, made elaborate greetings and then, "How come you didn't get me when Lacie was out this afternoon?"

"She and Nurse Ingram were doing all right. Victoria, Neala has just suggested to me that she could...wait, is it all right to say this?"

"It's a bit late now to ask if you can say it. Victoria, I trust you won't tell any of your friends but I would like to spend the night with Archie. Now, I'm rather shy about all this in that I have never spent the night with a man before and we may well have sex and I don't know how that's going to go. I don't know… Anyway, I wonder if you wouldn't mind terribly staying with your mother tonight so Archie and I can have the caboose to ourselves."

"Okay, okay, umm… I'll get my clothes and stuff. Oh that's all right, I got everything at Mom's anyway, other clothes and stuff, I mean. Okay, I'll go now."

Archie said, "Victoria, you don't need to go right now. Tell me about your day, about seeing Lacie."

Victoria turned at the door, "She says she doesn't know how to walk, that she has to think about every step, about how to do it. Good night."

"What about the weather?"

"Oh right." She scrambled up to the cupola. Archie smiled at Neala and, in seconds, the lack of conversation got awkward.

Neala called up to the cupola to ask what was wrong with Therese. "The school got a note from her mother saying she would be off sick for a few days."

"Oh shit…oh sorry… I was going to go to see her. No, I don't know what's wrong but yesterday she had that cough really bad."

Neala said, "Are you going over? If so, give her my regards."

"Where shall I say I saw you, in school?"

"Good point. Never mind, don't give her my regards. Do they have a phone yet?"

Victoria said, "Yes, they just got it." Victoria filled in little squares in her weather report. "Archie, when we've got time and we want to make a phone call, can we go to Therese's instead of to the Grumpies? Mrs. Deveau can't afford that phone and she could use the money. We could pay her phone bill."

"All right, dear, we can do that." Victoria scrambled down the stairs from the cupola and went to her room to get a different jacket. She asked Archie for a half dollar so she could get a treat for Therese. Neila said, "Oh let me. Here." She gave Victoria a five-dollar bill. "Get her something nice but don't tell her it's from me."

"Oh, cool, thanks." There was a glimpse of some white silky fabric sticking out of Neila's leather satchel. She usually carried schoolbooks or convent documents in it. Victoria kissed Archie and then kissed Neila who was, with a bashful smile, stuffing the white fabric back in her bag. "You two love birds have a good night."

When she closed the door, Neila said, "Therese is always sick. That's why they had to get a phone, for hospital calls."

Archie looked out the window, "It's safe, now. She's halfway to the bridge, already." They laughed at their shared embarrassment.

***

"Sure you can stay. To what do I owe the pleasure of your company?"

"Can't say. Big secret."

Juliette said,"Well, well, Neila is going to get it tonight. She is my age and she is going to lose her virginity tonight."

"I don't think so, Mom. I think they got a hotel room in Halifax one afternoon. Archie supposedly had business but I know she was away, too. I heard that at school. Archie didn't tell me anything about that day, so it's not a secret, is it?"

"You love to get technical when it suits you. Anyway, I am happy to have you here tonight. Did you have dinner?"

"No and I'm starved. I went to Therese's. She's exceedingly sick. You know my eyes get itchy every time I go there and I remembered, tonight, that Lacie always got the sneezes and sniffles there. I kind of think she gets a headache, too. Do you think it's germs in the house? Did you see Lacie out walking?"

"No, I would guess it is not germs and yes, I did see your friend walking. I wanted to get you from school but I thought she would be embarrassed by too much attention."

"Archie didn't come for me either. Lacie said she would have loved it if we were there."

Juliette said, "I fucked up, again. Sorry, my love."

"You're forgiven this time."

"They say mould in a house can cause a reaction. That might make Therese ill."

Victoria said, "That's what I was thinking. It's a damp and smelly house even on a nice sunny day."

"Yes. They take her to the hospital and give her this, that, and the other thing and she gets better. But maybe she just needs to be out of that house. Her mother is quite sickly, too. I know she sleeps till noon and spends the afternoon at her friend Angela's house and then, at night, works sweeping at the school. She probably spends less time at home than Therese does."

"Wouldn't that be something if Therese got all right?"

"Shall we go get her?"

Victoria said, "What? Ya mean take her here?"

"Yes, I will keep her here and see if she gets better."

"Miss Mc Auley will think you're magic."

The walk to Therese's took fifteen minutes and they talked all the way. Talk came more easily for them, lately. Victoria tried to restrain her animation and Juliette tried to restrain her annoyance. "The person who was not staying at Archie's tonight gave me five dollars to buy something for Therese but I couldn't get anything here."

"You will think of something. I could put some money in and you could put some in, too, and get the little waif a pair of shoes, a decent pair of shoes. I have never been in their house and I am not sure which one it is. What is Therese's mother's name?"

"Mrs. Deveau."

"That will do for now."

Mrs. Deveau wasn't home. Juliette called her at work. As a janitor's helper, she swept all the classrooms in the school at night. The school purchased a vacuum cleaner and cut Mrs. Deveau's hours in half. She now worked two and a half hours a night at sixty-five cents an hour. She also worked eight hours scrubbing and waxing two classrooms each weekend.

A tired, sad voice answered the phone, "Sterling Reserve School."

"Mrs. Deveau?"

"Yeah?"

"I am Juliette Cameron, Victoria's mother. Victoria wants Therese to stay with us a few days. We are at your place now." There was no response from Mrs. Deveau. Juliette continued, "I wonder, would you object if we take her to my place."

"Okay."

"Good. We will have her back in a few days and we will take good care of her."

A pause and then, "okay."

"Well, goodbye, Mrs. Deveau." Mrs. Deveau gently hung up the receiver.

The walk to the parcel car, getting a bath ready for Therese, letting her soak in the tub, and getting her into one of Victoria's night dresses took an hour and fifteen minutes. A hot drink of lemon with honey and Therese's cough eased a bit. She brightened up to the degree that Therese got bright. Juliette said, "Therese, we figure your house might be the problem. It seems quite damp and mildewed. That can affect your breathing."

Victoria said, "Mom's right. My eyes get itchy at your house and Lacie sneezes."

"That's great. It's just my house. I'll just go live in a tree and everything will be all right."

Wry humor was pretty new for Therese but it suited her. Her reserve could cause her to evaporate.

Victoria said, "You're not going back to that house." Therese was a girl of low expectations. Her strength lay in acceptance and endurance but she got used to the idea that these two friends of hers could make things happen. Gary and Melvin stopped beating her up after she passed Lacie's note to Melvin.

"Gee, Victoria, that would be swell. Can Mother come live in a tree, too?"

Juliette felt compassion for Therese but it took her aback that Victoria, with such vigor, seemed to commit her to the task of finding new accommodations for Therese. She saw Victoria's second thoughts in her posture, on her face. Her daughter thought she might have said too much. Victoria never did this before so Juliette followed her lead. "Therese, we will get you a tree suitable for a small family."

Victoria added, "A family tree" and giggled.

Therese didn't sleep with Victoria in case her illness was infectious. Juliette tucked the little girl away in her room and planned to sleep on the couch. Victoria got up at eleven- thirty. Juliette was drinking moonshine with a homemade beer chaser.

Victoria said, "I'm sorry I put you on the spot with… well, a bold statement that Therese would not go home."

"It was bold, it put me on the spot but you were absolutely right. I do not usually recognize pride in myself but I felt pride in my daughter. I still feel proud." Juliette smiled at her. Victoria stuck her head under her mother's drinking arm and snuggled up against her on the couch. Juliette passsed the drink to her other hand and put it on the table. She leaned back against her daughter. They drifted off together and slept for an hour.

"Honey, Victoria, honey, I must piss."

"Mom, okay, yeah, good night." Victoria staggered off to her room. Juliette went to the bathroom, then finished her drink and poured another. She drank and made plans for the Deveau's future.

Therese woke to the smell of bacon and the sound of mother and daughter making lists. Juliette hadn't slept. She was still drunk but she had a day planned for everyone.

She borrowed one of Lanks 'for sale' cars and he took another. By the end of the day, she'd spent a hundred and twenty three dollars on building materials. She made a phone call to Ontario at seven in the morning. The Grumpys slept through Juliette's early morning visit to use their phone. Therese and her mother could live in Ranny O'Brian's house for two years in exchange for Juliette, Lank, and Archie fixing the roof and a couple of windows and painting it in the summer.

Ranny moved to Sudbury after the silver mine closed. He couldn't find new renters so his house stood empty for five months. Juliette also convinced the head of the school board to push for restoring Mrs. Deveau's hours. She made the school board president aware that the bathrooms at the school needed constant attention, not the once a week or so cleaning they got now. She left a certain hint that little Therese got sick because of an infection picked up in the dirty, girls' washroom. Victoria took the day off school and Lank drove her and Therese to Halifax with a shopping list of clothes that could not be supplied from Victoria's or Lacie's old wardrobes.

Lank asked, "You think it's a good idea to leave the clothes shopping to Vee?"

"Oh hell, I gave her extra money to pick up a dressy skirt for me if she sees one at a good price. Victoria knows clothes. She has theories about clothes."

"What do ya mean theories?"

"Well, Victoria says that the length of the torso as compared to the length of the legs is the most important consideration in choosing styles. She says, you should buy things that look like what the movie and television actresses wore one to two years ago."

"Why?"

"Fucked if I know but when your daughter is well-dressed, you can thank my daughter."

***

After two weeks in the new house, Therese was no longer phlegmatic. She became a girl of action, getting involved in things at school, making better marks, and playing hopscotch and tag in the schoolyard. Therese and her mother, who also looked a little healthier, raved about Juliette and Victoria as great people, and they became great people to the community.

"It feels good in a way but I hope it fades soon. I'm just waiting for Mom to say something like 'Fuck off, I'm not a saint.' No no, sorry. 'Fuck off, I am not a saint.' Anyway, being a local heroine is kinda' awkward." Lacie and Victoria walked on the street in front of the hospital. Lacie no longer needed a nurse with her. She learned to walk again with crutches to steady her. "In a week, I get a back brace and say goodbye to my last cast." Lacie looked forward to it but just walking with Vee made her happy.

She easily endured the pain, the immobility, the specialty beds, and now, walking around wearing a body cast. Lacie enjoyed life through it all. People brought her great stuff in the hospital. She rarely ate hospital food because her father made her dinner most nights and Juliette often made lunch for her and for the staff and the few other patients who happened to be in the hospital. The cheerful and chubby Frank Cross embraced the chance to take a two-week vacation. Frank lived alone, making a living taking wedding photographs and refinishing furniture. He made money doing that but he liked his real job better as volunteer cook, server and dishwasher at the hospital.

Juliette researched foods to keep Lacie's bowels working properly. Before Juliette began supplying ripe pears, prunes, and bran to sprinkle on top of everything, Lacie had five enemas in three weeks. At one time, she lay on her back still impacted with a few pints of soapy water in her bowels. She felt intense pain but bodily discomfort became a familiar guest, unwelcome but tolerated. They turned her bed again and the nurse dug some hard little turds out of her with a gloved hand. The bed was turned, again. The bowel movement came in violent spurts, messing up the bed. That wasn't new. Using the pot under the hole in the bed or the slipper pan under her so she could pee, she didn't always get a clean shot. Lacie always showed great appreciation to whoever cleaned up her and her bed.

The only cure for what ailed her was going through all that. As an invalid, she needed help for everything. Lacie accepted it and started from there. She took to reading like never before. Faulkner's

As I Lay Dying challenged her reading abilities but she found special things in there. Lacie read it again and the book thrilled her. Archie bought her a record player that she could easily operate when lying facedown. Lacie didn't have many records of her own but people brought her all kinds of music. Archie got narrated books on records from the Halifax library. She listened to The Count of Monte Christo and A Tale of Two Cities. She liked to read aloud to hospital visitors and patients. Victoria resisted being read to in the beginning. She liked to be doing a lot of the talking but, after listening to The Count of Monte Cristo on record, she began to enjoy it more.

Lacie remained conservative about her treatment in spite of Doctor Lawley trying to push things ahead a little. Doctor Tobias, her surgeon, did not want to push. He wanted Lacie to take time to recover slowly, despite all the favorable evidence that her back had healed. "We want that fusion to be strong."

Lacie agreed with Tobias, so George Lawley let it go. When she read East of Eden to him, he asked her to call him George rather than Doctor Lawley. It felt awkward at first. Lacie's father called him Doctor Lawley, although Archie and Juliette called him George. Not many patients used the hospital that year and George worried that it would close. Only one nurse's aide worked the night shift. The weekend shifts were twelve hours. Juliette or Lank helped with Lacie's care on weekend nights. Victoria sometimes got called on as a second person turning her bed but George spent ten or twelve hours a day at the hospital. Time with Lacie was a pleasure for him and he spoke frankly to her about his wife's illness.

Elizabeth Lawley was eleven years younger than George. Two years after they married, she developed MS and the condition worsened. George admitted his wife to the hospital often. The nurses disliked her. Mrs. Lawley required a lot of attention and she criticized the nurses. She had mood swings but the range of moods passed from surly to nasty. Lacie visited Elizabeth Lawley when she spent a week in the hospital but it was a chore. People thought that Mrs. Lawley disliked them in particular. She often apologized for her nastiness but new insults followed each apology. Lacie continued to visit Mrs. Lawley, although she didn't know how to act with her.

George confided in Lacie that he hoped she would die soon, that she talked about suicide but never could go through with it. "If she ever asks me for an overdose of morphine, I will oblige. Her life is miserable and she makes everyone else miserable."

George Lawley was an unhappy man. Each day, he dragged himself away from work to attend to his wife's needs. He seemed happy only when he drank with his friends at The Tracks or when he sat in Lacie's room. Juliette maintained that he needed to leave Elizabeth with her family and get away from Sterling Reserve for six months. He said that made perfect sense but he could not bring himself to do it. George had a woman in Dartmouth he visited, not quite a girlfriend, not quite a prostitute and not quite a mistress. Elizabeth became aware of it and often, in any company, berated George for taking up with that 'nigger whore'.

By June, Lacie got out during the day but slept at the hospital where a small bed with rails on both sides restricted her nocturnal movements. If she tried to roll on her side with the body cast on, she might roll right off an ordinary bed. Smashing to the floor wouldn't do her any good. George was usually around when she woke up. She made breakfast for him in the hospital kitchen, where Lank and Juliette claimed a shelf in the refrigerator to keep things for Lacie. George came back from his first rounds of the day to crepes or Italian sausages and potato hash.

Lacie stood up to eat breakfast. The chairs in the small lunchroom did not fit her body cast. One morning, as George drank the good coffee supplied by Juliette, he began to cry. He regained his composure quickly but said, "I did everything I was supposed to do. I got my M.D. and worked hard to keep this little hospital alive but the only times I enjoy myself is when I'm on the receiving end of kindness bestowed on me by The Trackers, people who didn't do anything they were supposed to do."

"Your work though, that's worth a lot, helping people."

"Lacie, the number of people I help from this little cell I put myself in is about one-fifth the number of people a Nova Scotia doctor should serve. They consider me semi-retired. I came here to an active little hospital in an active little town. The company paid everything. This place should be closed but it's such a nice facility that no one wants to be the one to close it."

"Do you want more coffee?"

"No thanks, love, I'd better see Mr. Jackson. He's dying, you know. He knows that."

Lacie said, "I kind of thought so."

"I must go."

She pushed away the thought that George should allow her to mind her own business. Juliette thought that the family money trapped George but Lacie believed it was loyalty.

In the hospital lunchroom, looking at George Lawley's empty coffee cup, she decided to adopt a viewpoint she heard Juls express. She'd keep guard against duty and loyalty. Lacie knew she could give up her life for Victoria but felt that wasn't loyalty, not duty. She felt like that for Juls, too. For her father, she was not so sure.

Lacie couldn't remember exactly how things went for caterpillars, cocoons, and butterflies. When did they become free and beautiful? She reached the end of confinement. All wrapped up in a body cast, living like an inert sandwich filling on a Stryker bed, it was good. She became something. Her breasts felt real now, not just little bumps with questionable identity. She felt all kinds of possibilities. There would be bad things but she just proved she could take bad things without getting shattered.

For so many months, gravity sent simple messages. Gravity was the discomfort of lying in one position too long but walking made gravity complicated by balance, sequence, and expectation. For every footfall, she needed to actuate a foot launch and so much sweet effort from muscles she hadn't noticed before. Her body became a new friend. On a Thursday in early June, she walked Victoria to school and then went in the woods along the river. It was challenging topography for a girl recovering from a broken back. She used the cane her father made for her. The cane provided comfort and confidence. A big hardwood tree made a sound like a bird song as a branch rubbed against another part of the tree. The pines swished in the breeze.

Sharp, bright scents replaced the pungent smells of late spring when the decay of winter turned sweet. Discreet smells of new sweet fern, pine needles and spruce filled her whole body. Stepping along on the spongy soil covered with fresh moss, she heard the Tillman River. Thick bushes hid the river's edge. In the woods, she felt something like fear but it was a congenial fear, an old friend. Lacie reached a place where she had to give up the cues that automatically told her where she stood. She started talking to herself. /the river's over there/I'm heading downhill/where's the sun/where's the sun/ set a course/look back where I came from/. The raw pleasures of the woods filled her up.

Lacie knew from some early age, before her remembering, that she could be filled with all things at once: delicacy and strength, light and shade, silence and sound, wispy and solid all shared the same ground. She felt the unity in this engaging multiplicity which was, perhaps, enough to live for. Lacie picked her way through the trees and bushes to the river. Nothing took up her attention but she attended to everything. The feeling of weight on her feet and the changing angles of her ankles stepping over the uneven ground thrilled Lacie.

Duration in this exquisite state didn't fit into hours or minutes but it couldn't last. She understood the feeling was unsustainable but that suited her. One lived in the everyday.

At the Sterling Reserve School, they had a small graduation ceremony for the kids who passed grades six to nine. Lacie attended wearing a back brace. She sat in a chair with normal posture, still a bit stiff and upright but with none of the ungainliness of the cast. She had just started sleeping at home in her own bed. When Victoria and Therese got their grading certificates, Lacie stood up to applaud. No one else did that. She went to these things before and she knew people didn't stand up and she thought it would be unfair if people did. The less popular kids would be left out one more time but no one except her stood to applaud. That made it all right. Some things are okay for one person but you wouldn't want a lot of people doing it. Therese and Victoria would be in her class next year. Lacie lost the whole year because of her injury. That felt okay, too. She and Victoria always wanted to be in the same class.

Two weeks later, Lacie saw Doctor Tobias for the last time. The x-rays pleased him. "No more back brace. You must do your exercises for six months and be careful not to reinjure the area. Ease gradually over the months into any heavy lifting and avoid situations that could involve bumping and lurching, like bumpy roads or being out on a boat. Don't go horseback riding for six months. You can swim but don't dive, and absolutely no rough sports, not even baseball. You got all that?"

"Yes, Doctor, I have it all."

"I like you. You're a great kid but you almost lost the use of your legs. You should have been paralyzed below the waist; no feeling but you'd probably have pain, back pain that is. You owe it to good fortune and the people who exercised good sense after the accident. Most people would've wanted to pull you out of the snow first thing. Of course, you also had a damn good surgeon."

Her father waited for her in the outer office.

"I'm done with this, Daddy. I'm better. I just have to be careful for six months just so I don't reinjure it."

"You must be a happy Tracker."

"I am. Isn't it great?"

"More than I expected. The whole thing scared the heck out of me. Up until a few weeks ago, I was always braced for the worst."

"It still holds you, doesn't it?"

Lank said, "What do ya mean?"

"The worry has got a hold on you. It seems to have got you down and won't let you up."

Lank looked at her. They waited for the elevator, a one-minute wait. On the elevator, two women had a conversation that allowed both of them to speak at once. At the ground floor, the women got off and walked as fast as they had talked.

Lacie said, "Do you think either of them knew what the other one said?"

"What do ya mean, who?"

"The ladies on the elevator."

"Oh, yeah, them." They didn't speak on the way to the car but when he started driving, Lank said, "Maybe you're right. I can't seem to shake it. You asked me to have faith but faith is a gift. You either got it or you don't. I didn't have it."

"How can you get out of this now?"

"It jolted me. The thoughts of you being unhappy, of living a short unhappy life, I didn't know which way to turn. There were no solutions. But you're better now. I'll get over it. I don't care much as long as you're okay. It's hard to shake."

Lacie cuddled up against him as he wheeled the car over the bridge to Dartmouth. She looked up at all the suspension bridge steelwork of the Angus L Macdonald Bridge and thought about strength in tension, strain and weight-bearing. "Daddy, you are the sweetest man in the world. I guess you have to go through special pains to be like that. Giving a fuck about so much pushes you down but other things will lift you up. Did that make sense?"

"Yeah, it did. You always make sense."

"When was the last time you screwed?"

"God."

"You go too long between women. You should get a woman, take her home. You never take your women home. I'd like to meet your girlfriends."

"I never had anybody long enough to take home."

They had reached a clear part of the number seven highway. The slow car in front of them turned off to a driveway. Lank geared down to second, put his foot to the floor and popped the clutch. The little Chevy II with the big V8 jumped ahead, burning rubber.

Lacie said, "She's got the gams."

They got up past 100 miles an hour. The car started to shake. Lank slowed down. "I got to have another go at balancing those back wheels."

"You probably spun the leads off the wheels with that burnout. Victoria and I want to buy more chickens. Can you help us build a chicken coop? Lenny Ryan is going to loan us that mean German Shepherd for as long as we want. She guarded his chickens."

"What happened to Lenny's chickens? Did the Shepherd eat them?"

"Very funny. No, he said he didn't have time for the chickens after he started working for the highways."

"How many chickens?"

"A hundred."

"What?"

"Stay on the road, Daddy."

"That's a shit load of chickens. Not to mention a load of chicken shit."

"Yes, well, adults make money on eggs and there is nothing to it that Victoria and I can't do. Once, we had twenty-seven birds."

"But a hundred chickens at The Tracks? No, no way will that work. Twenty chickens were too many."

"Who said anything about The Tracks? We're going to put them at the crooked house farm. We can use boards from the old barn to build the chicken coops. Some of those boards are pretty good. Mr. James across the road will watch over it to make sure that nobody steals the chickens and that the dog is okay."

"Did you get permission to use the crooked house farm?"

"No, but it's not the first time we've tried adverse possession."

"Right. How much money are you going to need?"

"A hundred and twenty dollars."

"Okay, we've got that."

"You mean you could give us… loan us the whole hundred and twenty."

"Yeah. We've got over seven hundred dollars from fixing cars and selling cars."

"Holy smokes. I thought we would have to get the money in dribs and drabs from here and there and the other place."

"You expected the here and there and the other place to be Juls, I suppose."

"Well, I guess we thought most of it would come from Juls. Man, you must've worked hard for that."

"Not that bad. When I got into the capitalist way of doing things, making a profit rather than just charging for my work, it got a lot easier. I have probably two thousand, maybe twenty-five hundred, in inventory pretty much ready for sale. Most of them are at a guy's car lot in Dartmouth and he takes ten percent for selling a car. It's good. I'm going to keep doing it."

"Yeah. Daddy, that's great."

"I got the knack of buying the right vehicles, too. Sometimes, they only needed a day's work to get them running good."

"Is this for sale?"

"Oh yeah. They're all for sale. I bought this one with a blown engine and I dropped a 327 in it. Easy as pie. Some young fella will buy this and probably spend his nights burnin' up tires, street racin'."

"What's the quarter-mile time?"

"I don't know, fast with the right tires."

They turned at Brookfield going up to Sterling Reserve. Lacie asked him to go slow on that road because of the bumps. That was hardly necessary because Lank knew all the bumps and potholes and avoided them. The Chevy II eased along the road at twenty miles an hour, dancing around the bad spots. Lacie and Lank sang Elvis tunes and Runaround Sue and the Everly's Cathy's Clown. They sang well together in the past but this was the first time since Lacie's accident. They found interesting harmonies and often gave up on the words and kept only a hint of the melody as they weaved and bobbed around each other's voices. The sky clouded over but sunny spots on the road ahead looked like invitations. Twenty seconds in the sunshine and then back to the overcast. The Chevy II rattled over the bridge to The Tracks. Lank put on the parking brake which was entirely unnecessary and something he never used to do on the flat gravel of The Tracks.

"What a wonderful drive. Let's go in the car and I'll get you a hundred and twenty dollars."

***

The chickens became a struggle. The girls took a long time to get the bird's care and feed schedules right. Selling eggs at the local store didn't take much time or effort but the margins were low. Lacie and Victoria didn't lose money but it took a lot of time. By the next spring, they'd get better control over costs and manage to pay off Lank's advance.

During that year, Lacie gradually returned to her normal level of physical activity. Victoria caught up to her in height as Lacie became athletically feminine. Victoria wasn't chubby but not thin enough for her own tastes. Lacie didn't make much of her attractiveness, preferring plain clothes but Victoria often convinced her to wear tighter and shorter and more in style. In such cases, Lacie became teen sexy.

They tired of chickens. Victoria grew to dislike the birds. The girls hired Therese and Tommy Brian to do the feeding and chicken house work as well as some distribution and selling. Victoria and Lacie found better sources of feed, improved the health and productivity of the flock and continued to make a bit of money on their egg enterprise. They gave up collecting bottles except for a few older ladies who depended on them for company.

In the coalmine behind The Tracks, Victoria and Lacie picked coal strewn around on the mine floor. At first, they filled potato sacks with coal, dragging them out of the mine for the stoves at The Tracks. Juliette, Archie and Lank gladly paid them what they would normally pay to the coal hauler to deliver the few tons of coal they burned through the winter.

Lank and Archie designed and built a coal hauler from a leftover coal cart down in the mine. An old Ford truck with a cable going down into the mine pulled the mine cart up the slope. Archie went through extensive safety training with the girls. They expanded their coal sales to include customers outside The Tracks. Not only did they pick up coal left as debris along the floor of the mine but started digging lignite, a brown, soft, low-quality coal, actually a precursor of coal which did not burn as well or produce as much heat. They sold it at half the price of coal and felt lucky to get that. Victoria called it shit rock. They made more money on coal than on eggs and they liked it better.

CHAPTER TWENTY-FIVE

"Don't you have to go see principal McMoron?"

"Come on, Victoria, you could show a little respect for Mr. McLeod."

"Showing respect for him is a lie. I have to pretend at school, that's enough. He's a skuzz, always talking about himself when he should be teaching. I hate him. He's atrocious."

"No Victoria, you can't hate anybody. It's not allowed. You resent his authority, that's fine, par for the course, but just because you're intelligent, you don't get to look down your nose at the less fortunate."

Victoria screwed up her face. "Yeah, okay. I won't hate him but it's a 'big don't like him' I got."

"My my, Victoria."

Archie's tolerance didn't last long in Theodore R McLeod's office. The principal sat upright behind his desk. He didn't rise to greet them and didn't speak, just directed them to sit with what Archie took to be a dismissive hand motion. He suppressed a crackling resentment. Sister Jeanne d'Arc sat off to the right of the principal. She looked secretarial, fussing with papers on her lap. Sister stood up.

"Mr. Graham, Mr. MacKenzie, we have met before but in case you have forgotten, my name is Sister Jeanne d'Arc. I am Vice Principal at Sterling Reserve School." Archie smiled what he hoped would pass as a polite smile.

"Principal McLeod, this is Mr. Graham, Lacie's father, and Mr.

MacKenzie who is a neighbor and close friend."

McLeod raised his head slightly for half a second, his acknowledgment of the two men.

The words 'arrogant nitwit' passed through Archie's brain but the flood of warm feelings for his new lover and her gracious introduction dampened his anger. She sat down with her legs crossed under the long skirt of her habit. Sister Jeanne d'Arc raised her gaze from Archie's feet to his eyes and smiled at him. He was still standing. He stood up when she stood up, expecting a handshake from McLeod. Lank sat in a chair next to Archie trying hard to be anybody but himself. Archie watched the Vice Principal as she stole a glance at him and then looked out the window. An erotic thought ran through his head as he sat down.

McLeod reached down inside himself for the big notes in his voice and processed them in a rigid upper body, making the sound deep and rich but razor-sharp. "Lacie Graham is a bad girl. I don't suggest that she doesn't have some sort of ah, malady, nevertheless, she's a bad girl. Lacie is slothful and she's, shall we say, developing. I don't like to stereotype but let me say she's developing the way you'd expect, seeing that she comes from over on The Tracks. There's the short skirts, the tight sweaters and, the ways." McLeod enclosed 'the ways' in quotes with his index and middle fingers. "I know she's pugnacious with the boys and heaven knows what else."

McLeod stared at Lank as he spoke. He pressed his hands together at the fingertips and appeared to believe his speech was rhapsodic. Lank tried to disappear in his chair. McLeod took darting glances at Archie like a rodent sniffing for food or danger. Sister Jeanne d'Arc looked steadily at the principal, perhaps trying to hide contempt, perhaps offering the effort up as a prayer for the souls in Purgatory. Archie quietly interrupted.

"Mr. McLeod, you got your teaching diploma on a veteran's ticket, isn't that right?" Archie's elbow was on the back of his chair, his body turned a bit sideways towards Lank and his head turned the other way so that his line of sight seemed to include everybody in the room.

"Ah, ah yes, certainly, I served in…"

"I did that, too. I have a Masters in Philosophy thanks to the thanks of my country for my ordeal in France. I often wondered what would happen to idiots like you who acquired a diploma because of wartime service despite having a head full of nothing."

"Mr., ah, you… I'm shocked and dismayed…"

"Shocked and dismayed? What did you expect, you rude fucker?"

McLeod stood up, six-foot one, broad-shouldered and fit. His arms were stiff by his side and his voice thundered. "I'll not have that language in my school. Certainly, very inappropriate in front of Sister Jeanne d'Arc here."

"Oh, I don't mind. I don't find anything objectionable in what Mr. MacKenzie is saying. Nothing off the mark really." The souls in Purgatory were on their own.

McLeod struck his desk softly with his fist and stuttered, "Get out of m-m-my office. That girl Lacie is man-hungry. I can see by the way she acts when I come around but all she'll ever get from m-me is…"

Archie saw Lank spring up and brace his skinny knees against the enclosed front of the principal's desk. It was a stance that Archie saw Lank use in order to exert a surprising amount of force on a wrench or prybar. Lank grabbed McLeod's tie, the front part, and the little tail hanging down from the knot. He pulled McLeod forward until his face hit the desk. "I always thought of neckties as symbols of submission. Don't go near Lacie; don't think about her." Lank sat down again. He trembled. His eyes were on McLeod. What Lank might do next worried Archie. He put his hand on his friend's sleeve. Lank jumped and then, settled back in his chair.

"All of you get out." No one stood up. He got up himself. Archie watched his high-stepping robotic gait. McLeod stepped over landmines and barbed wire. He closed the door firmly but methodically as if that simple action had required study and patience.

"Neala, I'm sorry; I lost my self-control."

"There is no need to apologize, Archie. You looked good; I'm proud. And you're right Lank, everybody talks about ties being phallic symbols but you're right. It's like a tether anyone can grab." She spoke with cool composure as if discussing a book she just read.

Archie said, "Walking out of the room, he reminded me of all the confused boys; troopers, guys not sure of anything, doing the best they could, in way over their heads."

"No, Archie, my love, there is nothing complicated about this. Our fearful leader is simply despicable."

Lank said, "I'm a confused boy, Neely, Archie, my love?"

Sister Jeanne d'Arc said, "That's Neala with an 'a'. Archie and I have been lovers, twice."

"Whoa, didn't know that. Okay, okay. Is there anything to what he says about Lacie?"

"He insulted her, absolutely uncalled for. She's not a bad girl in any way. She is uncommonly intelligent, considerate, generous, imaginative… well, Lank, you know what I think of Lacie from our home and school meetings. She unfortunately thinks that she is Annette Funicello and she's getting to the point where she can pull it off. I hope her fast ripening body and her ways won't be her undoing."

Neala's four finger quotes around 'ways' was to Archie a tiny ballet full of elegant malice and mockery towards the principal. He said, "I feel bad for McLeod. He left here defeated; a shameful retreat."

Sister Jeanne d'Arc stared at Archie. Sister showed no facial movements but it was not a stone face. Her face was soft, ready to change, to accept, to venture. She held him in an affectionate stare which had something lascivious in it. Sister rubbed the side of her nose close to her right eye. "Mr. McLeod is a dolt. In my opinion, that doesn't forgive anything or not much, anyway. I worked with retarded adults for two years and you get your nice people and your jerks at all IQ levels. He spends most of his days intimidating the children with his big God damn voice and his ten-dollar words."

Lank asked, "Will you get in trouble for what you said?"

"No. Thanks for your concern, Lank, but we, I mean the convent, owns the school. McLeod works for me. He, as principal, is just a charade really so that it won't look too much like a Catholic school."

"I'll ask Lacie to dress a little less sexy. The school she went to in Halifax, the girls dressed like that."

"Ah yes, I can see that would do it. You can't take city looks and bring them to the country without standing out."

Lank asked, "What do you mean 'her ways'?"

"Lank, I was only joking. Although, she does move sexily, don't you think? Well, I suppose it's all natural. There's no put-on hair flicking or wiggle or anything stupid."

Archie said, "Lacie's mother was, probably still is, sexy without trying. Irma never put any effort into it; she was just attractive. She's just that way."

Lank said, "I'll tell her that you think she should… I don't know… tone it down a bit. She thinks you're great. Her and Victoria both love you."

Sister Jeanne d'Arc looked down at her lap.

/what a waste of time/all that garb the nuns wear/it's the face that blushes/the eyelids flush with sex/. This woman caught Archie by the heart.

She said, "I try to treat all the children equally but it must show that to encounter the Tracker girls makes my day. Besides everything else, like being smart and beautiful and charming and kind, they have that friendship between them. They make things better here for everybody, except perhaps the brainless one. My sweet Mary Mother of Jesus, he hates intelligence and imagination. He believes everything should come from plodding."

Archie said, "Marching. If you do enough of it you begin to believe in it. It's the perfect education for mummies."

"Don't blame me. I didn't hire him. Heck, Lacie should be principal here." She laughed a little too much. Archie was smitten all over again.

Lank said, "We should go. We should get out so you can get out, too."

"Yes. Tell Lacie the skirts and things are no big deal. Maybe some of us are jealous we don't have 'the ways.'"

"But you do." Archie thought that might've been too bold to say to Neala in Lank's presence.

Sister tilted her head and smiled. "It's been quite some time since a man has seen up my skirts. I don't know where this will lead."

There was a long silence and Lank said, "We must be going." Sister hugged Lank and he hugged back. She took Archie's hand, a handshake but she put her other hand on top of his. "I can't hug you without breaking a vow again but my vows are getting fragile. Perhaps sometime, soon, I'll give it all up. But maybe you don't want that. I know nothing, Archie. Just don't know what's going on."

Archie said, "Can we see each other soon, just to talk?"

"It all makes me afraid."

Lank said, "I'll leave you to it."

"Oh no, Lank, please stay. I don't want to be alone in here or be seen alone in here with Archie."

Archie said, "I don't know much either, Neala, about the future but, well, I'm in love. It's not the first time for me, I guess, but this is more powerful than ever before."

"Jeez, I'm sorry, I gotta go."

"Okay, Lank, let's go." Archie kissed Neala on the lips. It baffled Archie how a kiss communicates messages that aren't passed on in any other way.

***

Out of earshot of the school, Lank said, "Interesting afternoon. Before we get to the other things, will that guy have me arrested for grabbin' him like that?"

"No, he won't bother you. He'll be afraid of you. He'll give you a wide berth."

"Oh shit."

"What?"

"I'd rather be arrested. I don't want the poor guy to be afraid."

Archie reached up to his friend's shoulder. "Maybe you shouldn't have nearly broken his neck."

"I know that; first time in my non-assertive adult life that I took violent action. I'd been prepared for violence, by times, but I never did anything like that before. I expected it to feel better than this."

"You impressed me. You were fast, strong, clever and effective. It got the job done. Neala didn't object at all and, if her assessment is correct, it's the only way to deal with him."

"Deal with him? He just wanted to give his opinion and that made his personality flaws glare in our eyes. Blinded me, brought on an attack of righteous indignation. Oh well, so it goes."

"Do you think I should stop wearing suits and ties?"

"It's become your identity tag. What do ya need a tag for? I never understood it."

"Well, at least you never tried to break my neck."

"It didn't take long to get a reputation as a neck breaker. What about Sister? I hope you're not just fulfilling a nun-fucking fantasy. She's serious, and seriously troubled by it."

"No man, it's a big deal for me, too. Entirely different from any other affair...affair, hell, we made love twice. I mean two different occasions, one day and one night at my place."

"Who knows about it?"

"Victoria. I don't know who else. I think Sister Mary Ignatia knows."

"She's ready to leave the convent, is she?"

"Hell, I don't know. We haven't addressed that. It was grand, up until today. Now, it needs serious thought. I sure as hell don't want to hurt Neala. I know that."

"Her name is what?"

"Neala, like Neal with an 'a' at the end."

"Go see Juliette. She'll help you plan how to proceed."

"Yes yes, you're right. She'd be good."

 At The Tracks, Lacie stood outside the open caboose door. She called back inside to Victoria, "It's okay. I've got enough." She didn't see Archie and Lank.

Lank said, "Maybe, Lacie should dress like that for school. Nothin' sexy there."

"They're not allowed to wear slacks. Well, work pants in this case. But even with a dirty flannel shirt and work pants, she does look attractive, you know."

Lank said, "It's the miner's helmet. God, I don't know about her going down in a coal mine with her back. Geez coal mines are where you get a broken back, not where you let it heal."

Archie said, "She's okay. I asked Victoria about it the last time they went down. She said Lacie is real cautious. It's almost a year, Lank. As of Christmas, she won't even have to be careful about her back. Lacie's doing everything right."

Victoria saw them and came out of the caboose to put on her work boots. She asked, "How'd it go? Did you get a strapping?"

Lank said, "He thinks Lacie dresses too sexy but Neala says it's no big deal."

Lacie turned to Victoria. "See, I told you."

"Ah, such bullshit. Everybody around here is such a dip, especially that stupid fucker. He's the definition of square."

Lacie said, "I don't want to stand out. I don't want to be sexy except when I want to be sexy."

Victoria said, "Yeah, well, cut your tits off. Look, if anybody is offended because Lacie looks too damn good, it's my fault. I pick out her school clothes because she doesn't wanna bother and Lacie has no style sense."

Lacie asked, "Who's Sheila?"

Archie fidgeted with his tie. "She's my girlfriend or something. Sister Jeanne d'Arc. Her name is Neala."

"Your girlfriend!" Lacie, in a half crouch, put her hands on her knees looking up at Archie with a big smile of spontaneous delight.

"You see, Lank, she is sexy. She looks sexy, now."

"Hell, I guess. I don't really see it. She's my daughter, after all."

"Well Lank, I'm not aroused or anything but Lacie, you are just naturally sexy. It's a gift really."

Victoria slapped Lacie's bum, "See, I told ya. It's not the clothes, it's you."

Lacie said, "Your girlfriend? Did you know that, Vee?"

"Yup, sorry, I couldn't tell you. I was sworn to secrecy." Victoria made her voice deep and said, with something like an English upper-class accent, "Isn't it stupendous?"

"Yes it is. Congratulations, Archie. Sister Jeanne d'Arc, is it Neala?"

"Like Neal with an 'a.'"

Lacie said, "Sister Jeanne d'Arc is the greatest. You and her will be, oh you will be sweet."

Archie felt a pressure in his throat and a tear forming in his right eye. He hoped it didn't show. "It's very much a secret. It's only the four of us know."

"Mom's on to it."

"That's okay, Victoria. I have to consult with her on matters of the heart, anyway."

Victoria said, "This sounds serious, Archie." She was subdued, not smiling.

"Don't worry, dear, whatever happens… I mean, you're number one. That will always be."

She stared at him for several seconds and then looked away at nothing. No one seemed to have anything to say. Victoria leaned into Archie; she dropped her miner's helmet. The lens cracked. "Don't worry, it'll still work. The bulb's okay. Sorry about the dirty clothes on your clean suit. I thought about what would happen if you ever got married or something. I guess this is the best I could do, except maybe if you married Mom."

Lacie said, "Come on, Vee. We have to get some coal up."

"Yes, boss ma'am. Thanks for being Archie, Archie."

"No trouble, dear, couldn't help myself."

Lank found this enormously funny. He laughed himself into a spectacle. Still giggling, he said, "Another secret, I near broke the principal's neck."

"He did you know. Grabbed him by the tie and slammed his face on the desk." The men both laughed.

"Daddy, you didn't?"

"Oh, yes."

"That's terrible. Why?"

"I lost my temper. He insulted you."

"Oh Daddy, I'd expect that from him. I don't need protection from him."

Archie asked, "Lacie, do you try to be nice to him?"

"Yes, and I may be the only one in the school. The rest are afraid of him, like Tommy Brian, or they show that they despise him like Vee and Sister Mary Ignatia do."

"He thinks you're trying to seduce him; that you're man hungry."

"Oh."

Victoria said, "Arse fucker. I'd love to see his head slammed on the fuckin' desk."

Archie, still holding onto Victoria, said, "Does your language deteriorate as soon as you put your mine clothes on?"

"Sorry, your virgin ears."

Lacie said, "Well, it shows that McLeod doesn't get decency from anyone when he mistakes, what I intend as common courtesy, for me trying to get him. It's creepy but it only goes to show."

Victoria let go of Archie and brushed the side of his jacket where she had been leaning. She picked up her helmet. She flicked the switch. The light came on. Victoria stared into the light coming through the shattered lens. "It's our biggest disagreement. Lacie thinks there's good in everybody. I don't."

Lacie said, "The poor bastard never gets a smile. That's why he misunderstands. Do you have to deserve a fucking smile? It's got to start somewhere."

Victoria flicked off the lamp, put her helmet on her head and her arm around Lacie's shoulder. They walked off to the coalmine. By the time they reached the entrance to the slope, they were banging their helmeted heads together in some silly game.

Lank asked Archie, "Drink?"

"Oh yes."

***

Victoria and Lacie continued to miss school often. They did things with the adults at The Tracks and they had their own business interests. Most Saturdays, the girls made a quick bottle run to the people who looked forward to seeing them. It became more like visiting than bottle collection; not worth it for the money but they liked to greet and be greeted. Only one of the regulars was something of a chore. Mrs. Bavetta talked too much and with a heavy accent they found hard to understand. She usually had only one or two bottles but they knew she was lonely. She told them so. Occasionally they stayed long enough to have a sweet or salty treat. Together, the girls were quite resourceful. They had Mrs. Bavetta teach them some Italian. Unfortunately, most Italians would find Mrs. Bavetta difficult to understand. She came from rural Sicily and spoke with a thick local accent and she used lots of idioms.

The chickens required some of their time even though Tommy Brian and Therese did most of the work. They tried to keep the flock at about eighty laying hens. Therese and her mother, whose boyfriend had left her as her husband had ten years earlier, sold most of the eggs.

Victoria and Lacie spent much of their time in the mine picking coal and increasingly digging out lignite as the stray coal left on the mine floor got depleted. The girls made good money at this and they enjoyed the coal mine but had little time for their friends.

After the last weekend before Christmas vacation, they missed school on Monday and Tuesday. On Wednesday, the kids said Therese was home sick. The girls planned to visit her after school but Sister Jeanne d'Arc came into their classroom at two o'clock and told them Therese died, presumably of pneumonia.

Lacie didn't intend to go to the funeral but Victoria wanted her company. The Sterling Reserve School got the afternoon off so the students and staff could attend the funeral in the small Catholic church. Many of the kids barely knew Therese and didn't care a lot but the deal was you had to stay in school if you didn't go to the funeral. It was a snowy day, the first pretty snow of the year. A couple of days, in late November, had rain mixed with snow but on Therese's funeral day, large snowflakes gently fell. The afternoon was not sunny but not dark either. By one o'clock, a beautiful blanket of good snowball snow covered Sterling Reserve. The older kids drifted into the church after enjoying the fresh snow and that special freedom of being outside on a school day. It became a bit of a circus with talking, horsing around and making jokes. No teachers were there ten minutes before the service. Juliette got up to walk over to the noisiest kids with no particular intention in mind. Sister Mary Ignatia entered the church and swept the crowd with a look that had the power of a fire hose going full tilt. The kids went quiet in seconds.

"Did you do that, Mom?"

"No. Sister Mary Ignatia came in." Victoria bobbed her head in acknowledgment.

Therese's mother shared that same quiet reserve her daughter had shown but with Mrs. Deveau, it extended to bland. She had problems comprehending ordinary things. Mrs. Deveau had so little sparkle that you could not attribute her dull quiet to shyness. It would be hard to imagine her having emotion robust enough to cause shyness. Yet, you could see where Therese had gotten the soft, low-lustre patina.

No other family members came to the church. Mrs. Deveau's boyfriend had gone back to his old job as janitor for a trucking company outside Toronto. He and Therese had been close but Mrs. Deveau didn't have a phone number for him and no other way of contacting him was apparent to her. Therese's older brother, Rory, moved away years before. They would not have known Therese died. After the service, Lacie, who talked to Sister Jeanne d'Arc about what happened at funerals, took charge of standing at the door thanking people for coming. She thanked the noisy kids, Sister Jeanne d'Arc, the rest of the teachers and everyone else. Victoria and Juliette stood with her. For the girls, it was their first death, their first funeral.

Juliette thought they handled their friend's death very well but Lank worried about Lacie. "She's awfully quiet now; I mean, she's always quiet but, I don't know."

"Did you talk to her about it?"

"No Juls, I wouldn't know where to start."

Juliette said, "I will do it if you want. I talked it all through with Victoria."

"Yes please, Juls. I'd appreciate that. Thanks, Juls."

She peeked into the compartment where Lacie slept in her little bed. As she turned to leave so as not to wake, her she heard, "Juls?"

"Yes, dear, I am here."

"I'm awake."

"Lacie, you are outgrowing your bed and your compartment. We will have to get you more space."

"Are you drunk, Juls?"

"Two modest drinks; I am not drunk but I can talk to you in the morning with no drinks."

"No, that's okay. You're not drunk."

"Your father is worried about you. He thinks you took the death of Therese very hard."

"What does that mean?"

"Taking it too hard?"

"Yes."

"I suppose I do not know the answer to that question."

"Thank you, Juls; you and Vee never bullshit me."

Juliette squeezed in on the small bed. They faced each other. Juliette rolled on her back, lifting Lacie up above her so they could see each other and then she eased Lacie down. The two were cheek to cheek. "Have you cried, love."

Lacie popped her head up again to be able to see Juliette. "No, I guess not."

"Would you cry with me? We could cry for Therese, together."

"Why?"

Juliette answered by saying, "Think of your eyes. Feel your eyes. Think of tears coming out of your eyes. Feel the tears." Lacie began crying in seconds. It took Juliette a minute.

"Me and Vee were good to her."

Juliette wanted to say something helpful or wise but she could only cry. She wished it was Lank doing this. /a sad and terrible beauty/ Lank should have this sacrament/not me/. It hurt, a stinging and exhausting pain. She didn't know if it could have any lasting value for Lacie.

Three days later, Lank said to Juliette. "She made my breakfast and kissed me good morning. An omelette covered in fried apple slices, those yellow wild mushrooms and coriander on the eggs, cinnamon and pepper on the apples. She kissed me on the neck, right here just above the collarbone. I've never been kissed like that before. Thanks for talking to her, Juls. I think that's what did the trick."

Sentences were sewn together in her brain; she colored them, washed and dried and pressed them. /Lank there is no need to be shy with your daughter/Lacie will always guide you/she will take you where you need to go/ or /Lank my sweet man/we just cried/no talk/ no trick/. But Juliette said nothing.

CHAPTER TWENTY-SIX

Tommy Brian quit school at fifteen years old. He had no other prospects so the girls gave him the chicken farm. TB provided them with seven dozen eggs a week at half price. Lacie used a lot of eggs making baked goods that Victoria sold in Sterling Reserve. They also supplied Archie, Juliette, and Lank with eggs. City got half a dozen at a time. He didn't have an icebox or the good sense to throw out two month old eggs.

Juliette received a good income from her ownership of Our Pet but she and her father made most of their money brokering fish through Cameron Fisheries.

Archie and Lank also earned good incomes. Archie did contract work for Cliff but he, too became a competent broker. He sold saw logs to mills, secured pulpwood for paper mills, and brokered house lots of finished lumber from sawmills to retailers and builders.

Lank's income varied but he did well. His was a working-class income, Archie's middle-class and Juliette's upper-middle-class but Archie and Juliette were tightwads in many ways. They decided to avoid buying things like houses, cars, or getting electricity strung to The Tracks. Archie and Juliette thought some acquisitive fever took over North America and they felt good letting most of that pass them by.

Lank bought and sold cars. If he didn't do that, he would just buy cars. Lank loved cars. He moved his repair site to an actual building after Lacie recovered from her back injury. He could walk to work but usually took a car. Each car he bought and repaired, he drove for a week or so, ostensibly to check it out but Lank simply had an appetite for different vehicles. At one time or another, he used everything from a tiny Fiat Topolino to a big Blue Bird sixty-passenger bus as everyday transportation.

Lank made Juliette and Archie happy when he set up the repair shop in Sterling Reserve. He used an old Glover building with lots of room inside and an acre of land outside to keep parts vehicles and vehicles waiting to be repaired. It pleased Archie to walk or drive by the old mine storage shed and see all Lank's junk there rather than at The Tracks. But Archie and Juliette also turned into kids with toys when Lank got a vehicle they liked. Station wagons, small buses, and vans meant extra trips for the girls and their friends. Juliette willingly spent money on trips. She encouraged Lank and Archie to take the girls, one of them or both of them, anywhere. Lacie and Victoria flew to England with Lank and Victoria flew to the Bahamas with Archie. Lacie took buses and trains to New Orleans with Lank where he bought a big old Cadillac. They drove home in it. The five of them drove across the country towing a trailer behind an International Travelall in the summer of nineteen sixty-four. They had a toilet and rudimentary cooking facilities in the trailer but, when anyone wanted to get a motel or hotel room, they did that. When anyone wanted to eat in a restaurant, that was okay. They didn't spend any more money on the road than at home maintaining three different residences.

After establishing their long-haul-travel patience, the five of them enjoyed the trip, particularly their time together. However, while they stayed at a campground outside of Vancouver, Lacie went off for two afternoons with a boy. She spent an overnight with him in a pup tent on his parents' camp lot.

"Honey, do you want to drive down to the city for the night? It would be just the two of us."

Victoria shook her head, "Thanks, Mom, but that would be so obvious. It must be obvious it's bugging me that she's with him?"

"To me, yes, and probably to Archie but I doubt if Lank will pick up on it."

"Oh great, that means Lacie will know, for sure."

"For sure. You should tell her how you feel since she will know you are upset."

"Yeah, shit a brick. I'm so embarrassed. I wouldn't know what to say. It's too stupid. What's wrong with me anyway?"

"If I were you, I would be scared shitless that I would someday have to share her with someone." Juliette said in a pretend whisper, "He is not even cute."

"No, he's got pimples. But he's nice."

"Tomorrow, tell Lacie you missed her and the two of you will sort it out from there."

Juliette tried not to notice that the next day the girls were inseparable but they didn't attempt to hide it. Victoria hung in close when Lacie and Juliette cooked the evening meal. "Juls, can Vee and I have a motel room to ourselves for a night?"

Juliette proposed that they get the ferry to Vancouver Island and go directly to Victoria. "After all, since they named the city after you, we should go there and spend a little time in your city."

"Yeah right, my city. I'll get dressed up like the fat old Queen of England."

Juliette said, "I have a brochure for a great looking hotel in downtown Victoria. We can have as many rooms as we want. We should leave the trailer here and use hotels and motels on the island."

They took three rooms; one for the girls and two for the adults.

Staying three nights gave Archie, Lank, and Juliette each a chance to have a room to themselves for one night. Juliette was the only one to take someone to bed on her night alone. Frank had breakfast with them the morning after. They all said he was a jerk. Juliette agreed. But they were drunk when they decided to sleep together.

Juliette surprised herself by going to a lingerie shop. She bought a black lacy slip and matching panties for Victoria and a shimmering gray camisole and panty set for Lacie. Juliette didn't know exactly why she did that but when she gave Lacie the camisole set, Lacie lowered her eyes and said, most demurely, "Thank you, Juls." She looked up at Juliette again with a sweet, naughty smirk. Victoria was not demure.

"Oh my god, Mom, it's sooo risqué." She put it up against herself and looked in the reflecting brass walls of the elevator. Victoria posed and squealed. "Oh Mom, you're the greatest. Can I wear your lipstick; I left mine in the trailer." Juliette went back out and bought three shades of lipstick, a small makeup kit and a tiny bottle of Chanel perfume. /what the hell am I doing/I hope I never have to explain this to Archie and Lank/.

It was Lank's turn to do the laundry on their last day in the city. Juliette checked the laundry bag before he got to it and, sure enough, she found those four sexy little things in there and in need of cleaning. She took them out, resisted an almost overwhelming urge to sniff and gave them to the hotel laundry service. She picked up the items just before they left the hotel and brought them to the girls. "You can tell me if you need to but I do not need to know and I am sure Archie and Lank will not need to know."

Victoria gave a light and cheerful, "Okay".

"We are about ready to leave. Lank is going to bring the Travelall around front. The rest of the laundry is in the bag and we can sort it out later." She thought the girls giggled as she went to check one of the other rooms for left-behinds. Juliette felt sure they took some sort of enjoyment from her discomfort.

They drove to the beaches on the western side of Vancouver Island and then back to pick up the travel trailer for a long, relaxed drive home. They also picked up letters, seven of them from Neala. Archie wrote her every second day during the trip. Juliette addressed the envelopes in her very feminine handwriting with return addresses like 'Juliette and the girls somewhere in Western Ontario' or 'Juliette in a cloud of mosquitoes, Manitoba'. The campground outside the city of Vancouver was the first address Archie could give where he would have any chance to pick up mail. Juliette also got a letter from Cliff.

They returned to The Tracks two weeks late for school, with work piled up and lost opportunities for their various income generating ventures and all very happy to have made the trip.

**

The girls spent most of their time together, constant and compatible. It appeared to Victoria that her friend always had some illness that sent her running off to the doctor's office. Victoria said it was all in her head. Lacie didn't argue.

Victoria and Lacie put little effort into school. Lacie's attitude often slipped into what looked like indolence. However, Victoria came first in her class, and Lacie usually second in average marks but she made the highest marks in English, both grammar and literature. She often sat in class with a textbook propped up in front of the book she read. Lacie had a capacity to remember, for a minute or so, what the teachers said, even though she paid no attention.

"Miss Graham, are you listening to this?"

"Yes, Sister. You were saying that 'vous' is not only used as a plural but sometimes to signify a level of formality, n'est-ce pas?" But she hadn't paid attention at all. She concentrated and tried to figure out what Simone de Beauvoir meant by 'the other' and 'the look'. She borrowed existentialist books from Archie and talked to him about them. Lacie didn't like the way the existentialists made her feel but she still wanted to know. Victoria thought it made no sense to read things that made you worried about stuff beyond your control. "For fuck sake, Lacie, it's just nothingness. Don't fret about nothingness; it's nothing."

Enrollment fell at the Sterling Reserve School. Kids dropped out, particularly the ones who failed a grade or two. There were only ten grade eight and five grade nine students. The school combined both grades in the same classroom and the school decided that Lacie would do both grades in one year. Nine was the highest grade in the Sterling Reserve School which meant that Lacie would go to Brookfield for grade ten the next year. The girls would be in separate schools. The arrangement didn't make them happy but no one could deny that Lacie needed more of a challenge. School work bored her since the age of five. She lost a year with a broken back and was two years older than many of the kids in Grade eight.

Sister Jeanne d'Arc asked Victoria and Lacie to step out of the highest marks race in her subjects, English and mathematics. They became assistant teachers. Victoria helped the slow kids in math. For years, she did their homework and passed them answers on tests and exams. Victoria knew what they didn't know. She knew how they tried to bullshit their way through. Her students wouldn't get to the grade eight work but she successfully got her class caught up on stuff they should have learned from grades three to grade six or seven.

Lacie had the smarter kids in her group for English. It took her a month to get down to earth enough for the smarter kids but they loved her classes. Lacie taught Victoria and her four other students in the school's auditorium, along the riverbank, inside some old mine building and occasionally in a classroom.

After her father's grabbing the tie incident, Lacie continued to be nice to Mr. McLeod. She kept saying, "Good morning, Mr. McLeod" and, "A lovely day, isn't it?" By the end of the sixty-four, sixty-five school year he could be seen chatting with Lacie and Victoria. Victoria even admitted that McLeod was "not so bad, not so dumb". Sister Jeanne d'Arc began to believe it.

Archie and Juliette had been a delight for a very few librarians at university but out in the real world, librarians hated to see them coming. They borrowed regular sorts of books but the librarians got tired of looking up and ordering odd books and articles on inter-library loan. In nineteen sixty-one, Archie discovered Mrs. Gill. She worked in a small library outside of Dartmouth where she lived with her husband but she had been head librarian at a Montréal University. Mrs. Gill loved to see Archie or Juliette coming in the door. Lacie was still making her way through Archie's book collection and very often finding it heavy going. She rarely required Mrs. Gill's expertise but the librarian could see the potential and tried to be helpful.

She brought Lacie's attention to a small book called, Getting a Degree. "This little thing has no philosophy of education, no theories of education and it is totally amoral. You may find it abhorrent but, if you ever want to get the institutional requirements of educational certification out of the way so you can get down to education, this nasty little book is useful."

Lacie and Victoria read it together. It contained tips like; 'read all the exam questions first, making notes of what pops into your head', 'pay out-of-work academics to write your papers' and 'Benzedrine is useful for all night study sessions followed by morning exams'. Victoria loved the book but Lacie was not a competitive girl.

"It's all bullshit, Vee. Why get a college degree if that's all it is?"

"Come on, Lacie, you'll educate yourself no matter what but you still need that piece of paper to open doors for you."

"Maybe, I don't want to go in those rooms."

"God, Lacie, exams don't bother you."

"No, I mean the rooms the doors open on to."

"Oh, yeah, cute. But let's say you wanted to teach a college course on existentialist novels. They wouldn't let you do it without a degree, probably a Masters or PhD. By using some of those tricks, you could study the stuff you wanted and less of the stuff they say you have to study."

"Well, hopefully, they, whoever they are, know something about what it takes to get educated."

"Hah. If they do, you'll know it and you could follow what they say. Jesus Christ, Lacie, with your brains and this tricky shit, you could have a job and learn plant biology and Japanese while you get a degree in psychology."

"I might want to be a doctor."

"You never said that before."

"No, but I'm thinking about it."

Victoria used the little book's suggested methods, except the things like Benzedrine and messing up other students. Her marks became ridiculously high. Lacie also tried it and it just seemed to make sense to do a lot of those things. She surpassed Victoria half the time so she started sabotaging her own exams by answering only some questions and writing poetry for others. Sister Jeanne d'Arc told her that was arrogant and Lacie had to agree.

"Juls, what do you think? I don't want to make real high marks."

"Is that so you will not beat Victoria?"

"No, Vee would love a race. It's something else. Maybe I don't want to be a freak."

"You are a freak. Your intelligence alone makes you a rarity. I was also a freak, not as smart as you at your age, certainly not as well read but I excelled at many things and like you, I was unusually attractive. We both try and have tried to be good people, whatever that means. I failed to get a degree because of my weaknesses, primarily drunkeness. I know you want to be good and generous and I believe that it is a positive thing for people to look up to generous people, to see someone truly outstanding and know you are a good person."

"It's for the greater good that I beat my friends in the institutional rat race?"

Juliette recovered from laughter and said, "It might be a general good if you excelled with dignity rather than showing disdain for what matters so much to others. But, of course, you know what a nest of questions and contradictions that poses."

"It's hard, isn't it Juls? Life, I mean." Juliette stood behind Lacie where she sat on the edge of the parcel car's deck. She stroked Lacie's hair. Lacie twisted around and leaned into Juliette's thin cotton skirt. "All your smells are lovely, Juls. Thanks for you and Daddy not being bad drunks anymore. You both drink too much but it's not like it used to be. Vee doesn't even remember the way it used to be. You fixed that. Thanks."

***

Principal McLeod taught history to the grade eight-nine class. "I want you all to do a heritage project. It will be a report on some aspect of history that affects our world right now. It can be

Canadian, about Nova Scotia or something local, and don't forget that history is being made today."

Victoria decided to do a report on the history of The Tracks but the principal suggested otherwise. "You'd have to either whitewash it or you would, eh, embarrass people. For instance, would you tell about the excessive alcohol imbibing and other things that might be sensitive? You could do a project that would be just dates and measurements but that's not your style."

"Yes sir, you're quite right."

Giving up the idea of researching the history of the fifteen years people lived at The Tracks disappointed Victoria. Archie suggested that, in the spirit of the little book she and Lacie read on education, she could rewrite an old paper of his on Joseph Howe.

"Okay, I know a little about him. Joseph Howe was cool. Great, yeah. But I'd still like to know more about right here, just for myself."

"Well Lank and I know it all. We were here..."

Victoria interrupted, "I was thinking more like you and Mom. I guess maybe that's what I want, the history of you and me and Mom. I mean, I know you don't talk about your early years. As Mom says, that's closed to the rest of us but just since you moved here. Just tell me what you want to."

Victoria planned a series of interviews with Archie and Juliette. They bought her a new Norelco Compact Cassette Recorder.

***

Victoria: March sixteenth, nineteen sixty-five. The Tracks interview number two.

Yeah, okay. Archie, you were selling meat when you decided to live here, is that right?

Archie: Yes, for Canada Packers. I drove around the province in my Chevy. It was like a station wagon but without windows in the back; a sedan delivery they called it. I had my files with me and some samples in an ice chest and sometimes, deliveries. The car had no refrigeration or air-conditioning so it had to be a short run for deliveries or else just packaged meat. The ice chest didn't have room for a lot of fresh meat but I always had bologna. The little stores in the country often wanted bologna. It would keep without refrigeration and the company hated sending a truck with nothing but a couple of rolls of bologna. My degrees didn't give me a lot of job opportunities outside academia or government and I didn't want to do either.

I loved the job. I was out on the road, Halifax, Truro, and south to Yarmouth. I developed good relations with the storeowners and managers and meat managers and I met a lot of people, including Cliff. During that time, I started getting his discarded suits. A lot of salesmen wore suits in those days but mine were better than almost anybody else's, except one insurance salesman and drug salesmen sometimes had nice suits.

Juliette: It sounds too good. What were the bad points?

Archie: None, or not much. I got to stay at hotels on the company's dime. I didn't really have a home then. I stayed at Cliff's sometimes and I had a girlfriend in Liverpool and I stayed at her parent's house once in a while.

Victoria: Were you screwing her?

Juliette: Victoria, you can see why I think these interviews can become voyeuristic.

Victoria: A voyeur is like being a peeping Tom, isn't it?

Juliette: The meaning can be extended to any sort of peeping Tom activity, even if there is no ladder, no window and no sex.

Victoria: Well fuck, Mom, why shouldn't I be interested in whether Archie was screwing his girlfriend. Shit, that's just interesting. We've been over this. I don't tell anybody anything. I'm not even tempted to tell. It's not just a game, it's important to me and you don't have to answer any question you don't want to.

Juliette: Okay, okay, I do not want you to take it lightly.

Victoria: No. That's crazy…okay; of course…you're right. I'm not taking it lightly but I should ah, be aware and make you two aware that I am aware that this is sensitive. I know I am getting a gift here. That's it. I know that you are doing something very special and unusual for me. I don't think many kids would be able to get this sort of thing. I'm not sure exactly why. No, I really don't take it lightly.

Archie: All right, Juliette?

Juliette: Yes, I am sorry dear. We went through this before but I appreciate your explanation. Thanks.

Archie: To answer your question, not much. I didn't have sex with her often and it was a halfway thing. I would get on top of her and rub my penis on her just above her vagina, no penetration. Both of us did a lot of hand work. We had fun. In her mother's house, we didn't openly sleep together.

Victoria: Right, hmm, yeah, eh, where was I?

Juliette: Archie's job selling meat.

Victoria: Yeah okay, ah, did you make enough money?

Archie: It could vary. I worked on commission and expenses as long as I kept them low enough. I made as much as my contemporaries who got jobs by virtue of their degrees. The ones teaching college got less starting out as assistant professors than I made as a salesman.

Victoria: And you found this place here on your travels?

Archie: Yes yes, that's right, much like Columbus bumping into the Americas.

Juliette: Columbus drove a Chevy? Did you form the idea when you first saw it, that you would try to make a little community grow here?

Archie: Before I saw it. I heard about these abandoned cars and that's the reason I came to Sterling Reserve. A store like Old Pricey's would, in those days, start a regular order and they just called Halifax if they wanted to change it but I used to like getting to the little places. I asked around to find semi-abandoned places, mostly mining towns. There were some in Queens County but far out of the way and nothing much left of them really. There was a run-down place around Digby called Electric City. Really interesting place though. They had a wooden-tracked railroad for transporting lumber and they had their own electricity generated by a water wheel long before any other place in that area had power. My God, that place would've been great to do your project on. But, anyway, this place right here looked ideal for me.

Victoria: How did you know you wouldn't be kicked off as a squatter?

Archie: You mean, haven't yet been kicked off. It could still happen. The necessary adverse possession against a foreign owner is forty years. Part of it comes from my view of land ownership. People looked for some sort of half-life immortality in owning land, even just a house lot. I believed you were never settled no matter how settled you looked.

Here, the CNR owned the cars and the tracks and the bridge. The land belonged to Glover Metals Mining Company. Both owners seemed to want it all to disappear. The bridge deteriorated too much for a railroad bridge or any heavy traffic. Even getting the scrap metal out of here wouldn't have been worth it. Well, it would have been but I knew the CNR didn't want to bother with it. I did a lot of work here on this caboose right off but I knew it could be taken away. It became a worthwhile risk, I would say.

Victoria: Mom, your first job was in the fish plant? Oh thanks, Archie. That was sharp. You should have a statue as founder of The Tracks. Mom, you started in the fish plant?

Juliette: I suppose so. It was not really a job. I helped my father when I was eight and I got good at a lot of things so, if a big catch came in, I cut fish at the plant. I often went out with him, at first just day fishing, jigging cod or hauling lobster traps.

Archie: How the hell would you haul a lobster trap? How old were you?

Juliette: I probably started lobstering at eleven. I most often baited the traps and put in the lobster plugs but soon I steered the boat and pretty early on I could haul as many traps as a man. The trap weighs the most when it first comes out of the water. I jumped up on the gunwale to get my knees into it, and hauled on the line until I was almost lying on my back on the deck. We used to slide them along the gunwale, take out the lobsters and somebody would plug them. I re-baited the trap, checked it for damage, and then slid it back over the stern. Father Jimmy and I did that for eight or nine hours, spelling each other off between the wheel and hauling. At the first of the season though, we could have a crew of five. We started to get more reasonable pay for lobsters in those days but it was still hard work for little money.

At seventeen, I had only been offshore overnight four times with my father. He asked me to take a boat to Georges.

Archie: Georges Bank?

Juliette: Yes, Georges Bank. My first trip to the banks. The skipper of Father Jimmy's second boat got drunk, on a real bender for a week. It happened a lot with him when the fishing was good. He made a lot of money and started celebrating. They got good prices for cod and haddock around that time and they had great fishing off Georges. Father Jimmy did not want to lose out, so he said, "Juliette, you take My Cod Girl." I said yes, no hesitation.

Nobody on that crew could be trusted to skipper. A new guy who was a fine worker, could not navigate or steer well. He did not know enough about any of it. Shucks McNeil was an idiot. I would like to say that if you showed Shucks a simple task, he could repeat it but he could not. Nobody respected Monte House so I became skipper.

My father told me later that, as soon as he asked me, he regretted it but the wheels turned and I went out. He left port two hours behind me. He figured he would catch up and the two boats would go out together. He never caught up, never found me on the banks, and he was afraid for me and my crew. He hailed another boat and they told him they saw me steaming for home loaded to the gunwales with fish. Father Jimmy told me he had never been happier or more proud. I believed him.

So anyway, my father sent me out as skipper of a not-great boat with a not-great crew and planned to stay by my side; he planned to catch up and we would steam out together. Jimmy planned to show me where to find the fish and we would steam home together. That was his idea, not mine. I wanted to get out there, get a load of fish and get back to the plant. The next time he saw me, I just finished unloading my catch in Glace Bay. He had a pretty good load of fish but ours weighed in at one and a half tons more than his. He gave me the boat right then and there.

Archie: Then you quit school, right?

Juliette: Yes, I quit. I finished grade eleven, a pretty good education in those days.

Victoria: Were you a good student?

Juliette: Spotty really. I made the top of the class in subjects I liked but history and algebra bored me. I generally failed algebra but they paired that with plane geometry, which I loved. A bit like you with your great English grammar marks but not so great in English Literature. Well, you never made bad marks in anything but I did.

Victoria: How long did you fish on the old boat, My Cod Girl?

Juliette: A year. I got great catches and developed a good crew but My Cod Girl was old and due for a new motor or its third rebuild and those old wooden hulls had a limited lifespan. I planned on the motor rebuild to get another couple of years from her but my Uncle Alfonse from Petit de Grat had commissioned a new boat by a builder on Prince Edward Island. When the builder finished, Alphonse would not take possession because he thought she was too tippy. Alphonse still owed the builder over half the price of the boat. He refused to pay and the builder knew he had fucked up. The boat was too radical. They both hired lawyers and it looked like a court battle. Uncle Alfonse, my mother's oldest brother, is so very shy. He hated this fight as did the PEI builder, I guess. In any event, I got the boat for sixty percent of the cost of construction. The boat yard and Uncle Alfonse shared the loss. I called her Slipper.

Archie: Was she tippy?

Juliette: I did not think so. They built her narrow and five feet longer than the other long liners out of Glace Bay. The narrow beam, her hull shape and light displacement made her sway from side to side, especially when she had nothing aboard but bait and fuel. Slipper had limitations but she had speed. Unladen, she ran three knots faster than anything else out of Glace Bay and one knot faster with a load of fish. Slipper was uncomfortable but reasonably safe. In her first year, she made over twice the profit My Cod Girl made.

She had the best of gear but Slipper beat up the crew. She rocked and bounced a lot on the trip out until we got some weight of fish aboard. We drove her hard. We set and hauled nets and trawl and long lines if we had any hope of fish. A five-day trip included three days of absolutely brutal, hard work. She did that to you. Slipper had an urgency that got inside you. Her relatively small diesel was tuned up and balanced to run five hundred rpm's faster than usual. Monte and I talked about how Slipper got you all keyed up. The engine sound and her lively motion got you going but we never fully got it pinned down. All boats have a personality but some more than others. Slipper, tied to the dock, looked absolutely pissed off that she was not going flat-out. Is that too much about Slipper?

Victoria: No, it's interesting. I don't really know much about that part of your life. But the tape is coming to an end so maybe we can continue this, ah, what about Saturday afternoon?

CHAPTER TWENTY-SEVEN

Victoria: March twenty-eighth, nineteen sixty-five, interview number four.

In the last interview, we planned to talk about Mom and her boat Slipper, which sounds like it ran on coffee and diet pills but we got distracted talking about Irma and Custard Head. I'd like to get back to your hard-working youth.

Archie: What do you know about diet pills?

Victoria: Just what I read. Why?

Archie: I was just wondering. You've lost weight lately. Those amphetamines are dangerous, you know. They have lots of negative side effects.

Victoria: You think I'm so fat, I would take diet pills?

Juliette: Archie, you got yourself in a mess here.

Victoria: How do you know so much about diet pills, Archie? You know you're just pleasantly plump.

Juliette: (laughing) Victoria, leave the poor blob alone. He has a condition, just like City.

Archie: I did gain a few this winter, so yes, don't belittle a big fella.

Victoria: We've heard about your few pounds; can't see them but heard lots about them. Anyway, I don't take diet pills and I wouldn't consider it.

Archie: For the information of you two nasty bitches, if I put an inch on my waist, I'd have to start buying chocolates for Cliff so he would gain, too. His suit pants just fit me now. Okay, enough of that. Let's get back to Slipper. So you owned this boat, lock stock and barrel?

Juliette: Eighteen years old and I had a brand-new boat which proved to be the best, well, the most productive, fishing boat from Glace Bay, the big draggers not included. They are a different story altogether. She was not good for lobsters or catching bait so I let other people do that. I bought her with money earned on My Cod Girl and the bit of money I made selling that old boat, as well as a loan from the Cameron fish plant. Old Isobel acted like the loan was an ill-conceived personal favor from her. The plant loaned money to all kinds of people to buy boats. It was part of our business. It bound the fisherman to our plant as long as they owed the debt. Anyway, I saved every cent I made in the first month. I had a monthly repayment schedule and I planned to go out again two days before the payment came due. A new boat always screams out for dozens of little things you have to buy. I fitted her out on credit. Isobel enjoyed nagging about my upcoming default on the first payment. Well fuck, no fisherman ever pays anything on time. It is bad business. She threatened to seize my catch. I went a little overboard. I told her she was too old for that, no longer had the gumption. I knew those seizure orders take a month if everything goes easy and Father Jimmy had the final say but I wanted her to beat around the Bay seeing lawyers and such.

We did not catch as much fish on the last trip before the payment date but my crew loaned me six hundred dollars. Six hundred dollars was a fortune for those working fisherman to scrape together. I paid off the whole debt to Cameron Fisheries and took four days off. We all needed the rest. Isobel did not know I paid the debt. She kept harping on it; said she would sue me and get my boat and that Jimmy had no right to give My Cod Girl to me and that I had no Cameron in me what with that French whore of a mother. She got up at four-thirty in the morning to bitch and threaten before I left for the next trip. I said, "Oh that loan. I already paid that." Isobel called up the plant bookkeeper at home. Actually she called his next-door neighbor because the bookkeeper had no phone. Anyway, she got all those people out of bed to have her worst fear confirmed. She had nothing on me.

I learned a lesson. After working like a slave at a crazy pace and driving my crew too hard, the satisfaction of seeing her deflated was not worth it. Thereafter, I never played her game again and consider myself to be an absolute fool to have done it once. Winning at a game you did not want to play and did not need to play is pretty stupid. Anyway, on the next trip, I paid off the money my crew loaned me plus twenty-five percent. Slipper was all mine.

Victoria: You gave her the name, Slipper?

Juliette: Yes.

Victoria: Nice name for boat.

Juliette: Thank you. I liked it. The name held some irony because a slipper should feel more comfortable. It also appealed to me because it was a woman's boat and Slipper had a certain fairytale femininity and you might say she slips through the water but, with that diesel full bore you could hardly call it slipping along. However, unladen, she hardly made any wake compared to other long liners. But for the most part, I called her that for the rhyme. I wanted to be the Slipper skipper.

Archie: What was Slipper like in dirty weather?

Juliette: In a storm, she got treacherous. Arnold Steele went out only in perfect weather. My own crew considered her a crazy boat but they put up with it. Great crew really.

Victoria: How dangerous was Slipper?

Juliette: Have I, perhaps, talked too much already? I seem to be monopolizing this.

Victoria: No, this is great but hold on a minute. I have to change the tape.

[pause]

Juliette: How dangerous was Slipper? She was wild in a storm. She did a lot of things wrong. Her bow dug into some waves and it would be like you put the fucking brakes on. It took me months to get the hang of avoiding that. Arnold would never get it if he sailed her for a hundred years. Broadside waves in a storm could slew the boat over so much she took on water over the lee side. Arnold did not take her out if anybody forecasted twenty-five knots within eight hundred miles. He used her like an inshore fishing boat. Slipper was not a good inshore boat.

We kept hauling gear in thirty-five knots. Crazy really but that is why we caught so much fish. We put everything into it. That is not the only reason. The fisherman, particularly the older men from Arichat and Petit de Grat, told me everything they knew. They helped me out anyway they could. People think they would have resented a young hotshot female whose father owned the plant but no, the old French guys were proud of me.

Victoria: Did they all support you?

Juliette: We were fishing. I had competitors. One of them was my father but nobody did me dirty and I did not brag or try to fuck guys up. I loaned guys money to get them by a bad stretch. They all treated me fairly and often better than fair.

This knife, which you have both seen, my Uncle Alfonse gave me. He had a dream about me getting in some sort of trouble or needing to help someone else. He never made the contents of the dream clear but he was positive about the results of it. He had to make a knife for me. Alphonse is a great craftsman. I got accustomed to it. I cut fish differently. It is so wide you can lay the fillet over as you cut. The trick is that your cut does not necessarily go in the same direction that your blade is pointing. He made it for fighting and throwing as well as filleting. See, along the back here, it has little grooves and the metal is soft so as to keep the other guy's knife from sliding up to cut your hand in a fight. It has this hook at the hilt on the sharp side for the same reason. I thought he used some sort of lead mixture for the back but apparently it is a soft silver amalgam. Uncle Alfonse is so sweet. He had a heart attack. I visited but had difficulty talking to him. I write to him. The knife has been great. It is like a good luck charm, I guess. Thankfully, I never had to use it in a knife fight.

I am sorry. I get carried away. I sound like an old fisherman talking about a life passed.

Victoria: It's great; it's great to hear this stuff.

Juliette: Whatever the question was, did I answer it?

Victoria: I lost track too. Were there dangerous storms?

Juliette: Yes.

Victoria: Tell us about one.

Juliette: In March of my last year fishing, we went out with a bad marine forecast. That is not particularly wise but you do unwise things when you fish hard. It blew twenty-five to thirty on the way out. One other boat went out, too. We traveled together. I think you do that as much for company as for safety but you can also watch how the other boat handles the weather. You might see an option that might not have come to mind otherwise. Two Glace Bay boats heading for the Grand Banks; a long trip, none of us needed to go. It was that fishing cupidity; go go go.

Anyway, we were all beat up on Slipper by the time we got there. Slipper needed some fish aboard to steady her out. About ten minutes from setting our gear, with everything on deck ready to go, bad shit weather dropped on us. A small, weird weather system, only lasted four hours; ice pellets, thunder and really fucking cold. It hovered around freezing on the way out but dropped ten degrees, with freezing spray at the end of it. We had no idea it would only last four hours. The other boat, G B Folly, set a long loop of nets off the bow as a sea anchor. It worked great for the first hour but the waves built in no time and the waves were sharp, square-edged things. They built up straight walls of water and then flew apart like somebody blew them with dynamite. Wayne Aucoin skippered G B Folly. They had to cut off their sea anchor because the bow got buried in those hard, square waves. We were steaming into it but I got us turned around to run before it. That seemed worse right away but it was the right decision. G B Folly sent a man to the bow, an old salt, John R Murphy. He was fifty-five, strong as an ox and good on a boat. I often wished John R crewed for me. He crawled forward to cut away the sea anchor. A big wave came over G B Folly's bow. John R went over. We saw him thrashing, going astern of the boat at about two knots. A wave broke over him and that was the last anybody saw of John R.

Wayne sent another guy forward. He got the lines cut and got back all right. Wayne tried to turn her and she broached. G B Folly looked like a boat going down but Wayne saved her and got the pumps going.

Slipper kept getting pooped. We took on tons of water over the stern, way too much for the scuppers. It took more than a minute to drain off the afterdeck. We closed everything up tight. I stayed outside, at the wheel. We had an inside steering station but I would have lost her if I steered from in there. I had to track every oncoming wave and predict the gusts. It blew a steady fifty-five knots but the gusts felt like getting hit with a huge baseball bat. When Slipper was not getting pooped, she raised her ass onto an oncoming wave. At one time a big gust hit us with her stern up and out of the water. I had no rudder and my prop churned foam. I almost lost her there.

Victoria: Were you scared?

Juliette: Yes.

Victoria: Just in this storm or were you scared in other big storms?

Juliette: Yes.

Victoria: Ah, were you… were you always afraid fishing in storms?

Juliette: Yes.

Victoria: Like from when? How long were you afraid?

Juliette: Since I was twelve.

Victoria: Afraid out fishing since you were twelve?

Juliette: I have fear since I was twelve. I am afraid.

Victoria: Mom, Mom not just out fishing? Are you afraid now?

Juliette: Yes, all the time.

Victoria: Mom, what…?

Archie: Turn off the machine dear.